Obsidian

Obsidian

K.F. Breene

Map by Cartographybird

Copyright © 2025 by K.F. Breene

All rights reserved.

No part of this book may be reproduced in any form or by any electronic or mechanical means, including information storage and retrieval systems, without written permission from the author, except for the use of brief quotations in a book review.

ALSO BY K.F. BREENE

Demigods of San Francisco

Sin & Chocolate

Sin & Magic

Sin & Salvation

Sin & Spirit

Sin & Lightning

Sin & Surrender

Leveling Up

Magical Midlife Madness

Magical Midlife Dating

Magical Midlife Invasion

Magical Midlife Love

Magical Midlife Meeting

Magical Midlife Challenge

Magical Midlife Alliance

Magical Midlife Flowers

Magical Midlife Battle

Magical Midlife Awakening

Finding Paradise

Fate of Perfection

Fate of Devotion

Deliciously Dark Fairytales

A Ruin of Roses

A Throne of Ruin

A Kingdom of Ruin

A Queen of Ruin

A Cage of Crimson

A Cage of Kingdoms

Demon Days, Vampire Nights

Born in Fire

Raised in Fire

Fused in Fire

Natural Witch

Natural Mage

Natural Dual-Mage

Warrior Fae Trapped

Warrior Fae Princess

Revealed in Fire

Mentored in Fire

Battle with Fire

FAERIE

◉ CASTLES
◆ ORACLE

DIAMOND
KINGDOM

RUBY
KINGDOM

EMERALD
KINGDOM

T H E   F R I N G E

OPAL
KINGDOM

SEA OF
STARS

SAPPHIRE
KINGDOM

TOPAZ
KINGDOM

AMETHYST
KINGDOM

OBSIDIAN
KINGDOM

For the women who wear their darkness like a crown.

Chapter One

Daisy launched herself at the enemy before he could prepare. She was a non-magical Chester fighting a huge magical man twice her age and size; fighting fair was just irresponsible.

The business end of her knife pierced his stomach. He grunted and reached for her, ignoring the painful wound. She was already moving. To stay still in this situation was to be overpowered and die.

Dodging his reaching arms, she took the hilt of the dagger in both hands and slammed the blade into his body. It squelched as it came back out, and then she jammed it in again, aiming for a kidney and a quick death. Her aim on this part of the body was terrible—she knew she'd miss—but it would hurt like hell, and if he knew what she was going for, it would freak him out.

Welcome to being mind-fucked, my friend.

A fierce snarl nearly pulled her focus. Her brother, Mordecai, was engaging his guy just down the beach. Sand flew into the air. She couldn't watch, though. One slip and she'd be toast—the reason Mordecai hadn't wanted her in this fight in the first place. She'd be damned if she'd die and give him a complex.

"Stupid bitch," her big-eared enemy wheezed.

Big ears...

Maybe she'd cut one of those off, just for shits and giggles.

Ducking behind him, she bent and stuck her knife in his inner thigh, *really* close to his nut sack. If the kidneys didn't freak him out, this would.

His high-pitched scream made her smile. She jumped, slammed her blade into the top of his shoulder, and climbed him like a tree. He spun while reaching around, trying to throw her off. But this was why she'd embedded the knife—as a handle.

He spun the other way, slowing a little. It was too good of an opportunity to pass up.

Working faster than she ever had in training, she scrambled up to his shoulders, wrapped her legs around his head, clutched the knife, and spun her upper body down and to the side, ripping her legs with her. Gravity helped her to the ground. Before she hit, she pushed her arms wide so the knife didn't end up in her middle.

The impact cracked something and knocked the air

out of her. F*uuuck*-ing *ouch*! Her execution of that move needed work.

Struggling for breath, she clambered up. To give in to the pain was to give in to death—or so Zorn always said. Right now, she believed it.

She barely caught the sight of a black animal rolling across the white sands, leaving a bright red trail in its wake. A panther, struggling for life. Mordecai in wolf form was on it a moment later, his snarl sending a jolt of uncontrolled, primal fear through Daisy's middle. That was new. She'd never heard that note in his growl during training.

Then again, she'd never felt this sort of unbridled intensity during training, either. This fucking thrill of adrenaline. It was a high unlike anything. A calling, maybe. Good thing she'd ended up in the magical world, where people thought this mentality was somewhat normal. Otherwise, she'd be ushered into a jail cell.

With Mordecai still busy, she took two side steps, spun, and attacked, dagger ready. The enemy hadn't gotten up yet, so she pounced on his back and dug the knife between his shoulder blades.

She yanked it free and bounced off, waiting for his movements to determine where to strike next.

He didn't so much as twitch.

A howl of pain grabbed her attention. Mordecai ripped across the panther's belly with his claws before going for the jugular. The panther struggled feebly, beaten.

All Daisy had to do was stall before Mordecai handled the other half of her guy. Well...more like a quarter at this point. That was the deal: he'd said he could handle one and a half of these guys—older and more experienced shifters looking to pick a fight. They weren't as dominant as her sixteen-year-old brother, though! Mordecai had wanted to do the responsible older brother thing and stand down for Daisy's sake, but fuck that! This was an ego boost for him—a coming-of-age moment that Mordecai needed. That he was overdue. He was too humble to seek it out himself, and so she was happy to help serve it up for him. He deserved the win!

The man still lay prone, unmoving.

Worry crept through her. She really hoped he was playing dead to surprise her.

Except...shifters didn't play dead. They were like the god Zeus in that way. Their egos couldn't handle standing down.

Zorn's voice sounded in her head: *One must never be greedy for a kill.*

That didn't really apply. She was trying to keep the guy alive. The guy, and herself.

She inched closer as a more useful Zorn quote trickled into her mind: *One must never let down one's guard, even when the enemy is on the very brink of death.*

Well, yeah, obviously.

She darted in and pierced him in the shoulder, good and deep. That strike would hurt like hell. Even the most stubborn person would react. Nothing.

"Shit," she whispered, kicking one of his arms out of the way. It was heavy and lifeless. "Oh shit. Mordie...I think I fucked up."

This time something entirely different caused the rush of adrenaline.

After killing, be ready for remorse. Be thankful if it doesn't come.

But it wasn't remorse fluttering in her stomach. She'd killed once before. She knew the feelings that would come. The nothingness and knowing that in this life, it was kill or be killed. There was no room for emotions when surviving.

No, the fluttering was the fear that her mother figure, Lexi, would find out about this and raise hell that Daisy had put herself in danger and that Mordecai had let her.

"Oh shit. Mordie..." she said as he padded over, leaving the panther on its side, its bloody, glistening body rising and falling as it struggled to breathe. "Is that one going to live?" She pointed at the panther.

Mordecai sniffed the man's face before his head came up, his intelligent hazel eyes meeting hers. She knew the situation without having to ask. The crack she'd heard when executing the move hadn't been her back during the bad landing. It must've been this guy's neck.

She'd accidentally killed him.

Fuuuuck.

Her stomach started to roll. She would get in *so* much trouble for this. Lexi would *kill* them for fighting big guys twice their age. Kill Daisy for fighting at all when she wouldn't take Demigod Kieran's offer of blood magic, something that would give her speed and strength and quick healing. It would also tether her to him forever. That guy's dad had gone crazy, and they'd all nearly died stopping him. If Kieran followed in his family's footsteps and tried to trap Lexi, Daisy needed to get them out of there. She couldn't have the permanent connection of blood magic with a guy like him. He was levelheaded now, sure, but Demigods weren't to be trusted. Which Lexi understood...to a point. She would not be so understanding if she found out about this minor debacle.

The day swam before her. The sun bleached the color of the crystalline ocean, the white sands.

"Zorn will help us get rid of it," she said in a rush. "He won't tell anyone. He's really good at keeping my secrets. Should I go get him?"

Fuck, she hoped that was true. They'd only been training for a year or so, and he was a buttoned-up sort of guy. She didn't know him half as well as that claim implied.

A strange feeling rolled over her—a humming sort

of vibration that sang along her nerve endings, both soothing and ominous. A pleasurable tingle ran down her spine like ice-coated fingertips dancing along her skin, equally chilling and diverting. It was a familiar feeling, one she'd grown accustomed to. One she'd committed to memory, relishing in it, delighting in its terrifying pleasure.

A presence had joined them. *The* presence. Beautiful and wicked. Exciting...but dangerous. Death incarnate.

It called to her. Begged her to look at it. To notice.

She'd felt the same presence yesterday before the courtyard battle in the convention building at the Demigod Summit, a huge meeting for all the top magical people in the world. It had stood just off to the side, noticed by absolutely no one, a spectral brilliance that not even Zorn, a Jinn, could manifest on his best day. But they had the same roots, at least partially—of that she was certain. This was a fae.

For a moment—a brief, mind-spinning moment—a pair of vivid green eyes flared into existence. The face of a boy a few years older than her—she was just fifteen—stood close by, his body sparkling and shining within its glamor. His severe cheekbones would break a fist crashing against them, and the soft cleft in his chin pleasantly contrasted the strong jaw. His gaze was like a brand upon her skin, awakening something she didn't want to set loose, sparking something primal and setting it ablaze. His rugged, almost cruel handsomeness was nothing compared to the sparkle of deviousness in his eyes.

Her heart beat too fast. She'd never felt this feverish without being sick. Never felt this terrified, but she wasn't afraid. She couldn't tear her eyes away, wishing a body would manifest, wanting him to speak.

In another moment, everything vanished. The face, the presence, everything. Magic too incredible and too potent to track or maybe even acknowledge blinked out.

"What was—what..." Mordecai, having changed into his human form, took two quick steps forward, shock on his face. He looked at the beach.

The bodies were gone. Both of them. The blood, the messed-with sand—all of it. It was as though the skirmish hadn't happened and Daisy hadn't killed someone five feet from where she stood.

She opened her mouth to explain—

Shh, little dove. The fae's voice was strangely familiar in her mind. Deliciously familiar. *It must remain our secret, or it will be your group that I must silence. See you soon...*

Daisy gasped and jerked awake. The dream—a memory from four years ago but still so vivid—drifted away. The feeling of that fae's presence remained, though, left behind like a landmine. The image of his face, those eyes, the feeling that'd erupted in her...

She shook herself and wiped the sweat from her forehead. She hadn't told a soul about him...and he'd still done her dirty. Two days after she saw his face on that beach, he'd shown up amongst her crew—her family—and set loose an unspeakable magic that had nearly wiped them all out.

Served her right, she supposed. Only a fucking moron messed with fae. She should've known he'd fuck her over. It had been stupid to even be curious. Dumb to constantly think of those eyes and their devilish sparkle. His presence—

She flung her covers away and sat up, scrubbing the images from her mind. Four years later and she still had dreams. Still had moments when his memory —the unspeakable *feelings* of his memory—drifted into her mind and took root. It wasn't daydreaming when the subject was a human's nightmare. It was just so damn pleasurable, though. She couldn't seem to forget it.

After dressing, she headed downstairs. Mordecai sat on a stool at the island, hunched over his phone.

"You're here again, I see," she said, opening the fridge and peering in. If she waited long enough, maybe breakfast would make itself and fall into her hands. "Didn't want to stay at the new lady-love's house last night?"

He didn't answer. He'd never been very open about his love life, but he'd been gone for a few nights about a week ago, with only a few grunts for an explanation. Clearly he was getting some action with his new lady of choice.

A pair of green eyes flashed through her mind, accompanied by a flare of heat.

She shook herself out of it. Those dreams were incredibly disruptive. She wished she'd stop having them. Hell, after four years, she *should've* stopped having them. She needed to find a lobotomist.

"What time is training later, do you know?" she asked, pulling out some grapes.

His silence drew her focus. When it came to training, which directly related to her safety, he wasn't the silent-treatment type. Even if he was mad at her, he usually answered.

Currently, he had no reason to be mad at her. Not yet. Not until later, when he got a taste of her newest booby trap. It was a fun little game she liked to play, and he hated to be part of. He'd then try to pound her during training. Sibling rivalry. They might not be blood, but they'd been raised in really hard times and for long enough to act like it.

Mordecai didn't look up, bowed over his phone. His black, tightly curled hair was mussed in spots and his dark skin was dry and flaky. He wasn't taking care of himself like he usually did. At twenty, he was something of a (very sweet and respectful) lady-killer. The girls thought him handsome and a gentleman, not to mention rich and *very* well connected. He could essentially get anyone he wanted, even with this sad-sack disposition. He went to great lengths to live up to the family name, elevated to the world of Demigods even though their roots were as humble as a gutter rat's. This situation with him was...unusual. Worrying, even.

Frowning, she closed the fridge door and wandered closer, stopping beside his stool. She popped a grape into her mouth as she kicked the stool leg.

"What's your problem?" she asked. Soft light filtered through the kitchen windows in the residence they mostly called home. They could multiply their old house four times and it still wouldn't be as big as this one. Neither of them had ever taken their turn in fortune for granted.

He didn't react, continuing to doomscroll on his phone.

"Hey." She kicked the chair harder this time.

"Would you stop?" He cast her an irritated glance. Dark circles lined his red-rimmed hazel eyes.

Not taking care of himself and not sleeping very well. Only danger to their family or girl trouble usually created this. Given she would've been apprised of any danger, it was clearly the latter.

"What'd she do?" Daisy demanded, yanking at his shoulder to get him to turn and face her. "Tell me."

"Nothing. It's fine."

"What's fine?" Jack asked as he sauntered into the kitchen holding a brown grocery bag with something green sticking out the top. He was one of about a dozen people she thought of as uncles, brothers, nieces, a mother figure, or a stepdad type. None of them were blood. She'd been abandoned by blood when she was small and then shuffled around the Chester "care" system, the social services for magic-less orphans. Lexi had found her in the dual-society zone, the crack between the magical and non-magical societies where people struggled to coexist in order to escape their respective governments or law enforcement agencies. She'd been starving and half dead, ready to do unspeakable things for a meal, just to stay away from those horrible and abusive care homes.

Lexi had been her miracle, and Mordecai with her. It hadn't mattered that Lexi's house was beyond tiny, or that they lived in poverty, or that they had to scrape and steal just to eat. Lexi and Mordecai's kindness, their love, had felt like heaven.

So when Lexi had gotten into trouble and needed to move into the magical zone so a Demigod of Poseidon, who was at the peak in power of their magical world, could protect her, Daisy hadn't balked. She'd marched right into the fire alongside her family, ignoring the fact she was the only non-magical person allowed here. This was where she belonged, regardless of blood. Regardless of magic. It was where she'd stay, the dangers inherent in being a magic-less "Chester" in this brutal world be damned.

Besides, when Lexi had then gotten a magical upgrade, Daisy had finally taken the blood magic. Lexi's blood magic. Being tethered to Lexi was a comfort, and the benefits from the magic were sensational. She was faster now. Stronger. Able to heal *much* more quickly. She wasn't nearly as breakable. It didn't close the gap between her and real magical people, but it lessened the danger just a touch. Enough to keep Lexi from forcing her to live with people of "her kind."

Because of that Demigod, now Lexi's fiancé, their family unit had grown. First with Kieran's Six, the guys who'd pledged a blood oath to protect their Demigod, and then Bria and Dylan, Amber and Jerry—their crew. The people she'd fight beside until her dying breath.

Daisy ignored Jack while shoving Mordie this time. "What'd she do?"

"Leave it alone, okay? It's none of your business," Mordecai said a little too loudly, his face creasing in misery.

"Oh, his woman?" Jack lifted his dark brows as he set the grocery bag on the island. His bronzed arm, thick with muscle, stretched his shirt as he lifted out a carton of milk.

"Whose woman?" Donovan walked in next, lean and blond and very good-looking. All of Kieran's original Six were.

Zorn entered right behind, dressed in a button-down shirt and slacks. His wavy brown hair had been freshly cut, and his gray eyes were their usual sort of intense and piercing. His gaze swept the room, taking stock of the surroundings and assessing for any danger. He did it constantly and had taught her to do it, too. Very little escaped his notice.

"Rumple Sad-Sack here has girl problems, it seems." Daisy put a hand on the edge of the counter so she could lean over Mordecai to see his face. He'd gone back to scrolling through his phone. "Hey. What happened? I can help."

"Do not let her help." Donovan smiled as he reached into a cabinet and grabbed a frying pan. Oh good, at least they planned to make breakfast.

"Why?" Daisy's brows lowered. "What do you know?"

It was Jack who answered. "We know it doesn't matter what that girl did. You'd slit her throat for it if Mordecai let you."

Jerry, whom the magical world referred to as "the Giant," walked into the kitchen behind the rest. The nickname wasn't because of his size, though he topped out at six-foot-six with a large breadth of shoulder. It was because of his abilities with rock. He could literally move a mountain, bit by bit.

He sat at the kitchen table as Mordecai made a disgruntled sound and pushed to standing. Apparently the whole crew would be eating at this residence, taking a break from ruling Magical San Francisco for the day.

"It's fine," Mordecai said testily. He gave Daisy a hard look. "It's none of your business. Just *leave* it."

She put her hands on her hips as she watched him walk from the room.

"I don't blame him," Jerry said in his deep baritone,

resting his forearms on the table. "What that lady did would crush any man's ego."

Daisy turned toward Jerry slowly.

"You weren't supposed to say anything, *Jerry*," Jack said, emphasizing his name. It was a joking sort of mocking they'd been doing since they met the giant a handful of years before. Jerry, alone and lonely on his solitary mountain, had been an instant addition to their crew, belonging with the rest of the misfits.

"Yeah, *Jerry*," Donovan intoned, chuckling. "We aren't supposed to let the angry little gremlin know the situation for fear of her retaliation. Mordecai and his broken heart said so."

Jerry's eyebrows slowly lifted. "Oops," he said unapologetically.

He clearly wanted revenge for Mordecai, and the others knew she would get it for him. No one fucked with her family and got away with it.

"Spill, Giant," Daisy demanded as Zorn slipped into another seat at the table. "Tell me everything."

Chapter Two

Cold rage slithered within Daisy as she moved through the darkness. Zorn drifted just behind, down the deserted alleyway. The cobblestones shone in the low light, wet with moisture from the heavy fog. Golden-yellow street lamps glowed with diffused halos. Somewhere a cat screeched before a garbage can rattled and a glass bottle rolled across cement.

With Zorn's help, it hadn't taken long to formulate a plan. Half a day only. All the information they needed on her target, Mordecai's snake of an ex-girlfriend, was right at their fingertips. Daisy even had a picture so she could identify the woman easily. Tonight, slightly more than twenty-four hours later, she would take out the trash.

Near the end of the alleyway, Daisy paused and glanced around. Not a soul in sight.

Respectable people didn't come to this corner of the dual-society zone. There was nothing but crime and criminals hiding from the law.

Her target was three floors up in the corner apartment. A known criminal's apartment.

Turned out, Mordecai's ex-woman dabbled in stolen antiques and collectibles. Her fuck-buddy on the side did, at any rate. Given it was the dual-society zone, this area wasn't subject to Demigod Kieran and Lexi's jurisdiction. They weren't responsible for policing this area, and neither was the non-magical government. These people slipped through the cracks in this world and hoped no one bigger and stronger took notice.

Well. Now someone had. The woman deserved Zorn and Daisy coming after her, and the criminals she hung out with deserved to go dark. Permanently. Given the area, no one would give two shits about it. Kill or be killed. The nature of the game.

Daisy jumped up and grabbed the top of the fence. In a second she'd pulled herself over and landed almost silently on the other side. Zorn was at her side in a moment, making scaling a fence look graceful and easy. Garbage littered the walkway behind the building. She watched where she stepped and ducked under a lit window.

The fire escape barely hung down past the bottom of the second floor. She paused under it and waited. Zorn grabbed her thighs. She squatted and then jumped. He lifted, hoisting her up so she could grab the bottom rung. He guided her back down to a soft landing and access to the higher levels. Easy-peasy.

On the second-floor landing, it was a cinch to then get up to the correct floor and step out onto the wide ledge. With light, confident steps, she made it around the corner of the building. Light spilled onto the ledge from a window up ahead. Just beyond, voices drifted out through an open window.

She slowed and glanced back at Zorn. His piercing eyes shifted down to her. Very little expression showed on his face. She knew very little emotion bubbled under the surface, either. At just over six feet and with a medium build, it was easy to underestimate the absolute beast he became in a fight. He'd imparted that knowledge to her early, starting when she was just fourteen. He'd taken her under his wing when usually he didn't have time for anyone.

She tensed a little, and he nodded. After five years of training together, fighting together, doing jobs together, and getting into a hairy situation or two, they didn't need words to communicate. He wasn't much of a talker, anyway.

He fell back a bit. For the first time, she was taking point on a job. It was her right as Mordecai's sister and backup. Adrenaline and pride surged through her, along with an antsy feeling, like standing at a starting line, waiting for the pop of the gun.

She took a deep, steadying breath as she pulled a

switchblade out of her pocket. The blade *snicked* as it sprang up. She stopped at the first window and tried it. Unlocked, as expected for a residence this high up and housing the people it did. Derelicts crashed here. They met their employer's buyers, they partied, and they lounged around. That was the sum total of their existence. Or so it seemed on paper. Mordecai never should've gotten involved with people like this. He had a huge heart and he always wanted to help—people like this took advantage of guys like him. *Had* taken advantage.

Would die for taking advantage.

Daisy didn't sense any souls in this room, so she lifted the window slowly.

Lexi's blood magic gift had given her the usual perks—enhanced strength, speed, healing, and the ability to understand any language anywhere. But each Demigod also passed down something relative to their specific type of magic. In the case of Lexi, a Demigod of Hades, she'd passed on the ability to feel and identify souls, the thing Hades snatched as a person died and shed their skin. Or some such thing—she'd never been very interested in how it worked. Ghosts freaked her out.

Thankfully, she could only sense the souls of the living. Unlike Lexi, she wasn't plagued with feeling or seeing the dead.

She climbed over the pane. A waft of *funk* assaulted her. She screwed up her nose in disgust. It was like someone had put dirty socks and a wet dog in a bowl and heated it up. Laundry lay strewn across all available surfaces. Soda cans and wrappers littered the ground. She had to watch her step to avoid stepping on anything and alerting the residents of her arrival.

Murmured voices drifted down the hall. She paused at the door to listen. The window stayed open behind her. Zorn stood at it, waiting to make sure the breaking-and-entering portion of their plan went off correctly.

A man was speaking. Another burst out laughing. Finally came the sultry voice of a female. *Bingo.*

Down the other way, a light glowed from under one of the doors. The bathroom, if she wasn't mistaken.

A light splash caught her attention. Then the movement of water.

Yes, the bathroom, and someone was relaxing and taking a bath. Hopefully they wouldn't get the urge to get out just yet. She'd deal with that person later.

She glanced back at Zorn again. He drifted from the window like a phantom, still on the ledge. He'd peer in through the living room window, ready to help if she needed it.

She hoped to fuck she wouldn't need it. She'd looked up their magic and knew how to quickly combat it—none of them were anything special. But she never knew. Not in the magical world. One wrong move, a bad decision, a mis-thrown knife—and she'd be vulnerable. She could never afford to take any chances.

She slinked through the hallway, her switchblade in her hand. They were such a romantic sort of knife, switchblades. Close and personable and cool as all hell. Definite style points when used for grisly (though righteous) murders.

More laughter.

"When is he supposed to pick it up?" one of the guys asked.

"An hour, give or take," the other answered, sounding bored. "He doesn't tend to be punctual."

"I'll wait all night," the woman purred. Daisy gritted her teeth against the rush of anger. "He is..." She made an appreciative sound.

"Is that why you showed up?" the first guy asked.

The other guffawed. "What's that, Max? You thought she came for you?"

Daisy's fingers tightened. She edged closer to the corner at the end of the hallway. The room opened up beyond. She could just make out a pair of run-down sneakers. The owner was stretched out on the couch right around this corner. The others were on the other side of the room.

"You were fun, don't get me wrong," a woman, probably Ava, told Max, "but I'm kind of over it."

The other guy guffawed again.

Daisy burst into action. She recognized the two guys from the pictures easily, one near the window and the second belonging to those run-down sneakers. Green light for night-night.

She slapped the light switch and doused the room in darkness. The woman screamed. One of the guys said, "Ohhh whoa ahh." Very strange reaction.

Moonlight fell over him, but she'd already memorized his location and lined up her body. She pulled a throwing knife from the holster on her thigh and flung it. It lodged in his throat. Perfect shot. No one in this room had a Demigod's blood magic—except her—or fast healing like a shifter. That dude would bleed out sooner rather than later.

But the blood loss wouldn't kill him.

Acid spit gurgled out of his mouth and over his chin. It rolled into the wound and seeped in.

He had terrible genetics. Usually acid spit didn't affect the spitter. Not with this guy. Getting it on his skin was fine, but if it went into his bloodstream, it would kill him. He couldn't tolerate his own magic, something very unusual for magical people.

The guy on the couch started, his eyes wide. Daisy was on him in a moment, peppering him with knife strikes and quickly ending his flailing.

Low-hanging fruit, these characters. This was beneath her and Zorn in every way. It was good practice for her, though. A nice, easy steppingstone for her first semi-solo job.

She slowed, walking toward the woman. Ava. Very pretty, this lady. A knockout by anyone's standards. Mordecai had surely stopped thinking the moment she smiled at him.

She wasn't smiling now.

"I know who you are," she said, her voice quivering. "What do you want?"

Zorn pushed the window open and climbed in gracefully, nearly invisible despite the moonlight.

Ava let out a surprised sound, hurrying away from him and into the corner.

"Who's the guy in the tub?" Daisy asked her.

Zorn started moving toward the hallway immediately. He'd make sure the guy in the tub stayed put until they were ready to deal with him or her. They weren't implicated in all this. Yet.

Ava's body started to shake and then her voice changed octaves. A wave of sadness washed over Daisy. Ava was a magical mood changer.

Yawn.

"This is the last time I'm going to ask nicely." Daisy took a step toward the woman.

"He wants to meet the buyer," Ava said quickly, flinching toward the wall. "He works for Randall. He's higher up on the chain of command and wants to make sure the buyer feels comfortable."

The emotion changed to rage.

Daisy laughed. "Really? You want me to show you rage?"

Ava's face paled. The magical emotion she was pushing switched to depression. Her fear was messing with her control.

"The buyer of what?" Daisy asked, ignoring the changing emotions.

"A-antique. An antique. Don't come any closer! I'll tell you everything."

"Yes, I know." Daisy stepped forward and yanked Ava around until her face was pushed into the crack of the corner. She ripped the woman's hands behind her back before sliding the point of her bloody knife against the hollow behind Ava's ear. She pressed hard enough to break the skin.

"A goblet," Ava said frantically. "He called it a chalice. I don't know which one it is. Honest. I'm not on the payroll."

Daisy leaned into the woman, pressing the blade a little deeper. A thin rivulet of blood traced down the woman's neck. Her terror rose, her breathing becoming choppier and more panicked.

"You know who I am," Daisy said in a low voice, "and you certainly know who Zorn is. You must also know who my brother is."

"That wasn't my fault!" Ava trembled. "I told him I didn't want to be tied down. I told him! He said he'd be exclusive, but I didn't."

"Did you also tell him that you were with him so you could pass information to your boys? To make it easier for them to rob him?"

She froze.

"Yeah. The cheating thing is bullshit, obviously," Daisy went on, "but you were upfront about that. Fine.

Having someone filming you doing it while talking shit about my brother? Not good. That sort of thing gets under my skin. But setting him up to be jumped and robbed?"

The anger nearly dragged Daisy under.

"He's the type of guy who suffers in silence," she said with a constricted throat.

The picture Jerry had taken seven days ago flashed through her mind. Mordecai hadn't been with a woman at all. His whole body had been battered and bloody, his nose broken along with a few of his bones. He'd hidden that from Daisy and stayed at Jerry's while he healed so she wouldn't know.

The guys thought it was because Mordecai didn't want Daisy to claim vengeance on his behalf. That was probably partly true. But she knew Mordecai better than anyone. She knew what made him tick and why he did the things he did. He'd hidden because he was ashamed. He'd allowed himself to be caught off guard, and despite the rock-solid training they both had, they'd taken him down. It didn't matter that it was eight against one. He knew Daisy always tried to build him up, and he'd hate causing her pain by seeing him torn down. If he hadn't had the blood magic and the naturally fast healing of a shifter, he would've died. That was what had frozen Daisy's insides. He'd been done dirty and he'd suffered for it. That was inexcusable.

"You have him jumped, you take his shit..." Daisy

clenched her jaw as the rage swelled and twisted. "Then you make a sex tape while mocking him for it. He got that yesterday morning, right?"

It had crushed him. He had liked this chick for some fucking reason. He'd been over the moon about her. And she'd gone and shit all over him.

"Who talks shit about another lover while actively banging someone? No one. You were trying to hurt him emotionally after these assholes hurt him physically. What sort of hell spawned you?"

"He's nothing but an exiled shifter," Ava said through her teeth. "And you're nothing but a dirty Chester!" Magical self-loathing swamped Daisy. "It was embarrassing when he sang a Chester's praises in front of everyone. An angel? Yeah fucking right. He should've known better. He got what was coming to him."

He certainly should've known better. Mordie was too lovely to see Daisy for what she really was—the devil with razor-tipped heels. Death walking. That was his error, but this bitch was not the right person to call him on it. Daisy alone had that privilege.

The fake magical emotion couldn't beat out Daisy's very real fury.

Her voice was low and intimate. "First of all..." She shallowly jabbed the woman in the thigh with her knife, then in the side. Ava cried out and fell harder into the wall, back to being docile. "He was exiled *as a child*, right after his parents, the alphas, were murdered. Now he is working with Demigods. He could have a pack if he wanted, but he's choosing to stick with a very powerful family. He leveled up, you ignorant twat. Second, just so we're clear about the type of guy you fucked around with, he wanted to walk you home to make sure you got there safe. He didn't like this lifestyle for you. Is your air freshener actually a flaming dog turd? Because that's what it smells like. He's kind and lovely and gentle, but even if you hate that, he's very good-looking and has a stellar body. Like...what sort of stupid are you? That guy Max is dumpy as shit. Do you actively *try* to make bad decisions?"

Daisy gave her a few more shallow cuts, numb to the violence but wanting this message to be crystal clear. Fuck with one of her people, and you fucked with her directly. She didn't have compassion and she didn't play games. Zorn had taught her well. This chick wouldn't die, but she'd be laid up for a while. She'd have *plenty* of time to think about what she'd done. Plenty of time for the fear to take on a life of its own.

"You're going to send him an apology. Is that clear?" Daisy shook the woman. "You will send him an apology for being human garbage. After that, you will never speak to him again. You will never go around my family again. If you do, for any reason, I will finish this job I started. Get me?" She pressed the blade against the crying woman's throat.

"Yes," Ava whispered.

"What?" Daisy prompted.

"Yes!"

Daisy used the woman's slinky dress to clean off her blade before stepping back.

"Out of curiosity"—she put the knife away—"do you still have the watch or car you took from him?"

Ava sank to the ground in a tapestry of blood and defeat. "I don't have it. Randall took it and gave us cash. He's got it. I don't have it!"

Randall, hmm? Daisy might just look him up. He was the big fish of the operation. Actually, Zorn might want to handle him. She still had to go after the other six turds who had helped these dead guys take down Mordie.

The rage simmered.

Daisy turned her back on Ava, a signal that the woman was no threat. Doing that as a Chester was the gravest of insults to a magical person.

Zorn waited in the darkened hallway, no moonlight reaching this far.

"You left her alive?" he whispered.

"She needs to send an apology to Mordecai. You heard Jerry. He said Mordie feels betrayed. I don't want him to lose faith in women or people in general. Besides, he'd flip out if I killed her. He'd take responsibility and feel guilty and it would be a whole thing. I don't have the patience."

"Careful. Your big heart is showing," Zorn murmured.

Obsidian

She rolled her eyes at him.

He jerked his head at the closed bathroom door. The light was still on. No splashing came from inside.

"The shades are pulled on the window," he said. "I couldn't have a look. He must've heard the screaming. He didn't get up to investigate."

She hooked a finger over her shoulder. "They were utterly useless. Killed by your own acid? Give me a break. Mr. Bathtub is probably scared."

"Probably."

"He's part of the organization, so he's fair game, but we don't know what kind of magic he has."

"Correct."

Daisy bit her lip. Zorn stared down at her, no expression. He'd take point if she wanted. He was silently asking if she was up for this.

Nervousness roiled in her belly, but she didn't back down. This was her life. Sometimes, part of that life was walking into danger blind. With Zorn as backup, she should be able to handle it.

Should being the operative word.

"I'm on it," she said, not allowing the nervousness to quiver her voice. She headed that way.

Chapter Three

"Right, then." Daisy pulled a paracord from one of her pockets and checked the placement of her weapons. She'd have to move fast and not get blasted by whatever magic that guy had going. "Let's see how well you've trained me, hmm?"

Zorn's lips quirked up at the corners, his version of a chuckle. He liked that she was ready to blame her failure on him. He'd always had an odd sense of humor. It was probably why they got along so well.

A dagger was secured to her hip in a sheath. She slipped the switchblade into her pocket and retrieved the dagger. She might need more reach.

The cord dripped down from the other hand. She paused next to the closed door, her hand with the cord now on the handle. She took a deep breath, then another, before she surged into the room.

Steam hung heavy in the air. A man lay in the free-standing tub near the center of the space, a hand gripping each side. His neck was tense, holding up his head nervously. He was probably wondering what was going on in the outer room. Very strange that he wouldn't get up, get dressed, and either go investigate or climb out the fucking window. There were a lot better options than nakedly waiting for an attacker to find you.

"What the hell do you want?" he growled, but he couldn't hide the uneasy quiver in his voice.

He released the fingers of one hand from the side of the bathtub. Daisy worried he might mean to do magic.

She rushed him, using all her speed. Her blade bit into his shoulder. His eyes rounded. Deep crimson oozed into the clear water. He thrashed, swinging his hands forward to protect his middle.

She ripped the dagger from his body and tossed it out of the way with one hand while looping the cord around his wrist with the other. He grabbed for her, faster than expected. Ares magic, maybe? Too soon to tell.

She leapt over the rear of the tub and yanked the cord with her. His free hand lost purchase on the slick porcelain, and his body jerked toward her sideways in the water. She ran to the base, dragging the cord with her and getting his arm at the correct angle. She didn't have the muscle to easily counter this guy. She had to rely on leverage and positioning.

No matter. She was used to it from training with big, powerful guys.

His arm went straight behind him but his legs were bending. He couldn't get his knees under him or it would be a different kind of fight. A harder kind of fight.

She stepped into the filthy, bloodstained water as she yanked on that cord, keeping the pressure. Her shoes and pants went soggy with the lukewarm water. Her foot fit nicely in the crease of his back, and she stepped with all her body weight, pushing his face into the water. This was a risky move. Any of Kieran's inner magical crew, her trainers, would ignore the danger of drowning and buck while twisting to throw her off. She was banking on this guy not being as good under pressure.

He continued to thrash. She pulled on his wrist, forcing his elbow to bend. His arm worked up his back. Good news. She grabbed the other, gripping the edge of the bathtub near his head. He finally bucked, his butt coming up and throwing her forward.

Her head crashed against the edge. Fucking *ow*.

"Piece of shit..." she grumbled, struggling to get back into the right position. She was suddenly rethinking this whole strategy.

He twisted. His captured hand almost pulled free as his other hand pushed under him to lift his body into the air.

"Yes, exactly, that's what I needed," she grunted as

she pulled up both knees and rammed them into the center of his back.

His body met his hand on the bottom. That elbow bent, and she quickly grabbed it, putting all her effort into wrestling it back with the other.

"You...are not...making this...easy," she groused as she shoved both hands as far up his back as she could get before wrapping the cord around his wrists and forearms and tying it off. Red bathwater sloshed and spilled over the sides. She still had about ten feet of cord dangling from the knot.

She pushed to standing and grabbed part of it, breathing heavily. The guy started to turn over, having gone without breath for a while now. The only thing on his mind would be getting air.

She set about tying his ankles as he turned, flapping his legs like a merman, since he couldn't use his arms. Those tied together, she then roped up to his knees until the cord was all used up. That really oughta hold him.

By the time he got a sweet mouthful of air, he realized her switchblade was pressing against his balls.

Zorn glided farther into the room, liquid stealth. He lifted an eyebrow at the water drenching half her clothes.

"Yeah," she panted tiredly. "That really could've gone better. I still don't even know what kind of magic he has."

"Wh-what do you want?" The man's eyes were

wild with fear upon seeing Zorn. He always stole the show.

"We have a few questions," Daisy said, flicking her blade to get his attention.

He flinched, but his eyes didn't leave Zorn.

Zorn leaned against the wall, content to watch.

"What sort of work does Randall do?" she asked.

"Special antiques, collector's items, art. H-he acquires hard-to-find pieces that have a specific value to our customers."

"He *steals* hard-to-find pieces, you mean."

The man's eyes got cagey.

"Where'd you get the chalice for the client coming tonight? And also..." She shifted against the tub, so confused. "Why the hell did you think it was a good idea to take a bath, of all things, when he might show up at any time? You don't even sleep in this cesspit and you thought you'd take a break out of your workday to soak in the tub? What sort of strange outfit are you people running here?"

"I...I..." His gaze flicked back and forth between Daisy and Zorn. He hadn't expected this new line of questioning. "I came from working out. I needed to freshen up. The shower doesn't work."

Daisy glanced at the stained shower stall in the corner with the dirty, foggy glass and the grime between the tiles.

"Okay, fair enough. About the chalice..." She pushed the blade harder against his balls.

Once again, he only had eyes for Zorn.

"I don't know much. They don't tell me much!" The water sloshed as he twisted, struggling against the cord. "All I know is this guy's outfit wants the crystal chalice. If they can find the crystal chalice, they can get through the Faegate."

A jolt of adrenaline zipped through Daisy's body at hearing the term *Faegate*.

Zorn's whole body tensed. He straightened slowly. This had just gotten a whole lot more interesting. Or terrifying, depending on how one looked at it.

"What about the Faegate?" Zorn walked toward the tub.

The man licked his lips. "Just that— Hey, look, I'm just a peon. I'm a nobody. I'm here to make sure things go smoothly. They're offering a lot of money for—"

"What about the Faegate?" Zorn repeated. His rough voice held a warning.

He was not a person from whom anyone wanted a warning.

"The dark fae king... W-well...well..." the man sputtered. "He's looking to pierce the Faegate or something. To come into the human realm, I mean. To escape the Cerebrals or whatever they are."

"Celestials," Zorn said not so patiently.

"Ce-celestials, yeah." The man's eyes watered, fear drowning his gaze. "The fae type that rules all the kingdoms and guards the borders or whatever—"

Daisy nodded, motioning for him to move on. "We're all aware of the setup."

At least, people now obsessed with the fae were. People like her, ever since that *one* set loose an unspeakable danger that nearly killed her whole family. Since he started continually showing up in her dreams. Since his memory would not fucking diminish.

She'd been learning all she could about their realm and their kind, but the so-called scholars didn't know much. Humans who crossed the Faegate—what the fae called the "fringe," a sort of magical borderlands to keep their species put—didn't tend to return. If they did, it was because they'd made a deal with one of the kings or queens. A deal that usually went sour—part of the cunning fae's plans—and resulted in a fae rummaging through the deal maker's mind and then killing them gruesomely. There'd been a few instances.

Fae weren't supposed to cross the fringe unless they had a binding contract with a human. That would permit them entry, but only allow them enough time to carry out their business. If they lingered, the guardians of Faerie, the Celestials, would force them home or kill them outright. At least, that was what the books said.

Only a fool got involved with the fae and their meddlesome, malicious gods. Only an absolute moron invited them into one's life.

This guy was clearly both, and his boss was a dead man walking. Which, whatever. He'd get what was coming to him.

But trying to find magical objects with which to bypass the Faegate? Did he not realize that faerie magic would take root here and twist their reality into something nightmarish? There was a reason the realms needed to be kept separate. All the texts agreed. Hell, even the old gods agreed. They'd made the fringe, after all. They'd created the magically superior "star children" Celestials to guard it. If the fae got through, they'd enslave what they thought of as lesser beings, kill anyone they had no need of, and twist the fabric of reality to suit their needs. The whole place would become unlivable. And for what? A few bucks dealing cups?

She said as much.

"A few bucks?" The man's loose jowls wobbled with tremors. "Try a couple hundred thousand for each chalice. More if we track down one they really like. The crystal chalice? Over a million."

"Right but...then what?" Daisy's fingers tightened on her knife. She really wanted to slice something off to get the point across. "How's money going to help you? If that king gets through the Faegate, there's nowhere for you to hide. No other safe realm for you to go to. Not that we know of, anyway. You'll be as influenced by their magic as anyone else. You'll see friends turn into creatures. Non-magical humans get a magical upgrade and probably lose their heads with the power and declare war on the magical governments. There're a million different ways it could all go wrong, and I probably haven't thought of the worst ones. Money won't do you any good if you invite that sort of horror into these lands."

His eyes narrowed, looking at her fully. Stubbornness set his jaw.

"Obviously we'd be protected," he said indignantly. "Randall isn't stupid. He—"

"I beg to differ." Zorn stepped a little closer, and the man visibly quailed. "You'd be the first to fall by the king's hand." Zorn's hard gaze hit Daisy. "Clear out. Find that chalice. I want to see what it is. Leave it in the middle of the living room floor. Once you do, take the fire escape and head back to the car. Wait for me there."

Shivers rolled down Daisy's spine. Zorn didn't usually shoo her away from the job. Not for any reason. When you trained with Zorn, you lived by the sword. She'd seen some gory stuff. Daisy didn't have a squeamish stomach, and she didn't have much in the way of morals. She was made for this role, same as Zorn. Same as Amber, their partner in espionage and sometimes assassinations. His asking her to leave meant he planned to send a message to this Randall guy. To get colorful. This was the reason Zorn was greatly feared.

Or maybe he planned to ask for a few more details he didn't want her hearing. Zorn had fae blood, she was almost positive, and he was very private about his roots. This situation was probably touching very close to home. He might want to find out if he was in danger.

Whatever the reason, she put away her switchblade and collected her dagger. After slipping it into its sheath, she headed for the door. It clicked behind her, and she immediately heard the man start blubbering for his life.

He should've thought of that before inviting the fae into this territory. Now they had a potential nightmare on their hands. One that might show up at any time to collect a magical chalice that could ruin the human world as they knew it.

Well, this evening took a horribly unexpected turn... she thought as she reached the living room. Ava was long gone. She likely wouldn't be back. Not that it mattered. All Daisy cared about was that apology video. And it better be heartfelt! Or at least seem like it, anyway. Mordecai was too good of a person to lose faith in humanity's overall goodness. That was Daisy's job, and one she took to with great vigor.

She flicked the switch to bring up the lights and scanned the various rooms. It was in the third bedroom that she found what she was probably looking for. Tables had been set out in rows. Objects of all shapes and sizes adorned the velvet-covered surfaces. Old rings not cute enough to be hot vintage items, old lamps, vases—the usual subjects of the antique world were present. She wasn't much of a collector. They all looked like junk to her.

"Chalice..." she murmured to herself as she perused the farthest corner. Honestly, she didn't even know what a chalice was. Like a goblet, apparently. A big cup of some sort…

She glanced at each item. Nothing fit the profile on the first table, so she moved on to the next. Nothing there, either, though she did see a very cool vintage watch that would look stunning with a particular outfit she was thinking of.

"Yoink," she muttered, grabbing it up. Finders keepers. Last one to steal it wins.

A couple of gems, in bad need of a polish, caught her eye, but nothing too remarkable. Until she got to the far edge of the room.

A strange pulse of energy made her stop. A somewhat flat object lay against the black velvet, three inches long and two wide. The edges were jagged and one end curved up to a flat point. A black sheen covered a core that looked almost green, like it had hidden depths of deep emerald.

When her fingers brushed against the surface, the strange pulse materialized into a pleasant hum. The object looked dirty and bumpy, but the surface felt glass-smooth. She slid her thumb across. The hum intensified, vibrating up her palm. A basil-green light throbbed in the middle, transfixing her.

She pulled it closer, a sheen of sweat covering her brow. "What…" The glow blinked rapidly for a moment before fading away as though it had never been there. She stared, wondering if it would come back and feeling that hum continue to vibrate up her palm. Nothing.

It was magical, though. It must be. Nothing else in the room acted like this. Zorn might know what it was. Regardless, it wasn't a cup and it wasn't crystal. It wasn't what she was looking for.

"Don't mind if I do," she murmured, checking to see which pocket might fit it best. None were long enough, though. It would fall out.

She slipped it into her shirt and nestled it into the little holding place in her bra, between her breasts. There was a lot of space to work with. Puberty hadn't done a whole lot for her in that department. A custom-made bra and here she was, hiding shit in her boobs. Usually it was a weapon, but whatever. Desperate times…

At the end of the last table, she still hadn't found what she was looking for. As she turned for the door, she noticed the stool peeking out from just behind. It was clearly intended to be missed when walking into the room.

After swinging the door out of the way, she looked down onto a purple velvet pillow holding a thick-walled goblet with a sturdy base.

"Hello, chalice," she murmured. Clearly the idea was for the buyer to peruse the tables, grab anything of interest, and come back here for the item of the day.

It lay on its side, and the overall color looked almost pewter, with etchings of flowers and leaves on the sides of the cup portion and geometric designs down the stem and around the bottom. The surface was cold to the touch and seemed heavier than it appeared. Areas looked worn, as though this item had long been in use and been somewhat polished to a smudged shine. Nothing else seemed inherently magical, but it might be that the user needed natural magic to unlock it. She didn't qualify. The blood magic from Lexi didn't count. At least, that was what she'd been repeatedly told, often accompanied by a sneer from people who hated a Chester being on their side of the magical line.

She secured her new watch around her wrist to use both hands and then bent for the pillow. A scream floated out of the bathroom. This wouldn't be any fun for Mr. Bathtub. Zorn had a flare for ruthlessness. Hopefully the neighbors weren't overly curious people...

She put the pillow in the middle of the living room with the chalice on top. Zorn would know not to take it with him. No one needed a fae tracking them down, not for any reason.

Hopefully he was about done.

She glanced at the apartment door but headed for the window. This building had two working cameras. She didn't need proof floating around of her involvement in Mordecai's life. He'd be really annoying to live with if he knew she was playing vigilante on his behalf.

Outside on the ledge, she worked her way to the corner. A soul, out of sight, popped up on her radar.

Someone was out here with her, on the same ledge. Her scalp tingled in alarm as a hint of nervous anticipation wormed through her.

It was probably a neighbor wanting to see what the commotion was about without actually confronting the person causing it. It was what she would do. The fae client would just use the door. Their glamor would get them past the cameras, if they cared about them at all. Plus, only forty minutes had passed and this buyer was apparently not punctual. She and Zorn should still have time.

Regardless, she didn't want to meet a new friend unprepared. Even low-powered magic could be fatal if it hit her head-on.

She pulled out a throwing knife. Stab and run. It was always the best practice for a Chester.

She kept walking until she was close enough to the corner for a good shot. The person continued nearer until reaching the turn. There they slowed to navigate going around. After a brief pause, a tall man with impossibly broad shoulders stepped into view.

Her stomach dropped out, and her world exploded in color. Her knees nearly lost their strength, making her wobble toward the wall. A delicious thrum she vividly remembered flowered in her body, competing with shock and surprise and incredibility.

No, not a man. A fae.

Her fae.

Moonlight highlighted his straight, fine features,

elegant yet dangerous. Regal death. Dark, windswept hair draped the sides of his face before curling just under his jaw. In the back it was longer still, dusting his neckline. His dress shirt was stretched tight across his chest, showing defined pecs, but fell loose at his trim waist before tucking into black trousers.

His casual dress sneakers didn't make a sound against the concrete and were an interesting choice for scaling buildings and breaking and entering. A very fashionable choice that she really wanted to adopt, damn him.

His eyes were lost to the darkness, but she knew their color all the same: vivid green leading into a burnished gold ring around the iris. Intimately expressive. Absolutely gorgeous, like him. Like he'd been the first time she'd seen him. And the second, when he set loose a chain of events that had nearly killed them all.

Words slithered through her mind like a lover's caress.

Hello, little dove. Did you miss me?

Chapter Four

Imagine finding you here... His voice was like a soft lick inside her head.

He slipped his hands into his pockets casually, devilishly, and took another step closer. He clearly wasn't worried about pitching off the side, even though his shoulders were not making it easy for him to hug the wall. She took in his uncomfortable handsomeness and the play of muscle with each movement. Memories came rushing back: the crystalline beach and the delicious feeling of his proximity. The dreams and the waking pleasure-nightmares. She remembered the feeling then, similar to now, with hot and cold shivers running her length. Heat raced across her flesh. It was hard to think, hard to breathe.

Fuck, but he was startlingly attractive.

Her memories of being near him didn't do the

feeling justice. Couldn't compare to the sweet slide of pleasure lacing across her skin.

She struggled to get her mind back on track. Fought to remember what was actually important. His actions at that convention had burned a scar into her. Her family had barely escaped. Lexi had nearly died. All because this...*creature* standing in front of her had needed a distraction. A *distraction*!

Now here he was, trying to help his king get across the fringe to a land they'd ultimately corrupt and tarnish. He didn't deserve her fractured focus. He deserved death.

His full lips twisted into a smile. *I see you remember me.*

His eyes roamed her body slowly before resting on her face. "You've grown since I saw you last." His voice was billowing black satin. He seemed equal parts seductive and dangerous. Teasing but with a hint of maliciousness.

He'd grown, too. He still looked only a couple of years older than her, but he'd shot up in height. Out in breadth. He carried robust strength now. Loose, supple muscle earned from years of fighting. Of killing. His was a terrifying beauty filled with dark secrets and violent deeds. She'd witnessed it those four years ago, and he was clearly still at his games in the human realm, hunting down prey for his ruler. Trading memories for death.

He stepped closer, only a few feet away, looking

down into her hate-soaked eyes with a cocky, insufferable grin.

"You've changed." A slight accent rode his words, the vowels somewhat softer. He tilted his head, studying her. "When I met you last, you didn't have magic. It never mattered, though, did it? You always noticed me. No matter how tightly I wrapped my glamor around me, your gaze found me every time I was in your presence. In the halls. In the garden. There was no hiding from you. Your gaze and yours alone. I thought that curious, so I sought you out. Do you remember the first time we met face to face?"

Memories crowded in before Daisy could do damage control. The thrum of her body, the fire in her gut.

His lips curled devilishly. "Yes, exactly. I felt just like that. I *feel* just like that, right now. Curious, isn't it?"

Curious? Maybe. Frustrating? Absolutely.

His hand blurred when it moved. An artfully decorated, curved blade appeared in his palm.

Her training *finally* kicked in and she reacted. Her hand swung forward, the throwing knife with it. Her fingers relaxed at the right moment, releasing the knife.

He realized it too late. His twist wasn't fast enough, and the knife lodged into his side.

He hissed as he stepped forward.

She swiped her hand away and ducked into the fight, her dagger in her palm as if by magic. She sliced across his chest and angled the blade, shoving up to get him under the jaw. His height made the move easy. His longer reach made his counter in such close proximity more difficult. She'd learned to use her smaller stature to her benefit.

Both of her hands were on the hilt. She'd need all her strength.

Right when the blade neared that incredibly handsome face—such a waste to slice it off—a shock of pressure stopped her limbs. Her hand was forced open, letting go of the dagger. Tingling air slammed into her body, but it didn't feel like what Kieran could do with Poseidon's magic, a wall of air. This felt wilder. Unruly. Uncontrolled, almost, like it was writhing and twisting over her skin.

Fae magic, obviously.

An earthy fragrance coincided with her slamming back against the wall. Her hands were glued to the hard surface, as were her feet. An invisible band of dark air, shimmering with golden hues, wrapped around her waist to ensure she stayed put.

Well, shit. This fight hadn't gone well.

She sucked in a deep breath and tried to relax, pushing away the fear. There was no point in struggling while magic secured her. She'd have to wait for an opening to try again. A slip-up. Even the most experienced fighter made mistakes. One just needed patience to take advantage of it. She had to believe even fae made errors.

"Ouch," he said with obvious humor as he plucked the throwing knife from his side. "Look how vicious you are! Adorable. That was a very hard love bite, little dove. Wrong type of weapon to make the effect permanent, however. This won't slow one of my—" He paused as he looked at his torso. "You've ruined my shirt! What will my new friends think?"

He glanced at the apartment down the way to relay who his new friends were.

"It doesn't really matter," she replied. "They're all dead. Or nearly, at any rate."

"Oh. Well, that's good, then. Saves me the trouble." He tossed her throwing knife off the ledge and bent to pick up her dagger, balancing precariously on the edge. He hefted it once, twice, and then put his own knife away. "This is well made. Still the wrong type of weapon, obviously. The gashes you created are nearly gone already." He paused, looking down at her. "You are very fast, little dove. I am truly impressed." He wiped the blade free of his blood, further ruining his shirt. "Fast, vicious, and exceedingly beautiful. Like a fragile vase—when broken, its shard will slice a vital point and spill all of one's lifeblood."

"Poetic," she said dryly.

"Yes. I moonlight as a bard." His grin was mischievous. "Just kidding. I kill people and take their possessions. It's nearly the same thing, don't you think? Anyway, back to our friendly conversation that you ruined by trying to kill me. The feeling when I was around you at that convention caught me by surprise. And it clearly caught you the same way, both then and now. You weren't magical at that time, correct? Now, however..." His eyes narrowed as his gaze delved into hers. "What has happened? What has changed with you? I feel the magic, but it isn't yours. How is that possible?"

Tingles washed over her body. Pressure pounded behind her eyes.

"Are you shuffling through my memories?" she said warily, trying to hide the panic.

She'd known from four years ago that he must possess the mindgazer power, something necessary in his line of work, given he ransacked people for their knowledge. Demigod Lydia had mentioned something about that...before she forfeited her end of their deal and her life with it. She was the reason this fae had needed a "distraction."

Not all fae possessed the ability, she'd read. The texts said it was usually the more powerful fae, often the nobility, kings and queens, and of course the Celestials. This one, as nothing more than a glorified errand boy and assassin, had probably gotten lucky with genetics and found placement with his king and court.

His smile stretched, frustratingly dazzling. "My goodness," he murmured, his gaze snagging on her lips. "What a cutting though accurate analysis. Quite intelligent, aren't we? You'll do nicely. And yes, I was shuffling through your memories. I would've thought that obvious. When I gaze into a future lover's eyes, I'm not usually so constipated looking."

She swallowed thickly. Hearing his voice inside her head was one thing, but his knowing her inner thoughts or memories was entirely another.

History had taught her to keep that stuff bottled up and hidden away. Exposing the deeper parts of herself made her vulnerable. It gave people somewhere to aim when they wanted to hurt her, or her family through her. She'd learned long ago, within the many foster homes and their abusive residents, that the world loved a punching bag. Emotions were a liability. Joy was always short-lived. If she presented a hard front, fewer people tried to pick on her.

"Interesting," he said softly, and the pressure reduced. "Not about your fear of being vulnerable. That I get. I didn't know Demigods in this realm could impart magic without an oath. It's not usual they should do so, I think. But she clearly loves you very much and wants to protect you. How sweet. Let's make sure, shall we?"

He stepped closer, dousing her with his heat. Shivers flowed over her suddenly flushed skin. His body nearly touched hers, pushed in close to fit between her and the edge. The soles of his heels kissed the air.

"While we're here," he said softly, pulling the dagger up between them. The tip dragged against her neck. "Regardless of this feeling we both find intoxicating but highly annoying, I find you exceedingly beautiful. Did I mention that already? I can't seem to stop thinking it." The blade continued to travel, down her throat to her breastplate, where it paused, over her heart. A hard press and that was the end of her. "Dainty and pretty and harsh and ruthless, all at the same time. It is such a complement to my own pretty face and vicious brutality."

"With the size of your ego, it's a wonder you can fit on this ledge at all."

"That's how I got so strong. By carrying around my enormous ego." His grin was devious. "I know you noticed my physique." He winked.

The tip of the dagger sliced into the base of her throat. A little nick.

She wrapped herself in a cloak of nothingness so that the sting of the dagger didn't register. So that his dangerous presence and the magic trapping her to the wall didn't inspire fear. She locked her gaze on his and lifted her chin a little, defiant. She was blissfully desensitized to his actions while still on alert for an opening, *any* opening, with which to save herself from this predicament.

"Intriguing," he murmured, his eyes darting between hers, reading her. "You are fully aware I could kill you right now, and you have zero fear."

Zorn's words rose to the forefront of her mind: *Fear is a waste of one's last moments.*

Too true, he cooed, like a whisper in her mind, fully

expressing the texture and tone of his voice. She got the distinct impression he was teasing her. Taunting her about this feeling he'd identified. This reaction she seemed to have to him.

He brought the blade up slowly. A drop of crimson wobbled on the tip. He smeared it across his tongue, and now she reacted. Her look of disgust matched the *ew* in her mind.

"I am assessing your magic. Your magical people can do that, can they not? They feel it." He clearly caught her unspoken answer. "Just some of them, fine. But then they need their machines and procedures to know what type. It is mostly beyond human abilities, other than genealogy, to determine exactly how a person came by said magic. Mother, father..." He paused, and his entrancing eyes sparkled. "This magic was a gift, freely given..."

He nodded, as though answering a question. The blade dragged across her throat.

She steeled her voice so it wouldn't waver with uncertainty. "Are you going to kill me now?"

He tsked. "Why would I kill you before taking all that you are? I, at the very least, have to fuck you first."

"All that I am? If you mean my virginity, you're too late."

He chuckled darkly. "Good. Fuck the whole town if it suits you. When I claim you, I want you to know how to please me."

He slowly dragged the dagger's tip down the slope

of her neck. Her breath hitched as he turned it, and then the flat side slid against the bare skin on her chest. The metal was cold, but the shivers racing through her body were from the heat of his proximity. With a flick of his wrist, her top button detached and fell away. Her shirt minutely parted, catching his gaze. The knife continued to move, traveling over the swell of her shirt-covered breast. Pleasure jolted through her as it caught on the budded peak.

Her heart beat quickly, the urge to flee strong. The desire for him to lean closer equally so. Her chest rose and fell, her skin humming with a strange but pleasurable current. Her thighs rubbed together to stem the odd eroticism that flowed through her and burned along her skin. Transfixed, she watched him watch the knife as the point moved ever so slowly down her front to her stomach. At any moment, he could thrust it forward and spill her entrails. For some strange reason, though, she had no fear of his doing so. Knew he wouldn't. The touch stayed light. Dangerous. Strangely erotic.

The dagger paused at the opening of the sheath at her hip. Then he pushed it home in a slow, deliberate slide. Tingles and heat raced across her skin. She'd read that the fae were good at destabilizing their prey. This one was fucking *amazing* at it.

The object tucked into her bra started to hum against her breastplate. She could barely see the green glow through the fabric of her navy-blue shirt.

She felt more than saw his smile.

"You have something of mine," he said. "My chalice. I require it."

His large palm touched down on the base of her throat. She jolted at the shock of intense pleasure. His breath became heavy as his fingertips trailed down her skin to the neckline of her shirt.

"What a very curious feeling this is," he said quietly, as though to himself. "It is unlike anything I have ever felt. So...incredibly...intense. I almost can't resist it. What strange magic is causing it, I wonder?"

The hum of the object intensified before he pulled it away from her skin.

"That isn't a cup," she said, mouth suddenly dry.

"So it isn't. I need it all the same."

"You'll ruin this world if you shepherd the fae across the fringe."

"No, no." His other hand came up to rest just below her jaw line. His thumb gently stroked the edge of her lip. She barely held back a moan. "Not *across*. That would take more power than any of the seven kingdoms possess. The gods made sure of that when they tied the Celestials to the fringe. *Over*. A bridge, up where the magic is weakest. It still takes a lot of power, both to build and to thwart the Celestials, but with the right equipment, it is possible."

"Why? Why come here?"

"There are plentiful spoils in this realm. Slaves to do our bidding who don't have the power to revolt.

Freedom. The Celestials and their high sovereign, their glittering Diamond Throne, are no better than jailers. Their version of balancing the realm is suffocating. Restrictive. Here we would have vast lands to conquer. Whatever size territory we want with more all the time. Can you blame us?"

"You have the wrong magic for this place. There's a reason the old gods shored you up in that realm and built a barrier to keep you put. There's a reason they created an overall ruling body to keep your kind in check."

"But was it a good reason?"

"You'd destroy this place. I think that is a pretty good fucking reason."

"Nonsense. We wouldn't destroy it. We'd remake it in our image."

"Your image would be a nightmare."

"For you. And a haven for us. Come now." He tilted his head at her. "It's too early in our acquaintance for a lover's spat—"

He tensed and then ripped his hand away. It jetted past her and slammed against the wall beside her face. He twisted, looking behind him. She followed his gaze.

There, carving a slice into the bottom of the crescent moon, she could just make out wings. In a moment, she noticed the glittering golds and tangerines of more, moving in the moonlight. The wingspans were immense, too big for any bird.

"What is that?" she asked in confusion.

Obsidian

He spun back, all humor from a moment ago gone. His eyes took on a severe intensity. The mocking, teasing tone disappeared from his voice, replaced with panicked urgency.

"Celestials! Even a very clever assassin sometimes gets caught sneaking across the fringe. You now bear the flavor of my magic. Run! Flee! Hurry! They are nearly as powerful as one of your gods. You do not want to find yourself in their clutches."

The magic pinning her vanished. He stepped backward into the empty air. A gasp was pulled from her lips as he dropped. His fingers caught the ledge, he swung, and he was gone. She barely heard his footfalls on the ledge below.

There was no way she could duplicate that move. No way in hell. She had to get Zorn and then get down the slower way. Hopefully she had the time.

Chapter Five

Hand on the wall for stability, she ran back toward the apartment. Zorn stood in the living room, the chalice in his hands.

"That's worthless," she said through the opened window. "We gotta get outta here."

He glanced up, brow furrowed.

"Hurry!" She made a circle in the air with her finger. "Celestials are coming. We gotta get—"

She cut off in surprise as he darted toward her and ripped her through the window. He looked at the sky before shoving her on.

"Go. Front door. Follow normal human protocol." He dropped the chalice on the ground as he hurried with her.

"I didn't know they flew." Her voice jiggled as she ran. She reached the front door and jerked it open. "None of the books said they had wings."

"They're the only ones who fly." He kept his hand on her shoulder. "It's fine. They can sense fae magic and scent their kind, but no fae entered that apartment. They won't know to look there. They won't know we're connected to it."

She grimaced as they reached the stairwell, then gripped the handle and took the steps two at a time.

"About that…" On the second-floor landing, she swung around toward the next set of stairs. "I met one of them. He pinned me to the wall with his magic. He took the item I'd grabbed from the apartment. It wasn't a chalice. I didn't know he might want it—"

Zorn's firm grip on her arm stopped her before she could descend to the next level.

"*What?*" It was as close as she'd ever heard him sound to panicked.

She stilled even though everything in her wanted to sprint down the next set of stairs. She stared up into those hard gray eyes and saw his worry for what it was. That gaze dropped, finding the nick from the dagger.

"It's fine. He didn't hurt me." The opposite, in fact, as shameful as that was to admit. "He took the thing I'd grabbed and, after he noticed the Celestials, told me to run. It sounded like he wasn't supposed to be in this realm. He snuck past them but didn't escape their notice, however that might work."

His threat from all those years ago hung heavy within her, though she wasn't quite sure if it still applied.

Shh, little dove. It must remain our secret, or it will become your group that I must silence.

For some reason—fear, most likely—she worried about divulging too much information.

"What you grabbed..." Zorn swore softly. "He used his magic on you?"

"To pin me."

"Did he touch you?" The growl was ferocious. This man would battle a fae, regardless of if he'd lose the fight, if that creature had crossed a line with her in any way. Zorn was the same breed of loyal as she, and just as desperate for vengeance if his family was wronged.

The warmth in her heart was a stark contrast to the chill in her blood at what was coming. At the danger they might be in because of her chance meeting.

"Only to get that...rock thing, whatever it was. When I stabbed him, he said it was with the wrong weapon. I lodged my throwing knife in him and slashed him with my dagger, and he was barely fazed. Though those wounds wouldn't have slowed you down, either. Maybe just not enough holes in his body."

His gaze was conflicted. He looked skyward, as though seeing through the ceiling to the coming danger.

"Okay. Go. Hurry! Maybe we can get to the car before they descend." He marshaled her on, staying right behind her as she hurried down the steps.

At the bottom level, she slowed to a walk. It was never good to draw attention to oneself by rushing. Once she was through the ramshackle lobby and outside, she picked up the pace just a bit. She barely stopped herself from looking at the sky. Zorn would do it much less obviously. Besides, if she caught sight of them again, she might stare. She'd barely viewed them from a distance, but the pretty sparkle on those dawn-like wings, even in the moonlight, had been a sight to behold.

"It wasn't a chalice?" Zorn asked so quietly she barely heard.

"No. It wasn't anything. Just...like...a rock, kinda." She explained what it had looked like as they walked. What it had felt like and the momentary illusion of it glowing.

"Why'd you grab it?" He took her arm and kept her from turning the corner. Instead they walked straight on, toward the nearest fence and the fastest way away from the building.

"I wanted to ask you about it. It was weird but... cool. It had this neat...hum. I knew it was magical in some way, and since it wasn't a chalice, I figured it wouldn't matter. I grabbed a watch, too." She showed him her wrist. "He didn't care about that at all. Didn't even notice it."

"They aren't looking for chalices, then," he said, reaching the fence. He threaded his fingers together and dropped them low to cradle her foot.

He was taking care of his protégée and pseudo-niece, which was cute, but they didn't have the time. She jumped, grabbed the top of the fence, and quickly hauled herself over.

He dropped down next to her a moment later.

"They aren't looking to go through the Faegate, either," she murmured, unable to help herself from glancing skyward. "They want to go over somehow. A bridge, he said. He sounded confident that it was possible."

Puffy clouds slowly drifted across the night sky. Stars glimmered and the moon hung low. Nothing disturbed the light.

"Oh god," she breathed without meaning to, pulling her gaze away. "They must've landed. Can they really go that fast?"

"It'll be fine," he said, directing her with a hand gripped on her upper arm. "It really should be fine."

Should be fine?

She looked at his face, seeing no emotion. He didn't offer any other explanation.

They reached a main road and turned right. They'd gone a couple of blocks out of their way, but at least they were putting distance between themselves and that apartment complex.

"How long does it take for the flavor of his magic to go away?" she asked, chancing another look up, this time at the rooftops.

Zorn's face ripped toward her, his gaze sharp.

"What?" she asked.

He looked away without comment. Only after the next turn, closer to the car and their safety, did he offer a reply of sorts.

"Twelve hours if he is of decent strength. Twenty-four if he is powerful."

She swallowed. "Would an assassin for a fae king be that powerful?"

"Not usually. Twelve hours should do you—"

"Even if he could pluck out memories from four years ago?"

He jerked as though struck. His gaze didn't swing down to her in the following stretch of silence. He was contemplating her words, debating what questions to ask. His next words terrified her.

"Twenty-four, then, and we need to hurry. They'll be able to feel that magic from a greater distance."

By not asking questions, he was essentially telling her to keep her mouth shut. Clearly he realized the fae were prickly about information sharing. Hopefully she hadn't already said too much. The last thing she wanted was to give that fae male any reason to go after her family.

"Distance will help," Zorn murmured, his hand on her arm tightening and urging her to go faster. "Constantly moving air currents will, too. We'll go directly to Demigod Kieran. He can play with the weather and provide some shelter."

Her released breath sounded loud in the still night.

"Are you in any danger?" she asked softly. He'd know she was talking about his heritage.

He didn't respond. She couldn't decipher his body language.

She didn't push. There was no point. If he didn't want to answer, he'd ignore her quite easily. When he got stubborn, nothing in the world could move him.

They reached the next corner. A street lamp showered the cracked sidewalk in a murky amber light. The car was just down the way, around the bend.

"Can they still scent or sense or whatever the fae magic if it's locked up in a car?" she asked.

"Ye—" He jerked to a stop.

A tall man calmly strode around the bend, directly at them. A deep crimson jacket was molded to his broad chest. Sparkling scroll looped down on either side of the edges of his jacket in the same material. A high, rigid collar crowded his neck, and gray cuffs were a thick band around the bottom of each sleeve. Under, he wore a gray waistcoat in the same color as the cuffs, with the same loopy scroll, this not glittering. Shiny black pants completed the ensemble, ending in strange shoes made of something like velvet, but the material rippled like water as he walked. His crisp blond hair, utterly straight, dusted his shoulders. There were no wings in sight. They must be able to retract them somehow.

She had an eye for fashion. Had drooled over magazines when she was too poor to buy a pair of shoes. She knew jewelry and cars and all things expensive. Now it was a hobby, a flippant way to exist in her current life while hollowly drowning in her wildest dreams. The clothes on this guy were made of the finest stuff, and that glitter was diamonds, she'd bet her life on it. He wore this strange but perfectly cut and tailored suit like armor. His bearing screamed prestige and pedigree. Importance. Nobility.

His pointed ears, sticking out of his thin hair, said he was not of this world.

How did the suit work with his wings?

His gaze rooted to her as he casually strolled closer.

Zorn went that scary sort of liquid, his limbs loose, ready for action. He didn't move position. He never advertised what was coming next. He held her arm and watched the Celestial approach.

The man—could she call it a man without it being human? Creature? Thing?

He slowed, ten paces away, and held up a hand to Zorn, warning them to stay put. His eyes remained rooted to Daisy. He then lifted his other hand, his long, delicate fingers clutching her throwing knife—the one the earlier fae had tossed over the ledge. The fae's blood crusted the blade.

This belongs to you, does it not? the Celestial asked in her mind. The texture of his voice was smooth like satin. And rich. And not welcome.

"Use your words," she said, hiding the quiver in her voice.

The Celestial studied her. "Very well, human. Does this belong to you?"

His nails looked manicured. Pristine, like the rest of him.

"You know it does," she responded.

"Yes." The Celestial took another moment to study her. She didn't feel any power wafting off him. No magic. If he was digging through her mind, she couldn't feel it. He could've been a regular human guy with a penchant for cosplay and a silver spoon firmly embedded in his keister.

He tossed the blade at her feet.

"Enlightening," he said. "And yes, that is the wrong weapon. You'd best arm yourself a little better if you hope to take on one of his kind."

So he had been digging into her memories. He knew whom she'd stuck with that knife and how ineffective it had been. Good. Maybe they'd catch that other asshole and put a stop to his kingdom's plans.

The Celestial looked at Zorn but clearly didn't find much of interest, because in the next moment, he turned. As he did, wings surged from his back without disturbing his clothes at all. They flowed down to nearly the ground before the tips lifted into the air, giving Daisy a view of their incredible beauty.

Deep gold colored the base near his body, slightly translucent in the streetlight. That color spread out like veins into the rest of the wing, thicker in some places than others, the shape a combination of bird and butterfly wings that somehow worked so beautifully. Between the veins were nearly see-through, the wing almost dainty, the substance reminiscent of a dragonfly wing. The golden hues gradually changed from base to tip, morphing into pinks and oranges and then blues and purples. The colors reminded her of a sunset, almost. Or even like the crisp sky at dawn. Sunrise or sunset, so remarkably similar if she thought about it.

He bent at the knees and launched into the sky, the wings going active. He soared over the rooftops and away, probably to join the others, wherever they were.

A heavy breath rolled out of Zorn. He bent and scooped up the knife before cleaning it with his shirt and handing it to her.

"That was..." Daisy just blinked at nothing for a moment.

"Unexpected." Zorn started forward. "Reassuring."

"Reassuring?" She hurried to catch up.

"They might have let that fae you met slip through, but they are still effective. They realized their error and are working to right it. They also know what that fae and his kind are planning, thanks to you. They'll be able to handle things from within their own realm." They reached the car. He opened the door for her, looking skyward. "Hopefully."

Black BMWs to match Zorn's lined both sides of the street as they reached the houses near the dual-society zone. The house on the left, where Daisy often stayed, was Lexi's. On the right was Kieran's, both residences housing their close-knit chosen family when everyone got together out here.

The porch lights glowed in both houses, but only Lexi's had warm, buttery light spilling onto the pristine front lawn from the kitchen window. The living room, too, was illuminated, even at the late hour. Or the early hour, depending on how one looked at it.

Zorn put the car in park but didn't reach for the door handle.

Daisy unclicked her seatbelt but paused.

"The fae you met..." he said as he turned off the motor. "If he can read memories, I'm assuming he can speak within your mind? It usually goes hand in hand."

She didn't know that some fae could only do one of those. Zorn might just know more than the books she'd found.

"Yes," she responded.

"He pinned you with his magic, you said?"

"Yes."

"Why didn't he kill you?"

She wasn't sure if she should mention that she'd met him before. That they had history. She definitely didn't want to mention the draw of him. That seemed... too intimate, somehow. Maybe too damning.

Then again, did it really matter? Those things

shouldn't be enough to stop him from killing her. Fae didn't seem like the kind to care about that, not with a human, a creature they deemed *lesser*.

"I don't know," she said honestly, trying to recall the nuances of the conversation. The teasing and taunting. "He could've been playing with me. I seem to pose no threat to him. Not with these weapons."

Zorn stared straight ahead for a long moment. Leaves shivered in the yard at a slight breeze.

"You trust me?" he said.

"Obviously."

"I can trust you."

"I am sure glad that wasn't posed as a question, or I might've slipped a knife into you while you slept."

Zorn huffed, probably delighted by her spunk. He always had been.

He dropped his chin and looked away, out the window. "My biological grandfather was fae. Of the Sapphire Throne, located in the Sea of Stars. One of the gentry—what they call nobility, I'm given to understand. He met my grandmother by chance and took her against her will. My father was the result. He was wild, my father. Human blood greatly and quickly waters down the wildness of fae blood, but even still, he was vicious. Ruthless. He liked to play cruel games with my mom and me. When his amusement ceased, or any time he was drinking and gambling, he'd beat me bloody. Sometimes he'd beat me senseless. It never seemed to bother him. He never showed an ounce of remorse. Not ever. I wanted to know if that was because of his blood or his personality, and so I did a lot of research into the fae. As much as I could. They are all eternal, and immortality has made them cunning creatures. Brutal creatures. They scheme and plot—"

"They sound like the Demigods here."

"The Demigods of old, yes. Before they created laws and rules to curb some of the worst social infractions. Now Demigods are lambs compared to the fae nobility, and fae royalty is the worst of all. To rise in their hierarchy, they kill. Sometimes the assassination is face to face. Oftentimes, however, it is handled via the shadows, where the knife is hidden until their victim is dying. They'd kill their granny to take her place if the rewards were plentiful enough. And that is with their own kind, whom they respect. Humans are nothing to them. A distraction. Sludge under their boot. 'Lesser' doesn't even begin to describe how little they think of us."

She'd known some of that and guessed at others. Except for his father. She knew there had been abuse in Zorn's past, but not the brutal extent of it.

She took a deep breath but swallowed down the pain and sadness she felt on his behalf. The desire to reach out to him. He wasn't a man who cared about the sympathy of others. He wouldn't appreciate her gushing or saying she was sorry for what he'd been through. He'd gotten out of there. He'd granted himself his salvation, helped by Kieran. Then he'd seen the same hardness in her. The same trials by fire and the unwillingness to say die. He'd seen it...and he'd reached down for Daisy to help her out of it, as Kieran had helped him. He'd become her solid place in a scary, shifting, dangerous world. Her safety when nothing was safe. He'd taken a hand out, and then offered that hand to another. He was the very best kind of man.

So instead of gushing or anger or the dreaded compassion, she used a flat tone and said, "What's your point?"

He grunted, his version of barking laughter. "That fae is definitely toying with you, and when he tires of the game, he'll enslave or kill you."

A flash of unease wiggled in her belly.

"Then let's hope the Celestials start doing their job, I guess," she said evenly.

He ran his hand along his jaw, the sound like rubbing sandpaper. "We're not going to hope for anything. We're going to figure out what the *right* kind of weapons are, and then we're going to solve your fae problem."

Chapter Six

Heat rolled through Daisy, blistering her in the most intense, delicious of ways. She looked around, knowing exactly what she'd find. Half afraid to find it.

Unlike the memory, however, it wasn't a boy standing close to her, sparkling and shining within his glamor. This time it was a man—or a fae's equivalent of one. It was the creature who had held a knife to her throat. Who'd teased her and was now toying with her.

Six months had passed since she'd seen him on that ledge. Six months of almost constant dreams about him. Often they weren't connected to memories. Many times there were no clothes, him kissing down her body and between her thighs. Or sometimes showing her exactly how he liked to be pleasured.

After each one, she woke up feeling hot and languid...and frustrated with herself. Unfulfilled, craving the real touch, the buzz of his proximity, but shamed by how much she wanted it. How much she needed to hate him and *not* get lost in the memory of his warm hand touching down on her bare flesh.

People shouted within the hallway, necromancers yelling about a spirit that had the power to rip souls from people's bodies. To kill them with a small sliver of magic. It was the same kind of magic Lexi had, but this one wasn't on their side. This being, if it got free, would kill them all.

The memory was distorted. The dream dulled the danger. For she *was* dreaming, she knew that much. He'd stepped into her sleep time, yet again. This time, though, the feeling of his presence was amplified. Delicious.

"Hello again, little dove," he murmured. He stepped closer, his heat blanketing her body. "Keep yourself safe. You are important to my plans. I will need you before long. I want you...right now."

"Something isn't right," said Dylan, one of their crew—her family—standing next to Daisy. He wasn't aware of the intruder. "Do you feel that?"

She couldn't help but feel it, so fresh after meeting the fae again. So savory. Her reaction so terrible.

The fae winked, and his wicked smile grew.

In a moment, he was gone, all hazy air and sparkling wind, rushing forward...toward the barely contained Soul Stealer.

"No," she said breathlessly, transported back in time. Transported to that horrible moment.

It must be done, little dove. There is no better distraction on these grounds.

The haze that was him dodged around Thane, a level five Berserker who could destroy the whole place. When he changed, friend turned into foe. All he saw was red. The presence—her fae—slipped past Bria and stopped right before the body currently animated with that horrible, deadly Soul Stealer magic.

Zorn started and stepped forward, his hand landing on Bria's shoulder protectively. He'd clearly recognized the shimmer of the fae.

The fae darted so quickly that Daisy couldn't keep track of him. And then she could. He stopped next to Thane, and a strange though lovely, earthy smell tickled her senses.

"Shit—" Zorn lurched in that direction, but he was too late.

The fae zipped away again, much faster than Zorn could ever move in his gas form.

Thane sucked in a startled breath, flexing his biceps as he did so.

"Fight the urge, Thane," Daisy called out as the body in the hall cocked its head. The spirit inside the rotting flesh ignored the bells tolling through the hallway, desperate necromancers trying to keep it contained. If it could better work its mouth, Daisy knew it would be smiling.

"Oh no," she said in a release of breath.

"Get control of it!" one of the necromancers yelled. "Get control!"

"I'm trying! I'm *trying*!" the other hollered.

In a heartbeat, the two necromancers in charge of controlling the body slumped to the floor. The spirit had ripped the life right out of them. It was always the price for something like this.

The Soul Stealer's head came around, and then it was looking at her family. The only people she cared about in the world.

Thane grunted and groaned. Started to grow. The berserker was about to emerge.

Her heart leapt into her throat. "Fuck!" she yelled, grabbing Dylan. "Run! Go! Get out of here!"

"Distract Thane!" Bria shouted, turning toward Daisy and starting to run. "Make him follow us or that Soul Stealer is going to take him first!"

That fae had helped set two monsters loose, one who destroyed with a touch of magic, and another who destroyed everything in his path. The fae had intentionally put her entire family in danger.

Images flickered as the memory dissolved. A delicious feeling crept through her body.

Keep yourself safe, little dove, the fae whispered. *Keep my toy in one piece until I am ready to collect it.*

Her eyes snapped open, and she immediately looked at the window, half expecting to find him standing there. Half expecting him to be advancing on her.

The afternoon sun glowed from around the shades, the space empty. The dream had disturbed her nap, nothing more.

Her heart beat too quickly as she sucked in a breath to relax.

It was good they weren't relying on hope. The fae male was proving to be very cunning indeed. The Faegate and its Celestial guardians could not keep him contained. He'd snuck in at least a dozen times. He was after the crystal chalice and scooping up anything magical in the meantime.

It wasn't clear if he killed every person he visited. Those he did get rid of were marked, though. Placed atop each grisly murder...was a snow-white dove's feather. He clearly knew she and her team were paying attention and was making sure she knew where he'd been. Laughing about it, probably. He was playing a game of blood, and she was the audience. Eventually she would likely be a participant.

She pushed away the blanket and climbed out of bed. They hadn't made great strides in finding the *right* kinds of weapons. After procuring and poring over old texts, it seemed there were several that might work. The easiest were blades of iron. Apparently that material not only sliced up a fae good and proper, but it also burned their skin while doing so. The resulting wound took longer to heal, making it easier to kill them.

Better still? Magically treated iron, keeping the metal constantly cool and always sharp. Etch the right runes on the blade and it increased the punch.

The bitch of it was, hardly anyone made those types of weapons. If they found some with runes, the blades were chipped and dull. The craftsmanship was lacking. The human world didn't realize they had a fae problem, and so the market simply wasn't there for specialized weaponry to combat them. Worse, no one seemed inclined to try. Daisy and Zorn had tried to contact several people, to no avail. The artisans didn't care how much money was on the table; they didn't want to deal with anything relating to fae. Make a weapon to kill them, and one might show up on their doorstep with a dove's feather in hand. She couldn't fault the logic.

Zorn had found a lead, though. An elusive sort of guy who dabbled in antique weaponry. He supposedly had a store of them in his warehouse. It was that man she'd meet with tonight.

She headed for the shower, the catnap not refreshing her as she'd hoped. Fucking fae invading her dreams.

Sometime later, she stopped in front of the mirror and adjusted her relaxed black blazer cinched at her waist, secured with an inch-thick black belt. Her straight leg pants ended just above three-inch heels that were easy to kick off. A lacy black bra peeked out from the blazer lapels, and the gold buckle on the belt gave the ensemble an elegant pop. The fit was tailored, sleek, sexy, and perfect. *Boss bitch.*

Her brown hair, with artfully placed bronze highlights, was parted down the middle and slicked down straight, draping the sides of her porcelain face. A matte, baby-pink blush and glossy lip enhanced the extreme paleness of her skin. To add a little fashionista flare, she'd done a dense, smokey palette around her blue eyes and accentuated it with long black lashes and a thick brow. The entire *look* was calculated, playing up her doll-like appearance. Young and fragile. Vulnerable. Prey. It should serve her well on her job tonight.

She tugged at the bottom of her blazer before turning for her bedroom door. As her fingers wrapped around the knob, she heard the door down the hall squeak as it swung inward. Mordecai's deep voice grumbled something Daisy couldn't make out. Probably had to do with his door always squeaking no matter how often he lubed it up.

She grinned. The door was her doing, obviously. She liked to know when he was coming and going. He had a terrible habit of listening at her door when she was talking to contacts and too distracted to notice him. He worried about her, which was cute, but then he tattled, which was really fucking annoying. The latest had almost gotten her taken off this detail. She was still pissed about it.

Which was why she waited with her hand on the knob. His feet padded softly against the plush cream carpet in the hall, heading for the stairs. As he passed by, she swung the door open and stepped out quickly.

"Rawr!" she yelled at him, waving her hands.

He made a high-pitched sound of surprise. A fist jutted toward her, his impulse to attack what had scared him.

She laughed and batted it away. He was so predictable.

"Damn it, Daisy!" he hollered. "I hate when you do that!"

"I know." She shoved his big shoulder to get him walking. "And I hate when you eavesdrop."

"Maybe try growing up." He continued on, his size dwarfing her. This kid used to be skinny and sickly back when they lived in Lexi's tiny house. He'd had Moonmoth disease, a condition where his non-magical side fought his magical side. When they couldn't afford the expensive medicine to help him, he'd endured life in constant agony. They'd nearly lost him a handful of times, stealing and scraping to afford the only thing that would keep him alive.

Once Kieran had gotten him the treatment to save his life, he'd grown into the shifter he was always meant to be. Six-three, stacked with muscle, and a vicious fighter. His roots came from alphas, though—leaders—and so he was also levelheaded, balanced, smart, and positive. He saw the good in everyone, somehow. It was mystifying.

"I'm only a year younger than you, dickface." She shoved him again.

"I'm going to tell Lexi you swore." He turned and reached out to shove her back. She grappled with him for a moment so he couldn't get purchase.

Per Lexi and Daisy's "agreement," which Daisy had no choice in, Lexi got to punch Daisy in the face if Daisy swore. It had started when Daisy was fifteen or something, because she was apparently too young to swear, and continued until now because Mordecai was a saint. He never swore. Ever. It was fucking weird.

"Stop, would you? You're going to mess up my hair." She batted his arm away.

"Good. Maybe you won't go."

She rolled her eyes. "I'm going to tell Lexi you're using a made-up name and secretly dating someone outside our social circles because you're embarrassed by your family."

He froze at the top of the stairs.

He'd gotten that apology video Daisy had very politely requested of Ava, and then thankfully forgotten about her. Now he'd found a non-magical girl who didn't have a clue who he was. He'd gotten a fake Chester identity, created by their pal Bria, and pretended to be non-magical and mundane so he could have a chance at a normal love life.

Daisy had looked into the matter thoroughly. The

chick was cute, cool, not from a lot of money, and seemed totally normal. He was in safe hands.

"Stop getting involved in my love life," he ground out, blocking the stairs.

"I'm not involved in your love life. I have nothing to do with your secret trysts. But maybe now you know how it feels when people won't mind their own business, hmm? Move." She pushed him to press the point.

He flexed to keep himself put. "You need to be reined in. I know the guy tonight dabbles in antiques sometimes, Daisy. It's dangerous to meet him on your own. You're only nineteen. You shouldn't be doing stuff Zorn and Amber do. They have a lot more experience than you, and they are *magical*, Daisy. They are powerful. You are not. You're in danger just living in this territory. You shouldn't be making it worse by dealing with dangerous people."

Her anger rose. Zorn had stepped up her training in light of the fae situation, pushing her as hard as she could take. She needed it if she planned to survive whatever that fae had in store for her. Mordecai's worry about her had skyrocketed, though, and it had turned suffocating.

"I know what I am," she said between her teeth. "I know what I am up against. I don't need you mothering me. Now *move!*"

She fit her hands into the groove of his broad back, put all her weight behind it, and *shoved*.

His huge shoulders led the charge down the stairs,

his legs running on air as they followed. He grabbed the banister with a "whooooa!" as he fell. His side hit the carpeted (and therefore soft) steps and bounced. His legs tried to fly over him. He tucked as much as he could. His back hit the banister as his body kept rolling, thunking and thudding down the steps.

He'd been down this road before. The best was when he was sleepy and she rigged a booby trap.

She made her way down after him, chuckling at his uncustomarily clumsy fall.

He reached the bottom and sprawled on his face. In a moment, he bounced up and spun. His fists were clenched, and the muscles on his arms popped. He stared at her angrily.

"What happened?" Lexi ran around the corner, her brows pulled together in alarm. She wore black leggings and one of Kieran's wool sweaters that draped down her athletic frame. Her blond hair, with strategically placed lowlights, was pulled into a messy ponytail. She was planning on staying in tonight, it seemed. A gated community did wonders for privacy.

Lexi took in the scene. Alarm bled into suspicion.

"Daisy," she said ominously, "what did you do?"

"Me?" Daisy blinked innocently. "Nothing. I'm not the one keeping secrets."

Mordecai's eyebrows settled low, promising vengeance. She narrowed her eyes at him, tit for tat.

"It's nothing," Mordecai gritted out. "I tripped. I'm fine."

Lexi frowned at Daisy. "Don't antagonize your brother."

She stopped and put her hands out. "What did I do? He tripped. I saw the whole thing."

"Is that because your foot was connecting with his ankles when it happened?"

"No." It wasn't a lie.

Lexi's deadpan stare said she knew tomfoolery was afoot. She was only ten years Mordecai's senior and probably less mature than Mordecai himself. An eighty-year-old was probably less mature than Mordecai these days.

"Are you sure you want to take the lead today?" Lexi said slowly. "I know everyone is confident, but so much can go wrong."

A smug expression crossed Mordecai's face. He crossed his arms over his chest in an "I told you so" way.

Daisy sighed, containing her frustration, both at the repeated questioning and doubt, and at her magic-lessness. She couldn't blame them—she *was* the weak link in this family, after all. She was dead weight. They all worried about her because she didn't fit into this world. She didn't have all the tools to survive like they did. But hell, she'd been training her ass off for *years*. She had studied religiously since she'd moved into the magical zone, learning all the various types of magic, how they worked, and what their weaknesses were. She was at a disadvantage, but she wasn't without strengths. She was far from helpless.

Still, she tempered the reaction. Lexi and Mordecai were worried. She wouldn't shrug them off for caring about her. Lord knew not many people jumped on that train.

"We planned everything out, remember?" She reached the bottom of the stairs. "It's a charity event with a lot of influential witnesses. Even if something goes wrong, there is security. But nothing will go wrong because I'm just making contact and talking. We're not actually exchanging goods or money. It's a meeting. That's it." She pushed past Mordecai. "E*xcuse* me."

He shoved her. "Not excused."

"Mordecai, don't push your sister," Lexi admonished him automatically.

"No, no. By all means, Mordecai." Daisy showed him her teeth, an aggressive thing shifters did. "Go ahead. See how that works out for you."

"Would you guys *please* stop fighting?" Lexi put a hand out to stop Daisy. "I get that nothing will likely go wrong and that it is all planned out, but I don't see why Amber can't handle this. It's in her wheelhouse."

They weren't worried about the meeting or her contact. He was a level one Reflector, like Henry from their crew, but with hardly any power. His magical type pushed a person's magic back on them. If you could attack with acid, so could he. Given she didn't have magic to reflect back, he was just an ordinary guy when in her presence, one with a lot less training in hand-to-hand combat. She was golden where he was concerned.

No, they were worried about the fae randomly showing up and leaving a dove's feather on Daisy's bloody corpse. Without the "right" weapons, she couldn't fight back.

"This guy doesn't have any antiques or relics on hand right now," Daisy told them for the millionth time. "We asked about it, remember? He *only* has weaponry, and the fae isn't interested in that. Amber and Zorn did the background on him to make sure. There won't be any goods or money exchanged, either. He's not bringing anything to the actual event. There is no reason for a fae to show up and cockblock—cock isn't a bad word, Lexi. It's a body part."

She gritted her teeth, hoping no fist came flying at her face. Thankfully, Lexi was too distracted.

"But what if…" she started. "What if the fae is around and—"

"We've checked it all out, remember? You were in on the meetings. Zorn and Amber have visited every relics dealer in the area. None of them have heard of this fae, and the one who had is dead now." Along with those other idiots who jumped Mordecai. She'd seen to the matter personally. If Mordie knew about it, he hadn't mentioned it. "I'm good, Lexi. Honest."

Nervous jitters filtered through her body, but she didn't let them show in her bearing. In reality, no, she wasn't totally good. There wasn't any reason for the fae to show up...except to grab her. She had no idea when that might happen. *If* it might happen. He could've been toying with her on that ledge until the Celestials chased him away.

Part of her worried about those dreams—how real his voice sounded in them. How vivid his presence was. Part of her was convinced that the fae would come calling any day now and take what he wanted. Her. Horribly...she wasn't entirely sure if she was anxious because of the danger...or because of the anticipation of seeing him again.

But if he did want what this contact was peddling? She'd be damned if she'd send someone in her place and get her family harmed. It didn't seem like the fae would kill Daisy. Not yet. She knew in her gut that the same wouldn't be true of the others. Zorn agreed. This was a necessary risk to keep everyone safe. If they had to lie a little to do it, so be it.

Lexi studied Daisy, uncertainty clear in her eyes. She sighed heavily. "I know. It's just...I know you don't need the reminder, but if you go into a situation that is over your head, the penalty is death." She swallowed thickly, as though that sentence had taken a physical toll to say. "There are no second chances in this field. Remember what Zorn says? You can never relax. In a world with magic, the magic-less are always in danger."

Zorn's voice echoed in Daisy's mind, finishing his quote: *Your life depends on your vigilance.*

"Yes, Lexi," she said patiently, "but Zorn also always says that I will be underestimated, remember? Being underestimated is my greatest strength." She held out her arms before gesturing to her face. "I'm young, I play up my dainty look, and this makeup accentuates what you call my big blue doll eyes. People who can't relax around Zorn or Amber can relax around me because of my perceived fragility. It's an act. It's a persona. I've explained this. I got this."

She hoped to hell she had this, at any rate.

Lexi nodded. "I know." She stepped aside so Daisy could pass. "Just be careful. That's all I'm saying."

Daisy walked past her toward the kitchen. It was time to go.

Mordecai hovered close. "I still don't know..." he started, obviously seeing through her front. He'd always been able to. That was what happened when you spent a large portion of your youth sharing a bedroom with someone.

She created a distraction.

"Who's that girl you're seeing, anyway, Mordecai?" Daisy entered the kitchen. "She's pretty. Young, though, right? Is she legal?"

"What's this?" Lexi asked with an edge to her voice.

Mordecai tried to hedge. "Daisy swore earlier."

"I would *never*," Daisy said dramatically, knowing

dating a minor was way worse than a little slip of the tongue.

The woman wasn't a minor, of course. She was older than Mordecai. But one question would lead to several as Lexi learned all about his new squeeze. She'd found the love of her life in a dangerous, stalking Demigod. She wanted the same bliss for everyone else.

Daisy's family filled the kitchen. Boman, a light bender, stood at the island. He wore a black T-shirt to match his black cargo pants, the pockets stuffed with all the wonders of a Mary Poppins's carpetbag.

"What'd you do to make Mordecai rat you out?" he asked Daisy.

"He's got an underage girlfriend, apparently," Lexi said to the room.

Bria, sitting at the island beside Boman, spat out a laugh.

"She's not underage," Mordecai said adamantly. "Or my girlfriend."

"Bang-buddy?" Thane asked, his smirk showing through his bushy beard.

Dylan sat beside him at the end of the table, watching the show with a grin.

"Who is this girl?" Lexi asked Mordecai.

He gulped. "She's a woman and I'm getting to know her, that's all. She's a friend."

"Friend with benefits?" Donovan stood at the stove with Jack. He looked over his shoulder with a glittering smile.

Zorn sat at the table with his back to the window. Kitty-corner to him, at the end, sat the Demigod of Poseidon, co-ruler of Magical San Francisco and extreme political player in the magical world. Kieran.

He had the power to change the tides and control vast quantities of water and the air under which it moved. He could bring in clouds and control the weather. The pain his magic administered could kill (and had). This man's power had a literal undertow. His grandfather was an actual god, said to have been placed in this realm by the old gods to rule the humans, an easily manageable lot compared to what festered in the wylds.

He sat at the end of the table in a white T-shirt, with tousled hair and threadbare jeans. Only their family ever got to see him like this. It was the only place he was relaxed and casual and real.

"Terrible weather we're having today, *Demigod* Kieran," Daisy said as she stopped beside Boman. "Didn't feel like bothering to make a pretty day?"

Kieran shrugged. A little smile played at the corners of his mouth. "Not really, no. It's my day off."

Half the guys in the kitchen huffed out a laugh.

"I think I have fog burn," Bria mumbled.

"No, no, no." Lexi grabbed the back of Mordecai's shirt as he tried to scoot out of the kitchen. "No way. Who is this girl—woman, I mean? I want to hear more. I'm so excited for you!"

Daisy's heels clicked across the tiled floor. She

stopped behind Henry, Mr. Charming. His magic as a level five Reflector wasn't why he was so useful to this crew. His powers of espionage and information gathering had few rivals. Papers were spread across the table between him and Zorn. Henry's open computer showed several grotesque images Daisy had already seen. The little dove feather lay atop the person's ruined chest.

"What's going on?" she asked.

It was Amber who answered, standing in the far corner. "Another death, as you know." She lifted a manicured eyebrow at Daisy. "I almost didn't notice you going through my files. If I hadn't been on my computer at the time, I wouldn't have. You need to wait until your subject is not using what you are after before you try to slip past their defenses. How'd you get my passwords?"

"By being sneaky," Daisy answered, then mimicked Amber's expression. "While you were cleverly forcing me out and blocking my re-entry, I grabbed what I'd actually been after. But thanks for the pep talk, coach."

Amber's eyes narrowed slightly. The twitch of her head was barely noticeable. The woman hardly ever showed emotion. When she did, it meant she was thrown off her game.

"Ooh *burn*," Jack said delightedly, his big arms flared as he cooked. "Gremlin, one. Amber, eight hundred and sixty-three."

"You just killed her moment, bro," Donovan told him, laughing. "She'll get you for that."

"I do love me an angry gremlin." Jack's laughter filled the kitchen.

Daisy had gotten the garage code to Amber's secret residence. Now she needed to decide how she'd unnerve Amber with the information. These little games kept them all vigilant. Also, they were fun. She'd gotten very good at them.

Zorn, wearing all black, smirked as he stood. It meant Daisy had done a good job.

"Time to go." He picked a pair of gloves off the table. He would ride with her in the limo before switching to the car he'd left close to the event center. There he'd wait in case something went wrong. Hopefully he wouldn't be waiting long.

"Be careful," Lexi called after them as Daisy followed Zorn to the door.

"Don't take any chances," Kieran added, his stormy blue eyes concerned.

"I got this," Daisy told the kitchen at large.

The guys whooped and cheered her on, and she felt that warm glow of family. She loved this place and these people. She loved it when they all gathered together for dinners and cheer, celebrating their tight group. Most of all, she loved that they would take time out of their busy schedules to support her. This was her second mostly solo job, and they were giving her encouragement for it. That meant so much.

Now she just hoped everything she'd told Lexi a moment ago was true. She hoped that fae had other things to do tonight, like stay in his own realm far away from her.

Chapter Seven

The charity event was held at The Gala, a swanky and prestigious hotel in a prominent location downtown. The grandeur of the building could be seen from down the block, its artfully placed lights shining up its luxurious façade. Perfectly sculpted and maintained shrubbery lined the wide, circular driveway. The limo glided to the red carpet, and the hum of anticipation filled Daisy.

Time to shine. Her life had pushed her toward this, pressed on her until the result shimmered like a diamond. Then she'd trained. Oh how she'd trained. She was ready for this.

Fuck, she really hoped she was ready for this.

Nervousness rolled through her stomach as she connected eyes with Zorn. He sat near the window separating the passenger area from the driver. She touched the subtle earpiece in her left ear. Zorn tapped a button on his phone, eliciting a tiny beep. It was live.

She nodded before touching the location device sewn into the waist of her pants. He mimicked her nod. On and tracking. The panic button was sewn into the other side. She waited for him to push buttons on his phone before she touched it. He nodded again. All was active. She was covered, just in case.

The limo stopped between the red velvet ropes. Zorn watched her quietly as the attendant on the curb approached her door. No expression flitted across his face.

"Be safe," he murmured.

She inclined her head. *I will.*

The event included a five-course meal within the esteemed hotel's restaurant. She hoped to have wrapped up her business by then. For the last several years, she'd been sticking to the outskirts when she attended these things with the Demigods and their crew. She wasn't important, and so she was seldom noticed when they were on the scene. She had no interest in sticking around long enough for people to pinpoint who she was.

She approached the sprawling hotel lobby lounge. A marble masterpiece of a bar took up the back left corner. Three bartenders were in various stages of mixing drinks or taking orders. Guests sat or stood, chatting and laughing, all looking around at who else they might want to talk to. Soft strains of live music drifted between the words and occasional barks of laughter.

Daisy slipped between two well-dressed men without sparing them a glance. She sought the bar, finding a corner and letting her gaze roam. The bartender, a handsome guy a few years her senior with a sexy smile and a cute dimple, approached.

"Hello, gorgeous. What can I get you?" he asked, his mannerisms easy. He was used to being a favorite.

"Dirty martini, two olives, and maybe your number for later." She held his gaze before allowing a grin.

His eyes sparkled. "Coming right up." As he moved away, his smile stretched, utterly genuine. If she needed a bartender's attention in a hurry, she'd have it.

Bodies in expensive dresses or tailored suits, some glittering with jewels, moved and shifted. She scanned the crowd, not finding who she was looking for.

"Here we go." The bartender came back and set her drink on a bar napkin. She could see the digits peeking out from under the base of the glass. He winked. "On me."

She let her sultry smile grow. "I'll tip you later."

His smile matched hers. "I look forward to it." He turned away to the next patron.

She actually might, she realized. It had been over six months since she'd dated anyone. Since she'd felt the touch of another. Her mind constantly strayed to places it shouldn't. To dazzling green eyes and devious smiles. To the rush of adrenaline and passion that accompanied *his* very presence. It wasn't healthy, feeling that way—remembering his every touch in exquisite detail. It wasn't welcome. But this guy was… cute. A good distraction. Hopefully. Mercifully.

She sauntered through the crowd, aiming for a look of arrogance. Her chin was tilted up, and her drink was held a little too far from her body, showcasing her form. Her haughty expression would hint at her ego—she intended to look like a frail thing who didn't do much to hide the vulnerability beneath. She picked at the hem of her jacket with her free hand to accentuate the image, boosted by her obvious youth.

Nearly at the other side of the room, she spotted the man she needed to meet. Rutherford. He was lodged in the plush seating at the far corner. Two men sat opposite him, one with a gaudy gold pinky ring and the other with a suit stuffed to bursting with muscle. She wasn't the only meeting of the night, it seemed. Damn.

She angled her trajectory, intent on stealing Rutherford's focus with her appearance. That would help her claim his attention when she got close.

Before she could make headway, a man stepped in her path. His salt-and-pepper hair was artfully styled, falling rakishly over his forehead. His lips were pulled into a cocky grin and wrinkle lines fanned out at the edges of his eyes, exposing pale skin underneath an obvious tan, highlighted by his keen interest sliding over her body.

She knew the type. Rich, powerful, important, not used to hearing the word "no" and less inclined to listen. He was undaunted by the twenty-year age gap and probably turned on by her apparent fragility. She crossed paths with such people far too often. It always made her slightly uncomfortable, which made her violent. Now wasn't the time for either.

"Hello," he said, using his size to hunch over her in a way that projected caging her into his notice.

She met his gaze...and let her confidence leak back into her eyes. Violence lurked in that sparkle, she knew. A warning.

His smile wilted, uncertainty replacing the confidence. She stopped in front of him, her fingers itching for the small knife hidden on the inside of her waistband. That sentiment would be transmitted in her slightly manic smile. Not all doll-like creatures made good playthings. Some came alive in the middle of the night and killed you in your sleep.

His eyes widened as his bearing turned rigid. She lifted her right eyebrow slowly, silently asking what he was doing in her way. Zorn was a master at the expression, and she tried to leak just as much hostility into it as he would've.

"Ex-excuse me," the man stammered before clearing his throat. He shuffled away.

Huh. That had been easier than expected. Maybe he recognized her? Or maybe he just recognized Crazy. She was the type of woman who, when her feet hit the floor in the morning, the devil said, "Oh shit, she's up." She'd seen that on a mug once and never forgotten the analogy. It fit perfectly.

The way up ahead parted. She continued her slinky walk, keeping the pace slow in hopes her target would glance up. He leaned forward in his chair, gesturing at the men he was talking to. The men stayed straight, holding the power in that dynamic. Good. To grab Rutherford's attention, all she'd need to do was offer him his power back, an easy illusion to create.

Haughty arrogance flowed away from her expression and her posture. The ego flittered away, as well. Vulnerability turned into demure sophistication, money in the hands of youth, soft-spoken and reserved, eager to please and follow his lead. This was why she was so slow to be recognized in public. Her face might be the same, but circumstances changed everything else about her. She could seem like an entirely different person at the drop of a hat. Amber had taught her well.

The man leaned back, his eyes flicking away from the others in irritation. It was then he caught sight of her, his gaze passing her by one moment, then snapping back. It slid down her body, a spark of interest igniting. When he finally noticed her eyes, she was biting her lip with a little smile.

His attention fell away from the men immediately, as though they'd gotten up and walked out of the room. Nearly upon them and she still held her target's focus, his eyes gleaming. Getting him away would be no problem.

She gave him a smile of hello as a strange shimmer caught her notice out of the corner of her eye.

Her focus shattered. Her blood felt like it had frozen solid, shock and surprise and delight and fear rolling within her in turns. The air glittered in a familiar and beautiful array of gold and tangerine and rose with sparks of violet and cerulean, reminding her of the sky at dusk. It sparkled and glowed, entrancing. So incredibly obvious...but not noticed by anyone else in the room.

Adrenaline poured through her body.

As if recognizing he'd been "made," the sizzle of color bled away to reveal an uncomfortably handsome fae in a perfectly tailored suit adorning his incredible physique. His hair was styled loose and tousled and somehow made his almost severe, chiseled face elegantly jaw-dropping. It also hid his otherworldly ears. No one in here would know what he truly was. His poise was regal in a way no one here could be, and his clothing, and the way he wore it, was dapper in a way everyone was attempting.

Small beads of sweat coated her forehead. He shouldn't be here. There was nothing here he was supposed to want.

Except her.

The fae's perfect lips curled into a mouthwatering

smile. A welcoming smile. Ice formed in the pit of her stomach.

"Hey." A man ten years her senior diverted her attention for a moment, approaching her with a slick grin. "I'm Andy. I see you have a drink, so I guess you don't need me to buy you one." He laughed. "Do you come to these things often?"

She felt the force of the fae's presence suddenly wash over her. His wild, potent magic curled around her, the smell like freshly churned earth waiting for seed. It hummed across her flesh and vibrated through her middle. The air shivered with a dark cloud of menace.

"You are beneath her, Andy." The fae reached them with all the swagger of nobility. His voice lowered into a vicious snarl. "Never speak to her again or I will wipe you from this realm. *Leave.*"

The magic surrounding them amped up, twisting and violent. It seeped into Andy's skin, slithered across his face, and clawed at his throat, dark shivers of air currents carrying out its master's unvoiced orders.

Blind terror slackened his expression. Wine sloshed out of his suddenly shaking glass.

"Sorry, sir," he said quickly, backing up. "You're right. I knew she was. S-sorry. It won't happen again. Forgive me."

He offered a bow before turning and practically running in the opposite direction. At almost the same time, the magic dulled somewhat, turned from that dark, ominous cloud into the vibrant colors of dawn, beautiful. Playful now, where before they'd been treacherous.

"That was overkill," Daisy said. "He didn't mean any harm."

The fae tsked. "And he did not come to any. You didn't welcome his advances. It was written in every line of your body. I was merely facilitating a speedy exit."

Daisy quirked an eyebrow, all of her worry and anxiety from the moments before bleeding away entirely. It was as though, when she was in his proximity, she didn't have the ability to feel fear. She didn't have to try to be calm in a sticky situation. The effect had to be magic, but nothing about it felt imposed upon her.

People were looking his way, angling their bodies to better see. The men likely thought he had riches, and the ladies probably wanted to see what was under the suit.

"But *my* advances are clearly much appreciated." The fae's smile softened all his hard edges into something truly stunning. "Hello, little dove. Did you miss me?" he asked in a deep murmur. He looked down at her attire, his gaze not sticking to any one place. "You look beautiful. Very well put together. We make a very handsome couple."

"Except, of course...we aren't a couple."

He stepped a little closer. His otherworldly scent

invaded her senses, and the delicious feel of his presence danced upon her skin. His heat melted the ice that had formed in the pit of her stomach. His voice pitched low and intimate, for her ears alone.

"Imagine watching you walk through the room. I was riveted. You changed so eloquently from one situation to the next. Truly a master. I am impressed. You're almost working as hard as I am."

"Almost?"

"Yes. It is easy for you to exist in this world. I have to sneak, steal, and kill to accomplish my business here. But it is worth it every time I catch a glimpse of your fragile beauty. Like a porcelain dove in the hands of an anxious child."

"I am anything but fragile."

His smile was devious. "We shall see." He dropped his head a little closer, inhaling deeply. "Equilas help me." It sounded like he was appealing to one of his gods, a name she didn't know. "I desperately want to see if you taste as good as you smell. I've missed the feel of your intoxicating presence. I dream of you."

His words slid sinfully across her skin. She clamped down on a response, not wanting to admit she felt exactly the same.

"Now tell me, what are you doing here?" he whispered, his breath dusting her heated flesh.

"Everyone is staring."

"Of course they are. We are the most interesting couple in the room. Why are you here?"

She tried to think of a song to block out the answer, but she needn't have bothered. No thought could form while her brain buzzed within his closeness. With his fingertips ghosting across her hips. His proximity warning away all others.

"Hmm." It was a rumble in his chest. "What a curious effect." He paused. "I should step away to get my answer, shouldn't I?" He breathed her in. "I find I don't care enough to do so."

"Why are *you* here?" she countered, not pulling herself away either. She would forever claim it was to protect her thoughts. That reason was better than the alternative. It seemed that every time she was near him, she played with fire. Danced through the flames. He represented more danger than she'd ever known—than the world had ever known—but the gravity of that, the reality of it, never seemed to seep in. She was on a self-destructive road. A passenger on the train of bad decisions, as Bria might say. Toot fucking toot.

"To see you, of course," he replied easily, his tone teasing.

"Is that the real reason?"

His dark chuckle shimmied down her spine. "Partially. I like to mix business with pleasure. That's what you were doing earlier, wasn't it? With your handsome bartender? I wouldn't meet him in a dark alley, if I were you. He likes to hunt non-magicals—Chesters, like you—and kill them for sport. He probably thinks you're magical, but you wouldn't want him to find out otherwise."

It was like cold water had doused her. She pulled back, trying to judge his truthfulness. His sly grin made her narrow her eyes.

His shrug was ever so slight. "Believe me or don't, it's up to you, but I would certainly bring the knife currently hidden in your *chic* trousers if you meet him for a nightcap. I do recall you being quite good with those. Unless you'd like me to kill him for you? It would be my pleasure. Just say the word."

She tensed with the need to look back in the bar's direction. In that moment, the fae took her hand, snapping her focus back to him. He bowed elegantly and ghosted a kiss across her knuckles. The move was graceful and debonair, old-fashioned and oddly sensual. The feel of his cool lips against her flushed skin weakened her knees. She stood frozen in place as her middle erupted with frenzied butterflies.

He stepped back. "Don't get too comfortable, little dove. I'll see you soon."

He gave her a scorching smile and strolled from the room.

She stared after him. So did many others. It wasn't just his appearance that was arresting, but his charisma. His sophisticated aloofness. He screamed *important*, from his poise to the way he didn't deign to notice anyone he passed, as though they were nothing.

She'd attempted to affect the same sort of air earlier but realized she had come up woefully short.

The relief of his leaving made her sag. The breath whooshed from her lungs. He hadn't taken her, and he didn't stop at Rutherford. Whatever the reason for his presence, it wasn't her. She had time. Not much of it, but some.

She needed those weapons. *Now.*

Gathering herself and turning, she re-sighted her target and hoped that diversion hadn't unraveled all her plans.

One thing curled through her mind...

I'll see you soon.

Chapter Eight

Zorn was quiet in her ear. He must've heard all that, but he wasn't raising the alarm. It meant he needed more information. That, or he planned to go into action and check out the fae himself. Whatever his plans, his silence meant she should stick with her directive.

Her target was just getting up. She inwardly cursed but headed for him anyway. She could still salvage this. *Had* to salvage this. She could, of course, find another time to meet this guy, but he traveled a lot and was often busy, and her time was running out.

"Rutherford," she said, sticking out her hand to stop him.

Rutherford's gaze caught on her, then skimmed her person eagerly. His eyes sparked, but he tensed. In a moment of indecision, he glanced back at the guys he'd been sitting with as they headed away. He was expected to go with them. *Shit.*

"Rutherford," she said again. "Hi." She turned her hand for a shake while giving him her best demure yet interested smile. She'd practiced it often in the mirror over the years. She hoped it masked the desperation creeping in at that fae having shown up. "I'm Sally. Sally Hawthorn. You'd said to meet you."

Rutherford had no idea who she really was. Zorn didn't think Kieran's and Lexi's offices should be implicated in case something went wrong.

A pleased smile lit his expression. He took her hand lightly, his palms sweaty.

"Sally," he said, like savoring the taste of her name. "I've never dealt with someone so radiant."

"Thank you," she purred, playing into it. "I wondered if now was a good time to chat? I won't take much of your time. I thought we could get to know each other and see if we might do business in the future."

His smile turned lewd. That wasn't a good sign. She needed to pull *way* back on the charm.

"I have business to attend to, sweetheart, but I'll tell ya what." He fished into his jacket and pulled a pen from an inner pocket before drawing 803 on her wrist. "Why don't you meet me after?"

She frowned down at the numbers. *Yuck.* That wasn't at all what she wanted to do.

"I can stay here, if that would be better?" she tried.

His gaze turned predatory. He sensed a little mouse and that he had the upper hand.

"This bar closes, baby doll," he lied. "I don't know that I'll be done in time. Tell you what..." He ran his thumb over her wrist. "Why don't you decide if you really want to do business, hmm? If you do, come on by."

He attempted a wink, half squinted instead, and left her standing there.

She stared after him, disgust eating at her.

"Go to his room," Zorn growled in her ear. "Kill him but don't leave any evidence that might incriminate the Demigods. We'll look up his warehouse location and take what we need. The world will be a better place without filth that uses his position to lure women in. He fucked with the wrong family."

Fair enough.

She wanted to ask Zorn about the fae, but thought better about it in a public place. If someone heard, it might cause panic or implicate her. If Zorn hadn't mentioned anything yet, he didn't plan to right then.

She glanced over at the bar and caught the cute bartender looking at her. He gave her a smile before helping a customer. She headed that way. She had an hour to kill. She wanted to see if what that fae had said was true.

. . .

An hour and ten minutes later, she walked out of the elevator and headed right, toward Rutherford's room. The fae had been correct, damn him. That bartender downstairs was a piece of shit. It had taken no time at all to get him talking about his distrust of Chesters. Then his outright hatred. Then the antics with which he treated them. He didn't come right out and say it, but yeah, he had a body count. It was easy to tell. He'd need to be dealt with, and brutally. But that wasn't her task right now. She had more important things to handle first.

She carried a leather folder that Rutherford would think held paper for notes and maybe stats or prices or who knew what. It didn't matter. It actually held weapons, some particularly nasty. She'd stashed it in a safe spot in the hotel the day before in case one of a few things went wrong. This wasn't exactly one of those things, but it was close enough. She wanted a knife bigger than the one she had previously stashed on her person.

At the door she paused, feeling his soul inside. Stationary. He was waiting.

She knocked softly and nearly let the grimace show when he opened the door in a hotel bathrobe. Fucking hell, this guy was something. She might've gone a little too hard with the mouse routine. No originality among perverts.

"Oh..." she said as though taken aback. "I didn't—"

"No, no. It's okay." He held the door wide for her.

"Don't mind me. I had to get out of the penguin suit. My clothes are being dry-cleaned. They should be here any minute."

A penguin suit was a tux, which he hadn't been wearing, and the clothes thing was a really shitty lie. He thought she was dumb or desperate.

"Okay." She edged past him and was not surprised when he flicked the extra lock on the door. To continue playing the part, she really should ask about that. It was what a nervous woman in her situation would do. But she didn't have the energy for any more of his shenanigans. "So...here?"

She pointed at the desk in the corner with the single chair, lifting her eyebrows to ask where she should sit.

"No, not enough room. Here." He walked between the double beds, sat on one of them, and motioned for her to sit opposite him.

Huh. She hadn't seen that coming. She had thought he'd want her to sit on the same side.

"Oh...ugh..." She cleared her throat as if debating, then hesitantly sat down, scanning the room for his laptop. That would make things ten times easier.

He sat with spread knees, revealing what little was between his thighs. Fabulous. His leer said it had been on purpose. He liked flashing.

Oh, fuck this.

She mumbled something about it, feigned embarrassment so he wouldn't go on the defensive just yet, and opened her leather folder in such a way that he couldn't see what was inside.

"Let's talk about that later…" He leaned closer and put a hand on her knee.

"Oh!" She stood as she snapped the leather folder shut, the knife she'd freed pressed against the back, out of sight. Ideally, she should do this in the bathtub to make cleaning up easier. Wrestling him to that location, though, would be a huge hassle, not to mention she might not have the strength. In her situation, surprise was always the best method.

"No, no, it's okay." He followed and stepped forward, lifting his hands to cage her in.

There wasn't enough maneuverability here. She slipped by him easily but slowed near the wall. This was better.

He hastened after her. "Shh, shh," he said as though to a frightened cat. "I won't hurt you."

He already had. Her retinas were burned from the image of his horrible lack of manscaping.

He pushed in close, reaching for her. She dropped the leather folder, knife in hand. She tilted her body and balanced just before—

Rutherford's body was ripped to the side. He flew through the air like a rag doll. His head slammed against the wall, splattering red on the white surface, and his body crashed into the nightstand as it fell. He slumped to the ground silently and lay deathly still. It was very likely he wouldn't be getting up again.

Daisy's breath caught. The fae stood in front of her with a look of carnal rage on his handsome face. Power blistered and crackled all around them but didn't touch her. His gaze slid down her body. It wasn't sexual. It seemed as though he were checking for handprints.

"My, my…" His voice was a vicious snarl. "What is my little dove doing here with slime like that?"

She swallowed the egg-sized lump in her throat as heat pulsed through her at his fury. His power. The sleeves of his dress shirt were rolled up, his jacket having been taken off somewhere along the way, exposing his forearms. Muscled, veined, and coiled with strength, like his whole body. His eyes delved deeply into hers, searching.

She didn't speak. Found that she couldn't. Then again, she didn't need to voice her thoughts. Not with him.

The rage clouding his features slowly faded. Understanding lit his eyes, but he paused, tensed as he continued to look at her. His head tilted, and for a moment he looked utterly lost.

He blinked and glanced back at Rutherford while a crease formed between his brows. Rutherford's robe lay open, and that was the second time she reeled from the sight.

"I apologize," the fae mumbled, waving his hand. Blue fabric fluttered as it winked into existence, covering the man fully. His breath stuttered, as though he had caught himself. "For interrupting, I mean."

His chest rose with a deep breath, and her gaze snagged on the defined pecs outlined in his stylish shirt. In a moment, his muscles loosened. His mood shifted back to the relaxed and arrogant guy she'd spoken with downstairs, or on that ledge. She'd glimpsed the other part of him, though. The wild and vicious part, ruthless and feral, hiding under this regal and posh exterior.

"I couldn't have him putting through a certain business transaction, you understand." He faced her fully again, but though his voice was back to being cocky and teasing, his eyes seemed troubled. Unsettled. "You didn't think I was trying to be chivalrous, did you?"

She cleared her throat and wondered if the look in her eyes matched his. If her uncertainty about the strange allure of him, the worrying magnetic pull, showed on her face. In her gaze. Her voice was just as unaffected, however. She at least had control over that portion of herself.

"Kinda, yeah. Chivalry makes men sexier. You can open locks, huh?"

She could feel the texture of his gaze as it roamed her face. "I don't need any help with sexiness, as you well know. I look very good naked, by the way. I know you've thought about it. I'll show you sometime. But about these weapons you seek... Why, in the favor of the gods, would you subject yourself to *this* to get subpar weapons? I can provide you with whatever you need."

"First, you didn't give me your phone number." She paused. "Do fae even have phones?"

"Of course. They just work a little differently. And look a little different. Okay, they aren't phones. They are mental receptors, but they achieve the same result."

"Well, I don't have one. Second, why would I trust you to provide me with weapons? You can clearly read why I want them."

He clicked his tongue. "You wouldn't kill me. You lack the conviction." He stepped closer so that the tip of her blade pushed against his stomach. "You're too mesmerized by this curious feeling."

She stared into his unsettling green eyes, the color so devastatingly vibrant. The buzz between them filled her with pleasure. With longing to feel *more*. Deeper. It sucked her in and threatened to drag her under.

"What is this feeling?" she murmured. "Is it magic?"

His voice was just as subdued, his gaze still troubled. "I don't know. I am not causing it, whatever it is. I don't have the power to control someone in this way. Not as I am. Not like this."

"Not as you are?"

He ignored the question, leaning in a little more. The point of the knife stayed pressed against him, but she let his body push the weapon back, allowing him closer. "Does the blood gift of your gods allow you to control those you covet? Is this *your* magic, little dove?"

She'd spent the past five or so years learning every

type of magic in this realm. She'd committed to memory all the facets of each, how they changed based on power level, and the best ways to combat them. She'd had to. It was the only way she could exist in this world, especially in her chosen line of work. She'd met people who could alter emotions, including class fives, the strongest of the power levels, besides Demigods. They'd never felt like this. Their effects weren't so complex, so consuming. So devastating.

"No," she said, not bothering to elaborate. He would've heard all that. At least his abilities saved time. "And let's get one thing clear: I do not, even remotely, covet you. I'd happily do away with this feeling. Any ideas on how I might do that?"

His lips curled wickedly, but she didn't mistake the disquieted frustration in his eyes. "Maybe it is chemistry, then. Who would have thought that was possible between a fae and a human, hmm? If anyone found out, I'd be laughed out of the court. How embarrassing." He studied her for a long moment. "To get rid of it, it seems I'll have to kill you."

She huffed out a laugh, ignoring the delicious buzz. The delirious hum inside her. It was a race to the death, then, was it? Because she had a score to settle. There was that little issue of revenge from all those years ago, and then his trying to help his kind flock over the Faegate, and now this huge inconvenience? Oh yeah, there was a score to settle, and she'd be the one filling out the toe tag. She hadn't gotten this far, and survived this long, to let some arrogant fae with an Adonis complex decide her fate. She had plenty of conviction, and when she got those weapons, she'd prove it.

A smile soaked up his features.

"Well then," he said softly, "I guess we know where we stand. Magic, a horrible joke by the gods, chemistry and attraction—it doesn't really matter what is causing this feeling. In the end, one of us will kill the other. What is that human saying? 'All is fair in love and war'?"

He leaned ever nearer, and that damn hum turned into a full-body vibration. She tried to hold on to her logic before it swept her away, but his eyes fluttered closed, and he let out a tortured groan that she felt across every inch of her flesh.

"It is truly a pleasure, though, isn't it? While we are sharing our truths..." His voice was low and rich. His eyes drifted open, finding hers, burning. "I enjoyed watching you earlier. Gliding through the room, playing those people like a perfectly tuned musical instrument. You made that man move with nothing more than a look. Masterful. You're a natural. You'd do well in court, playing the gentry like puppets. You'd like it, too, wouldn't you? You'd like making them dance to your tune before you stabbed them in the back and let them bleed out in front of all their peers." He leisurely reached up, sliding his hand against the side of her neck. Electricity sparked within the touch, sizzling across her. He hooked his thumb under her jaw and gently lifted, angling her face away. "I'd watch you from my throne, my crown crooked in mockery of the position."

It was hard to breathe through her tight chest. Hard to keep her eyes open. "Your throne?" she asked in little more than a whisper.

He matched her volume. "The Obsidian Throne in the dark fae kingdom. Do you know it? Currently ruled by the wicked king and his miserly queen. Set to be inherited by his rotten, strategizing children, the scourge of the realm. Ignored by the Celestials because of a trade that should've never taken place and is now left to run amok. They have ruined that kingdom, and the imbalance is spreading. It is time someone stronger rips the royalty from their perch."

"And yet...you're attempting to amass power to cross the Faegate?"

"It is time for a fresh start. Here, you could be at my feet. My treasured pet. A queen of her kind. You'd fill the role so perfectly..."

She could still hear the teasing in his voice, marveled at the blasé way he spoke about killing a *king* and taking the power for himself. She wondered how much of it was true, if any. How much of it was him dreaming. Despite the myths, fae could lie, even to themselves.

He chuckled darkly. "True enough," he said in answer to her thoughts, his hot breath dusting her as he lowered his head to beside her neck. "We all dream, do we not? Me of getting out of this suffocating, demeaning position, and you of one day fitting in. Of one day not having to constantly look over your shoulder, worried that someone stronger, more powerful—which is everyone in your life—will finally cast you out of this life in which you do not belong. I see your struggles. I feel your pain. I am not the only one lying to myself, am I?"

Something dark and raw opened up inside her. She had never before voiced those thoughts. Never before given light to them. Hated that Zorn might hear them through the comms now. There was no point in thinking like that. Her family was magical. It didn't matter that she was not. Despite her situation, she would always stay with them, danger or no. Looking over her shoulder all the time or not. Their love was worth any price.

But yes, she had to admit, it was exhausting constantly being vigilant. Never really belonging, even within her home. Always being different.

"I know," he whispered, and in that heartbeat, she believed him. Truly. Heard his own pain. His heartfelt understanding. She felt heard even though she'd never uttered a word. She felt *seen*.

He laid a hot kiss at the base of her neck, and her body exploded in pleasure. She struck forward with the knife without meaning to. The blade dug into his side about an inch. He groaned as though it were foreplay.

"Equilas, help me," he breathed. "You taste... *divine*."

He kissed her again, dragging his lips up her neck. His tongue left a trail of heat that seared her flesh until his lips were looming over hers, until he shared her breath. Heat and magic pulsed around them. Desire and attraction, and that new understanding, that new parallel between them, hung heavy in the air.

Her breath came in shallow pants, and she couldn't hold herself back. She leaned forward, needing those lips. Wanting his kiss. Just this once. Just right now. She could collect herself later and reassemble her thick steel walls, but in this moment, she needed to give in to this incredible ache.

He angled at the last instant, though, and she connected with his jaw. The knife tinkled as it hit the floor, and she fisted his lapels to drag him closer. He complied, and it was her turn to kiss the scorching skin on his neck. To taste his fevered flesh, like daffodils and sunshine, spun honey and morning dew. Her groan was every bit as tortured as his had been. His mind was probably every bit as confused, as delirious, as unapologetic as she reveled in the unquenchable pleasure.

"You should stop," he panted, his hands braced against the wall, his chest heaving.

"Why?" She ran her palms upward, one stopping

at his collarbone and the other tangling into his hair. Time slowed. Their lips aligned.

"This craving... It is almost unbearable," he murmured. A little louder: "If I take this kiss, I will own it. No one else will taste your lips, or delight in the gratification of your kiss, without being killed for the pleasure. These"—his nose brushed against hers as he cut the distance between their lips in half—"will forever"—her eyes closed—"be mine."

She pulled him to her. She needed this. Craved it. Couldn't live without it. Existing without the feel of his lips *was* unbearable. Unimaginable. She needed it like she needed air to breathe. Food to nourish. She needed it as though it were life.

His lips crashed into hers. She moaned as his magnificent body pushed her hard against the wall. His head tilted, and his lips slotted into hers like a puzzle piece. Electricity and adrenaline surged, pounding between them. It crackled against her skin, like his magic had done to the air not long before. Seeped in through her pores and electrified her blood.

His large hands cupped the edges of her jaw delicately, his thumbs rubbing gently. He pulled back slightly, and his eyes roamed her face once more. "You are so fucking beautiful. The pleasure is so sharp that it almost pains me to look upon your face."

He sucked in her bottom lip again before switching to her top lip playfully. He ran his tongue against the seam of her mouth, asking for deeper admittance. She opened to him eagerly. Desperately.

Emotions overwhelmed her—desire, longing, the feeling of belonging in a way that had been completely foreign to her until now. It felt as if time stood still. They existed in a bubble of intimacy that excluded the outside world.

His hands started to shake where they held her. The kiss deepened until she was lost within it. His tongue swept through and tangled with hers, a dance of erotic tension. Of soul-clenching passion. Her body ached for him to fill it. To become one with her.

"Enough," he murmured against her lips.

She felt glued to him, afraid to let him go. This feeling *had* to be magic. But whose?

He ripped his hands away and pressed them against the wall on either side of her head. "Daisy, we must stop. I'm losing what's left of my shaky control."

He didn't listen to himself, capturing her lips and thrusting his tongue in. She lifted her knee to hook around his hip. He ground his hardness against her. She moaned at how good it felt. This small moment, clothes intact, none of their secret places explored, felt ten times better than anything she'd yet experienced.

"A kiss is enough," he said, as though begging for forgiveness. "I cannot take more from you. I will not. Not now."

"Take it all," she begged, past reason.

He wavered, pushing against her again, dragging another moan from deep in her throat.

"No." He yanked his head back, sucking in a deep breath. Rivers of liquid gold sped around his pupils, nearly covering all the vivid green. The point of his ear peeked through his tousled hair, and for some reason, the "otherness" of that fanned the flame. His body was tense, as though he were in great pain. "*No.*" He pushed himself farther away, his eyes squeezed tight. Fighting the desire, she knew.

She watched him, breathless, her chest heaving and her lips tingling and swollen from his fervor. Her back pressed against the wall behind her as if that alone were holding her up. She'd never received a kiss like that, had never felt like this, and wasn't sure what to do with it. With him, her enemy. The danger of the realm.

His eyes leisurely came back to hers, the passion within them burning. His gaze stamped her parted lips.

"That kiss—those lips—belong to me now," he said, and something clicked into place. She couldn't identify what. "If they touch another intimately, you will have granted them their death tag." Hardness stole over his expression, like he was getting himself back to reality.

She wished it were as easy for her. Her body still ached for him. Shivers continued to run her length. The haziness of passion wouldn't clear from her mind.

"You are a human, my little treasure," he went on, "and therefore, you must be a toy. My toy to play with however I like. To do with as I please. In the end, however, I will be forced to break you. It is the hazard of dealing with my kind. It cannot be helped."

That sobered her up, the words ebbing and flowing around her pounding core and his dizzying proximity. She laughed, remembering what she'd thought earlier. Some dolls came to life in the middle of the night and killed their owners. She wasn't the type of toy good little girls and boys would want lying around.

His lips tweaked into a panty-dropping grin. *I am not a* good *little boy.*

He winked, leaning closer again.

"When you wake," he said with a devious sparkle in his eyes, "you'll need to run. They aren't the sort to let you live. Welcome to the game. It starts now."

"When I—?"

All went dark.

Chapter Nine

Loud pounding dragged her to consciousness. Shouting pierced her cluttered mind.

She lay on one of the beds in Rutherford's hotel room, her hands resting on her stomach. Deep night layered the window, as though the embodiment of blackness itself looked in. A soft pillow cradled her head. Little bits of tape covered each fingertip.

The banging kept in time to the pounding of her headache. A strange smell perfumed the air, metallic almost. Like rust?

She rolled off the bed, groggy, and paused when she noticed the splatter of darkening crimson against the wall. Blood, obviously. She remembered that happening. Liquid, darker still, clotted and cooled like gel, pooled on the multicolored hotel carpet near the end of the bed. A mangled body lay within the large puddle, the face still pristine. Rutherford.

Obsidian

No dove feather lay atop his chest. She knew who'd done it. He didn't need the talisman.

Duct tape covered his mouth. In black Sharpie was written, *Shhhhhh*. A joke, clearly. Dead men told no tales, after all.

A laptop sat open on the desk. Duct tape was stretched across the blackened screen. This one read, *You're welcome*.

She glanced at the tape on her fingertips. Still more writing, one word on each finger. *D-o-n-'-t* on one hand and *t-o-u-c-h* on the other. He'd made it so she wouldn't leave fingerprints. How nice. He must've snatched Zorn's instruction from her mind. Memory-thieving fucker.

More shouts came from the door. A beep signified the mechanical lock disengaging.

When you wake…you'll need to run.

The door bumped open, caught by the additional lock. The sound of men's shouting intensified as they became frustrated that they couldn't get in. Another piece of duct tape stuck to the back of the door. *Danger*.

Her eyes widened as the situation came into focus. That fucking fae. He'd magically dosed her and left her to whoever was trying to break in.

They aren't the sort to let you live.

"Fuck!" She rolled across the other bed to avoid the pools of blood. At the desk, she slammed the laptop shut and scooped it off the clean surface. Her knives had been put away neatly and placed on the floor in front of the open balcony door. Yet another piece of tape, containing a happy face, was stuck on the leather folder.

Why the hell would he make her scramble like this?

Welcome to the game. It starts now.

He was playing with his new toy.

The hotel door banged against the interior metal lock again. A body slammed against it; someone else yelled about busting it open. She didn't have time for the panic button, and it wouldn't make sense to press it now anyway. She couldn't really wait around for Zorn to come rescue her.

That was nice of him, she thought sarcastically. The fae had given her extra time to save herself. Just not enough time to be saved.

She stepped out onto the balcony. The city lights twinkled and blinked below, a dizzying reminder of the height. She pushed the door closed behind her so no one would immediately assume she'd left this way. Hopefully the Celestials weren't part of this clusterfuck.

Nothing for it now, though. She didn't want to think about the sort of people—or creatures—that a fae considered dangerous. She had to get out of here.

She stopped at the waist-high metal railing and tried to fit the laptop into the waist of her pants. Not ideal, but her pant legs would keep it mostly contained. It would have to do. She needed her hands.

A loud bang made her heart lurch. The door to the hotel room burst open.

Daisy quickly stepped into the corner so they couldn't see her through the glass. She pulled off her heels and flung them over the balcony. They somersaulted through the air. She'd pick them up when she got to the ground level. The knives, too. Too bad the computer wouldn't survive that fall.

With no time to spare, she hoisted herself up onto the railing. Her hands were slick with a cold sweat. The next balcony over was three feet away. Between them, the agonizing drop seemed to go on forever.

She steadied herself with a breath before jumping. Hesitation would be as dangerous as the jump itself. Maybe more so.

Her hands hit the railing of the next balcony over. The jolt ran up her arms. Her toe hit the bottom and vibrated pain through her foot and into her leg. She climbed over and dropped down, careful not to disturb the table and chairs. No lights were on in the room. She didn't bother trying the door. This room was much too close to the scene of the crime.

After a glance at the thankfully empty night sky, she adjusted the computer and then leapt to the next balcony railing. Then the one after that. Her palms burned. Her fingers hurt from her desperate grip. All the duct tape had peeled off and fluttered away.

A sliding glass door rumbled along the rollers from the direction she'd come.

She paused, her breath catching in her throat. A head preceded shoulders out of Rutherford's hotel room.

She flattened herself against the sliding glass door at her back before slinking to the corner of the balcony. The wall at the edge jutted out just enough to hide her body. Only a slice of her head would be viewable in the darkness as she peeked around.

The contour of a man was fully on the other balcony, looking away from her. His head swiveled around, and she kept totally still. Movement of any kind would catch his eye.

He walked to the edge of the balcony and looked at the distance between it and the next before looking toward the ground. That done, he stepped forward to look over the edge at a different point. His hand bounced on the railing twice before he headed back into the room.

She wasn't the only one who could make that jump. Not even remotely. She was a Chester, for fuck's sake. If she could do it, a great many could. He didn't have a solid lead, though. To cover all their bases, they'd have to start knocking on doors.

The sliding glass door didn't roll shut, and she wasn't that far away. They'd be able to hear her plight if they were at all paying attention.

She swore softly as she crossed to the other side

and once again looked down. Her best bet would be to get to a floor below. At the corner of the building, there was an emergency fire escape. That was her goal point if none of the rooms had an open sliding glass door. Getting to a floor below, though, was a helluva lot more dangerous.

A mental image of the fae dropping from the ledge played through her mind. Did she have that kind of strength? Or dexterity? Likely not.

She reached for the button that would connect her with Zorn, then froze when she didn't feel the earpiece. That fucking fae.

The panic button, the location device—all removed from her clothes. He'd cut her off from help.

Fine. Fuck him. She could get herself out of this.

Muffled banging made her freeze. Was that knocking on the interior door? Were they already checking the rooms around the crime scene? If they checked out the rooms, they'd check out the balconies. It was only a matter of time before she was found. She had to get down a floor. At least.

"Fuck, this is a bad idea," she said, looking over the railing at the balcony below. If she jumped to it, her weight plus inertia would be too much for her hands to hold. She'd slip and surely fall to her death. No good. She'd have to drop down at a measured pace. That meant dangling toward the balcony directly below.

She crawled over the railing as her heart picked up speed. That fae had made it look so easy. He'd essentially stepped off the ledge and caught himself, and away he'd gone. The amount of strength that hinted at was beyond her.

Movement caught her eye as she tried to lower herself little by little. The curtains of her balcony shifted. A hand speared between them, moving toward the side and pulling the curtains with them.

"Shit," Daisy whispered. A cold sweat broke over her forehead. Her hands were slick against the metal as she quickly crouched down. The computer pushed up, threatening to break free from her pants and fall.

She'd rather it hit the ground than her. She didn't let it distract her.

Curtains were ripped out of the way. Light washed over the balcony floor, with the shadow of a man positioned at the door, trying to get it open.

Shit, shit, shit! She braced herself and let her feet fall. Nearly at the same time, she lowered the rest of her body, her arms shaking with the effort to go slowly.

The lock on the sliding glass door clicked over. Her feet dangled over empty air.

The door opened as her hands slid the rest of the way. She barely kept the panic at bay as she took a moment to ensure her body was swinging toward the balcony below, still a couple of feet from her toes. This was not a good time to be on the shorter side. With her momentum going in the right direction, she held her breath and let go.

Her body fell. Her feet missed the balcony. She knew a moment of abject terror before her hands were racing toward the railing. Reaching out, she grabbed it just in time. Her weight yanked at her grip, but she held on and scrabbled up and over. The computer broke free, clanging against the metal. It followed her onto the balcony, where both of them were dumped onto the floor.

The slide of shoes echoed against the ground above her. Hands slapped down onto the metal railing. The person was trying to get a glimpse of her. From that vantage point, there was no way.

The clock was ticking. They'd wait a second before running to get to this floor. She could either try to drop down to another floor, or race him.

She dared not try dropping down again. She was nowhere near as good as that fae. The next time she might not be so lucky as to grab on, and if she did, her grip might give out.

A slice of light outlined the heavy curtain on the sliding glass door. Someone was probably inside.

Something popped as she rolled to her knees and then crouched to try the door. The curtain parted before she could. A confused man looked out. He must've heard the thumping of her body landing. Upon his seeing her, surprise and increased confusion creased his face.

Seeing an opportunity, she forced terror to bleed into her expression and crawled toward him. She reached out, a young woman in trouble needing a savior.

The action worked immediately. He quickly reached for the lock on his door before sliding it open. She grabbed the computer before stuffing it back into her pants. Still no footsteps sounded from above. The guy was trying to figure out what was going on below.

"Are you—"

"Help!" she said in a frantic whisper, cutting the man off. Her words tumbled out, aiming to confuse him further. "I fell. He's after me. The mob. It's danger—"

She launched forward. Her two hands hit the center of his chest, shoving at an upward angle. His weight went off balance and then the force of her push moved him backward. She clamped a hand over his mouth to muffle his outcry of surprise.

A shock of magic blistered the air. The hotel room shimmered until ridged mountains topped with snow took its place. An illusion. She'd gotten lucky this guy's magic wasn't something painful.

She kept pushing until his feet caught, and he tumbled over. His body disappeared into a crystalline lake with a mirror-glass surface.

"Sorry, but he's after me," she said with a frantic edge to her voice. She hit a solid but soft shape that her eyes didn't see. The bed. "My ex-boyfriend. He'll kill me if he finds me."

She felt her way toward the end as the mountains disappeared and the room clicked back into reality.

"Wait, calm down." The man was struggling to right himself.

She jumped onto the king-sized bed and ran across.

"Wait—just wait a minute," the man said as she hopped off the other side.

"Thank you for helping," she said, grabbing the door handle and yanking it open. "Thank you!"

In the hallway, she pulled the computer from her pants and sprinted for the elevator alcove in the center of the floor. The hallways existed on either side of it. It would be faster to take the stairs, which was why the guy from a floor above would likely be in the stairwell.

Instead, she crossed through the alcove to the other hallway, passing a very confused woman in a bright pink dress. Once there, she turned right and aimed for the stairwell on the other side of the building. The building had four, one in each corner. By the time the guy on the floor above realized she'd fled the room, he'd have no idea exactly where she'd gone.

Her breathing became heavy as she reached her destination. Her heart pumped at an unhealthy speed. Everything in her said to burst into that stairwell and take two stairs at a time until she reached the bottom. Instead, she forced herself to slow down. She'd put distance between herself and her pursuer—now she needed to erase suspicion. She couldn't let anyone see her hurry.

The handle clicked softly as she swung the door open and stepped in like she had a right to be there. No one waited on the other side. She paused to close the door gently and quietly before starting down the stairs. No other sounds greeted her. No footsteps or other doors opening and closing. No breathing, even.

The coast clear, she picked up her pace. Her right foot touched down on something sticky. She grimaced as she smoothed her hair. She needed to look presentable. One floor down...two. Still no one entered the stairwell.

She was passing a large white 2 when echoes of a door opening way above reverberated against the walls.

"He didn't see who it was?" a woman asked loudly. Footfalls—two, maybe three people—clattered against the concrete.

Daisy descended faster.

"Or *what* it was, no," a man answered. "A fae creature of some kind, they said, judging by the look of the body. Instructions are still to kill on sight by any means possible. There've been too many instances in this realm lately. They don't know how to stop it."

She reached the ground level but paused before opening the door, listening for anything else. She hadn't heard that creatures had been seeping into this realm. Amber's computer didn't contain anything about that, not that Daisy had seen. Did the Demigods know and were keeping it from Daisy, or were they in the dark too? If they were...who were the people policing that and so far keeping it quiet?

Her mind spun as the voices disappeared behind the thunk of a closing door. She'd ask Zorn about it. He might keep her in the dark sometimes, but if she asked him a question point-blank, he'd tell her what he knew, or he'd tell her she couldn't know.

She let herself out of the stairwell, gingerly closing the door behind her, then put on a haughty expression. Her posture screamed *important, don't mess with me*. She adjusted her stance and walk so her presence also read *bitch*. Hopefully people would leave her alone and not notice her lack of shoes.

From the preparations, she knew the layout of the hotel. Turning left would take her toward the lobby. She went right, acutely aware of the cold marble under her bare feet. Various hotel residents were scattered around. Some glanced her way. Only two people looked harder, noticing her hair and then glancing down her body. Based on their huffs and grins, they probably thought she was doing a walk of shame. Great. Whatever helped explain her appearance.

Farther on and the corridor narrowed. Around a turn and past a service stairway, she found her safe haven. The exit.

Her sigh was audible.

Keeping her decorum, she pushed out into the night. Chilled air and silence greeted her like an old friend. A smile flitted across her face. She'd made it. That fae had thrust her into a very sticky situation, and even though she hadn't specifically prepared for it, she'd still made it.

Something shimmered on the walkway up ahead, hidden in a glamor. The fae's glamor, to be precise. She knew that beautiful twinkle.

Her stomach dropped when she recognized what was spread out on the ground before it. Duct tape. Three lines of it, each written on with black Sharpie.

Great work getting this far, the first said, with a happy face drawn at the end.

I got you a present, was the second.

Let me know how it works...

Just beyond that was a dagger lying in the center of the walkway, as though waiting specifically for her. The blade was tucked into the most beautiful sheath she'd ever seen, with metalwork in a bending, twisting sort of overlay. Within the loops and circles the design created, stones sparkled and glinted like crystals, glowing a soft turquoise or speckled cerulean blue. The hilt sticking out was wrapped in what looked like supple leather. The blade promised to be a work of art.

She didn't bother to ponder how he'd known she'd be on this walkway. This was the rear exit, seldom used by anyone but hotel personnel escaping for a cigarette break. Of course someone in her situation—the situation the fae had forced her into—would want to sneak out this way. Understanding how no one had grabbed the knife before her was also obvious. He'd affixed his glamor to it, magic that no one else seemed to notice but her.

What she did wonder was what would happen when she picked up that blade.

Let me know how it works...

Another game. Surely this was a trap of some sort. There was no way she was taking the bait.

Veering right, she gave the knife a wide berth. Decorative stones poked the bottoms of her feet. She still needed to pick up her shoes and knives from where she'd tossed them.

As she passed the object in the center of the walkway, however, her face smacked into a solid surface. The air was acting as a barrier. She couldn't go any farther.

"You've got to be kidding me," she whispered, putting her hands against the invisible surface. "Please be an air elemental. Please be a normal magical type whose weaknesses I've already studied—"

You didn't spring the trap. The fae's textured voice rang within her mind, his tone teasing. Taunting. *Very good. You can never trust one of my kind. You can also never free yourself once you've been ensnared. And you, my treasure, are definitely ensnared. By me. Pick up my gift. It is yours.*

"If I refuse?"

There is no need to draw attention to yourself by speaking out loud. People will think you're hearing voices. Think your responses. As long as you are close to that knife, I'll hear you. The telephone, remember? If you're ever in trouble—trouble I didn't create, of course—you can reach me through that means. I will come to your aid. That knife will grant me passage to do so.

She narrowed her eyes, thinking that through. Hearing the unspoken truth.

The knife will only grant you communication, she surmised. *My asking for help, and your granting that help, is a deal struck. The deal allows you admittance into this realm. The deal also puts me in your debt. I'd be at your mercy unless specified otherwise, and if I was in actual trouble, I wouldn't have time to specify.*

His mind was quiet for a long beat.

My, my, he thought softly, and she could hear his amusement. *You are a quick study. Yes, you are correct. I will be lenient, however. You are mine now. Mine to play with. Mine to break. I do not share. If someone threatens you, they are threatening my property. I will deal with them in kind.*

Shivers raced across her flesh. Dread settled in her gut.

Yes, little dove, he purred. *It is quite a predicament you've gotten yourself into. Do not worry. You were always going to end up in this situation. Fate has had a hand in our affairs, I think. A heavier hand than we might've liked, but at least we got that kiss out of it.*

Don't you agree? I thoroughly enjoyed the feeling of your lips. The rush of your spiraling out of control. I'll dream of it often. Now, be a good little pet and pick up your knife. I want to see the extent of your battle prowess. It'll help me plan.

She ran her thumb across the cloth that used to hold the panic button. She wasn't proud. She could admit things had gotten out of her control. She desperately wanted help out of this situation.

I removed that, yes, the fae said. *And the location device, as you've noticed. I am not like others of my kind. I've been in and out of your realm for years. I know how your technology works. Your teacher has no idea where you are, what you are up to, or if you are okay. I dropped into his head a while ago and informed him that if he interfered with my plans for you, I'd kill you. He is not handling it well. You can put him at ease if you just pick up your knife.*

Anger was a live wire surging through her blood. *You really should know better than to bring my family into this. Your death will be my very great pleasure, and I will use that knife when I slice you open.*

What fun would it be if I didn't cheat? She could *feel* his devious smile in every inch of her body. *Good luck, my treasure. You might need it.*

She marched over to the weapon, shimmering and beautiful. Without another thought, she bent over and snatched it up. Her palm nearly compressed into the supple leather as she wrapped her fingers around the hilt. She pulled it free and couldn't help marveling at the sheer beauty of the blade. The edges were like rivulets in a stream, ebbing and flowing down its length. The metal, whatever it was, glowed a phosphorescent seafoam color with lighter streaks running within. Down the center was more metal scrollwork to match the sheath, with intricate designs curving around twinkling gems. Diamonds, if she had to guess.

With her free hand, she touched the blade. The surface of the weapon was ice cold. That certainly boded well for using it on the fae, though she'd thought iron was a key component in the recipe. She wasn't sure there was any iron in this one, unless that was what made up the scrollwork.

There was no belt with it. Where would she put the sheath if she had to use...

Her thoughts trailed away. With a deadpan stare at empty air, she slipped the sheath into her shirt. Even though it should've been too large, it fit perfectly between her breasts, almost as if it could shrink enough to fit. She could carry it, hidden, in her bra. The same place he'd found the rock-chalice thing.

Cute, she thought dryly.

His chuckle was a ripple of black velvet.

Rolling her eyes, she reached in to grab the sheath again. Before her fingers could close over it, though, the darkness around her changed. Liquified, almost. She watched in horror as solidified midnight slid across the ground all around her. It shivered, as though someone had disturbed the fabric of the night, before crawling into the air. One by one, blots of obsidian took shape into twisted, horrible creatures.

Were these what the other people were looking for?

Let me know how it works...

Chapter Ten

The building lights clicked off, dousing her in darkness. Only the paltry moon illuminated the makeshift battlefield. Horned beasts rose before her, each topping her height by a couple of feet or more. Black on black, she couldn't make out their details, merely the long, curved claws adorning spindly arms.

Emotions from the moment before calmed. Tremors of unease subsided. She'd trained for this. Not horrible fae creatures with distorted bodies and unknown magic *specifically*, but for the human counterpart. She'd trained in total darkness, her eyes useless, and with only one small weapon in her hand. She'd been accosted on city streets, in gutters, in a swamp without proper footing. Zorn had subjected her to every horrible situation he could possibly imagine, and with practice, she'd risen above them all.

If it was battle prowess this fae was looking for, she was about to show Zorn's magnificence as a teacher.

She calmly placed the computer to the side and bent her knees, her knife held aloft.

"Your move, asshole," she murmured, watching the largest of the creatures. It stood directly in front of her, and with her words, it cocked its head, five horns moving within the night.

A shadowy hand rose from the concrete at her feet. It latched on to her ankles to keep her put.

Without her heart so much as kick-starting, she bent in a smooth motion and sliced through the solid, dark mass. A high-pitched squeal accompanied the substance shrinking away.

The forms of the beasts on her sides wobbled before they launched. The claws on their feet clacked against the concrete. The first creature reached her and swung its spindly arm. Claws swiped through the air toward her face.

She leaned away as she stepped, her knife elongating into a long, curved blade. The change stopped her for a moment, and she blinked stupidly at the weapon.

Another creature slashed at her. Its claws raked across her back, digging into her skin. She sucked in a pained breath before she spun away, dancing around another reaching creature to give herself space. The sword elongated just that bit more, enhancing her reach within the creatures' long limbs.

"Far out," she muttered, a term that strangely annoyed Mordie to no end, before she stepped toward them again, altering her stance. A purplish glow pulsed from the blade right before it parted midnight flesh. A sizzle preceded a twisting line of smoke and the creature's shriek. There was almost no resistance. She wondered if that was relative to these creatures, or if this blade would go through her fae just as easily.

She slashed at the next creature. The blade cut through at the shoulder, severing the limb and sending the beast careening to the side. It was almost as though the weapon had added a small explosion to the strike. Better and better.

The next creature reached her. The others were on its heels. She ducked a strike and spun, cutting into its stomach. Another handful of claws raked down her arm. The searing agony seeped into her, through her, and dissipated into the background. Part of staying alive was mastering one's pain receptors.

It swiped again, but she was already moving, working around it and slicing into its back. Spinning again, she jabbed her sword through a creature's chest and pivoted to swoop low, separating a leg. Shrieks and howls existed all around her. Creatures shook and writhed on the ground, those still standing now backing away, fearful of being burned. She dispatched the last and looked on, breathing heavily with the exertion, ready for more.

The lights clicked back on, flooding the scene. She

squinted against the sudden brilliance but didn't drop her stance. There was no telling when the game would end. The beasts vanished as though they'd never been there. Her sword pulsed a pale blue before shrinking down to its original knife size.

Stillness hung in the air. Her breathing slowed.

Well done, said the fae in her mind, his tone appreciative. *Give my regards to your trainer. He is currently waiting in his BMW around the corner with his hands gripping the steering wheel. Remember...if you share my secrets, it will be your family I must silence.* His tone lightened. *Snitches get stitches.*

She felt his touch slip from her mind, as though his attention was turning elsewhere. The space in her cranium felt strangely hollow in the aftermath.

Dropping the knife hand to her side, she glanced back at the door, then up. A camera peeked down at her. She'd need to get Amber or Henry to erase whatever footage was there.

She finally dropped her guard, noticing the duct tape had changed configuration again. Where there had been three strips, now there was a circular sort of clump.

"A rose," she murmured to herself, recognizing the shape he'd created. In the middle, like a bee rubbing within the pollen, awaited her earpiece.

* * *

The BMW was right where the fae had said it would be. Zorn was, as well, his hands on the wheel and his knuckles white. He stared out the windshield, unmoving.

She'd never seen him so amped.

She knocked on the passenger window with her knuckle before pulling the door open.

"Gremlin." His voice would have sounded its customary calm, always cool and collected and in control, if not for the intensely relieved sigh that rode each syllable.

She tossed the earpiece into a cupholder. She'd used it immediately to tell Zorn she was okay and that she'd meet him shortly.

"I expected you fifteen minutes ago," he said, not looking over at her.

"One of my knives escaped the folder. It was hard to find." She closed the door behind her.

He grunted and turned on the car. It wasn't until he'd pulled away and turned a corner that he finally spoke, breaking the silence.

"Tell me what happened. Don't spare any details. If you won't be finished by the time we get home, let me know and we'll take a detour."

As ever, Zorn was prepared to do damage control. He would decide which secrets she could keep, and which she'd need to tell everyone else. The problem was, some of the secrets she couldn't tell even him, lest that fae decide to silence them all.

She finally glanced at the clock on the dash. Nearly two in the morning. The fae had spent a couple of hours with Rutherford's computer. What were the odds he'd left behind incriminating files as to what he'd been looking for? Probably slim to none.

Then again, that fae was not from this realm. He might know what a communication device was and could clearly find and disable tracking devices (probably with the help of her thoughts), but effectively wiping a computer was very likely beyond him. Erase files, sure. But that wouldn't stop Amber and Henry from recovering whatever had been stamped on the hard drive. In this, the fae was outclassed. And in finding that information? That was outside of what she knew. It would be his shoddy work that snitched, not her. Every fiber in her being said that mattered. She was growing a sixth sense where his deals and candied words were concerned.

Maybe, just maybe, if Kieran and Lexi's team could figure out what the fae was going after next, they could get there first and destroy it. And now Daisy had a weapon. If she also had the upper hand, it would be him walking into a trap this time. And he wouldn't be walking away after she got through with him.

* * *

A week after the charity function, she paused beside her car in a dimly lit parking lot following a grueling night out. Her whole body vibrated with anger and disgust, her fingers itching to close around the knife tucked against her thigh, hidden by her fashionable but slightly billowing dress.

"I think you should come over," Liam said, standing beside her, leaning heavily against her car. His gaze roamed her face, never pausing very long on her eyes. His interest was more in her lips, or her bust. Her butt when he didn't think she'd notice. In undressing her with his eyes.

She'd accepted a date with that hot bartender from the charity thing. Normally she would've killed him for what he'd admitted to her, or let Zorn do it. Zorn could be oh so colorful. But...she had questions.

"I mean..." He lifted a hand to trace a finger down the line of her arm. She stopped herself from shivering with unease. When he reached her elbow, he yanked her closer.

The breath nearly left her with the unexpected force of that move and the aggressive lust burning in his eyes. If she'd been a normal girl on a first date, this would've made her incredibly uncomfortable. His manhandling her like this, the two of them all alone, implied strongly that he was dangerous. That he would ignore rules when no one was looking.

But she already knew all that. In hushed, gleeful tones, he'd relayed all that over dinner. Over drinks a week ago. He enjoyed what he did to those Chesters, mutilating them, tying them up, and beating them until they stopped struggling. Worse, probably.

But she wasn't normal, and she didn't like her prey knowing they were being hunted. And so she smiled when she half fell against him. She laughed, pretending this was okay. Pretending these antics didn't matter. And in her gut, her fire burned brightly. His time on this earth was drawing to an end.

"We're just getting started," he murmured. His breath smelled like fish, and his cologne was sickly sweet. "I want to show you my dungeon."

She couldn't help the shiver this time. How the fuck was this kid still alive, seriously? How had no one killed him before now?

Then again, she wouldn't have known to manipulate a confession if it hadn't been for that fae. She'd have almost certainly been blind to his "hobby" and ended up beating the shit out of him for manhandling her like he was currently doing.

He reached around her and squeezed her butt. He turned and pushed her against the car, trapping her body between it and him.

"You're so fucking hot," he groaned, smashing his groin against her hip.

Let's just get this over with.

She angled her face up.

"Oh yeah," he said, crashing his lips onto hers as he ground against her. His tongue shoved between her lips and did a strange sort of swirl in her mouth. His jaw opened and closed in a strange rhythm, and she wasn't sure what was actually happening, just that she should've forced a breath mint on him beforehand.

"Come on," he said, pulling back and trying to drag her with him. "Leave your car. You're coming over."

She smiled, batted her eyelashes, and did a twist-yank to get her arm out of his grasp. He stumbled backward in surprise.

"I have to go. I'll call you. I promise." She opened the door as he was regaining his balance, and slipped into the car as he started back toward her.

He stopped beside the closed door, leaning down to the window. His eyes cleared of their lust, but didn't lose their determination. He nodded, grinned like this was a game, and lightly tapped the top of the door.

"Okay then, play hard to get." He stepped away like it was no biggie, slipping his hands into his pockets. "You'll be mine yet."

"We'll see," she said, playing the game.

She'd repeat that back to him before lights out. If she got the chance...

Her mind raced as she drove home. She crept through the quiet neighborhood to the house near the dual-society zone. Strangely, cars lined the curbs and a few windows in both residences glowed their welcome.

What was everyone doing here? There weren't any family dinners planned.

She glanced at her phone. No missed calls. There couldn't be any emergencies.

The front door was unlocked. They were clearly expecting her home. Very presumptuous of them. She'd told Mordie she was going out on a date. Granted, she'd also told him it was with the Chester-hating bartender she'd met last week...

Ah, how stupid of her. Everyone was here because they were worried about her. Or worried she'd have a body on her hands and need help to make it disappear.

If it wasn't for those questions she had...she would've. But she had to know. She had to know if that fae had been blowing smoke that other night in the hotel room...

He must have been, right? How would he even know when she kissed someone? The books said magic didn't travel across the divide between the realms. It couldn't. That was what kept humans safe from the wyld fae magic. If he wasn't here, if he didn't physically *see*, he couldn't possibly know.

Right?

Shivers ran down her length, chilling her blood. She didn't belong to anyone. No part of her did. She certainly didn't belong to a fucking fae.

Did I unknowingly strike a deal? Without words?

Warm light and the familiar smells of home greeted her. Voices murmured softly in the kitchen, past the foyer. The door clicked softly when she closed it. The voices hushed.

Yup, they were here for her.

Bria sat at the island with a half-finished bottle of

Jack Daniel's beside her, her fingers wrapped around a glass of mostly ice. She swayed when she spied Daisy, and a smirk played across her lips.

"Well hello there, little masochist," she said, slurring her words. "Hanging out with people who hate everything you are, I hear. How'd that go? More importantly, did you take Zorn's teachings to heart and ensure not to leave any evidence at the crime scene?"

Thane sat at the table with his back to the window. A beer bottle was sweating in front of him. At the end of the table sat Dylan in a rumpled shirt he wore so well, with tousled hair and bedroom eyes. The guy did *sexy* without trying. He probably wished he could turn that facet of himself off, though. He certainly wasn't ready to be touched by anyone other than supportive family members for a short hug. He'd had a tough past.

The only other person in the kitchen was Zorn, sitting at the end of the table with a scotch on the rocks, or some other brown liquor. He wore sports sweats and a white T-shirt, like he was just about to go to bed. His gray eyes missed nothing as they assessed her.

"Hey," she said as she pulled out a chair. "What's the occasion?"

Thane's eyebrows lifted. He thought that was a stupid question.

"Do you want a drink?" Zorn asked. He wanted the gossip. They probably all did. Tomorrow, Lexi or Mordecai—or both—would probably lecture her. She had a great many mother hens in this outfit.

"Sure, why not?" she said breezily, sitting. "A nightcap might be nice."

"You didn't have one of those earlier with your new beau?" Thane asked, his voice laced with a growl.

"Another nightcap, then."

Thane's expression darkened.

"On it!" Bria gently slapped the island. "What're we havin'?"

"Whiskey on the rocks, please," Daisy replied.

"Outta whiskey." Bria pushed to standing, wobbled, then gave Thane a thumbs-up. "See? I'm good. I have the tolerance of a Scotsman at a wedding." She grabbed the Jack bottle by the neck. "Here we are. Here's a balm for terrible decisions."

Thane scratched his cheek with unease. "Daisy, you know Lexi won't be okay with your dating a Chester-killer, no matter how hot he is."

Daisy lifted an eyebrow at Zorn. She hadn't told Mordecai about the bartender's appearance. She *had* told Zorn, and he'd clearly passed on that nugget of information.

He hadn't known why she'd really gone, though. The fae had apparently deadened her devices. She hadn't filled him in on *all* their dealings.

He didn't show any expression, but his eyes started to sparkle. He found humor in some part of this.

Bria took a glass from the cabinet, wobbled a little harder, then stared at the fridge. "I've done this in the wrong order." Bottle down, she zigzagged to the fridge with the glass. "Don't scratch, Thane. You sound like you have fleas."

"He probably does," Dylan said with a grin that didn't reach his troubled eyes. He leaned back. "How'd...it go?" he asked Daisy.

"Don't ask the secretive little gremlin such vague questions, Dylan. Don't you know anything?" Bria's ice cubes missed the glass. "Balls."

"Sure, yeah, great tolerance." Thane huffed and shook his head.

"That ice didn't pass muster." Bria pushed her platinum-blond, shoulder-length hair out of her face. She'd been on the booze train for a while, it looked like.

The next fistful of ice cubes tinkled as they hit the bottom of the glass.

"You gonna clean up the ice you spilled?" Thane pointed at Bria's feet.

"Then what would you do to help?" she replied, heading for the bottle again.

He grinned and stood. "Give me some too, yeah?"

"Yup." Bria stopped and stared at the cabinet, swaying. She then looked down at her hands, one with the glass and one with the bottle. "First thing first," she muttered. "Daisy, you're into Coke, right? Coca-Cola, I mean. Not the hard drug. You like to water it down, right?"

"You don't water down with Coke." Thane bent for the ice, his shirt sending up the white flag as it struggled to stretch across his muscled girth. "You Coke it down."

"I'll Coke you down," she muttered, pausing with the glass held up. "But I'll switch the 'e' to a 'k.'"

"You'll cok— Oh." Thane frowned at her. "That's not how you spell—"

Bria wheezed out a laugh, folding up on herself. Daisy couldn't help chuckling.

"Anyway." Bria straightened and assumed a very dignified expression. "What is the verdict?"

"Straight, thanks." Daisy swished her fashionable dress to the side just to see it move. It really was a work of art, custom-made by an up-and-coming designer. "Coke is bad for the teeth."

Daisy faced forward as Bria leaned over her. The glass hovered near the table, touched down once, came back up like a helicopter not sure if it really intended to land, then settled. "Nailed it," she murmured. Her breath could've ignited fire.

Thane retook his chair, his gaze coming to land on Daisy once again. "Seriously, it isn't smart to date a guy like him. All he has to do is look you up and he'll know what you are. I'm surprised he hasn't already."

"He has a fake name. He did look me up and got the corresponding fake profile. My face doesn't come up in Google searches any more than yours does, you know that. Amber is thorough. It's fine. I'm just having fun. Blowing off some steam."

He leaned forward. His muscles bulged. He meant business. "You could blow off steam with anyone."

"Yeah, but he's really cute." She winked at Thane, whose face turned red in frustration.

Dylan adjusted in his seat, highly uncomfortable. He was clearly just as worried but letting Thane handle it.

"He is also a Chester-killer," Thane reasoned. "Those types initially think of it as a sport. Then a high. It becomes less about Chesters and more about killing, so when they run out of easy pickin's, they go for the low-hanging fruit in the magical world. Fruit like your fake profile. It would only take one moment of you not paying attention for him to slip you something that would render you vulnerable. Just *one* moment. This isn't smart. You need to either deal with him permanently or give me the name and I'll make sure our offices handle him."

"You guys worry too much." She put steel in her eyes. They'd be expecting her stubbornness. "He's hardly magical. Level one. And I've made it so he won't want to do away with me." She waggled her eyebrows. "Trust me, I've got this."

Thane stared at her incredulously before looking at Zorn. "Really, bro? You're going to stay silent about this? I know you like her to deal with her own mistakes, but this is going too far. Not only is it utterly messed up getting with a guy like that, but it is incredibly dangerous for her."

Daisy turned her head toward Zorn slowly, fighting a smile. *How* did no one see the sheer fireworks of mirth going off in Zorn's eyes? He was so very obviously having fun with them, the same as her.

"Yeah, Zorn. Are you going to stay silent about this?" she asked in a hostile tone. It was how she usually fought him on decisions she didn't much like.

A tiny smile threatened his lips. "She's an adult, and this is her personal life. She needs to make decisions on her own."

Thane's mouth dropped open, and Dylan's eyebrows drew together.

Bria started laughing before singing, "I know something you don't know..." Unlike the others, she could read Zorn. She was in on the joke. "Look, I agree." She burped, then groaned. "Garlic might be good for the heart, but it is not good for the aftertaste."

"Gross," Daisy muttered, and took a sip of her drink.

"Yeah," Bria replied. "Tell me something I don't know, right? Anyway, look, Daisy can take that guy. It'll be fine. She's an adult. All that stuff."

Dylan scratched his head. "Be that as it may, I really think you need to give Lexi a heads-up. This is potentially dangerous, and she should know about it."

Daisy frowned at him in surprise. "Mordie didn't rat me out?"

"Mordecai told me," Zorn said. "I explained to

these guys why I was waiting up. They insisted on waiting up as well."

"And for good reason," Thane murmured.

"I just wanted to keep drinking because sometimes it is a pleasant fog, isn't it?" Bria said.

"Oh. Then why is everyone here?" Daisy asked.

"Henry and Amber made headway on Rutherford's computer," Zorn answered, the twinkle in his eyes subsiding. "We're going to go over it tomorrow and make some decisions."

A chill ran through her, then excitement. Decisions meant they had something. It meant she might get a crack at that fae, like she hoped. They'd just have to navigate the treacherous waters of dealing with one of his kind.

"Back to the issue at hand," Dylan said, his tone reasonable. "I really think Lexi needs to know what's going on. I mean...I get wanting to engage in dangerous behavior, and even wanting to...get intimate with someone that...hates your kind..." He struggled for words.

"He doesn't get it." Bria shook her head sagely with a crooked grin. "He doesn't get it at all."

Daisy waved it away. She had other things to think about. "I only kissed him. It's over."

"It's over?" A small crease formed between Zorn's brow. His gaze swept her person again. "Did you kill him?"

He thought he'd missed the signs. She laughed.

"Not yet. I was just getting the lay of the land. That's all. I'll finish it when I have a moment."

Thane and Dylan let out a relieved sigh.

"Thank fuck," Thane said. "I really didn't want to tattle."

Daisy finished her drink in one shot and stood. Butterflies filled her stomach at the implications of that computer. Of what they might've found. "Thanks for waiting up. And for worrying about me. No thanks for thinking I am that horribly stupid and self-loathing. I thought you knew me better."

Now the guys were working their mouths, not sure what to say.

Daisy excused herself to her room. Once there, she glanced at the area near her window. Small pieces of duct tape made a semicircle against the wall. Outside and to the right, kept in a satchel and nailed to the wall by the roof, hung the knife the fae had given her.

When she'd gotten it, she'd tested the proximity within which he could hear her. Once she had the distance, she set to work putting the weapon in a place where she could get to it in a hurry, but that was far enough away to allow her some privacy.

Now, as she thought about the new things she'd learned and ways she could trap him, she definitely did not want him hearing her thoughts...and knowing what was coming. She hoped to fuck this would be the end of it.

Chapter Eleven

Early the next morning, Daisy awoke to thundering footsteps echoing down the hall. Blinking open heavy lids, she noticed the surveillance screens lining her desktop across the room all blazed with activity. They'd caught something in the yard.

She burst out of bed and quickly threw on her sweats. Her door swung open and a harried Mordecai half filled the open space. "Hurry. Something is happening!"

Her adrenaline kicked up. The first thing that ran through her mind was an attack on the Demigods.

She squished down the fear as she ran for the door. Fear had no place in a situation like this. Cool logic would win the day. The whole family was on hand, and Kieran was excellent at strategy and battle, not to mention Lexi could handle armies. They'd be fine.

"What is it? Do you know?" she asked as Bria ran by the open door.

Mordecai waited for Bria to pass. "Property breach, I think. I overheard someone yelling about it."

She followed Mordecai down the stairs, taking two at a time. Confusion seeped into the moment. A property breach could be anything, but given that Lexi's ghost sentinels were on duty, roaming about the yard undetected by normal people, they had clearly reported something extreme for this much activity. Yet...no one had told Mordecai and Daisy to get to safety. That was the first thing Lexi would do. Always. Then they'd argue about Daisy and Mordecai wanting to help...

This couldn't be an active battle. This had to be something else.

Butterflies swarmed in her belly with implications. Dread was a heavy weight in her gut.

Produce and other breakfast items littered the kitchen counters. Cutting boards and knives lay strewn about, the breakfast prep abandoned. The front door stood open, people having run in from the other house and down the hall to the backyard. Daisy could feel their souls gathering there.

She was right behind Mordecai as they burst out through the back door. The yard stretched before them, with a large patch of cut lawn surrounded by bushes and then trees, obscuring the brick fence at the perimeter. Everyone gathered in one location, looking down at something in their midst or around them in the empty yard. Soft billows of fog rolled and tumbled through the air, leaving dampened kisses across Daisy's exposed skin. A chill slithered across her, leaving goosebumps in its wake. She wasn't exactly sure if that was from the fog...or the situation unraveling before her.

Zorn glanced back at her and Mordie, his expression guarded.

Fuck. That wasn't good.

"What is it?" she asked, out of breath as she joined everyone else.

"Yes, Frank, I can see that," Lexi said, talking to one of the resident ghosts that had followed them from the old house to this one, and now just kinda loitered around Lexi wherever she went. "Obviously it means something, yes. That token, or whatever you want to call it, has been marking murders across the world for the last six months. But what we need to know is how it relates to *us.*"

Another shock of adrenaline rolled through Daisy, and she pushed forward, needing to see what everyone was looking at.

"Here comes John," Kieran said, his voice full of authority and command. John was another of the sentry ghosts, this one much better at his job. Having shared power with Lexi, Kieran could see and talk to the ghosts nearly as well as she could. "He'll have talked to the others."

Jerry twisted a bit when he felt Daisy's hand on his arm before stepping back so she could get a look.

Her world bled of color, so many emotions running through her that she couldn't process them all. Didn't know how she felt.

A body lay on the dull green grass with its limbs twisted and broken, jutting out at unnatural angles. The man's lips had been shaven away in gruesome hacks by what looked like a dull blade. His handsome face was contorted in agony, even in death, and dried blood coated the sides. A green rope was tied around his throat, where it had once constricted him and now was in a bow. The color was reminiscent of the ribbons Chesters proudly wore to signify their lack of magic. A joke, probably.

"Cause of death?" she heard herself say, somewhat in shock. She'd wondered if something like this would happen. Wondered if she'd allowed herself to be trapped—to have made a deal only an absolute fucking moron would agree to.

Amber was studying her from across the group, almost as good at reading her as Zorn but usually much less inclined to get involved. Her past was somewhat of a sticking point with Kieran and the crew. She always made herself available to Daisy, though, and for that Daisy had forgiven any past wrongs. Not to mention she still had somewhat of a girl crush. The woman was fucking sensational at her job. It had to be acknowledged.

"Strangulation is my guess," she said, her onyx eyes assessing. She knew something was up. "Probably right before he was dumped on the property. It looks like he was still bleeding when he was put here."

"I've got a name." Henry glanced up from his phone on the other side of the cluster. "Liam Harrison. I'm just pulling more information now to see how he might correlate to the other bodies that have turned up."

"He doesn't." Daisy's eyes flowed over the bare torso, the first time she'd seen it. All she'd done was kiss him. She hadn't felt him up, stripped him down, anything. Just a kiss, and then she'd left, wondering what would happen next.

The question had been answered.

Her heart thudded. *He'd* somehow known about the kiss—magic, probably—and she'd summoned him by breaking their agreement.

What had she done? What sort of absolute fucking moron was she to have landed herself in this situation?

She nearly groaned at the implications. She'd let him into their realm, past the Celestials, with a sanctioned pass.

The unemotional, logical part of her wondered who else she might wipe from this earth without having to do much more than offer a kiss. She wanted to pull a list of notorious crime lords and murderers and make her way through, forcing the fae to drop everything he was doing and take time out of his chalice collecting to do his duty as *kissing assassin*. It would probably annoy him to no end, both because of the time lost and because she wouldn't keep his "property"—her lips—off other people. Two of them had entered into that stupid deal, and she was plenty happy to join him in fighting dirty. This toy also liked to play games.

She read the message on the torso, cut into his flesh and wiped enough so she could read the bloody letters: *My pleasure.*

"Unless you'd like me to kill him for you?" the fae had said. *"It would be my pleasure. Just say the word."*

Everyone's faces turned toward her. Henry's eyes flicked up from his phone.

"What's that?" Kieran faced her full-on, dressed in sweatpants with no shirt or shoes. He was no less ready for battle.

Lexi's eyes tightened, and a pang of guilt hit Daisy's gut. This would worry Lexi. Daisy hated doing that.

"He doesn't correlate to any of the other murders," she repeated, pulling the ponytail holder off her wrist where she kept it and tying her hair back. "He's the bartender at the hotel where the charity event was held."

Thane, his hands on his hips, narrowed his eyes. "The Chester-killer you saw last night?"

"Yep," she drawled, nodding. "One and the same."

The sky darkened with clouds above them, Kieran

affecting the weather unconsciously while very likely trying to control his turbulent emotions. Finally, Amber broke the silence, asking what they were probably all thinking.

"It has the dove feather. Was it done by the fae who's been plaguing this realm?"

A nervous flutter stirred in Daisy's stomach. "Almost certainly, yes," she said, pulling her lips to the side and looking on the ground. She turned slightly toward Zorn but didn't dare look at him. She needed to know what and how much to say, but she didn't want them to know he was keeping secrets for her.

"And so…" Amber hesitated. "Why would the fae kill this person? The one you saw last night. If it doesn't relate to the other deaths, I mean."

Out of the corner of her eye, Daisy saw Zorn's very slight head tilt. A nod, of sorts. He was telling her to spill a little info.

Kieran's eyes flashed that way, noticing Zorn. A peal of thunder rolled across the sky. *Shit.* Worrying Lexi was one thing, but going head to head with Kieran was entirely another.

"Short story—"

"I'd like the longer version," Kieran growled. Lexi put a hand on his forearm.

"Short story," Daisy repeated, "is that he made an appearance at the charity event the other night and informed me that the bartender was a Chester-killer. I hadn't known. He offered to…dispose of said bartender for me. That it would be his pleasure. I declined." A few mouths dropped open incredulously. "I didn't mention it because I've been told not to say anything. By the fae. I've been told to keep his business private."

"Since when do you do what other people tell you to do?" Jack asked in a rough voice, his customary good humor utterly absent.

"Since it would put my family in jeopardy," Daisy replied sternly. "You know all you need to know already. Hopefully whatever is on that computer will help you learn more. The other stuff isn't relevant."

"Isn't relevant—" Lexi rubbed a hand down her face and slumped. Knowing her, her ire was rising fast and the need to do something violent to protect her "kid" was boiling her blood.

Kieran stared at Daisy, those blue eyes stormier than she had seen them in a long time, not since they'd found a moment of peace from the world of Demigods.

"Just to be absolutely clear"—Amber put out her hands, probably to forestall Kieran from blowing up—"this death has absolutely *nothing* to do with the other deaths within this realm. Zero to do with them. Even though it carries the dove feather..."

Her voice trailed off suspiciously, and her look was poignant. The eyebrow quirk was to clue everyone else in, and her glimmering eyes said she'd figured out what no one else had thought of. Despite deaths cropping up in this realm from as far back as four years ago, the feather hadn't started turning up until six months ago.

That had been directly after the situation with Mordecai's ex-woman, Mr. Bathtub, and Kieran's need to mess with the winds to ensure no Celestials changed their minds and decided to pay Daisy a house call. It had been right after they'd learned of the fae's plans and what magical item they sought.

Amber had probably been toiling away on that talisman, the feather, all this time, wondering why it had started showing up—if it was someone new killing people or another reason. This incident had supplied the missing piece and clicked everything else into place, clear as day. Damn it, that bitch was much too smart. This was why Daisy's girl crush on Amber never, ever waned.

She ground her teeth in frustration, though a smirk of respect slipped into her expression.

The other woman's lips tweaked slightly as well. This was payback for sneaking past Amber's radar the other week. Just wait until Daisy used that info. She'd regain the upper hand in their friendly battle yet.

"Nothing to do with each other except for the dove feather, yes," Daisy said, pausing before the part Amber was prodding her into revealing. "The dove feather has always been for my benefit." She took a deep breath. "You call me gremlin. He calls me *dove*."

Someone sucked in an audible breath of surprise, though she couldn't identify who. Magic raked through Daisy's middle, like it was trying to rip out her very soul. She winced in pain—they all did. Lexi's slip of control, no matter how minor, was terrible.

Amber nodded slightly. She'd been right. That fae had a personal connection to Daisy. Now they all knew it.

"Inside, *now*," Kieran said as a thunderclap shook the ground. Dark clouds rolled toward the city. The weather would not be great for Magical San Francisco today. "You're keeping information from us. I don't give two shits why. That ends now. Someone get rid of that body. He got what was coming to him."

"I call dibs on the body," Bria said quickly, raising her finger as Kieran stormed into the house.

Jerry's face crinkled in disgust. "You would. It's the right amount of messed up for you."

"You bet it is, buddy." Bria clapped him on his back, making him jump. "That note and the shaved-off lips are gold! I'm going to stitch that dove feather in, too. That's the perfect touch. It'll make people nervous just seeing him out lurching around. Wanna help me?"

He retched, shrugging her off. He thought the whole situation with animated cadavers, the necromancer's trademark, was gross. Bria found no end of entertainment in that fact.

"For such a big guy, you sure do have a weak stomach," she told him, following him into the house.

"What you do isn't natural," he muttered.

"It's just biology, *Jerry*. Before life, after life—it's all just biology. Flesh and bones and— Don't throw up in here. Lexi will kill you!"

Their voices drifted away as everyone else filed in behind them. Bria would be out later to magically seal the corpse into the ground, ready to be unearthed and animated should anything happen. She'd done it a few times before. They had a troubled past.

Jerry was right, though. The whole thing was pretty revolting. Daisy often wished for magic, but if that one was offered, she would probably turn it down.

She realized someone had waited behind with her, and it surprised her to learn it wasn't Mordecai.

Dylan stood on the other side of the body, his hands in his pockets and his eyes studying her.

"What's up?" she asked, facing him fully. "You okay?"

He didn't speak for a moment. "Do you remember how we met?"

She frowned at him. "Of course I do. It wasn't that long ago. You walked into the coffee shop and threatened us."

A crease formed between his eyebrows. "No, after that. When you guys were all pulling out of town. You offered me your bank account, and all that was in it, to give me a fresh start."

"Oh yeah, I remember. And you never paid me back. You're welcome for not holding a grudge."

His lips worked into a dazzling smile. The poor guy was just made to be noticed. "True. I kept the account as it was, hidden from everyone else in case something should happen. In case Kieran and Lexi were killed and my blood bond got released. If that happened, there would be more than a few Demigods swooping in to try to lock me into a new blood bond, probably against my will."

"Yeah. Tough break having one of the world's most special magics, along with one of the world's most pleasing faces. What a heavy load to carry, being prized..." Her voice was deadpan, as was her expression, but she did know the very real danger he'd be in if Kieran died and Lexi wasn't there to help. They all did. "What about it?"

"You were the reason I ultimately joined this crew. This family. Your selflessness that day convinced me that you'd always have my back. That I could trust you, and through you, that I could trust Lexi and Kieran. That I could trust you all."

She turned toward the door and waited until he had walked to her side. "And?"

"And now I want to be there for you." He stopped her with a hand on her shoulder, the touch signifying a lot more for him than words ever could. "I know you'll hold back with Kieran, and you'll definitely hold back with Lexi. I'm sure you've even held a bit back from Zorn. I know you want to protect everyone. Loyalty is hard won with you, but once you bestow that gift, you will do anything to protect those you care about." He paused, his gaze delving into hers. "But I also know what it is to be trapped. I don't want you to hold back from me. Do you understand? I don't care what danger it puts me in, Daisy. I've met the undertaker. I'm not afraid of death." His grin was slight. "I'm sure Bria could use the extra body to taunt Jerry with. Whatever it is you need—help analyzing the situation, talking about it, venting—I'm available. You aren't alone in this. I'm with you. Always."

A weight pressed on Daisy's middle from the significance of Dylan's words and the conviction with which he'd said them. Her heart swelled, filling her completely. She almost had to blink back tears, something not normal with her. She couldn't even remember the last time she'd cried. But this meant so much—his worry, his touch, his unwavering desire to help her despite the cost.

Yet she could only nod, thankfully, not sure what to say. Because she couldn't possibly take him up on that offer. Not when he was so much more valuable to Kieran and Lexi—to their protecting the family—than Daisy would ever be. But it was kind of him to offer.

Rutherford's open computer sat in the middle of the large dining room table, with the whole crew gathered around. As hoped, Henry and Amber had been able to recover various files from the hard drive that *someone* had recently tried to delete. They were files relating to

Rutherford's dealings with another entity, a company that had come across a batch of old weaponry with "runes, or some other odd or ancient writings" on them. Obviously it was those sorts of weapons Daisy had wanted to know more about.

But other things had come in the batch. Relics of some kind. Odd stones and rocks with strangely cut, "cloudy or dirty" gems embedded in them. Misshapen goblets with "strange writing" or chipped and pockmarked crystals. It was that which the fae was clearly trying to get his hands on, something their crew hadn't known about, even with their searches.

It seemed Rutherford had found a buyer for the relics—the two guys Daisy had seen him talking to. The fae had said he needed Rutherford dead so he couldn't complete a transaction.

Lie.

Rutherford hadn't signed any deals about the extra loot. The two guys he'd met had wanted more information, and from the notes, they'd seemed plenty interested, but no prices had been agreed to. Rutherford had been killed before anything could be set in stone. If the fae had talked to the other guys, he would've known that.

He'd been in that hotel room to get the information from Rutherford. A simple look into his head would've sufficed. But he'd killed the guy in a fit of rage instead and momentarily lost control because the man had been advancing on Daisy.

Her stomach dropped out. He *was* being chivalrous. He had been protecting her.

She had no idea how to feel about that fact, since he'd then essentially thrown her into the fire. She bet that fae didn't know how to feel about it, either. He'd certainly seemed tense and confused—frustrated—about the whole thing.

Would *he* have the conviction to kill Daisy when the time came?

"So what you're saying is," Kieran said, leaning his elbows on the table, "that computer didn't say where the goods are actually being stored."

Henry nodded, his own laptop open in front of him. "Correct. He has one small warehouse where he has stored some weapons for sale—"

"And we have that address?" Zorn asked.

"Correct." Henry nodded again. "We can ransack that at any time. The goods in question weren't stored there, however. It seems he got a tip that they might be in high demand among antiques traders, and a certain subset of those traders were prone to thievery. He hid that merchandise."

"And that isn't on his computer?" Jack asked, crossing his enormous arms over his chest. "You'd think he'd want to keep a record of it."

Henry peered at his screen where he'd typed all his notes. "He has the various items listed in his inventory. Each item is usually stored in one of three places—Warehouse, Shed, Garage. For the items in question, the tag is Sarge." He spelled it out. "They are the only items with that tag."

"We have some leads, of course," Amber cut in. "We cross-checked files and went through contacts. One of his friends is a Chester. Oliver Dawson, a former sergeant in the Chester armed forces. He lives in the non-magical zone behind a checkpoint that requires an ID. No magical people allowed. He has a small house but a big barn and a lot of land. Retired now. Another...creature of interest is a cat by the name of Sergeant Whiskers. It is owned by Rutherford's mother, who lives in Magical Arizona in a townhouse in a fifty-five-and-older community. She has a quaint two-bedroom, not much land, and no other storage areas."

"I'm betting on Sergeant Whiskers," Donovan said with a crooked smile. "That's fitting with Lexi's whole MO. If the mom is always wearing pajamas, all the better."

"Har, har," Lexi said. She'd been dubbed a pajama-wearing cat lady at one point, and the powers that be had made sure it stuck. Her two enormous magical cats came and went, hunting things in the yard or lounging around until needed.

"When's the last time he visited either of those areas?" Kieran asked.

"I was just going to mention that," Amber said, bent over her tablet. "He hasn't visited his mother in some time. Calls are infrequent and far between."

Boman tsked. "Not a very good son."

"He did visit the state within the time period, though. We couldn't get data from his rental car. It would've been a hike to his mom's, but not impossible."

"A car, not a van?" Kieran asked.

"Correct." Amber straightened. "He speaks to his Chester friend more often. The calls are short. No texts. Nothing else traceable. We have records of his leaving the magical territory after many of those calls. The Chester is within driving distance. We're looking for fake Chester identification, but regardless, I think we should check it out. That seems like a winner."

Kieran studied the table, everyone else falling silent. "How likely is it that the fae would've made that connection?"

"Slim," Henry said. "We're dealing with a creature that thought simply deleting a file also erased it. He didn't even erase the automatic backups. He's probably good for his kind, but he in no way can compete with the human world and is wholly outclassed by us. I doubt he knows about Sergeant Oliver Dawson."

"And he definitely doesn't know about Sergeant Whiskers," Donovan said.

Thane huffed out a laugh.

"If Dawson is holding anything, he might try to make contact before long," Henry said. "If he does, he might ask around after Rutherford. If the fae goes sniffing around Rutherford's home and meets a neighbor, all he'll need is a whiff, and then he can mind-hop to get the information he needs. He's not terribly tech savvy, this fae, but he is highly intelligent. He'll find what he's looking for eventually."

"Then time is of the essence," Kieran said. He pivoted his gaze to Daisy, expression tight. He'd asked a lot of questions of her since breakfast and had only partially believed the web of lies she'd woven to keep them from knowing more than they should. The fae wasn't the only one who was highly intelligent—Kieran was no chump. He knew when to stop pushing, though. He knew she wouldn't crack. Instead, he'd watch her more closely than she could wiggle away from. The guy went into overdrive when confronted with danger, which was a great thing...until it was her under the microscope. "Do you have anything to add?"

"I didn't know any of that," she said honestly. "But yes, checking it out sooner rather than later is a good idea. He's looking for a crystal chalice, and crystals are listed on the inventory sheet. He'll be doing everything he can to find those items. First, though, let's ransack that warehouse. We need weapons in case we do happen to meet him."

Chapter Twelve

The weapons they'd gotten weren't anything like the gift from the fae. The blades were iron, all with carved runes and hand guards of brass, but they seemed clunky in comparison. Clumsily wrought and totally out of balance. Only one was cold to the touch, but the blade was dull and chipped. Many were stupidly heavy and cumbersome to use. And forget being easy to hide—they were bulky things with fat sheaths. She hated to say it, but they'd never do. They had to keep looking.

Nothing could be done about it now, though. She couldn't use her gift because the fae might read her thoughts through it and know what she was doing, and they didn't have time to hunt down another possible supplier before they checked out the sergeant.

"I still would've preferred going after Mr. Whiskers," Donovan said from the driver's seat of the stolen car with Chester plates. They all had fake IDs to get through security. Kieran and Lexi could've asked for admittance using their stations, but they'd have been escorted. They needed stealth on this one.

"So dove, huh?" Jack said, in the front seat and smiling. Daisy and Jerry sat in the back. Here it came. The guys hadn't been able to razz her about that nickname because Lexi was so keyed up about the situation and Kieran was crazy intense about the possible breach in his protection of his family. No one wanted to set the Demigods off. But these guys added levity to everything. They took very little seriously outside of actual work.

Daisy shook her head and looked out the window, waiting. There really was no point in trying to head it off.

"How'd that come about?" Jack continued, turning in his seat to look back at her. "Clearly that ol' fae has seen a softer side of you than we have."

"Or maybe you guys are much softer than that ol' fae," she clapped back.

"Nah, that can't be it," Jack said. Jerry shifted uncomfortably. "That one can read thoughts, right?"

"Yeah," Donovan answered, his eyes crinkling as they appeared in the rearview mirror, looking at her. "What do you think, Jack? Reckon our little gremlin is actually thinking lovely, gushy things about us all the time? Think she has a mushy middle and big heart?"

"I think that ol' fae doesn't know her very well if

he's calling her a fragile sort of useless bird," Jerry murmured as he looked out the window at the dark night. "If he insists on calling her a dove, he deserves to have his eyes pecked out."

The SUV went quiet for a beat before Donovan and Jack started laughing.

"What are you trying to say, *Jerry*?" Jack said. "That you don't think the gremlin is actually a nice person underneath that hard exterior?"

"Yeah, *Jerry*," Donovan intoned. "It's not nice to say that you think the gremlin is just as hardhearted on the inside as she seems on the outside."

Daisy couldn't help laughing. In truth, she had no idea why he called her a dove. He certainly did think she was fragile, and yes, he deserved to have his eyes pecked out for it.

Heavy clouds blocked out the glow of the moon. Thick sheets of fog drifted around the road. Only their parking lights lit the way, not needed for much more than keeping off the wall of fog to their left and right. Near what must've been their destination, they slowed to a crawl and turned off the road onto a bumpy field.

Jerry clicked off his seatbelt. Jack and Donovan did the same, their humor having dried up in anticipation of the job to come.

"Hey." Jack turned in his seat to look Daisy directly in the eye. She could barely see him within the faint glow of the dash. "Stay safe out there, okay? If you see or sense danger, you get the hell out of there. You let us handle it."

"It's not me the fae will kill, Jack," she returned. "*You* get out of there. Let him have me. I'll have time to get away from him. You won't."

Jack's jaw clenched. Donovan's eyes flicked up to the rearview as the SUV bobbed and swayed, bouncing them around on the rough dirt.

"This is not the time to be stubborn, Daisy," Jack said. "Do what your elders say."

She held his gaze, saw the stubbornness looking back at her, then subtly twitched her head. Sure, why not? Obviously she wouldn't run while her family was in trouble, as he well knew, but they could all pretend. It would move things along much quicker.

He gave her a stiff nod and faced forward again as Donovan turned the wheel to follow the others in a semicircle. She still couldn't see through the fog out the windows. Kieran was laying it on thick.

In a few minutes, the SUV in front of them stopped. Donovan parked right behind, and then they all stepped out into the chilly night air. Donovan handed her a small flashlight as the fog peeled away from the backside of the barn.

"Hey." Mordecai stepped to her side, in a frilly purple robe that he would shed when things got rolling.

"Hey," she responded, keeping the light off for

now. She didn't need it with the others getting organized, theirs shining at the ground.

Lexi joined them a moment later. Her gaze was fierce. "If that fae shows up," she said, "you will run. Do you hear me? Let Kieran and me handle him. Together we will have more power than he does—than one of their Celestials, or so Zorn thinks. Okay? This isn't just your fight this time. This is *our* fight. We're a family. We fight together. Remember how many times you've told me that? Remember every fight you *refused* to leave because of that reason? Well, here we are. Family sticks together."

"Then why would I run?" Daisy quirked a brow, then nearly laughed when the glower lowered Lexi's eyebrows. "Okay, okay, I hear you. I'll let you handle it."

She was being honest. Lexi had made a good point. The fae had said that a Celestial nearly had the power of one of her gods. If that fae was scared of Celestials, he had less power than they did. Lexi and Kieran, not to mention the rest of them, really oughta be able to handle him.

Lexi nodded at Daisy, looked over at Mordecai, whom she also hated engaging in these things, and walked toward the barn. The others assembled behind her, except for Bria, who had opened the doors on one of the vans and was quietly pulling tarps off her pile of dead bodies. She'd animate them, or Lexi would, if something happened.

A dog barked in the distance. That must be the house. It sounded like a good bit away.

"No people or animals nearby," Lexi said into the growing hush as everyone stopped behind her.

Kieran worked his way around the rest of them and met her at the front. He glanced at everyone, then stared at something to the side of him like he was listening. A ghost, obviously. He nodded and looked back.

"We're good to go," he said. "No one is in or around the barns, as Lexi said. No animals. The doors at the front of the barn are open, though." He looked at Boman, the light bender. He could make it so that the opening stayed dark to the naked eye. The farmer would never know someone was poking around inside.

Boman nodded and scooted past them. Behind the wall of shifting fog, a hinge creaked. He was going in the back way first.

Kieran waited. It was Lexi who nodded, obviously following Boman's soul with her magic and knowing when he was far enough in that he'd be blocking them from view. Daisy didn't even remotely have that sort of range.

"Here we go." Kieran took the lead now.

Lexi flared out until they reached the doorway. She held up her finger to halt everyone before they disappeared inside. One of the large magical cats bounded in behind her. The other stayed near Daisy and Mordecai.

Donovan waited by the door for a moment before he went in. Jack paused and went next.

"We're waiting out here until the coast is definitely clear," Jerry told Mordecai and Daisy in a low rumble.

"They know the plan, *Jerry*," Bria said, joining them. She put what looked like a dead rat on the ground.

Jerry made a sound like *blech* before he shuffled backward. "Don't do that *here*! Do it over there by the van with the rest of your horror show."

"Oh, calm down," she murmured, pulling her backpack from around her shoulders and getting ready to animate the rat with her various incenses, candles, and sometimes bells. "It's just a little rodent. You won't even notice when it shakes to life."

"It's a *rat*," he groused, moving around to stand behind Daisy and Mordecai so his vision of it would be cut off. "It's possibly grosser than a— No. I won't even say that. It's definitely not grosser than a dead person, especially when they're all half rotted—" He gagged into the air and turned his back on the whole scene.

"You did that to yourself, bud," Bria said with a cockeyed grin. "That was all your fault. I was just minding my business that time."

"Did they tell you about the other night?" Mordecai asked Daisy in a quiet voice as the other two bickered. He turned to her, dropping his head so he could lower his voice even more. "When that guy was dropped on the lawn?"

Bria's eyes flicked their way, and her face lost all expression. She took a step away and bent to the ground, showing them her back, readying to work her magic. She was giving them space or pretending not to hear, indicating they weren't *supposed* to tell Daisy.

She watched Dylan glance their way before disappearing inside the barn.

"I looked at the security footage," she murmured.

"Amber downloaded that and erased it. You probably didn't see what the ghosts did."

"Amber doesn't know about some of my tricks. She got that over on me once. I've ensured she can't do it again. He dropped the body and looked right at the camera before placing the dove feather. He was making a statement. It was lost in my indifference."

"And then?"

Daisy's eyes lost focus, and she swallowed, remembering.

He'd walked around the house, sauntering almost, as though he had all the time in the world. As though he owned the house and the land it was on. Motion sensor lights clicked on and he let them, not concerned he would be seen. Not worried he'd be caught.

He'd gotten around the corner and stopped where he could stare up at her window. He'd known exactly which one it was. Maybe putting the knife there hadn't been such a great plan after all. The golden rays of dawn reached into the sky behind him, spearing through the deep indigo and coming violet. Rose and pink and peach saturated the horizon, making him stand out in relief. The image was a beautiful tableau, the subject outshining even the glorious sunrise.

He'd stared directly at her window for a time, then at the camera next to it and mouthed, *"I'll see you soon."*

"I said I saw. He's playing games. I told you guys that."

"You're in danger."

"I'm always in danger, remember?"

"Not like this. Lexi and Kieran are talking about moving you. I think it's a good idea. Hide you until we can get some protection in place or find a way to shut that fae down. I said I'd go with you. Not for protection but...just to keep you company so you didn't feel like you were exiled." He paused, looking down at her. "Daisy, Lexi and Kieran can combat that fae. They are talking to the other Demigods to organize a group effort. That's the best bet. Neither of us can help in this. We might as well get out of the way."

She jerked her face up to meet his eyes, solemn and serious and heartfelt. He would essentially exile himself to support her. He was such a fucking good guy.

She snaked her arm around his waist and squeezed him. He hugged her back.

"But you're going to say no," he surmised when she'd loosened her hold.

Dylan popped his head back out through the door, glancing at Jerry. He gave a nod. *All clear.*

"He'd find me," she whispered, the weight of that assertion settling heavily in her gut. She was connected to him. Maybe had been since the ledge. Hell, maybe had been since the Demigod convention, when he'd sought her out.

You were always going to end up in this situation.

At this point, it was not a matter of running or hiding. Right now, it was a matter of playing the game. Of winning. That was all that mattered. Maybe all that ever did.

"I can't explain how I know...I just do. It'll take me killing him. If you guys want to help, help me do that."

He paused at the door and pushed it open wider, his arm high. He waited until she ducked under it to go in first. "Okay," he said to her back.

The soft light of battery-powered lanterns placed sporadically on the ground illuminated small areas of the vast, airy barn. A large network of weathered wooden beams rose to the ceiling high above, connecting with the rafters. Rough-hewn wooden planks jutted out from the carcasses of old horse stalls, silvery gray with age. Cracks and gaps let the light from the other lanterns seep through the other side and join those nearer her. Compacted dirt and traces of soiled and soggy straw lay underfoot, some areas scuffed away from heavy traffic down the center of the space.

In the middle on the right, however, everything changed. Metal shelving gleamed in the diffused illumination, pushed back against glossy white particle board to block off the old plank walls behind it. That same style of board closed in the shelves on either side and bedsheets, the fitted kind, draped down the front. Odd choice of cover.

Daisy drew near, knowing this was what they were looking for.

"Looks like it definitely wasn't Mr. Whiskers," Donovan murmured as he pulled back the sheet.

"Let her through." Zorn put a hand on Donovan's arm, moving him out of the way. His eyes were on Daisy as he took over pulling the sheet back, hooking it on the corner of the setup.

She frowned as the others, even Lexi and Kieran, pushed away to the sides, giving her plenty of space.

"I'm no expert," she said, but her curiosity continued to propel her forward.

"You're the only one who's seen what the fae is looking for." Zorn followed her gaze to the shelves, six in all, somewhat like a metal bookshelf. Items of all shapes were spread out on various colored towels. She bent to look at the bottom, seeing stone textures with jagged edges. Some items appeared like geometric shapes, angling up at a diagonal, resting on the only flat surface. Others looked like rocks out of a decorative garden, shades of brown or gray or sand but with streaks of another color or smoother texture running through. A couple had the gems Rutherford's notes had mentioned, though from here they looked more like smooth or bumpy rock. Their colors ranged from deep crimson, to twinkling periwinkle, to soft jade... All the colors of the rainbow, it seemed, and not something that would fetch any sort of decent price with a jeweler. She knew precious stones. These weren't fit to be sold. Not as anything someone might affix in a ring or necklace, at any rate. No, their value probably lay in a different market.

The next shelf had smoother surfaces, like colored glass. Each was in a kind of block, clear on the outside but a moving, writhing set of colors within, twisting and turning around each other, and sometimes bubbling to the surface. At least, that was the impression they gave Daisy. None of the insides actually moved at all.

Next were the crystals, the most populated shelf. Most of these one might find on a Tarot deck. The colors here also varied, with a cloudy violet, a splotchy sky blue, or a streaked and hazy white nestled in a rough, rock-type base. The other shelves held an odd assortment, none of them really going with each other or anything else. The strange, gem-looking rock things were stuck in a few items, as though hammered there.

Daisy stared, transfixed, as one on the top shelf started to visibly vibrate. The air above it turned hazy, like heat rising from hot concrete on a blistering summer day. She reached out and felt it, the smooth surface slick and cool.

"Is that..." Jack put a hand on her shoulder and leaned over her, easy with their size difference. "Is it moving?"

She pulled it off the shelf, feeling the hum crawl through her fingers and up her arm. The inside started to flicker and then glow a pale blue.

"Oh wow," Thane murmured, pushing in as well. "That's magical. I wonder if the Chester sergeant could tell. He probably would've put nicer towels under them if he could."

"Well, *this* Chester can tell," Jack said as she handed the item back to him. He took it and stepped away, content to look at his new toy and give her more space.

"That is true," Thane said, each word clipped, basically calling himself an idiot.

Daisy grinned as she went back to looking at the items. If she waited long enough, they'd show themselves. That seemed to be how they worked.

Another glowed, this one a vibrant chartreuse, flickering from the middle of one of the twisty glass blocks.

"Ooh." Dylan pushed in, reaching around her to grab it. "It's vibrating. Here, Lexi. Feel this."

It was a crystal, the glow not much more than a dull throb of chocolate brown but ending with a little light show, like a disco ball catching and throwing the light. Three more, their glow or interaction all different, but no less special. No less obviously magical.

"It makes sense why he hid these away," Kieran said, hefting a stone item cut through with rings of blue that glowed like the deep recesses of the ocean, blue-black. Or so Kieran had said when he nearly shoved her out of the way to get at it. He was no more immune than anyone else to how cool these various items were.

Daisy looked over the rest of them, waiting, seeing if any more would show their magical ability.

"That might be it," she said, straightening from her lean. "They kinda call to you when they kick off."

"Yes, they do." Thane hefted an item with a mournful cherry glow, the longest-lasting performer of those they'd found.

"Take them all." Kieran glanced at the door. "Jerry, grab the duffel bags."

"Not like Mr. Whiskers's less impressive name-cousin really needs them." Donovan turned to go help Jerry.

"Where is Bria to tell you how stupid you sound right now?" Jack asked after him.

"Outside guarding Jerry's treasured dead bodies, thankfully. I'll never know."

"None of the others are probably worth anything," Daisy said, putting her hands on her hips. "The fae is looking for power, and that hum seems to signify that power. Without it, it's almost certainly just an ordinary crystal or rock or strange glass sculpture with a rock driven into it."

"Why were there so many of those magical items in this one lot, I wonder?" Lexi asked, her eyes traveling over the remaining items. "Didn't you say there was only one in that apartment?"

"Yeah. But who knows what he found in the other places he visited," Daisy said, stepping back and bumping into Jack. "Would you skedaddle?"

"Nope. You're short. Bend down and start collecting the rocks on the bottom shelf."

"I want to know how his supplier came by all of this." Lexi stepped away, chewing her lip in thought. "This seems like too big of a payload."

"We can cross-check—"

Henry's words fell away as Daisy closed her fingers over the mostly round rock in the far corner. The second her hand touched the strangely silky surface, a violent jolt flared up her arm and exploded within her body. Heat unfurled from her middle and crackled through her limbs, a feeling like her blood was flash-boiling and scalding her skin from the inside out. It rushed her length, came back to her middle, and lodged there with a heavy, white-hot flare of agony. The air pulsed around her, a sonic boom that blasted out and blotted out her vision. Something hard and unmovable hit her back a moment before her head thunked against it.

The ground. She'd fallen.

Pulses of heat, of electrical current, of raw power continued to pour into her body from where her fingers were still closed around the object, her thumb dipping in a hole in the side, the sharp points within blistering her fingers with heat.

"Get it out of my hand," she panted, darkness threatening to take over her. *"Get it out of my hand!"*

Chapter Thirteen

A foot connected with her wrist. If there was pain, it couldn't register. The orb shook loose. Her arm tingled in its wake, and her vision was still splotchy black, with the lantern glow filtering in around.

"Daisy, hey." Lexi bent over her, putting her hand under her head and peering into her face. "Daisy, are you okay? What happened? What was it?"

Daisy's body shook with the residual power, like she'd been electrocuted. Her feet felt numb.

"That's one of them," she managed from a scratchy throat. Had she been screaming? "Maybe don't touch it, though."

Lexi helped her to sit, kneeling beside her. Everyone had gathered around. The orb lay up against the metal of the shelves, and she could now see its details. What she'd mistaken for rock was actually crystal around the outside of the misshapen sphere. It glittered in the low light, grays and creams and whites creating planes and textures within. An opening in one side went through to the other, leaving the middle hollow. Glittering points, like princess-cut diamonds, flowed along the inside like a river and spilled over in three places, where it traveled over the surface and dipped into the other side. The overall effect was breathtaking, a piece of art or décor that would be highly sought after.

"That's it." She could barely understand herself through her numb lips. "That's it." Her breath still came in quickly. She couldn't get enough air. "That's the crystal chalice. That's what he's looking for. It must be."

Lexi didn't even spare it a glance, still looking into Daisy's eyes with concern.

"We got a curious sergeant," Boman called from the front. "He must've felt that blast of...whatever that was."

Daisy looked that way, her head still rattled, thoughts coming slow. "It blasted out that far?"

"It nearly knocked us off our feet." Lexi glanced behind at Thane.

"Yup." He bent and scooped Daisy up, hugging her into his hard chest. "Let's get you into the car, huh, princess?"

He knew she wasn't a fan of that nickname. He was trying to rile her up and make light of this situation, knowing she didn't like people to take care of the Chester. Knowing she hated proof of her weaknesses.

"I'm rattled, not incompetent," she said automatically, but didn't struggle away from him. She might be lying. Her feet were still mostly numb, and it felt like she had bugs crawling under her skin. She wasn't sure how walking would go just now. "I can still stick you with something sharp when you're not looking."

"There she is." Thane grinned.

"The sergeant has a gun," Boman called. "He can't see me, but he can hear me, and he's about to take aim."

"I got him." Donovan jogged in that direction. He was a telekinetic and probably intended to yank the gun away.

Daisy lost sight of them as Thane neared the back door.

"Don't use your hands!" Lexi hollered. "Are you crazy, Mordecai? You saw what happened to your sister. Use the sack or kick it in with your shoe or something."

Thane pushed out through the back door to find Bria standing above a body lying prone on the brittle grasses.

"What was that?" she asked, her brow pinching when she noticed Daisy. "What's going on?"

"The gremlin thinks she found the crystal chalice, even though there is nothing cuplike about it." Thane didn't take her to the SUV she'd come in. Instead, he hiked her up so that he cradled her in one arm while using the other to open the door of the SUV Lexi and Kieran had brought.

"What did it do?" Bria left the body to follow them to the car.

"Released what felt like a punch of power and knocked her flat on her ass. I had to kick the damn thing away."

She let out a breath, hands on her hips. "Well, shit."

"Yeah." Thane settled Daisy in, adjusting her so she was comfortable before trying to smooth her hair.

"I'm good." She swatted at his hands. "I'm fine. The tingling is going away a bit."

"Oh yeah?" Bria pushed in behind him to look at Daisy as the first person with a filled sack came out. Jack. "What was it like? Did anyone else try it? Maybe it doesn't affect magical people as much as it affects Chesters."

Thane leaned against the side of the SUV next to Daisy, leaving the door open. "Or it could be infinitely worse."

Bria nodded, turning to watch Jack load the sack into the back of the SUV Daisy sat in. The Demigods would be guarding the precious cargo.

"Good point," she said. "I vote you try it and see."

Daisy laughed as Dylan came out with the next sack. It didn't take long for everything to be packed up and their convoy to be on the way.

"We'll have to tighten up our territory defenses,"

Kieran told Lexi as he turned onto the highway. "Even if we destroy those...magical items, eventually that fae is going to track down who took all of this and will come knocking. We need to be ready when he does."

"We need to invite him over, actually," Daisy said, watching the world go by out the window. "First, we need to track down better weapons, and then we need to set a trap. Hell—that isn't a bad word, Lexi. That's a place. The weapons we have will probably do if we're prepared."

"How do you plan to invite him?" Lexi asked her guardedly.

Kiss someone, Daisy thought immediately. That seemed to result in a punctual visit. She had a list of people who deserved his attention.

She didn't mention that, though. She didn't want to get into the details, like why she'd kissed him in the first place. Why she'd practically begged him to keep going. How many times she'd thought about the feel of his lips and his hard body under her palms.

"I can call him through—"

Glass exploded next to her. Something large hit the side of the moving vehicle. The tires screeched against the road as the SUV was shoved to the side. Kieran swore, yanking the wheel to go straight.

"What the hell was that?" Lexi yelled over the cold wind flooding the cab. Her phone started ringing.

"Look out!" Mordecai shouted, sitting in the back with Daisy. He yanked her toward the center. Her seatbelt dug into her chest. Something slammed against the car again. Kieran's window shattered, flinging shatterproof glass across his face.

The SUV jumped on the road, the tires screeching when they landed again. It swerved wildly. Lexi's phone skittered out of the center console and fell to the floor.

Kieran yanked the wheel to keep the SUV from turning too fast and rolling.

"I can't feel any souls!" Lexi yelled, diving for her phone. "What's hitting us?"

The right tires bumped down onto the shoulder. Everyone in the SUV was jostled violently.

It couldn't be Daisy's fae, whatever it was. She'd felt his soul, as weak as she was at it. The Celestials had them, too. Lexi would be able to feel them easily and from a greater distance. She could even identify the dead. So what the hell was outside the vehicle?

Lightning rained down around them. Dylan was using his magic from the car behind them, clearly able to see what was attacking. The bright slices of white-yellow outlined a ghostly shape in a hazy cloud. It flew right at them. The face materialized into a ghoulish skeleton with gray, waxy skin hollowing in the eyes and at the cheeks.

"It's coming!" Daisy yelled, flinging out her hands even though she had no magic with which to bat the thing away. "Kieran, you need to—"

It rammed them. Another she hadn't seen came right

after. The side of the SUV bent in, shoving at her. The force knocked the whole vehicle farther onto the shoulder. Another creature flew into the side up front, swinging them around. Kieran hadn't stopped it, and the sides of the tires dug into the dirt. The force took the SUV onto its hood and over, rolling into the fields beside the road.

She held on for dear life as their bodies whipped back and forth with the impact. The vehicle spun and glass sprayed her side. Her blood rushed to her head; her mind became dizzied and disoriented. The sacks in the back flew through the air. Heavy objects peppered the inside of the cab. Something struck Daisy in the head and darkness rushed in.

A hard grip settled around her ankles, yanking her awake. Her body slid against a bumpy surface, pulling with her a fuzzy blanket. She opened her eyes, but fabric covered her vision, a hood on her head or something similar. Her head pounded and parts of her body ached, as though she'd been flung around. There didn't seem to be any serious injury, however.

Souls registered all around her, none of which she knew. Ten people in all.

The primal part of her wanted to kick out and struggle. To fight. That was the mild panic trying to eat through her logic—trying to derail her training.

Allowing panic to control her, though, was a sure way to die quickly. She had to keep her head and ascertain the situation she was in.

The hand left her ankle and closed around her upper arm as her body followed her legs over the side. Her feet hit the ground, and her knees buckled. The weight of her limply dropping body tore at the grip. Fingernails sliced across her skin and caught on her shirt. Fabric tore, pulling out the seam and yanking at her neckline.

Her legs hit the soft dirt, then her back, and she rolled slightly so as not to hurt herself on impact. Then she curled to the side and made herself smaller in case a kick came, shaking to mimic cowering.

"Blight," a man said, using the word like she might use "fuck." Soles shuffled against dirt and rock before two hands grabbed her, hauling her up. "Stand, you stinky human," he growled, jostling her as he dangled her on her feet.

He had no problem with her hundred and thirty pounds, and he'd nearly spat the term *human*. Not Chester, but human.

The image of the skeletal face materialized in her mind. She recalled the flying shape and wordless scream as the creatures had descended on the SUV, strong enough to knock the large vehicle off the road. She was either dealing with one of them, or someone they worked for. Fae, in other words, but not her kissing assassin. She still didn't recognize any of the souls around her.

Well, that's not good, she thought as she closed her eyes again and took a slow, deep breath.

In her nineteen years on this earth, this was the second time she'd been taken captive by an enemy. After the first time, Zorn had dragged her through countless practice sessions in case it ever happened again.

And look, here she was.

Just like in practice, his teachings came easily to the forefront of her mind.

The most important rule: do not panic. Panicking only wastes time and energy.

Very true. She took another slow, deep breath. The hood slid against her face, the musky, stale scent nearly making her choke.

Give them what they expect. Weakness can be your greatest strength if you use it properly.

Her feet remained close together and slightly askew, a stance no fighter would use. Fae thought humans were frail and useless. *Less than.* She'd play that part for now.

He yanked her around and pulled her forward. She half tripped, forced to stutter-step, and made herself shake even more. Dimming light appeared in the slice of visibility at the bottom of her hood, night falling.

Murmured voices lowered in volume the closer she

got. People—or beings—stopped their conversations as she appeared in their midst. The animals had been grouped off to the right, judging by the souls, probably tethered for the time being. The crackling of flame accompanied an occasional pop of burning wood, a fire probably newly started. They must've stopped for the night. Unless she was somehow already in a different realm, she'd lost a day from when she'd crashed until now.

"Seat her there," someone said, and the being directing her shoved her downward.

She crumpled with a whimper and started pleading for her life. She babbled about rewards for returning her, how young she was, and anything else she could think of, most of the words lost to terrified-sounding sobs.

A hard object crashed into the side of her head to shut her up. Daisy grunted as she splayed onto the ground, her head pounding from the impact. *Fuck*, that hurt. *Fuck those fucking fuckers!* A boot, most likely. These assholes meant business.

She gritted her teeth against the pain throbbing within her cranium. Fae were supposed to be ruthless, but her kissing assassin had never laid a hand on her. Not in violence, at any rate. Only magic to keep her put. She'd misjudged how much she could get away with. Another mistake like that might cost Daisy her life.

"Get up." The rough hand grabbed her by the hood

and hair, yanking her to sitting and making her squint with enhanced pain.

"Take off her hood," the voice said, the one who had indicated where to place her.

She flinched when the top of the hood was pinched, and winced again when some of her hair was ripped away with it. The scene revealed itself within the folds of early evening, and she drank it all in as fast as she could.

You need to be ready at all times. You'll never know when you'll have to move.

Horses were tethered to a nearby tree. Covered wagons were stationed in a semicircle. They cut out some of the breeze flowing from...the east, if she had to guess. Eight guys with pointed ears all gathered around the modest fire. That was all as expected...except for how strange the guys—or possibly male creatures, in this case—looked. She'd get to that in a moment.

Trees scattered around with ample space between them. Away right, a meager dirt road cut through their thick trunks, sparse with branches. A smattering of stars were just making their night's debut overhead, the same pricks of light that would be hidden in a city's bright landscape. Night birds called out their presence, and off in the foliage, small critters worried the grasses. The area was remote, offering a sense of isolation. That wasn't ideal. If she were to escape, she wouldn't have a lot of cover or anywhere to actually go.

She might've lost a day from when the SUV had

gone off the road, but if they were going by horse and cart, they couldn't be too far ahead of Lexi and the others. Lexi could find her in the spirit realm and direct the others to where she was.

There is no worse pastime than waiting to be saved.

Yes, fine, Daisy thought in annoyance. She had to help herself. She knew that. But still, Lexi and the others weren't the types to rest when one of their own was in danger. They'd come for her. If nothing else, there was that to look forward to.

What was likely the leader of this crew stood on the other side of the fire, and when she took him in, her breath escaped her in a slow whoosh. Very strange. Definitely not human.

He stood with his chest bared, his skin the color of seafoam and with the subtle markings of scales running along his breastplate, over his shoulders, and down his arms. What looked like kelp mixed with branches and twigs twisted in a rope and encircled his neck and left upper arm, just above the lanky muscle. His long hair was partially tied up, disappearing within a headdress of twigs and leaves lined with shimmering green metallic kelp and silver-tipped feathers. The hair flowing down around his shoulders was stringy and gray-black, with plant matter that looked like ribbons flowing within or sticking out.

Those gathered around had a similar tint to their skin. A water-type fae, ruled over by the queen of the Sapphire Throne, one of seven minor kingdoms in

Faerie. Or so the books said. What the hell did they want with her?

The crystal chalice.

The answer came to her before she'd consciously thought about it. Whatever she'd done had drawn their notice. That wave of magic had sealed her fate.

"Tell us...knowing, and we hurt none," the leader said in an accent that sounded like he had a mouth full of water. He was trying to speak English.

Had he somehow missed all her babbling that he could almost definitely understand, given her Demigod's gift cast it in his language? Obviously she spoke his language. Thanks to the Demigod's blood gift, she could understand and speak any language within any land. It clearly worked for fae, because she'd understood the creature who'd dragged her out of the wagon.

The fae in charge had sent idiots. Which was great—it would be much easier to escape—but also...how tedious.

The tears from a moment ago still ran down her face, and she added a quiver to her lips. She shook her head, brow furrowed.

"What?" she said in their language, nice and slow so they couldn't help but understand.

A crease formed on the leader's brow, where she realized no eyebrows existed, before he looked at the others. Back to her.

"How do you know this tongue?" he demanded aggressively. Suspiciously.

"Hu-human magic," she supplied, and tilted her head to show him the side of her neck. There was nothing there, but he wouldn't know that unless he could read her mind. Given he seemed clueless about her weakness charade so far, he couldn't.

His eyes flicked to her neck before he jerked his head. Her handler bent to her. He grabbed and twisted her toward the fire so he could see. They obviously didn't have night vision. With his other hand, he scratched at her skin, peeling away flesh.

The pain vibrated through her, and she cried out, gently struggling away from him. She had a ruse to keep up, but she really didn't want a kick in the face. The hand holding her let go, and she tumbled into the dirt. Her clothes would be *filthy*.

"Leave it," the leader barked, annoyance plain. "It's not important right now. Bring the trove."

Definitely couldn't read minds. Great news. Now she just had to figure out what kind of magic they had, and she was halfway out of here already.

The leader paused as her handler stepped away. Two other males rose from crouching and disappeared into the quickly falling darkness.

"Human female," the leader said, "stop crawling away like pond scum. If you tell us what we want to know, we won't hurt you."

Apparently pond scum traveled where they were from…

"I don't know anything. I swear," she bleated. "They don't tell me anything. I'm just a ward. They aren't even my parents. I'm just—"

"*Silence!*"

She whimpered and did as he said.

The two males returned carrying what looked like a stretcher. Upon it lay the stones and crystals and other objects her crew had taken from the sergeant's house. They were after the same things as the dark fae. Clearly it was a race to obtain the power and flood over the Faegate. The Celestials weren't as popular as the overall ruling throne, it seemed.

"Which one of these is it?" the leader asked as the stretcher was placed beside her.

She let her very real confusion show. Wouldn't *he* know what he was looking for? The other fae had seemed very knowledgeable about the whole thing. She'd just stumbled into this mess.

She again spoke slowly so he got her meaning. "Which one is what?"

Her gaze slid over the clustered items. A few were missing. Those had been the ones the guys had grabbed. They must've hung on to them, and this crowd didn't know that.

Interesting. She'd already surmised that she wasn't dealing with masterminds here, but now it seemed like she wasn't even dealing with knowledgeable creatures.

It was like their directions had been simply "grab the girl and all her shit." Now they were trying to put two and two together.

She nearly laughed. This situation was getting better and better.

The only issue was that one item *had* made it. *The* item.

The crystal chalice.

It was stuck in with the others, a gorgeous piece of art that belonged on someone's shelf. A hollowed crystal orb, glittering with a diamond river flowing within and over the sides.

Truth be told, there was no way she could know if it was the actual crystal chalice, the item her fae sought. Could her instincts in fae matters really be believed? Definitely not. It could've been just another magical power item like the others.

One thing could not be denied, however. It was more powerful than the rest. More powerful by far. Whether it was the one her fae sought or not, it was certainly one he'd want to collect. One that could drastically help them all. One that had to be destroyed, and fast.

She didn't let her gaze snag on it, and couldn't do anything about the flare of sea-green from within a mundane-looking rock nestled in the middle of the jubilee.

Someone sucked in a breath. They all leaned in urgently. Another pointed.

The leader hastened over, snatching the object from among the others and pulling it in close. His eyes widened a fraction, and a faint buzz signified the object in his possession had started to perform its magic.

"It is true," the leader whispered in awe as all of them shuffled closer or leaned in to see. "I feel its power."

His gaze flicked to her and stuck, as though he were thinking something through. He turned, and the others fell back, their gazes landing on her as well, waiting for something.

The leader approached her, the smell of kelp and sea salt permeating the air. He held out the mundane rock, still glowing merrily.

"Take it," he said, shaking the object at her.

The energy it took to bite back a snarky remark nearly undid her. Her hands and legs were bound, for fuck's sake. What did he think she was going to do, inchworm over on her face and take it in her teeth?

"Wh-why?" she said, at a loss for what she was meant to do. She was used to an intelligent captor, not...whatever was going on with this donkey show. "Why me?"

His nostrils flared in annoyance. He motioned at her handler.

Her handler took a step and backhanded her across the face.

Fu-cking hell!

She let the inertia carry her back into the dirt,

crying out for reals. Her teeth cut into her lip. A trickle of blood slid down her chin, and she snaked her tongue out to instinctually assess the damage. That fucker had a good swing.

His boot fit into the middle of her back, pressing her front into the ground. She breathed heavily, taking stock of the placement of her limbs for evasive measures in case they got rougher and she might be in danger of popping a shoulder out of joint. They clearly would not care.

Her cheek rested against the cold ground. She could barely see the leader approach and bend down to her side to fit the rock into her hands. Its thrum of power ran up the length of her arm and shivered into the rest of her body, not doing anything more than it had in his hands.

Ah, now she got it. They wanted her to point out the crystal chalice. They wanted her to receive its painful jolt of power. This was turning into a really bad fucking day.

The leader grunted and straightened again. "Try the rest of them. Keep only what works—"

He cut off. His right boot scraped the ground as he turned, and he immediately tensed, as though there were danger near.

She tried to arch up to see what was going on, but the boot at her back kept her mostly put. She scarcely noticed movement in the inky darkness between the trees. Then she saw a dim light. It drew nearer, a phosphorus glow slowly swinging back and forth.

A man—or what passed for one—drifted into the firelight, and she just barely contained a hasty intake of breath.

She couldn't make out details in the darkness, but she knew his vibrant green gaze sought her out. The plane of his face turned her way, a metallic sheen covering his chest, and his limbs gleamed in the firelight.

"You have something that belongs to me," the fae male said in a cultured voice with a dangerous edge.

Shit.

Her villain in shining armor had come to reclaim her.

Chapter Fourteen

"Tarian," the leader said, the name sounding regal and grand within the accent. Lofty. The tremor of nervousness in his voice was unmistakable.

She knew how he felt, but not because of a name or whatever position he held. She could've gotten away from these morons, she knew it. They weren't bright, they couldn't read her mind, they'd easily fallen for her antics, and they had absolutely underestimated her. All she'd needed was a direction, time, and a distraction, and she would've been long gone.

The kissing assassin—Tarian—was the complete opposite, and he knew how to track her down. Her odds of escaping had just shriveled before her eyes. She was at his mercy.

Tarian's focus slid from her to her captors. His

body stayed loose, his beautiful, glowing sword hanging at his side.

The boot disappeared from her back, allowing her to shift so she could better see. The leader licked his lips, glancing down at the stone he held, then at the collection of other items on the stretcher.

"You misunderstand the situation," the leader said urgently. "Your king expressed an interest in an alliance with Queen Liora. I am simply checking the validity of his claims. Given what I've seen—"

"I think *you* misunderstand." Tarian offered a lazy, arrogant smile. It didn't hide the violence that screamed in every line of his body. "The human female is mine." He tsked. "And it seems you've mishandled my property."

"No. Wait!" The leader looked down at her in trepidation. "No! I didn't know—"

A surge of power made Daisy's eyes sting, and suddenly Tarian was in action. His sword swung so fast it blurred. The outline elongated, from a sword to a staff, razor-tipped at each end. He leapt over the fire, the shortest distance between him and the leader. Flame licked his metallic leathers and very cute, thick-soled boots. How was the guy always so damn fashion forward, even in something resembling armor?

The leader flung out a hand, and his fingers flexed. The other hand held the rock tightly to his chest. The sheen intensified, and a hazy, mossy green hue colored the air.

Streaks of black cut through, slicing away the magic.

"What—" The leader staggered backward, but Tarian was on him.

He sliced across the arm that held the rock. Fingers loosened as the hand and rock both fell to the ground. The leader screamed as the others in the area yanked weapons from their belts or bent to scoop them up from around the camp.

Tarian plunged his staff into the center of the leader and wrenched, quickly cutting off the howls of surprise and pain. The body slumped to the ground, and Tarian straightened, not even breathing heavily.

The others in the area fanned out, weapons at the ready, eyes tight as they surveyed the enemy in their midst. Tarian stepped foot over foot to grant himself more space, perfectly balanced. His staff twirled beautifully, a blur of light. He might have the swagger and arrogance of nobility, but he had the hands and footwork of a master swordsman.

"It doesn't have to be like this," one of the green-hued males said, trying to circle around to Tarian's back. "There is plenty to go around. Despite what you did to Sharlo, we can still work out a deal."

Tarian's voice came out emotionless, almost bored. "Our courts might work out a deal, but you'll be long dead when they do."

"You think you're going to best nine of us?" another fae scoffed.

The first hissed, as though willing his brethren to shut his mouth.

Tarian didn't respond right away as they moved, the nine surrounding him, his staff twirling all the time.

"I'll make it painless. How's that?" he finally said, stilling in the middle of their circle. "Except for you." He pointed his weapon at the fae in front of him. "You laid a hand on my property. You, I will kill slowly, with as much pain as possible."

He stepped backward and thrust his staff. It plunged into the fae before he could get his sword up. Tarian ripped it to the side, ending any hope of his enemy healing, before stepping toward the next and swinging his staff around, blocking an enemy strike. Daisy thought he would finish that male, but instead he slid across the circle toward another, keeping them from pushing in on him too quickly. He dropped that one, swung to the next, and sliced. Back to the one he'd blocked.

He looked like a dancer, flitting amongst his enemy as though moving to a merry tune. His staff swung and struck, blocked or parried. Screams and moans filled the night. Firelight flickered against spraying blood or flailing bodies falling to the ground. None of the enemy had so much as touched Tarian, not even a nick. In no time at all, as promised, only one of the green-hued fae was left—the one that had struck and scratched her.

"I didn't know," he bleated, backing up. He held a

non-glowing sword in shaking hands. "I swear it. I didn't know! Sharlo told me to do it. It is his fault, not mine!"

"Sharlo is dead. You will atone for his sins."

They moved farther into the night where the firelight couldn't reach. The staff shortened into a dagger, the glow only bright enough to show Tarian's hard, cruel eyes. His dagger shot forward, and then there was screaming. Howling. It went on and on, varying in pitch and ending in a gurgle. Still there was thrashing, as though the tongue and vocal cords had been ripped out for a little peace and quiet, but the pain continued on.

Not one to waste this precious distraction, Daisy rolled toward the collection of bodies and stopped near the first viable weapon. She trapped the hilt with her hip and sawed away the ropes from her wrists. Hands freed, she made quick work of the ropes on her ankles. That done, and with no time to spare, she hopped up, ready to grab one of these horses and go. The cover of darkness would shield her until dawn. It was the only option she had.

But as she moved to the horses gathered to the side, completely unimpressed with all that had gone on here, she registered the utter silence behind her. Not even animal life moved within the darkness, as though a big predator had moved in and they didn't want to be noticed. She knew how that felt.

Slowly, her pulse too fast and the sweat standing on her forehead despite the night's chill, she turned.

Tarian stood next to the fire, his metallic clothes splattered with blood, watching her with a smirk. His weapon now resembled a sword and hung down beside his leg.

"Hello, little dove." His voice was deep and rough. His smirk twisted into a wry smile. "Did you miss me?"

She let loose a gush of breath, utterly deflating. She should've known he wouldn't be distracted for long.

"Not really," she replied, staying where she was. There was no point in running. He'd catch her. "How'd you find me?"

He relaxed his posture and glanced at his handiwork. She didn't follow his gaze. With a wave of his hand, everything disappeared.

He'd pulled that trick back when they first met. She'd been glad for it then, intrigued by the feeling of his proximity and his vibrant green eyes. She was nervous about it now, the power it displayed. The chasm between their strengths.

He didn't answer her, walking to the stretcher and surveying what was there.

"All that magic, yet you kill them with your sword?" she said, needing something to mildly distract her as he picked up the stone Sharlo had held and dropped into the midst of the others. It could've been a random rock for all the reverence he gave it.

"Yes." He prodded the stretcher with the toe of his

boot. The items resting on it tinkled as they jostled against each other. Several lit up, showing their power. "If I am going to make the effort, I prefer using my hands. It's much more gratifying when you best your opponent that way. Magic is inherited. Sword work is learned. It shows skill and discipline when you master it."

He crouched, looking the magical items over, before grabbing two and tossing them away from the others. Then the next two, leaving those that glowed within the stretcher. He was separating magical and non-magical items in the blink of an eye.

"Of course, I do cheat," he said. A dozen or so magical items were left when he finished. The hollow orb twinkled up at him, not glowing but from the firelight reflecting on the diamonds. He studied it for a long time. "I can read their thoughts. I know who is going to do what, when. With as much training as I have had, it's simply a matter of anticipation."

He pushed to standing and looked around the campsite.

"How'd you find me?" she tried again.

He made his way to the wagons. "I've been watching, obviously. When it was clear you wouldn't use my gift how I'd intended, it became necessary to keep tabs on you until you could figure out where our friend Rutherford kept his loot. Isn't that what you call it? Loot? A fitting term. I hadn't realized the Sapphire Throne was also watching. Very annoying, that. They clearly have an informant in our court. No one else knew I was waiting for your people to crack the code."

"For my people to crack the code?"

He pulled bedrolls from the back of the wagons and gave them a sniff test. His nose crinkled, and he threw them back in. Apparently, they didn't pass muster.

He turned to her with a half-smile. "You didn't think I was being a gentleman in leaving you that computer, did you?" The sentiment echoed what he'd said after he killed Rutherford. "I only deleted the files so you wouldn't suspect I was feeding you information. How were the weapons, by the way? The pictures of them looked atrocious."

She opened and closed her mouth silently, not knowing what to say.

"So you *did* think I was being a gentleman." He laughed. "You think better of me than my own family." He pulled food and skins of water from the wagons before transferring them to a large piece of fabric resting on the ground. "I didn't expect his records to be so cryptic about the chalices."

"You hadn't meant to kill him," she said. "You could've gotten the information from his mind. And why do you call them chalices? Not one of them looks like a cup. Not even close."

He gathered the corners of the fabric and moved the food and water items more toward the fire. "You're right. I hadn't meant to kill him. I had a momentary slip of control—" He tilted his head and corrected himself. "I had one of a couple momentary slips of control. Luckily, your team excels at espionage and technology. Do they not? Anyone of consequence in the human magical world thinks so. I knew they could get the files they needed from his computer and figure out where those chalices were being kept. That failing, I would've gone about it the hard way. Thankfully, your team came through. Kudos. It saved me *oodles* of time."

He approached her like he was advancing on a skittish animal. His movements were so fluid and graceful, entrancing.

"I will always find you, little dove," he murmured. "I've made it perfectly clear: you're mine. Your whereabouts are of the utmost importance to me."

"Why?"

He didn't answer as he stopped in front of her and reached out slowly. His fingers lightly glanced across her bruised cheek, her temple, where the boot had connected, and the scrapes on her face. Anger flickered across his expression, and his jaw tightened. She could see the violence sparkling in his eyes.

"These tracks of tears..." His voice was a low growl as he drew a line beside her nose and around her mouth. "Were they real?"

"No."

He smirked. "Of course they weren't. You're much too fierce to let a minor inconvenience like an abduction break you."

Down to her neck.

"Is this..." His voice turned deep and rough again, and his body tensed, like he was struggling to keep his composure. Like he might want to kill them all again. "Did they scratch away your skin?"

"They wondered why I could understand them." She told him what she'd said and why.

"Ah." He relaxed slightly. "Clever. When it comes to the power in a kingdom, not many outside of a court will have mindgazer magic. And members of the court don't trouble themselves with mundane affairs like acquiring chalices and diddling with humans."

"Except you."

"Except me, but I'm a rare circumstance."

"Why?"

He didn't answer as he pulled her torn shirt away from her arm to look at the wound. "At least you heal quickly. That's a blessing." His hand dropped, and his eyes met hers. "Chalice, in your tongue, is a goblet of sorts. Or the cup-shaped interior of a flower. In mine, it's more" —he toggled his hand—"myth, almost. It's given to mean an instrument that holds unlimited power. That isn't necessarily the case, as no power is unlimited, but that's the theory. There are many kinds of chalices—again, in lore. The most powerful is one produced by nature, enhanced by a human, and blessed by the gods, some say."

"The ones over there with the gems?"

He toggled his hand again. "They aren't exactly

gems, but yes, essentially." He looked beyond her at the horses. "We'll need to bring all these animals with us. I won't leave them here to die. Tomorrow, though. We can't travel any more tonight. It's too dark, and there are wild things out there that would give us trouble."

"You can't see in the dark, then?" she asked. "I thought dark fae could see in the dark."

"Not all. And while yes, I can mostly see in deep night, the horses cannot." He walked around her to the animals. "Besides, that fire is glowing merrily. We might as well enjoy it."

"What about the other group? You've been watching me, fine, but what about them? I was in the Chester lands when their…whatever they were attacked."

"Not *their*." He ran his palms along the horse's withers. "Those creatures were the minions of the dark fae, but not under my control. Further proof that the Sapphire Throne is dabbling where they shouldn't. And how did they find you?" He glanced back at her, his expression lost to the night. "They felt you. Any fae on this side of the fringe would've. You still radiate the power that coursed through you. Smell like it, sweet and savory and delicious. It adds to your overall allure, something I didn't think could be possible. It seems you've found the crystal chalice."

So it was true. She'd been right. And judging by how long he'd looked at it a moment ago, he knew which one it was.

Cold washed through her. This was it. He'd found what he'd been seeking, plus a host of additional powerful items. Now he could create that bridge and bring his kind into these lands.

Her chest was tight, but her resolve hardened. She was here now, in its vicinity. She knew which one it was. If she could destroy that orb, they wouldn't have the power to leave their realm. Their plans would be forfeit.

Not advertising her intent, knowing she was far enough away that he couldn't touch her mind, she raced toward the fire and the magical items. She barely paused to get her bearings, knowing he'd be coming hard after her. She planted her foot, lifted the other, and slammed it back down. It connected with the item, and she anticipated hearing the hard crunch of its cracked surface...except that sound never came.

A burst of power so potent that it made her eyes water exploded from the point of contact. It didn't seep into her body like before, but burst outward. She was lifted up and thrown backward, her limbs windmilling as she flew. She hit the ground and rolled, the breath knocked out of her.

Sputtering and wide-eyed, she pushed up to her elbow to look back toward the fire. Tarian wasn't there. He was still with the horses. He hadn't even bothered to turn around and watch her. The orb sat where it had a moment ago, twinkling like before, laughing at her.

"You can't destroy it like that," he said in a bored

tone. "You can't throw it in a fire or crush it in a human vise. It won't succumb to magic or tolerate being covered in spells to diminish its power. It is eternal, as far as you are concerned."

She pushed up to sitting. "What does that mean—as far as I am concerned?"

"It means it *can* be destroyed, but it must be taken to the Divine Collective, the seven gods of the Celestials, and they must be asked to retire it. Must be pleaded with, probably."

"What...like taking the One Ring to Mordor?" she asked incredulously.

He half turned to look at her, pausing in placing a feed bag. "I don't know what...ring... I'm not sure what Mordor is."

She scoffed and shook her head, remembering a long time ago when Mordie had gotten her to watch *Lord of the Rings*. She used to make fun of his name because of it—Mordie/Mordor. The memory was bittersweet at the moment.

"And these gods exist in the fae realm, obviously," she said, her heart dropping.

"Very astute." He was mocking her.

"And a human couldn't reach them within the fae realm?"

He shrugged. "Maybe a magical one could. But you? Only if you rode a flying pig."

She bit her lip, staring at the fire. She couldn't destroy it, fine. She could hide it, though. She could steal it when she was escaping and put it in a place his court couldn't recover it from, since he'd obviously have to be dead by then. There was still a way to salvage this. There had to be.

"What now?" she asked, pulling in her feet and crisscrossing her legs to sit comfortably. Absolutely *filthy*. "I suppose, since you have what you need, you'll turn into the perfect gentleman and drop me off at home and leave me alone forever?"

He didn't so much as grin at her antics when he turned to her. Instead, his expression was hard and sober. "I will caution you about this once and once only, little dove. I may have had a lapse in control in the past, but that will not happen again. It cannot. I am not chivalrous. I am not what the humans think of as a gentleman. I am fae, and our rules are brutal. They are vicious. To let down one's guard—to lose control—results in death or worse. My...whatever this feeling is for you will be shoved so far down that I won't feel it. *Can't* feel it. Come tomorrow, the game will truly and fully commence. Starting tomorrow, you will be fighting for your life, and I will be thrusting you into the fire. Purposely. Repeatedly. Soon, I'll be using you for a subtle and cutthroat battle in the faerie courts, taunting them with your aroma of power and your status as my pet. You'd best get ready, or you'll be broken before your game has barely begun."

Chapter Fifteen

The next morning, she lay on her back, staring at the wagon's cover. The soft dawn light crept in, announcing the first day of her new life. Her new captive status, at any rate.

Tarian had unintentionally woken her about a half-hour ago when carefully removing himself from her side and climbing out of the wagon. It was the first she'd known that he'd slept in her vicinity. Given he had magically dosed her at bedtime last night, she had slept incredibly soundly.

She supposed she ought to thank him for that. Otherwise she wouldn't have gotten a wink of sleep. She might've tried to escape, as well, disappearing into the darkness and the cold, likely getting lost in an unfamiliar place until morning, when he'd randomly show up and reclaim her. Or maybe just follow her around and taunt her. Who knew with that fae.

His movements in the camp were soft. He was likely making ready to depart. A horse huffed and stamped its hoof.

Her thoughts whirled. She hadn't said much to him after his assertion that she'd go to the faerie courts. What was there to say, really? He'd take her where he wanted, and she'd need to go along with it until she had an exit plan. Besides, it had been gratifying to ignore him when he repeatedly tried to get a conversation going. She didn't have much as a captive, but she did have the infuriating ability to act like a child and annoy him. It had been the only weapon in her possession worth swinging.

After another few moments of patiently staring, he appeared at the back of the wagon wearing a crisp button-down shirt with green ribbing and deep blue jeans. He probably had really cute shoes, too. He'd obviously spared some time to shop in the human realm because, judging by the Celestial attire, he hadn't gotten those clothes from Faerie. He was as vain in his fashion as she was, and good at putting an outfit together. Which galled her for reasons she couldn't explain.

His expression was hard, a battle commander going to the front line.

"Rise and blossom, little flower. It's time to go."

She didn't move for a moment, wondering if he would hasten her or drag her out. Instead, he waited patiently.

With a sigh she knew he heard, she pushed to sitting and hit him with a glower. A little smile peeked out from under his hard mask. Fantastic. How nice that he was getting a kick out of her bad mood.

When she crawled in his direction, he stood back and let her climb from the wagon. He didn't reach to tie her wrists or turn to shield the dagger that sat in a belt at his side. He wasn't scared of her.

Her mood darkened still. Of course he wasn't, but...it would've been nice if he at least didn't trust her.

I definitely do not trust you, he said softly in her mind. *Why do you think I haven't given you your weapon back?*

"What weapon?" she asked.

"Your gift. The one you stored outside your room where my mind couldn't reach you. You made it very easy for me to retrieve. Thanks for that."

She frowned at him. "When did you get that?"

"Shortly after the sluagh had acquired you. I was in no rush. I knew you'd be taken to this area. It is the best place to enter the fringe, after all—something the Sapphire Throne has learned from my travels. They have greatly trodden on my patience. Worse than that, however, is they have a leaky court, more so than the Obsidian Court. They have many spies that go unchecked. They believe that housing their court in the Sea of Stars will somehow shield them from outsiders, when their own court is anxious to win favor with other kingdoms. They are the ones who sell the most information. Their queen is shortsighted and her court badly run. The Celestials…"

His lips pressed together, cutting off the information. Everything he'd said soaked into her mind. She'd collect every scrap of knowledge he let slip from here on out. Even seemingly useless information could have a purpose if used correctly.

Then it was she who pressed her lips together, even though it was her thoughts that were the problem. She'd need to get used to a meditative state around him, keeping her thoughts from acting like words.

A very good trick to learn, he told her, the sun highlighting his beautiful face. *I have instruments to help with that as soon as we get to my chambers.*

A rush of heat flared through her, but she squashed it just as quickly. She'd be damned if this strange feeling between them made a fool of her. If he wanted anything from her, it would have to be forced. And if he came that close, it would result in his demise.

"Noted," he said teasingly, leading her toward the pile of ash replacing last night's fire. The rest of the camp was completely squared away. All the items had been cleared, magical and mundane alike, the crystal chalice with them. Sliced fruit waited for her on a slate board, along with nuts, cheese, and a butt of bread. The air this morning was crisp and fresh, and she watched the beautiful colors of dawn wash across the sky.

Last night, after he took care of the horses, he'd

brought his own horse out of the darkness. A donkey with pack saddles had followed. That would've been the ideal time to ask where they were and why they didn't use cars. Why everything seemed like her lands but different at the same time.

That, however, would've led to a host of other questions, like a general "What the fuck?" And "Why me, when I don't even have magic?" And "Have you always been the absolute worst?" Those wouldn't have helped, though, and fatigue had made her punchy, so she'd bottled up her words and emotions and been thankful when he put her under.

Now, though, it was a new day. Time to get to work.

"It seems like we're still in the human lands. Where are we, exactly?" she asked when she'd finished her breakfast.

He cleared away her empty containers and any trash before handing her a scuffed metal water bottle. Once she'd taken it, he finished preparing to leave. All his movements were fast and efficient but not hurried. He'd done this countless times, and it showed.

"It goes by many names," he said. "The borderlands are used most often. The frontier. The waste."

"This is the hollow alongside the fae barrier?"

He quirked an eyebrow as he latched the packs to the donkey. "That's one I haven't heard. The hollow." He pondered that. "I can see how that works. And yes, the very same."

"But the books said this place was a wasteland with…nothing." She slid her gaze across the tall grasses around the trees, spying a bright purple wildflower. "They said there was no animal life, no nature…a scourge, kinda. This can't be that place."

He directed her to the horses. "Here we go." He stopped beside the largest of them, a dappled gray male with a seemingly pleasant disposition. His horse.

She glanced between that horse and the ones behind. "I can ride one on my own."

"And untie your own, ride off into the abyss on your own, and get killed by a Celestial or twisted creature on your own, yes. But I want you alive for now, and so I'll ensure you stay in one piece, yes?" He gestured at his horse a second time.

She sighed but hopped up, feeling his hands on her hips to help.

"I got it," she murmured, trying to shake off the glorious thrum tightening her up.

"Besides," he said, easily hopping up behind her, his muscular thighs sliding in tightly against her legs, "you talked yourself out of running last night. I don't have high hopes that you'll refrain today. Not once you see the Faegate, as you call it. It'll be easier for me to keep control of you this way."

"Oh, well. Let's definitely make things easier on you."

"Yes, thank you. I'm glad you see it my way."

He prodded the horse to moving.

The dirt road running alongside the camp wasn't much more than tamped-down grasses and scuffs of brown. She thought about what she'd read and compared that to the sprigs of green budding on the nearby trees or the occasional shrub or wildflower that crept up from the beds of pine needles.

"This isn't at all a wasteland. I mean..." She shrugged. "It's not exactly a lush forest or anything, but I expected large tracks of dirt and not much else. Maybe desert." She'd expected the books to be *somewhat* right. Given that they weren't, it called into question everything else she'd read about the fae lands.

"Your texts will very likely be wrong in many respects, but the environment here does get more dismal the closer we get to the fringe. The Divine Collective made sure the magic was strong. Too strong, some think. That magic seeps into the human realm this close to the fringe and twists the fabric of your world. It's sectioned off by the portal, keeping it away from the rest of your realm, but it certainly affects this area."

She crinkled her nose, looking closer at the trees and the gnarled roots at some of their bases. "What about this is twisting the fabric of reality?"

He transferred the reins to one hand and dropped the other to her thigh. A thrill that wasn't welcome arrested her. She picked his hand up by the wrist and passed it back to his own thigh.

"The plant life isn't horribly affected, no," he said

after a beat, leaving his hand where she had put it. "It's not thriving, as you said, but it isn't turning to flesh-eating vines or anything, not like we have in the wylds. But the animals haven't escaped the magical influence. A hare looks somewhat normal until it is gnawing on your face in your sleep, for example. The wagons were a nice change. Usually, I have to set up wards and magical pitfalls to trap anything that gets close. It always wakes me up. I usually get terrible sleep the day before a passage. But today I feel as fresh as a morning lily."

"Bully for you," she groused, and he laughed delightedly. "There's nothing big enough to crawl or jump into a wagon?"

"Not anymore. Not like four human years ago, when this area was treacherous. More faeries have crossed in the last year, hunting the larger predators for food or killing them in self-defense. Some kill just for sport, I think."

Four *human* years? Their scale of time must be different. It wasn't important at the moment, though. She remembered the people in the stairwell talking about the creatures that had crossed.

"More faeries have crossed?" she asked.

"Yes. The Celestials are breaking down in their duties. The High Sovereign— That's the queen and king of the Fair Folk tasked with overseeing all the kingdoms and the wylds. They're in charge of maintaining the balance of our realm, a precarious affair.

You know, in case your books didn't cover it..." He was teasing again, in great spirits despite the seriousness with which he'd spoken last night. When she didn't respond, having known that already, he continued. "The High Sovereign are experiencing squabbles within their court and their family. That is always the case within a court, to some degree, but things have become a lot more chaotic. Politics aren't aligned and the kin are vying for the Diamond Crown. A push for power always results in instability. Given fae are immortal, and the Diamond Throne is usually the most solid of the land, upheaval like this comes but once in many of your lifetimes."

"But now, the more cunning of your kind will use it to their benefit."

"Exactly right. See? Humans aren't so dumb after all."

"Certainly not as dumb as the fae originally transporting me. It really is a shame you had to interrupt our party."

"Thank the Trinity I got there when I did, or I would've missed the pleasure of killing them for slapping around my pet. You would've systematically slipped a knife into their backs the second you had a chance."

"Or run, most likely."

He scoffed at her. "I doubt that. You seem to like holding grudges, and you're gloriously ruthless. The chance *would* have presented itself and you would not have hesitated. Tell me I'm wrong."

"Well...not if it had presented itself..."

His chest shook as he laughed silently.

"Who are the people—or fae—tracking down and killing the creatures that get through?" she asked. "We couldn't find any information about them, or any evidence that creatures had crossed at all."

"Ah. That." He let out a slow breath as though relaxing and looked out to the side. "The Celestials almost always handle the creatures that get through. Creatures aren't cunning like fae or crafty like humans. They are simple and unable to trick the Celestials, who have a magical means of tracking them. They are found very quickly, in most cases, and destroyed. The people in the hotel that night, chasing you around—they were employed by me. Humans will do a great deal for a little gold. They would not have hurt you, and if they had, I would've killed them gruesomely in front of all their peers, a fate they were well aware of when they took the job. I wanted to see how resourceful you could be. It turns out, very fucking resourceful. I was impressed, both by your escape and by your fighting the shadow wraiths on the ground level. I was not as impressed by the chances you took on that balcony."

She shook her head. She should've known. *Fucking fae.*

"I didn't realize I had a choice," she grumbled.

"Even those without a choice often succumb when they meet insurmountable odds."

"Yes, they do. Which is why I am sitting in front of you on a horse walking me to my doom."

He huffed out a laugh. "Yes, good point."

She watched the trees pass as they plodded along, nothing much changing in the landscape.

"I don't understand the logistics of this place," she said after a bit of silence. "You have to take a portal marker to get here, I know."

"Yes. The markers are spread out over the human world and, once activated, transport anything within their sphere to this place or one like it."

"So how is this still considered human lands?"

His puff of breath flowed over her shoulder as he took a moment to collect his thoughts on that. "It's a way station of sorts. It's like walking on a beach before one goes into the ocean. It is still technically human lands because it operates like they do. Mostly. It has similar trees and animals. It lacks its own magic."

"But motorized vehicles don't work here."

"No. Nor do technology and electricity. I can only imagine that is because the gods created this place, and while it doesn't have its own magic, it is created by magic. It remains as it does because of magic. But I'm not certain. I doubt anyone is. If someone is lucky enough to be granted an audience with a god, the last thing on their mind is how the human side of the barrier works."

She supposed that was true. "And on the other side of the Faegate? Is there no portal taking you to your lands?"

"No portal, no. The fringe leads directly into the wylds. If you can make it through those, the beauty of Faerie will open up to you. It is unlike anything you've experienced before, Daisy. You'll hate yourself for how much you'll love it."

"If you can make it through the wylds, you said. I've read that it is dangerous for humans, but I didn't realize it was for fae as well."

"It is usually death to humans unless a Celestial grants them passage. Before you ask, that only happens if a court permits a visit. You are being abducted from the human lands and smuggled through, and I got through unlawfully. If the Celestials capture us, we'll both be killed."

"They let me go after I met you outside of that apartment."

"You were an innocent bystander then. Now you've helped me acquire chalices and let me claim you. It's different."

She twisted to look at him and narrowed her eyes at the smug twist of his lips. His gaze dropped to her mouth, and hunger flared. The answering growl arose in her body, and she quickly faced forward again, flushing.

"I don't believe you," she said, wrestling with her composure. "I may have kissed you, fine, but I didn't know what I was doing. Their killing you would absolve me of that burden. And helping you acquire the chalices? Please. They can read minds better than you can. They'll know my intentions. They'll also know I do not desire passage through the wylds but want to go home and forget I ever met you."

"Oh you'll never forget you met me." His hand slid forward, running over her thigh.

Desire burned within her. His body pressing against hers was a delicious heat. His groin pushed against her butt, hard and hot and ready.

She once again picked up his hand by the wrist, but this time, she flung it away. "Maybe not, but I'll be glad once my dealings with you are over. A human—a Chester, no less—has no business messing with a fae."

He leaned his head closer, his mouth grazing her ear. She closed her eyes as an explosion of butterflies filled her stomach.

"You are so much more than a mere Chester," he murmured. His breath washed goosebumps across her skin. "So much more than a human. You have the radiance of a god."

Fuck, he was charming. It was unsettling.

She jabbed back with her elbow, connecting hard with his chest. "Stop or I'll walk. If I walk, I'll try to run. Then you'll have to chase me, and it'll be a whole thing. Let's just get to the Faegate so I can flag down a Celestial and get the hell out of here."

His chuckle was sinful and deep. "Is that what you

want?" His hard length throbbed against her. His chest coated her back. Electricity sizzled between them, and her mind started to buzz in a way that said he couldn't read it. Not like she could conjure up any thoughts anyway. There was only one thing drifting along the edges of her mind. One primal thing she could hold on to as carnal desire rumbled through her.

She leaned back harder against him, resting her head against his collarbone, sliding her hands up his thighs, and he quickly slid his palms over her hips.

"I want to run my lips over every inch of your skin," he murmured huskily, his lips still grazing the shell of her ear.

"I don't care," she whispered, lost in the heaven of his touch, sucking in a breath when his hand slid toward the apex between her thighs.

"I want to strip these clothes from your body and lick up your center until you are panting and begging to feel me deeper."

She continued to run her hands along his legs, on the outside of his thighs, reaching for his hips. For his butt.

His fingers trailed along the seam of her pants. He stopped at exactly the right place and applied pressure, and everything went fuzzy.

"I want to push into you, slowly, until I'm so deep that all you know is my touch." His voice was raspy and dark. Its texture promised secret delights she'd never known.

She reached his hips and kept going, applying pressure, wanting him closer. Wanting less fabric between them. She angled her head, and he immediately sought the hot skin of her neck with his lips.

"I want to take my time with you, little dove. I want to hear you moan so beautifully as our bodies tangle together. As I thrust into you, over and over and over again—"

Her breath came faster. Her resolve wobbled.

Before she completely lost control, she snatched the hilt of his dagger from his belt, ripped it from its sheath, twisted her torso and arm, and slammed it toward his kidney. It was a very difficult maneuver while sitting this way, and though she'd never practiced it on a horse, she'd become an expert in similar sitting arrangements. She was now eternally thankful for what she'd thought of at the time as somewhat odd training.

The dagger's tip dug just a fraction into his flesh... before her arm froze up. Before she lost the feeling in her fingers.

He groaned, continuing his ministrations, rubbing perfectly, speeding her toward climax.

She wrestled with the magic stopping her hand, tried to force that knife in deeper—

Her body exploded in pleasure. She shook with the release.

"I notice you didn't stop my fingers whilst trying to kill me," he said, his voice hinting at satin bedsheets and sweaty bodies. She wondered if his eyes had that river of gold that indicated his throbbing desire. Wondered if he'd feel as fucking amazing as this preview had hinted.

"An orgasm while you died was supposed to be the icing," she said as dryly as her labored breathing would allow.

His laugh rumbled through his chest, and his lips continued gliding along her neck. She didn't stop that, either. Didn't want to. Really needed to.

He sucked in her skin but pulled back, reaching around to dislodge the dagger.

"What do you have against my shirts? You keep ruining them." He took the weapon from her numb fingers. "And now look. It has blood on it. That'll never come out."

She wiped her brow. "Your shirt is collateral damage."

"Obviously." He cleaned the dagger and slid it back into its sheath. "I wondered when you would go for that blade. It's just been sitting there, grinning at you, all this time. I will say, that was very good timing. I couldn't have planned it better. If it had been any old fae blade, I'd be dead."

"Such a pity that it is different."

"So it seems." He paused. "Aren't you going to ask why it wouldn't let you stab me?"

"*It* wouldn't let me?"

"Yes, *it*. I wouldn't have reacted quickly enough to

stop you. Really, very good timing. Violence while orgasming is exceptional. I'm turned on all over again. If I hadn't checked your magic myself, I'd have assumed you had fae in you somewhere. You're wonderfully vicious. I adore it."

She leaned forward to get some space from the constant thrill of his presence. His touch. "Something is wrong with you."

"You're the one getting off while stabbing me. I'm just an innocent bystander in all of this. But yes, the blade is magical. It will not allow anyone to stab its owner. Well..." He twisted to survey his shirt again. "It's not supposed to, at any rate. You got the blade in a little. I didn't think that was possible. It must like you."

"It's alive?"

"It was forged in the wylds, my treasure. Of course it's alive, with, clearly, a very dark sense of humor."

"And the knife you gifted me...?"

"You cannot die by that blade. Given that it was forged for me and I gave it to you, I cannot die by that blade, either."

"Ah." She slouched, still pleasantly tingling from his earlier ministrations. "You gave me something with which to protect myself against all manner of fae... except you."

"Correct. While also having a way to communicate."

"And a way for you to spy on me."

"Now you're getting it." He grabbed her around

the middle as he reached forward, his hard length still pulsing against her, but he did nothing to satisfy his craving. He'd stopped at satisfying her. He grabbed the reins and leaned back again. "Any other questions? We're almost there."

She couldn't get her thoughts to stay in line enough to think about questions. Their chemistry was indescribable. Insatiable. She'd just climaxed from his touch, yet it wasn't enough. She wanted more of him. Less clothes between the press of their bodies. More time and no inhibitions, with none of their murky motives to muddy the waters. She just wished she'd found someone like him in the human world, where it would've been normal. And easy. And maybe lasting.

If he heard any of those thoughts, he didn't comment, for which she was thankful. Then again, he was probably thinking all the same things. She would've killed him just then, just as she would eventually take the chance again when it presented itself, but she'd lament the possibility of never feeling this heat again. She suspected he felt the same. She had a feeling they were battling this together while in complete opposition. Two sides of the same tarnished, scratched, fucked-up coin.

The dirt road continued on. They didn't see a single soul along the way. It wasn't until late morning that the vegetation started to wither, just as he'd said it would. Barren trees twisted cruelly in an increasingly darkening sky. Vines crawled along the ground and crowded each side of the dirt road, none of the reaching vegetation daring to break the plane.

"I've long suspected this road of being magical in some way," Tarian said, noticing her looking at them.

"And if you leave the road?"

"The magic of the wylds is weak here. Those vines are still mostly just vines. They grow slowly and don't have the ability to quickly grab you. They do not have any intelligence."

"And the vines in the wylds?"

"Would grab your legs, drag you to the ground, and thrash you viciously. They don't need mouths to kill—they can constrict around your body or throat—but some plants do, in fact, have mouths. And teeth. And move very fast. They like the taste of fresh blood."

She shivered, fear crowding close. Then, much sooner than she was ready for, they left the forest, and she got a look at the Faegate in the distance.

Without warning, her stomach lurched, and she barely had time to turn to the side before she lost her breakfast.

Chapter Sixteen

"*Shh,*" he said, his voice turning somber. He wrapped his free arm around her, as if his embrace would protect her from the sudden fear freezing her blood. "You're feeling its magic. The sight of the fringe is supposed to elicit terror in those who are not permitted to pass. With effort, you can force the effect away."

"The fringe? That's a fucking doom wall." But *wall* wasn't even enough to describe it. Fae*gate* was laughable.

She breathed deeply, taking it in.

A colossal barrier towered above the desolate land in front of it, nearly as high as the eye could see. It stretched endlessly in both directions, forming an impenetrable barrier between this realm and the mystical fae lands beyond. As they continued closer, she could see it was made of huge and ancient stones, roughly hewn and each taller than her. Briars and brambles and dark, thorny vines curled and twisted and snaked their way up and across. Sharp spikes jutted out at irregular intervals before hiding back in the wall again, each longer than her leg and their deadly thrusts hard to anticipate.

A grand arched doorway existed at its base amid the rocky and rough ground. Holes broke through beside, crawling with the brambles tipped with long and dangerous thorns. The air remained thick with the fear-inducing enchantment, the effect clawing at her worse than any level five magical worker from the human world. It felt suffocating, like it was sitting heavy in her chest and constricting her throat.

The dark and forbidding sky overhead boiled with clouds, announcing a coming storm that likely would never arrive. Within it, Celestials lazily sailed through the air, their wingspans larger than any bird's, incredibly majestic to behold. Gold and tangerine at the base morphed into fuchsia and then indigo and violet, a gorgeous blending of colors on a glittering surface. They almost seemed illuminated when against that dark, angry sky. Ethereal in how they cut through the air gracefully. She watched with her mouth agape, entranced by the beauty.

"Those are the fringe guardians," Tarian murmured, noticing where she was looking. His tone darkened. "There is but a fraction of what there should be. Someone from the Diamond Throne has ordered them elsewhere."

"Isn't that good for you?" she asked as they drew closer to a strange, murky area with dark purple, hazy air that rolled like fog. The sound of the horses' hooves dimmed, and their voices became muffled, as though they'd entered a vacuum.

"Very."

His voice sounded strained, as though he, too, were fighting his emotions within this place. Or maybe it was the sight of those Celestials, his nemeses when in the human lands and a blockade to getting her back into his.

None of the Celestials seemed to notice them, even though they were the only creatures dotting this vast expanse of desolate, dusty ground. They didn't even swoop down to the wall to get a closer look. They remained up high, where only their kind could go. They didn't seem to care if someone should use the massive, arched doorway or sneak through the various corroding holes and crevices.

"You seem to have a staring problem," Tarian said with a strange tone she couldn't identify. Jealousy? Frustration?

"I met one of them, after meeting you on the ledge outside of that apartment. They are..." She couldn't put words to the impression the male had made. To the impression these were making. "Their kind and what they can do is scary, but they're just so..."

The horse stopped, and Tarian pulled his leg from its back, hopping down. He grabbed her around the waist and lifted her. She twisted and braced her arms on his shoulders, her gaze still skyward.

"Why don't they come down to check us out?" she asked.

"So you can flag them down?"

"That...or maybe drool while staring, yeah."

His expression was unreadable as he gently nudged her out of the way. "The fringe is technically in the fae realm. It's at the very edge, hence the name. We are technically in the human realm, as I explained." He began to take off the horse's bridle. "We won't become visible until we step within the enshrouding magic of the wylds. Then we will have to run because they'll— They are supposed to descend upon us with their wrath. By the time they come close enough to read your mind, you'll be dead."

"What about the humans seeking admittance?"

"They aren't stamped with wyld magic. Not like you are from the crystal chalice"—he glanced back at her, his eyes flashing—"and my magic. I wasn't lying when I told you they'll kill you. I can't lie to you at all, actually. Not anymore. Not after I claimed your kiss. You give up some of your freedoms, and so do I. Luckily, I have a way with words." He winked.

"Why are we the only ones here? I thought you said more people come through the Faegate now?"

He made a kissy sound at his horse and began walking toward a spot where the hazy purple air darkened, as if preparing to go fully solid. "This is the waypoint, the place where you return your portal items. Horses, packs, yourself—whatever you either won't need when moving on or that can't survive in the wylds. Because of that, it's magically designed for privacy. There might be someone right next to us and we wouldn't know it. We'd never feel them, or them us. Once we step out of the haze, everything becomes visible again. That's when we'll know if we aren't alone."

A jolt of surprise made her look harder at that hazy, shimmering air. She could run into that, and it would grant her passage out of here. She could find a phone and call her family to come and collect her.

But then what?

She'd put her family in danger, because Tarian would almost certainly return to take her and likely harm anyone in the way. Not to mention he could just follow her through and grab her on the other side.

She put her hands on her hips as Tarian stepped out of the way and let the horse continue walking through. It vanished, as if through a door. He looked at her as he turned, smirking.

"No?" he asked as he passed. "You're not going to

make a run for it? You've talked yourself out of it again?"

She didn't respond as he collected the next horse. This one he led, first past her and then to the hazy purple area. Nearly to the almost solid mass, he stepped to the right and somehow went around, still pulling at the rope. As the horse walked through, he flung the rope up and over an invisible line, and it dragged on the ground behind the animal, pulled along through the portal.

"If not"—he passed her for the next animal—"you could always help me. It would make this go a lot faster, and we'd have more time to relax at the first resting place in the wylds. Assuming I can get you across the fringe."

She sighed and turned to help him. There was nothing for it. She was stuck in this venture for the time being.

"True," he said, and it was still as annoying as all hell that he could read her mind. "Because yes, I would just follow you. And reclaim you. And put your family in harm's way if you made it that far, which is doubtful. I will accomplish my plans. You will help me with that whether you like it or not. Running would just delay the inevitable."

"Yes, I realize all that, thank you. Which you know, because you eavesdrop on my mind." She trudged back for one of the next horses.

"Don't you like to be told you're right?"

She ignored him, eyed the knife at his side, then ignored that, too. It was a great shame it wouldn't work on him. "What happens if we aren't alone when we step out of the haze?" she asked instead.

"Some would say it depends."

"On what?"

"On if the person you're meeting is more dangerous than you. If they are, you'd typically run. If not, you'd usually try to kill them."

"And so we assess and be ready to attack or flee?"

His smile was arrogant. "I always attack."

In other words, he was always the most dangerous.

* * *

They started toward the Faegate with nothing but a pack each, cinched tightly to their backs. If they had to run for any reason, it wouldn't bounce too much. While he might always be the most dangerous of the fae he met sneaking through the Faegate, he wasn't more dangerous than the swooping Celestials, something he hadn't enjoyed her pointing out.

"Here." He held out the blade he'd gifted her in the human lands, the one he'd retrieved from her home.

"If this won't allow me to kill you"—she took it from his grasp and slipped it into her shirt, securing it in her bra—"why wait until now to give it to me?"

"I didn't want to ruin the surprise of your botched attempt to kill me with it. I also wanted to see how you'd react to being completely at my mercy. In case you're wondering—"

"I'm not."

"—better than I expected. Your fearlessness and confidence, not to mention what must be hours upon hours of training, is exceptional."

"I was dosed to sleep for most of it."

"Nonsense. You talked yourself out of trying to escape, you tried to break the crystal chalice at your possible peril, and we enjoyed a lovely horse ride together—it's been an exciting collection of hours. The only additional thing I could've asked for was to taste your lips while my fingers sought your deeper places, feeling you tighten and ripple around them as I brought you to climax. But I'll wait for that. I want to watch you unravel in the comfort of my chambers."

"You're getting tedious," she said with a suddenly flushed face. She knew full well that she *would* unravel, which was why it wouldn't be happening. Unless it was a means by which to kill him—

She jerked her face toward him in frustration, belatedly cutting off that thought.

He laughed delightedly as the shimmering purple in the air lightened.

"What a fun toy I have found." He slowed, checking the straps on his backpack and taking his knife from its sheath. "So grumpy in your resignation, yet still so delusional. I *will* watch you unravel. You won't be able to help yourself. I can't wait. Now..." He held out his hand to slow her, his eyes going skyward. "This is it. The moment we cross this plane, the fringe will be right in front of us. It is entirely an illusion, remember that. It is not actually a large wall at all. The holes you noticed aren't really holes. The archway is not as it seems. It is an illusion to cloak the fringe, to identify the barrier, and to seem very scary."

"And so when you say you are going over the fringe...?"

He squinted while tilting his head this way and that, thinking through how to explain it. "It's complicated. We'll be running toward what looks like a briar-covered hole, the *second* opening on the *right* of the large archway. So there is the archway, and we will take the *second* opening on the *right*. Do not get confused."

He paused and waited for her to nod.

"I have tried each and every one of those supposed openings. The first on the right is devastating. I barely lived through it. I have permanent scars to show for it. Okay?"

"Second on the right."

"Yes. Now." He held out a finger, the teasing and joking from earlier completely gone. "The moment we cross the threshold—are actually within the fringe—we will stop and collect ourselves. This is the important part. From now on, you will do exactly what I say, when I say it. No stopping to think. No grudging acceptance and dragging your feet. Your survival depends upon you following my orders to the letter, and immediately. I will keep you alive as long as you trust me."

She quirked an eyebrow at the last line. It was a very large ask for her to trust him in any capacity. He was her captor, her secondhand abductor, and he was taking her to her doom. Trusting a guy like this seemed like suicide. But it was clear he had plans for her, and they weren't just what he had planned within his chambers.

Besides, what other choice did she have? The bottom line was, she *was* at his mercy. Completely. Her weapon and his didn't work on him. Hand-to-hand was laughable—his magic would stop her before she could get anywhere. And yeah, the magic. He had the upper hand in all things. He could kill her at any moment anyway.

He waited patiently, his gaze jogging back and forth between her eyes. He was letting her work it out, wanting her to agree to this willingly.

It was that, above all, that made her offer him a crisp nod.

"Okay," he said, mimicking her nod. "Take out your blade. You'll need it. It'll save your life and, if needed, mine, because if I die, you won't make it out of this realm. Do you understand? I am your lifeline and you are my responsibility. We work as a team to keep each other alive."

She repeated her nod and did as he said. Once in

hand, the small knife grew to the size of a dagger, her weapon of choice. It clearly knew that.

"Okay." The word rode a release of breath. "This is the most dangerous part. That blade will cut through fae magic. Remember outside of the charity banquet hotel? The Celestials are no different. They'll just have more power and more cunning. Defend yourself however you can, and do it while running. They cannot follow us into the fringe. That is where we'll be safe from them."

He didn't say it, but his tone made it obvious—safe from them...but not safe.

"Try not to make any sound until you're within the fringe," he continued. "I will speak into your mind. Think any answers, and I will hear. I won't bother explaining why it's necessary. From here, we will sprint to the gate. Are you ready?"

Her stomach fluttered with adrenaline. Her body was amped up and a little anxious. A lot wary. She gave in to it for a moment, letting it run through her. Then she focused. She loosened her limbs and prepared for battle.

Yes, she thought.

"My gods," he said softly, his gaze appraising. "You are magnificent."

She didn't get a chance to wonder what had excited him because he thought, *Three...two...go!*

They pushed forward as one, weapons in hand. The haze cleared, and then the gate was *right there*, fifty yards away and looming like a great and terrifying barrier. The punch of magical fear nearly made her cry out, but she swallowed it down as her feet pounded the ground. The winged sentinels were much closer to the ground from this perspective, and she realized the view before was a trick, magic attempting to make the coast seem clear. It was anything but!

The thrum of those great wings vibrated the sky. Before she could look up, though, another group nearly crashed into them. Four of them in all, they looked like humanoid trees with branches growing out of odd places and bark for skin.

Kill them, Tarian thought, veering that way immediately. His knife elongated into the razor-tipped staff, light whirling. *Quickly. No need to make it pretty. Just get the job done.*

She didn't understand doing it any other way.

She spun and slashed, chopping off a limb and stabbing through the chest. The sword didn't go in far enough, though, the gray bark-skin much tougher than normal.

I need an axe, she thought, and no sooner were the words formed than her dagger turned into said axe. Fantastic.

She dodged a clumsy strike with a wooden spear attached to the creature's arm and hacked at the crease between its shoulder and its neck. It issued a high-pitched squeal. She did it again, jumped, and kicked it in the chest. The head bent at an unnatural angle, and the thing fell away.

The next closest had turned, ready to run away. She took two quick steps and cleaved it in the back. She left the axe stuck in there and jumped, using it to crawl up to its neck and wrap her legs around its neck. She'd accidentally killed a guy with this move right before she met Tarian, and for some reason, it seemed fitting that she do it properly now.

She swung her top half, leaned back, and ripped around. The neck cracked like a newly felled tree splitting. She swung again, and the body beneath her tumbled toward the ground. Job done.

She hopped off before hitting the ground and grabbed the axe from the middle of its back.

Go, go, go, Tarian said urgently into her mind.

He'd taken the other two down and stood with his eyes pointed at the sky. She didn't bother looking up. She was scared of what she'd see. Instead, she put on a burst of speed. He matched her, his long legs eating up the ground, but held back to stay even.

Thank you for not trying to hold my hand while we run like in all the action movies, she thought, gaze on that opening in the wall. Briars crowded the open space, their long thorns looking like spikes. Darkness pooled and gathered within the jagged bricks framing the hole.

What a stupid notion.

Despite the situation, she couldn't help her grin.

Duck! he mentally shouted.

She did, still not looking up. Air rushed past her, followed by the whisper of wings. The morphing colors of dawn shimmered as the wings passed by, attached to a regally dressed body that remained as straight as an arrow. A strange rumbling vibrated her bones. Fear made her heart quake, but she didn't succumb. She slashed up with her weapon, now a long staff, slicing through a strange haze above them and into the Celestial's leg. The blade cut in deep, hitting bone. The male jerked and looked down, his flawless features twisted in agony and blood dripped from the wound.

Tarian yanked her arm, getting her running. Wasting no time, she turned it into a sprint. Her weapon shrank into a short sword. The beating of wings grew louder against the rushing wind.

Here we go, Tarian said. *I won't let it kill you. Take the pain.*

A blast of power shocked straight through her middle, slicing into her heart and tearing at her organs. It felt like a rough version of what Lexi could do, only it wasn't attacking her soul. It wasn't threatening to rip out her life's essence. It was, at its peak, just pain, as Tarian had said. She ignored it easily thanks to a *lot* of practice when Lexi was still learning, or now when Lexi was too mad at her to control herself.

Tarian threw up his hand, and a new feeling rose. This one was spicy, but not painful. The opposite, actually. It was exhilarating, like lightning bubbles working through her legs and into her belly, where they heated up and spread. She sucked in a startled breath as a blanket of sparkly gold cut through with black spread out over them. Shards of indigo tried to slice through it from above but didn't make it.

Run faster, Tarian gritted out, the feeling of his exertion coming through.

She gave it everything she had, aiming for that opening in the wall. Aiming for safety.

A spear sliced through the magical haze above. It glanced off Tarian's arm before finding the ground and sticking there. He muttered a curse but didn't falter, his hand still held high, his sword out and ready. Her core pounded, but not sexually. A buzzing filled her center, but it wasn't pleasurable. Another spear sliced down and stuck, missing them.

The beating of wings let her know they were coming in fast. She created her own spear with her weapon and thrust it up. The beating grew erratic as the Celestial dodged. She tried again, and again, blindly aiming while running. She paused for a second, expecting their attack, then glanced up. A female with flawless skin dove in, taking aim. Daisy jumped and thrust, stabbing the Celestial in the side. She'd aimed for the gut, but that would have to do.

Veer right, Tarian said. *Right!*

She hit the ground and did as he said, at his side. His weapon had turned into a spear as well. His magic billowed out around them, gold cut through with black, slicing into the flailing creature and three others swooping down toward them. Daisy jabbed upward again, aiming for the wing. Her point poked through that delicate webbing, as fragile as a dragonfly. The face of the Celestial, a pretty male, screwed up in pain, and he flapped his wings wildly. He tilted left, the wing not working properly because of the damage.

She tried to get another, but the Celestial pulled up right before she could make contact, a crease forming in her brow, as if she were confused that Daisy was fighting back. Or maybe just that a human was somewhat effective.

Ten yards to go. Almost there. Tarian tripped, staggering. She grabbed his arm to steady him.

Teamwork, he murmured, and the thought made her grin for some reason.

One of the females twisted, readying her spear. Daisy jumped and thrust, missing but forcing the woman to push higher into the sky. Five yards.

Almost...there... Tarian thought, and Daisy could hear the fatigue in his tone. He must be putting everything into his magic to keep the stronger beings away.

The opening loomed, the vines and briars clearer. They twisted within the space. Feelers reached farther out as though looking for someone to grab.

"This is the least treacherous opening?" she asked, forgetting that she wasn't supposed to speak. Though she supposed it didn't matter. The Celestials already knew where they were.

Yes, Tarian said, slamming his knife into its sheath and using both hands toward the sky.

More Celestials descended, hovering over them, weapons at the ready. The opening was right ahead of them. They were nearly there.

A large male dropped in front of it. His feet hit the ground, and he readied to fight, blocking their way.

Chapter Seventeen

Usually, an attacker thought their prey would hesitate, startled into freezing. Daisy didn't. She assumed Tarian would handle the sky, so she sprinted for this new foe. Her weapon quickly shrank into a switchblade, and her manic grin would've been plenty to make the average person nervous. She reached the Celestial as he was pulling out his blade. Pivoted as his brow crumpled in confusion. Stabbed him in the upper thigh as the sword swung out in front of him.

She dodged it and struck again, in his ribs. Anticipating his reaction, she hit the ground and rolled, slicing his wing with the knife as she avoided his staggered sword strike. He really should've pulled those in. Right behind him, she went to work, slicing with one hand and ripping with the other—a shame to hurt those beautiful wings, but survival wasn't pretty.

He called out in pained panic as his wings finally pulled into his body. Tarian slowed as he met the Celestial, his eyes hard but his weapon still put away. He was keeping the others off him with magic. He needed both hands.

She cleared her mind so that the Celestial wouldn't know what she would do and kicked up. Her foot connected from behind, crunching his nuts. She was a human Chester—fighting dirty was her right. Then she stabbed him in the back right after her blade turned into a dagger. She loved this fucking weapon.

Tarian dove and rolled as the Celestial cried out again, bending. Staggering. She lifted her weapon for the kill shot as Tarian jumped up. She brought the blade down, only to have his hand catch her wrist. He pushed her farther back, into a cavernous darkness. A sheen, like the surface of a bubble, draped over the opening, showing the wilting, bleeding Celestial kneeling to the ground just outside.

Tarian breathed heavily, the front of his shirt slick with sweat. He'd put a lot of effort into that magic. His mouth was open as he labored, but his eyes were shuttered. He looked at her for a long moment.

"What?" she asked, adrenaline still coursing through her body.

"I've never seen a creature attack a Celestial so aggressively," he finally said. "So thoroughly. So... masterfully."

Pride welled up, and she tried to tamp it back

down. "Why not aggressively? What do fae do? Wait to die?"

"In some instances, yes."

"What's the point in that?"

"So the Celestials won't hold a grudge against their kin, usually. Once a fae is on the correct side of the fringe, past discretions concerning the fringe are forgiven. Hurting or killing a Celestial typically is not. Not socially, at any rate. It is lawful, but it is...frowned upon. As I said, they hold a grudge."

"Oh." She shrugged. "Well, they can hardly blame me. It wasn't my choice to come through here. I'm just protecting myself. And anyway, I'm human. Surely they'll be more embarrassed than pissed that I bested that one."

He studied her for another long moment. "Very likely." He glanced back at the mouth of the opening, and she belatedly realized the vines and thorns had pulled away, leaving most of the space bare. She mentioned that as the Celestial beyond the sheen straightened slowly, two more dropping to his side, before turning to look in at them. Except...it didn't seem like he could really see. He looked to the right of where Daisy stood.

"I chased away the opening's deterrent. They'll crawl back in as soon as I pull away my magic." Tarian looked at the side of his arm where the spear had glanced off. Dark veins spread from the wound, as though his blood had been poisoned. He glanced at her, straightening. "It hasn't been. It's my magic fighting the magic coating their spear. I'll be fine. This isn't the first time I've been struck by one of their weapons. I have the power necessary to thwart it."

He ran his fingers through his unruly hair, wilder with his loose curls than any of the Celestials, and a few shades darker. It wasn't cut straight across the shoulders like theirs, either. It made him look more rugged. Fiercer.

He looked out at the three Celestials still gathered at the barrier's opening. They leaned toward each other, speaking, but the words didn't reach beyond the sheen.

"How do you usually get past them without help?" she asked.

He turned to look deeper into the cavern. "I've never seen so many descend. Not since I've been coming through. Not even when they more thoroughly populated the fringe. If they'd come at me like this in the past, I wouldn't have gotten by. Not a chance." He shook his head, glancing behind again. "They don't usually guard these entrances, either. They don't land." He ran his bottom lip over his teeth before looking at her, his expression dark. Grave.

"What?" she said again.

"Nothing," he finally replied. "It's a good thing I have what I need, because I'm not sure I could make my way back out. We surprised them this time. They aren't often slow to compensate. They'll come up with a new strategy, and next time, they won't fail."

Her heart dropped. That didn't bode well for her future attempt to get out of this place. Then again, maybe they wouldn't be so hostile if it was just a human trying to go home.

He took off his pack and reached for the one she carried. He set them both on the ground before stepping back and putting out his hand to make her do the same. The air filled with a musty, earthy scent, and the packs vanished.

"Where'd they go?" she said, aghast.

"Somewhere safe...where you won't try to drop them and let the Celestials claim them."

She watched him pass. "Shit. I should've dropped my pack out there."

"It wouldn't have mattered. I had the main object of interest in my pack. Now we need not worry about it. Come along."

"Why make us carry them? You could've sent them *somewhere safe* before we were sprinting for our lives, weighed down by them."

"I can use my magic in the human realm, and I can use it in the fae realm, but I cannot use it across both at the same time. I cannot send items from the human realm into Faerie, and vice versa. No, I do not know why. I don't even know if that was by the gods' design or a happy accident for them."

"But how..." She felt dizzy. "How do you do it?

How do you make stuff disappear? There are only a couple types of magic similar in the human world, and those basically go through the underworld. Someone has to be carrying the objects."

"Sounds complicated." He didn't elaborate. Clearly he wouldn't be explaining the intricacies of fae magic.

She followed him deeper into the cavern, shoving the magical curiosity aside. It wasn't the most important thing right now.

"Why are there suddenly so many Celestials out there?" she asked.

"They sensed the magic. Mine usually draws one or two, only. It seems the crystal chalice magic called them to you in greater numbers. I hadn't known it would. Now I do. You'll be quite an alluring little pet within the court. The ripples of curiosity, jealousy, and desire will play into my plans nicely. The increased danger, though..." His words trailed off. "That'll take some additional planning. We don't want you killed soon after arriving, do we? Now, let's get ready for the next phase of the fringe."

Silence drifted in between them, and their footsteps echoed on the bare, rough-hewn walls. Strange bioluminescent fungi and small-leafed plants grew along the top, illuminating the jutting rock or pockets along the ceiling. Water dripped somewhere, splatting onto the hard-packed dirt floor. The cool, damp air carried with it a scent like ancient earth and moss.

Do not speak, he told her, his mind touch like a whisper. *The heart of the fringe is a treacherous place. You must always assume danger lurks around—*

A deep and mournful sound vibrated the ground under their feet. Tarian stopped with a hand in the air, looking up at the ceiling first, then at the walls. The sound continued, growing louder until dust rained down from the ceiling.

He turned in a rush. He sprinted back the way they'd come, barreling into her. His arm looped around her back, he lifted her and held her tightly. She didn't resist, holding him around the shoulders, her feet dangling.

Everything shook, and it sounded like a crank, metal grinding against metal, reverberating against the walls and groaning through their feet. They stopped at the mouth of the cavern, and he put her down. The Celestials still stood guard. Tarian didn't cross the bubble sheen. He pushed her against the wall right beside it, flattening himself over her as the vines and plants crawled back up the wall away from him.

What's happening? she thought, her face crushed against his hard chest and her back pressed against the wall.

The ground bucked. Rock pushed up under their feet. The wall shoved at her, but he held firm, keeping her pinned. She could feel his heart thundering. Two metallic *clunks* sounded deep within the ground, one and then the other, before the sound died away. The quaking of the cavern subsided.

Tarian's breath came loud and quickly. More dirt rained down from the ceiling.

That—he pulled back, looking deeper into the cavern—*was the Celestials cheating.*

What does that mean?

He stepped away and took her hand, pulling her with him. She didn't have the time or inclination to allow the delicious feelings to materialize from the warmth and pressure of his hand holding hers. *Sorry, I might have to be like one of your action stars. I need to keep you close without sparing you my attention.*

I know how to walk closely to someone. It's not likely I'm going to run now.

Run? Not likely, no. Something stepping out of the shadows to grab you? Very likely.

That shut her up. She held his hand tighter.

Celestials have the power to change the heart of the fringe, he said, each footfall slow, like he was hesitant to make too much noise. She followed his lead. *They haven't done it in...decades. More.*

And they just did it now?

Sounded like it, yes. We'll know in a moment.

They *really* didn't want her and Tarian making it into Faerie. In feeling the power of the crystal chalice, they must've known its potential to help fae over the fringe.

Just so, Tarian murmured in her mind.

When does the magic of the crystal chalice wear off?

He barely spared her a glance as they neared the area where they'd previously had to turn back. To her, it all looked the same. Fungi and moss illuminated the rough ceiling and jagged walls. Small weeds struggled out of the dirt near the base.

Never, he said, tugging her forward. *The magic stamped you. Now you bear its mark, like you bear mine. I will also make my mark visual, however. Official. Otherwise, you'd be used by the royals and then their guards. A pretty human, such as yourself, won't go unnoticed. I'd end up having to kill half the palace when coming to your aid.*

I wouldn't live long enough, she ground out, her whole body burning in anger. *The first person to touch me would die, and they'd surely have me executed shortly thereafter. There are some things worse than death.*

I know well, he said ominously.

She wondered about that as they walked, his incredible cautiousness for the first time she'd ever seen. Then her thoughts veered to what he'd said about his mark. She'd let his talk of claims roll off her shoulders, having seen the proof of what he'd do if she violated their absurd agreement, but he hadn't mentioned a magical stamp upon her flesh. He hadn't told her specifically that his magic would remain laced into her skin. It couldn't have been like a Demigod's mark, glowing and ethereal—noticeable. Her family hadn't said a word, and that was something they definitely would've noticed and picked apart.

The mark is not for humans, he said. *Though that would be helpful if the fae are to dabble among them. It is for my kind. It denotes ownership. You are mine. You will only be touched by me. Handled by me. As I've said, repeatedly, I don't share. My magical stamp, and my mark, will affirm what'll happen if they cross the line with my property. In case you're still not clear, it'll mean their death. Gruesomely, if I can spare the time.*

But...what about the green guys? They didn't seem troubled by any claims.

No, they didn't. And look what happened to them. A visual mark will help those too stupid to notice the magical claim.

And you don't plan to release the magical claim and save yourself the grief of my kissing my way through the castle?

His look at her was dark and tortured. *I would love nothing more than to choose how long that claim will last. To not apply it at all. That magic is not because I am fae. It is because I am, myself, trapped. Part of my servitude in the court comes with what the queen and her minions think of as a joke. A curse, by all accounts. Once affixed, I cannot release that claim. It is a brand upon you—upon any of my lovers. If you should grow tired of me and want to choose another, you'll be forced to repeatedly see your lovers die by my hand. I'll be magically forced to oblige. My first and only love felt the sting of the entrapment acutely until the court tired of their games and ended the claim themselves.*

How'd they do that?

He was quiet for a moment. *By killing her, of course. Torturing her while I watched. She'd lost her love for me. I am still, and will forever be, partial to her. But to be released from the claim, the court decreed she had to die. I was more valuable than her. Only the royals are immune to this...curse. This horror. I can never have a causal fling without sentencing someone to death or entrapment...except for them. They aimed to make me a plaything. To service the crown.*

His lip curled in a snarl, and she felt herself reeling with that revelation. Recoiling in horror on his behalf.

I would rather die than touch any of them, he thought, and she didn't blame him. She understood his desire to rip them off the throne and be done with them entirely. *My power is too great for them to force me, and so they taunt. Always taunting.* He took a deep breath. *But then, that's how the game is played. I have been working you in. You're smart enough, and hard enough, to be immune to those antics. Thank the gods for their mercy for that. Your life has already been spent in constant danger. You won't be out of your depth in the dark fae court. Not at first. Not until they seek to punish me by using you. I can only shield you so much, and then you must fend for yourself. It is the nature of faerie courts. The game ends when you are broken. When we both are.*

He fell silent, and she didn't disturb the troubled stillness in the aftermath. She took that all in for later contemplation. There was too much to unpack, too many revelations and angst for her to properly analyze right now. This fae had layers. Many of them. And pain. He was in a precarious situation in his court, and she needed to really dissect each nuance of that. It was too delicate to do right then, especially as he slowed. Their current situation needed all her focus.

There was just one thing that snagged her logic.

Why didn't she just kill you?

He spat out a laugh, then slapped his hand over his mouth to muffle the sound.

I mean... Daisy shrugged. *She didn't love you anymore, and it came down to you or her. I thought fae were ruthless. Why didn't she just kill you?*

She should've. You would've...and then died for your efforts. The royals like to taunt me, but I am valuable to them. But not all fae are as vicious and ruthless as we claim. Some are softhearted and kind. She was. She didn't deserve what happened to her. She didn't deserve the destruction I wrought in her life.

And I do?

He slowed as they reached a wide opening that forked into two smaller tunnels, one going right, the other left. His gaze found her and stuck. Darkness shielded his expression.

You are better equipped for handling villains, I think. He paused. *Yours is a situation out of your control. You didn't fall victim to loving me. You fell victim to fate. You can contemplate all this later, as you decided earlier. Focus now, or neither of us will make it across the fringe.*

"You were always going to end up in this situation," he'd said once.

He nodded upon hearing that thought, but didn't elaborate. She'd need to dig if she hoped to glean more.

She needed to stop him from hearing her every fucking thought.

She took a deep breath and did as he said, focusing. Live today so she might escape tomorrow.

The tunnels looked identical. They could've been cardboard cutouts placed side by side, each rise and fall in exactly the same place as the other.

It was clear the Celestials *had* changed the interior, because Tarian didn't know which tunnel to take.

Choose the one that smells the least foul, she said automatically. He quirked an eyebrow at her. She lifted hers in response. *The one that smells the least foul. Look, we're basically headed in a roundabout way to Mount Mordor, right? Well, Gandalf, when leading the Fellowship through the Mines of Moria, made mention of choosing the path that smells the least foul. And he did. And they eventually got out.* She started losing steam. *Though he did have to sacrifice himself to get the job done...*

His look was deadpan. *Is it because I am holding*

your hand that you think this whole adventure is out of one film or another?

It was a valid question.

His huff was amused as he looked back at the options. *There is no right answer,* he finally said, staring first one way, then the other. *Both ways will be terrible. One will almost certainly be longer, though. I'm thinking over which one that might be.*

She very nearly snapped her fingers. *Like a battle of wits with a Sicilian, right? Yeah, I saw* Princess Bride. *Lexi made me. She called it a cinematic masterpiece, and I've questioned her judgment on what a masterpiece is ever since. But I digress. Right. So let's just add things up. Do those Celestials know a lot about you? Personally, I mean. About how you make decisions?*

He was staring at her like he had in the tunnels. *Personally? No. Before now, our interactions were a lot vaguer. They were at a larger distance and didn't put much gusto into killing me. Only now are they actually doing their job properly.*

Because of the crystal chalice magic?

I am guessing so, yes.

She nodded. *Do you know how their kind operates?*

Yes, which is why I was trying to figure out the direction before we veered into problem-solving via the history of cinematic masterpieces.

She waved away his sarcasm. *Tell me about them, then. Don't hold back. The time you spend here will save you when I pick the right one.* He seemed unconvinced, and she motioned him on with her free hand. She still held his other, taking comfort in the rough skin of his palm and the solidity of his touch. It shouldn't have helped her relax, but she was thankful it did. *Problem-solving dangerous magical situations is my greatest strength. It's been my constant vocation for the last five years. I've had to read magical people, strategize their thought processes, categorize their magic, and make very precise decisions on what would keep me alive. This might be a different creature, but it won't be a different overall scenario. Trust me, I don't miss. Not in things like this. I can't.*

Maybe it was because he'd told her to trust him and was now trusting her in turn, or maybe he believed her —hell, maybe he didn't have any better options—but he hurriedly relayed the broad strokes of what he knew. Which, actually, seemed like quite a lot. More than mere words filled her mind. He relayed images of their flight and training, sensory details of the conditions, perceptions—it was as though she were seeing it herself, in person. Like he'd opened a window into his head and invited her in to sift through the details.

Celestials knew they were important from their first memories and held themselves above the rest of the fae. Tarian thought this wasn't arrogance but necessity, and she scoffed at his take. It was clear they thought themselves *more than* in a way humans were *less*. Regardless, there was no denying their duty—as he saw it, anyway. They were the peacekeepers, the oath takers. The balance of their realm, and the retribution should someone step out of line. Judge and jury. They didn't get the luxury of being idle, not even the royalty. They put their duty first and themselves second, training for their roles, be it guardian, nobility, court justice—whatever that was—or king and queen since their first steps. They'd die for the job. Die to protect their kind and their home. Die for their kin, which they thought of as all faeries, high- and lowborn, creatures of the wyld, even the smallest flower.

Or so he believed. Everyone always had grand ideals before they were put to the test.

It was the training that she homed in on. That was the meat of this situation. She slowed him down when he "explained" their flight training, how they learned their magic and how they practiced it. How they learned to fight and the degree by which they were held to excellence. This took longer than the first assessment, drilling down to the theory behind their actions. The muscle memory that had been with them since they first held a sword.

Gotcha, she said, stepping toward the two tunnels and letting her mind run through all she'd learned. He watched her patiently, and she thought that was curious. He really was trusting her. She wasn't sure she'd be so open-minded in his place, not trusting a human with twenty minutes' worth of hearsay knowledge tasked with deciding their fate. She didn't take it for granted. Couldn't. Their lives were on the line.

She closed her eyes and let the details trickle through, a few things catching, other things vying for attention. When a solid weight formed in her gut, she knew.

We're fucked either way, she said, and he slapped his hand over his mouth again to keep from blurting out a laugh. She grinned and shook her head. Zorn's voice echoed through her mind, then through his.

Being afraid is a waste of one's last minutes.

Truer advice, Tarian said, not finishing the cliché. He stood at her shoulder, holding her hand, looking at the tunnels. Looking at their combined fate. *So? Which shall we choose?*

Chapter Eighteen

She pointed to the left. *That one, obviously.*

Obviously?

Yes. Obviously. Assuming you're sure one will be longer than the other and that they will be different...

I'm positive. They have to end at the same place. One always goes nearly straight there. The other tunnel always arches around and takes longer.

Well then, if you are to be believed, in training—whether it be flight, hand-to-hand, bow and arrow—they engage the exercise from the right. They enter the battlefield, or they wait their turn at the target, or they wait in line to be squared off with an opponent, on the right. They exit the exercise on the left, to keep things organized. They've done that since they were young, right? She didn't wait for his confirmation. She'd seen it in his head. *When they engage in the exercise, they do so hard and fast. After, they recuperate while they head to the next thing. In flight, you said they took the long way to soar back to starting positions until they had to do it all again. This would be etched in their minds.* She pointed to the right. *Hard and fast and getting to one's destination quickly...* She pointed left. *Slowly getting to the destination with more opportunities for breaks. We need to go left because fatigue will be as deadly as whatever awaits us. We'll want a chance to rest, I'm assuming.*

Except...before this change, I've been through all the paths. The short and long tunnels vary. Sometimes the longer tunnel is harder. That doesn't follow your rationale.

Well, no, of course not. They can't have everything the same or you guys would catch on. But they planned all that out, right? They don't usually change things up, willy-nilly?

No... He drew out the word.

Right. In the past, they wanted to mind-fuck you, which included creating options that were easy and others that were harder. They had ages to perfect that, but this time, they only had a matter of minutes. Minutes to create a horrible and deadly obstacle course. Right? That's essentially what we're stepping into?

He nodded.

They didn't have time to think it through. They did whatever came to mind. They would've fallen back on their training, and I am almost certain they will throw in the worst of the obstacles from the other openings.

Those blueprints are already there. Grab and go. They'll want the ones that will kill the most gruesomely. Those arrogant fuckers will want to pay us back for what I did to their wings.

He turned his head to her slowly as more and more information tumbled through her head, reassessing her decision with facts she might not have considered, images or words she might not have properly analyzed. Each time she kept coming back to the same decision. Her gut said she was right.

"You have great instincts," Zorn always said. "You should trust them at all times."

Left, she reiterated.

"You are," Tarian said in a very low whisper as his thumb traced a line across hers, "truly exceptional. You are a rare, gleaming gem in a field of plain rocks. Nature chose perfectly."

"Are we talking now?" she whispered back.

No. It is best to stay as quiet as possible. I wanted to express that in a physical space so that you understood the gravity of my words. A feeling moved over her, his front pressing to her back and his arms wrapping around her, holding her tightly. He pressed a kiss to her head in quiet devotion. All the space between them filled with sparkling, zinging energy. She felt light and effervescent and carefree. That had to be his magic.

It is, he clarified. *I wanted another way to express my delight at your radiance. I hope you don't mind.*

Her belly flipped as she soaked in his words, not

really understanding how good it felt to hear them. But coming from him, a fae who was a master with a blade, contract killing, information gathering, fashion—everything she'd strived for when carving out her Chester life in the magical world—well, it felt really good to be noticed for her achievements. It felt amazing to be acknowledged for the results of her hustle, especially from someone like him.

And he'd heard all of that echo through her head. How utterly fucking embarrassing.

His mental laugh felt enormous, living in every cell of her body. In every line and seeping into every hard crack in her thick defensive walls. Before she could react, it drifted away, leaving her hollow in its wake.

She stared at the dark tunnels ahead, but her mind skittered back to the feeling of the magical touch. She wondered if it could be used sexually and from a distance. If—

She flung his hand away and took a deep breath. She needed to get her head in order.

Yes, it can. His mental touch was dark and seductive, but only in her mind. He didn't magically reach out to her body this time. She heaved a sigh of relief. *But thus far in our acquaintance, you've wanted my physical touch. That option feels just as good for me as it does to you, so I complied. Eagerly. Using my magic on you intimately will be just for you, and I'll watch you writhe in ecstasy—*

Awesome, super, great to know. Let's focus. She

wiped sudden perspiration from her brow. *What are we likely to experience in there?*

Rivers of gold circled his pupils. His body was tight in some places but loose in others, and she could tell he wanted to reach out to her.

She moved as if to slap him, going so far as to bring her hand up halfway. His hand shot up; his fingers wrapped around her wrist. He blinked slowly, eyes on fire, confused.

"You didn't plan to actually *hit* me," he whispered.

No, she thought. *Come on. Get your shit together. I'll let you magically give me a Big O after we get out of this if you want, but right now, I'm assuming I need you focused and alert.*

He switched his grip from her wrist to her hand as he took a long, slow, deep breath. *Yes, you do,* he murmured in her mind, the rivers of gold starting to slow and shrink. She realized he was struggling to pull his eyes away from her.

I find this feeling thrilling, don't you? he said. *It has a way of taking over my thoughts. My body. Everything. It's so consuming, and when I'm lost to the throes, I can't find my way out. Don't want to, maybe.*

That's not thrilling. It's a nightmare. It's a struggle to hang on to control. It puts us in danger.

His wide smile was dazzling. So incredibly handsome. He made the Celestials' flawlessness look plain.

Losing control is what is so thrilling about it, little dove. I've never let myself free-fall. Have you? I've never let myself get submerged in desire so completely that I didn't care to crest the surface for a mouthful of air. The rush is unlike anything I've ever experienced. I like it.

She didn't. She hated it, actually. It felt as though she would be swept away. It hazed her mind and made her do asinine things, like give away her kiss or get tangled up in all of this.

I heard your thoughts when fighting for our lives a heartbeat ago, he said as he inched them into the left tunnel. He analyzed the walls and the ceiling. *I saw your smile when the Celestial was presenting you with certain death. When you charged him. I honestly wondered if I was hallucinating. No fear, fine. But a smile?*

Her brows knitted together. Normal people would have given her a side-eye in unease. Not even Zorn smiled when he was in that situation. It made her seem utterly unhinged. And maybe she was. She'd never really worried about it. But Tarian's light, breezy tone said he wasn't done having fun with her.

Like when the guys teased her, she waited for the punch line.

I felt your elation at beating your foe. Your desire to quench the thirst for a battle win. The bioluminescent plants started to spread out, dimming the glow by which Daisy and Tarian could navigate. So far, the tunnel was nothing new, with its packed dirt ground and the rough-hewn sides. *I find your viciousness adorable. Your passion in battle endearing. When you do finally give in to that free fall, I will have a wild ride in store for me. We will battle, but we won't be fighting to get away from each other. We'll be fighting to get closer. You will give yourself to me completely like you give yourself to your knife. To the fight.*

She sighed softly. She should've known that was where it would land. Teasing. Always teasing. Or maybe he thought it was training. It all amounted to the same annoyance. *And I assume I'll then be tied to you with my body, as well? A sexual relationship with anyone else would be forfeit. Or it won't matter because you'll break me by then?* she thought sarcastically.

The illumination dimmed even more, and the tunnel sloped downward. He slowed. His fingers tightened around her hand.

You touching another is at an end, yes. In the courts, that must be so. Even his voice in her mind was hushed. He pulled his knife from its sheath. She took out her own, her eyes straining in the growing darkness. *But if you are to kill me in the end, as you claim, you might as well get an incredible night out of it, yes?*

Very full of ourselves, aren't we?

Very. Rightfully so.

The slope of the decline increased. The darkness encroached until she could barely see the ground in front of her feet. The walls turned into black blotches. He stopped moving entirely and tugged her closer. Her side bumped against his.

As quiet as you can. His mental voice wasn't much more than a murmur. *If you are right, the Celestials drew inspiration from the other caverns within the fringe's catacombs. If they did, and if the light completely cuts out in another handful of paces, we can expect a very large serpent to be stalking our every move. They can feel the vibration from our feet as we walk. No amount of light stepping will prevent that. But noise makes it hasten, and so if we are very quiet, we won't have to deal with it for as long.*

How do we kill it?

We don't. I'll blind it with light and we will run. It'll thrash. Avoid its striking tail. The spikes on the end will punch right through you. Do whatever you can to get to the other side of it. Once one of us passes a certain threshold, it won't be able to hear us anymore. That's safety.

Avoidance. She could do that.

Ready? He waited for her affirmation, and then he stepped forward.

Are we holding hands for this? His was starting to get slick with sweat. He knew what was coming.

Yes, until...we aren't.

Fair enough.

Their steps were slow and shallow. The light leached away from their surroundings until it was pitch black. She closed her eyes. They weren't any good now, anyway. Shutting them instead of straining them in the darkness would allow her other senses to become more dominant. Another step. Two. Nice and slow. Tarian was waiting for what he knew would come.

The slide of something against stone caught her ear. She slowed a moment after Tarian had. His grip tightened. He didn't utter a word in her mind. Another sound. Was it a slither? No. Almost like a click.

Click...click...click.

Claws. Claws on stone.

The texture below her foot changed with the next step. Became harder, with less give.

Click-click-click.

She hesitated, and Tarian did so with her. The noise stopped as well. It could see them. It was waiting.

Does this large serpent have little lizard feet ending in claws? she asked.

No. And neither does the hideous creature currently staring right at us.

Her eyes snapped open. Weak, pale gold light filtered in from who knew where, gently coating the walls and lightly falling across the floor. It didn't do much more than define the space, leaving the center of the roomy area thick with gooey black shadows. She spied what waited in the darkness, blocking their way.

A large creature had a single big eye with a faint yellow glow circling nothingness, probably a black pupil. Large teeth glistened from too big of a mouth, and those two items made up its whole face. It had two thick arms and hands with three fingers and a thumb, each ending in a claw of about two inches. Nothing too sinister, really. It probably moved fast because it didn't have an extended reach. The legs looked like frog legs, and the claws on its three toes were twice the size. They'd disembowel someone fairly easily. It hunched patiently, watching Daisy and Tarian, and different-sized spikes rose from its spine. Its height was around six feet, not too tall by monster standards, and so it would definitely be fast. Its intention was obvious—you had to earn your passage through.

The cavern had opened into a kind of sphere, with rounded walls and a domed ceiling. The surface was rough but didn't look like it had been chiseled from deep within a cave. The Celestials had made this, and it was obviously a fighting pit.

Fine. She could handle that.

Her toe was an inch away from the stone of the fighting "pit." She looked over at Tarian. He looked at her. They didn't need to communicate. He let go of her hand, and almost as one, they stepped onto the stone.

The creature burst into action, the clicks a chorus as it ran at them. Daisy cut in front of Tarian and took the lead, ready for the swipe of its hand. It didn't disappoint, the claws sailing through the air toward her face at lightning speed. She fell into a slide, passing it by and angling as she did so. Its foot kicked out to catch her and almost succeeded. If she hadn't twisted as she'd gone, it would have. Clever creature, and yes, very fast.

It nearly turned to follow her, and that was its undoing. Tarian was there in an instant, twirling his staff in a very pretty light show. He hacked at a limb as it swiped with the other. She hopped up behind it and plunged her sword into the center of its back.

I really need two weapons, she thought dismally as she was forced to rip it out again and spin away.

Why would you leave a weapon in...an...enemy? Tarian asked as he, too, cleared out of the creature's reach.

Oh...I don't know...

She darted in, caught its attention, and hesitated. Tarian did the same, but the creature knew he was the more dangerous of the two. Which kinda hurt her feelings.

Tarian snickered, having heard her.

Because of this. She sprinted at it and plunged the now-dagger into the creature's lower back, at the base of the spinal cord. It howled, the first time it had done so. That would hinder its movement. She envisioned what she meant to do, then spider-monkeyed up the creature's body, using the sword as a bracing point for her foot, wrapping one arm around the creature's neck and reaching out with the other.

Tarian tossed his blade to her. The second it was in her palm, it reduced in size to the perfect knife for the job. She slammed it into the creature's eye, dodged its agonized swipe, and fell away as it spun. She hit the ground hard, her hip flaring with pain, then rolled so as to present a moving target.

Tarian yanked her blade from the creature's back, left his where it was stuck, and swung. His muscles bulged as he hacked the head from the creature's shoulders.

She squealed, hoped he hadn't heard, and scooted away from the oblong head spraying the stone near her as it rolled by. The knife made a satisfying *clunk-clunk-clunk* as it went.

"Huh," Tarian said, looking around for something to wipe her blade on. "I see your point."

She pushed to standing and grabbed his knife. She looked down at her filthy clothes and thought, *Fuck it*. She ripped off her sleeve, which had been hanging on by a thread anyway, and cleaned his blade. He walked to her and, before reaching for his blade, wiped her now-switchblade-sized knife on the part of the shirt still on her body.

"Really?" she asked quietly, not knowing how loud they could be. "You couldn't use the part I *just* ripped off?"

Smirking, he tossed the knife into the air and took his before she startled and juggled it out of the sky. Unlike a normal blade, when this one fell against her hand, it was as dull as a stone.

"Cute," she whispered, keeping it in her hand.

"Shall we?" He indicated for her to go first, which would've been chivalrous had it not been more dangerous. His voice was at its normal volume. "That went much smoother than I could've anticipated."

She still whispered, "You say something like that after every skirmish."

"Yes. You continually surprise and impress me." He paused, looking down at her with annoyingly pretty, sparkling eyes. "You're not going to gush with that compliment?"

"Oh shut up," she muttered.

He laughed. "No, but really, I am surprised and impressed. You handled that creature like you'd battled it a million times."

"I handle every creature like I've battled it a million times. Confidence makes the arrow fly true." She tilted her head. Was that a saying or had she made it up?

"And you've earned it." He held out his hand when they reached the other side of the space. The walls condensed into a tunnel not unlike the one they'd come from. He put his finger to his lips, then to his temple.

We're miming instead of talking now? she asked.

We worked very well together against the Celestials. I wondered if that was a fluke. It seems it was not. I think we can expand our communication to nonverbal cues.

She twitched up her shoulder, something Zorn would've known was "yeah, sure, whatever," but that Tarian gleaned from the thoughts tumbling through her head.

Yes, you do have a dizzying mind at times, he murmured, his focus snapping back to the issue at hand. The bioluminescent moss was back, covering much more of the ceiling than at the beginning of the tunnels. It cast the two of them in an eerie glow. *And yes, I'll be able to cheat until we teach you how to shield your mind.*

She looked over at him with a quirked eyebrow. His gaze roamed her face, paused on her eyes, and stuck to her lips. *I don't know what that means, but I'm happy to be looking at your beautiful face.*

She rolled her eyes.

I do *know what that means,* he murmured.

You've never mentioned there was a way to shield my mind.

No, because I didn't want you to figure it out on your own and hide your thoughts from me. It's safer this way.

She didn't bother asking for whom. Obviously, it was for him.

Obviously, he thought.

The tunnel wound around and down, then split into offshoots that went in various directions. A maze, it seemed. Tarian took the lead on this, always seeming to know where he was going. Only twice did he take a wrong turn and berate himself for it. When asked how he knew the way, he described the stonework and the various tells the Celestials always used as markers for the dummy tunnels. He'd paid attention to the other mazes he'd had to travel, each set of throughways apparently having one.

As she'd expected, they had periods during which to catch their breath before hitting the next challenge. And the next. Each battle went like the first, the two of them working together seamlessly to cut down the creatures the Celestials had thought would pose a problem. For Tarian individually, and certainly for her, they would've. At one point, two three-headed, bear-like things with spikes for fur had chased them around a large sandpit. He'd had to use magic for that one, not trusting them to bring the creatures down without it.

She'd, of course, mentally yelled at him for not using magic up until that point, intentionally wasting their energy. To which he'd responded that magic took energy and she was a horribly selfish little nymph. It was starting to feel like he couldn't be serious for longer than it took to fell their enemy. That wasn't training. She didn't care what he said. He would've gotten along great with Jack and Donovan and the rest of the gang, joining in at poking fun at her. It would be a shame when she had to kill him.

It wasn't until what Tarian suspected was the final obstacle, when they were dead tired and splattered with the dried blood of dead creatures, that they encountered the worst one yet. Not for him, though. For her. For a human. The Celestials knew what he was smuggling into their lands, and they were making sure he wouldn't be able to get it through to the other side.

Chapter Nineteen

The tunnel was the same size and shape, with shadows draping across the open space, but it was no longer clear. Huge, briar-like plants dominated the walkway, squeezing out the walking area until there was barely enough room for Tarian to squeeze through.

Those are lethal to humans, he said, his tone somber. *They were cultivated a long time ago when humans were flocking to Faerie.*

Why in the world would humans flock to Faerie?

He barely shook his head. *I don't know. It was well before my time. And yours. Ancient times in human years. Fae created these plants as a passive line of defense. The plants required minimal upkeep and did the job very nicely until the humans realized what killed the plant.*

What kills the plant?

I have no idea. They've been mostly eradicated in the wylds. A few types of creatures feed on them and they don't grow back very quickly. When fae touch it, it stings badly but it doesn't kill us. Like a thistle would to you. Or...a thistle mixed with a cactus.

She was smaller than him, obviously, with a slimmer stature, but it left her no room to maneuver. No room to dodge an attack or even stumble and regain her balance.

The thorns resembled something like a thick needle, spaced every few inches and sticking out an inch. From each point welled a brownish-crimson liquid, enlarging until it was too big to cling to the end and then dripping down. Where the liquid touched the packed dirt floor, a wisp of smoke rolled up and a hole started to form, like acid.

Tarian stared at it, his expression a hard mask entirely devoid of any teasing banter. He didn't try to lighten the mood.

Please tell me I will surprise and impress you in this, she said, noticing the occasional metallic gleam on those "thorns". As if they actually *were* needles.

You'd have to be fae for that. He took a deep breath and approached the beginning of the plants. His eyes darted from one side to the other as he stuck his arm into the opening. Nothing happened. He then moved it a little to the right, then left, before pulling it back out. *They seem to be stationary. That's at least good news. They haven't been growing long enough to mature. They don't yet reach for their victim. Or...*

She waited for him to go on.

Or they've thought of other ways to shove you into the poisoned thorns.

It was her turn to take a deep breath. *How long will it take the poison to work?*

Instantly, I'm given to understand, but I don't know if that is true. Quickly, I would assume. Ancient humans learned how to kill it before finding an effective antidote...

Thoughts of this new issue rolled through her head. *And going back? The creatures along the way would've stayed dead, right?*

Most, yes. But Celestials can feel the presences within the fringe. They will meet us at the entrance if we go back, and if we dally too long, they'll rework the interior and crush us within.

Her eyes widened. She hadn't known that. *Why haven't they done it already?*

Changes to the heart of the fringe have a ripple effect into other areas, including the sanctioned pass-through beneath the arches. That might kill other creatures or innocent life, which they always try to avoid. Because of this, as defined by the natural balance, they can do only one large change every sunrise.

They still had some time to get through. It couldn't have taken them the last half of the day and a whole night to get this far. However, they *had* taken the long way, and they *had* rested between obstacles. Given the strength of her fatigue and the depletion of her energy, she wasn't just weary, she was sleep deprived. It must've been well into the night, then. They couldn't just sit around and count their toes until they were ready to brave this next situation. Not like they'd do that anyway. If they couldn't go back, they might as well go on. There was no sense in delaying the inevitable.

Meeting you was the worst luck, she thought gloomily.

That's a fair assessment.

You go first, she thought. *I'd prefer something grabbing me from behind than having to deal with whatever might pop out of the briars and push me into the poisoned needles.*

Very likely. His tone was once again somber. He held his knife in front of him, the blade smaller than usual. He was preparing for close combat and quick strikes. Her knife shrank to match. It was a good idea.

I will say... Even her thoughts were hushed as they crept silently into the mesh of impending doom. *This knife is absolutely the best present I've ever gotten.*

She could feel his smile through his mind touch. *It served me well. It's kinder than the blade I now wield. More helpful, I think. It aims to please. Mine is more cunning. Tricky. It won't do me wrong and ensures I succeed where it can, but given the chance, it'll let pretty little nymphs lodge the tip into my side.*

There's a dirty joke in there somewhere...
Let me know when you find it.

One of the needle-like thorns dripped next to her bare arm. The liquid wobbled before it succumbed to gravity and cut through the empty space. It splatted into the divot in the dirt. Based on the size of that divot, these plants were definitely new additions to this space. They hadn't cut their way into the ground very far.

Bad news, I'm afraid, he said in frustration. *My magic has been cut down to next to nothing. It won't help us here.*

How will this poison kill me, exactly? she thought, careful to step around the reach of a cluster of vines.

I don't know. Probably gruesomely and painfully, but how exactly, I am not sure.

She shook her head in frustration. *No, I mean...will it poison me if it touches my skin, or does it have to reach my bloodstream?*

Ah. That, I don't know. He paused in his mind-speak for a moment as he slowed. The brambles stuck way out directly in front of him, closing down the space. He didn't have enough room to walk straight through.

He looked back at her, his eyes ticking from side to side—sizing her up to see if she would fit, no doubt. If she went sideways, it would be no problem.

Realizing this, or maybe just hearing her think it, he offered a small nod and turned to try to squeeze through. He watched the front needles as he sidestepped by.

Careful in the back, she warned, stepping closer to touch his upper arm. His muscle flared against her palm, his bicep popping larger than her handspan. He paused and let her direct him, centering him through the passage.

Rustling made her freeze and him jump. Something lunged out of a dark space at his feet. A deep violet paw slashed with five long silver claws. He jerked backward. The needles stopped him from going far, shallowly piercing his flesh. The claws raked across his ankles, opening up gashes that quickly welled with blood.

He sucked in a pained breath as his knife elongated into a spear. He jabbed at the dark hole, the tip going in deep. A squeal meant he'd hit something. Rather than yank his weapon out, he slid it across the ground, dragging with it a strange, furry thing without a discernible shape. She couldn't find the head or even the paw that had made an appearance. It was like it had curled in on itself to become as small as possible.

Once the creature was visible, he reached a hand out to her. She supplied him with her weapon as she turned, surveying the way behind her, then her own feet. Her blade matched his, and he viciously rammed it into the creature several times. Its sounds of agony cut off before he kicked it back into the hole from whence it had come.

Harvest's blight, Tarian swore softly, his teeth clenched. He handed back her weapon as he gingerly pulled away from the needles at his back. Their poisoned liquid was gone, now injected into his back. *That hurts like a tarnihole wart.*

She wasn't sure what a tarnihole wart was, but it must've been bad, because Tarian had gone stiff, his muscles flaring and his jaw clenching hard. He rolled his head, cracking his neck. He gripped his weapon with white knuckles. His body started to shake as he put a lot of effort into continuing his sidestep past the rest of the plants. He didn't limp, which meant the slashes to his ankles were nothing compared to the poison in his back. On the other side, he shrugged out of his shirt and tried to look behind him at his back.

Pixie farts and swamp juice, that is... He grimaced in pain as he put a hand on his shoulder, twisting a little more. As he did, his back came into view for her.

She tore her eyes away from his big, well-defined arm and tried to corral her vision to the strip of wounds along the right side of his broad back, down the thick slab of muscle. Her gaze kept snagging on the wide expanse of art, though: jet-black ink covered the majority of his skin in an interesting and entrancingly bold design. A sword cut down the middle, the hilt starting at his neck and the tip lost within his trousers. Thick, dark swirls cut away from there, rounding on themselves to meet back at the sword or swirl up and around his shoulders. Between those designs were small, thinner lines like lace, giving the bold, simplistic lines a pleasing complexity. It ran over his shoulder but stopped, turning into one thick line down the side of his arm. Attached to that line, on each side, circled ten rings, spaced evenly, down to his elbow.

At your leisure, he thought sarcastically, not able to hide the pained tone.

She yanked her gaze away from his lats, then from his rear oblique, and finally from his perfect and round butt. She did love a good rump, but she loved a broad and muscular back more.

That's fantastic, he drawled. *I'm glad to hear it. But will you please stop eye-fucking me and look at the actual wound so I can get a visual?*

The lat tried to pull at her attention again, but she resisted, finally zeroing in on the smattering of angry red welts oozing pus onto his skin.

She grimaced. *Gross.*

Looks like it hurts, she said, her gaze drifting again.

It does. A whole fucking lot. He looked at his shirt. *I don't know if it is better to put this back on to sop up the discharge, or keep the wound free of a sweaty and dirty shirt so the fresh air can help it scab up and heal.*

I vote fresh air. Forever.

He turned to give her an annoyed eyebrow arch, but he couldn't hide the darkly amused expression. He balled up his shirt in a fist and moved out of the way, his weapon posed as a spear as he watched the dark and shadowy openings at their feet.

She turned to the side and slipped through quickly, careful to watch her feet and the tilt of her upper body. Once she was past the trouble area, he held out his shirt.

I'm not carrying that for you, she said in confusion.

No shit. He nudged her with it. *Wipe away the discharge.*

Ew. I don't want to.

He huffed in annoyance, but a grin tweaked his lips. *You're going to have to look at it, regardless. Would you rather look at a bunch of pus or a wiped back with only a little? I'm sure the wounds will close quickly enough, though the radiating burn is growing stronger. That's not ideal.*

She did want to look at that incredible expanse of back with the really cool design, but no, not the other stuff.

Fine, she said, taking the shirt. He turned his back to her, and she grimaced again. Her expression surely curdled into a look of disgust as she got the job done, then handed the shirt back.

Throw it on the ground. He walked forward. *I can't hold it, and I don't want something grabbing at it if I tuck it into my waistband.*

The plants pulled back some up ahead, leaving various-sized pockets filled with unnatural black shadow. Her eyes couldn't pierce the gathered darkness, and so she stopped trying, instead putting out feelers for presences or danger. For paws or claws poking out of those dangerous hiding places.

Tarian seemed to be doing the same. The wounds on his back wept, no longer pus but now blood, the holes not closing even though they were small. Even though his healing should've been as fast and efficient as hers. Skin had started to bubble and peel away, the acidic property burning anything in its path. The poison might not kill him, but it was causing a lot of destruction and pain. Good thing it was only on a small portion of his back.

The pain feels like it encompasses a lot more than just that, he murmured.

A small rustling was the only warning they got. Something large shook the plants a moment before an ear-splitting roar echoed around Daisy's skull. Panic gripped her, fear riding on a manic urge to flee.

Tarian's hand shot out to grab her arm and keep her put. She shook him off. She knew this was magic. She recognized the signs from encountering the Faegate. This was very similar, if not as potent.

An unnaturally large mouth burst through the plants. Anything in its way magically vanished, allowing it full admittance. Kinda like a tiger and very much not, the thick body came after it. Its trajectory would make it plow into Tarian, forcing him into the plants at his back.

Daisy charged, slamming her shoulder into it with all her might. Its mass matched hers, and it might not have budged if its four feet had been on the ground, but in the air, it didn't have anything to grip. Its body veered enough that Tarian could step to the other side and pierce the creature with his blade. This time, he didn't leave it in or reach for hers. He yanked it out and thrust it in again while grabbing the creature with his other hand, curling his fist into its stringy fur. His upper body flexed as he spun the creature into the other wall. If he was trying to impale it on the plants, he had no such luck. The plants disappeared entirely as its body went through. He yanked his hand back when they reappeared as his arm neared.

He halted, and Daisy stabbed her now-sword through the space between his arm and body. The blade pierced the creature. She pulled it out and did it again. And again until it stopped struggling.

All that muscle is very useful, she thought, panting with effort and adrenaline.

If my back didn't hurt so much, I'd make a lewd joke about what this muscle could do in a bedroom.

It's probably for the best. She stepped back to give him space. *I'd then make a small-dick joke at your expense. This way you get to keep a little dignity.*

I'm ecstatic. He wiped his forearm across his forehead, catching his breath.

She caught sight of his chest. It held a much simpler and smaller design that was no less beautiful and interesting. It draped around his neck and down like a metallic black necklace. It cinched near the neck, coming to a point, then looped down as far as the bottom of his pecs, like a breastplate. The middle portion was hollow, giving him something like man-cleavage. Within the thick band that might make up the chain of the necklace curled an intricate design with twists and swirls. Equally as beautiful—or maybe more so—was his fucking chest. *Holy hell.* She'd thought she'd been a back girl. Maybe a butt girl if the right one came along.

No, she was a chest girl.

Perfectly sculpted pecs curved atop his defined abs, leading down to delicious obliques that flared before dipping into his trousers. A dusting of dark hair ran from his belly button and down the flat lower portion of his stomach. The man was a specimen. She didn't even care that he heard those thoughts—he deserved the ego for all this. He deserved the praise. He'd earned it.

Staring is rude. His tone was fully amused, and his pecs popped.

She watched like a sex-starved woman. Drool escaped from the corner of her mouth, and she wiped it away in embarrassment. *Speaking of losing one's dignity...*

She didn't just jerk her gaze away, knowing it would wander back—no, she jerked her whole head away. She looked at the other side of the tunnel and then straight in front, desperately ignoring the new type of adrenaline gushing through her body. The intense arousal. The need to touch. Her desire for him was getting stronger the more she learned about him. His struggles and her compassion for his situation were fraying her resolve. She could feel it. She didn't know how to stop it.

Let's get through this and you can touch all you want, he said, starting forward again.

Obviously she wouldn't, but...she might dream about it. Hopefully she *would* dream about it.

They encountered another small creature. This time it let Tarian pass, and then Daisy before it swiped from behind. She took the strike, staying in one place, and then she turned and jabbed it. Like Tarian, she dragged it out and made sure to end it. She didn't need the thing crawling up behind her.

If the Celestials don't want to take innocent lives, why would they force these creatures in here to be killed? she asked as they continued. *Also, why leave these openings? Why allow people—or fae, whatever—the option of getting through?*

These creatures are twisted beyond what the wylds should produce. They need to be exterminated to maintain the balance. This purpose fulfills that need while also making it harder for the unloved—what they call the illegitimate or criminal—to breach the fae or human realms. As to why they allow it... He paused. *They didn't used to, I've heard. They shouldn't now. But the fringe needs the power and magic of the Celestials who guard it, and with a larger number of Celestials not doing their duty, the magic erodes. The power diminishes. These obstacles are put in place as a patch, I think. They can make the crossing more difficult, even though they can't entirely fix the issue. With each passing of the sun, it gets easier still—until this last passing, obviously.*

Do you know why so few are coming to guard the gate?

Unrest in their court, I believe. Differing opinions on where the guardians are best utilized, as well as dissent within the ranks. Though I don't know for certain. The Celestials, at their core, are an army. They can be mobilized against a foe. Within fae courts, that foe is often one of their own. Ripping away power is never pretty, and the resulting fallout is grimmer still. The Diamond Throne is bleeding. The effects are visible all over the land. The fringe is but one example, sadly. Faerie is in trouble, and the Diamond Kingdom, the supposedly overarching ruling force, is the cause.

Which is why you want a fresh start, no matter who you step on to get it.

He half turned, his gaze slamming into hers. His face was as grim as his tone had been, his eyes troubled but resolute. *Yes.*

They continued to make their careful way through the briars. Occasionally, he had to go sideways with her hand on his arm to guide him. He returned the favor, though it wasn't as tricky for her.

More creatures came at them from the recesses.

Both of them limped. Each was sweaty, filthy, and bloodstained. Her stomach growled, painfully empty, and her head throbbed from thirst. Exhaustion plagued them both, but still they trudged on. Carefully. Focused and pushing forward. Unwilling—unable—to give in. Trusting in each other to stay alive.

The larger creatures gave very little warning before they lunged or swiped. When Daisy and Tarian heard the rustle, she charged and he tried to get to the side. Only once were there two creatures, these medium-sized. One lunged for Tarian, and before she could help, another came her way. She'd ducked, knee on the ground, knife held up. She got its stomach with the blade and was flattened by the impact. The creature raked her right thigh and left arm with its claws as it squeal-roared and flailed. She continued the attack from beneath until the slowing creature's body was ripped from her and tossed back into the briars. Tarian had a few new punctures across that beautiful back, she had a bump on the back of her head and throbbing limbs, but they kept going. Despite the odds, limping, wondering how they were even standing, they pushed on.

Tarian dealt with the brunt of the attacks and continued to attempt using his magic to no avail. Something in the briars was siphoning it from him, or unraveling it, or some other thing to prevent him from using it. When she asked about it, he'd shaken his head in frustration and mumbled something unintelligible.

Given she likely wouldn't understand anyway, she'd let it go.

What felt like years into the winding, twisting sea of deadly plants and unhinged creatures, a soft glow with a silvery-blue hue coated the inside of the dark tunnel a ways up ahead. She spied clear tunnel walls with no more plants. No bioluminescence. The glow looked natural, like moonlight.

Is that... She didn't even want to say it for fear it was an illusion. Her mouth felt like cotton balls had been stuffed inside.

Tarian reached back. Dried blood coated his forearm and the heel of his palm. She filled it with her weapon and looked around for the coming danger.

He glanced over his shoulder. *No. Not your weapon. Your hand. I think that is moonlight. We're through.*

She could've cried. She definitely sagged against him, taking back her weapon and then his hand, not at all caring about blood or pus or piss—it didn't matter. Nothing mattered but getting out of his hellhole.

He must've sensed her waning strength or seen the tremor in her knees, because he asked, *Do you wish to be carried the last bit?*

It was an absurd question. They had another twenty feet or so to go, and there might be more creatures. They might've saved the biggest and baddest for last. She would've.

But before she could throw out the logical answer

—the tough-girl answer—one word floated to the surface, usually safely tucked away within the defenses of her mind and now on full display.

Yes.

He tugged her closer, turned for her, and reached, ready to reel her in. Ready to cradle her to his chest or toss her over his shoulder. It didn't really matter. She craved the closeness of his body in a way that, strangely, seemed entirely natural.

Before he could, they saw that the Celestials *had* reserved the biggest and nastiest for last.

But it wasn't a creature. It was so, *so* much worse.

Chapter Twenty

A wall of briars to their right swung toward them, cutting through the established briars like the creatures had and bearing down. This attack had waited until Daisy and Tarian were right in the middle of the massive scape of poisoned needles before starting its swing. There would be no way to duck under it. No way to hide.

Run! Tarian shouted, but she'd never make it. She'd have to go carefully to ensure she didn't touch the thorns. She'd never have enough time.

Her stomach dropped, and her heart hurt. She called up an image of Mordecai and Lexi, the first family that had offered her love. The first real home she'd ever known. Then Kieran and his Six, the first additions to her tiny world. Then Bria, Jerry, Dylan, and Amber—the people for which she kept expanding her circle of trust. The only people who would miss her. Who would lament her passing.

She called them up in her mind and held them close, soaking in her love for them in her last moments. Wishing them goodbye.

Tarian yanked her around and wrapped a big arm around her. He squeezed her to his chest as he jostled her toward the stationary wall of briars, away from the swinging wall.

"Do. Not. *Move*," he ground out next to her ear. He spread his legs, planted his feet, and reached through the thorns to brace his hand flat against the tunnel wall. Thorns scraped his skin. Blood and pus welled up. His flesh turned angry and red. Then his whole body popped, it felt like, muscles pushing into her everywhere, bracing around her.

"Wait—" she'd started to say, or maybe scream, when the wall slammed into him from behind. He grunted and pushed forward with the impact. His elbow bent. Sharp needles neared her body, her face. One was aimed directly at her eye.

His arm shook with the effort of keeping that wall from knocking them into the briars. His whole body trembled, whether from pain or maintaining his position, she didn't know. Probably both. Then his elbow slowly straightened. Bit by agonizing bit, he willed himself to push away from the wall. She felt the incredible determination through his mind. His agony, but his unwillingness to give up, to give in and let the Celestials win over him. In his mind, they were not above him, as their stations declared. They were his inferiors. They should be looking skyward at him.

He shoved away from that wall until his elbow locked. Until they had breathing room in the tent of his exertion.

"Go," he wheezed, carefully releasing her body. Even now he would keep her from falling forward and killing herself. "Hurry. Get to safety. Once one of us steps out of this obstacle, it's safe. It should release me." He paused. "It *should*. Once you escape its net, it *should* lose its ferocity. The wall of briars should disappear or diminish."

"What if it doesn't?" she whispered, stepping to the side while crouching.

"We'll cross that bridge when we steal the right chalice." It was a joke, and she didn't waste any more time. Couldn't. If she didn't help by getting out of here, she would help by finding a log or something to wedge into the briar wall that might release him.

She was quick but careful, the space limited and a few jutting briar patches in her way. She crawled for some stretches, slithered in others, and noticed the moving wall shaking, belying his extreme effort or pain. She could see the cleared tunnel up ahead.

She felt a snag on her shirt at the back, near her right side.

Her heart stopped. Had something poked her? Was she imagining it?

A horrible burning sensation spread across her skin. *Fuck*. No, she was not imagining it.

"A little wider," she yelled at Tarian, fear seeping into her words before she could shove the feeling away. "I'm caught. There's not enough space."

She heard him groan, like a bodybuilder lifting too much weight. The shivering wall moved an inch. Two. It was enough.

She crawled across the tunnel floor as fast as she dared. It felt like her skin was blistering. Like it was dripping away from her body. The pain throbbed, sinking into her ribs at her back. Deeper, into the very center of her, like a knife twisting. She couldn't seem to ignore it. To avoid it.

Zorn's voice swam into her consciousness.

To give in to the pain is to give in to death.

She gritted her teeth. She remembered his teachings and internalized the feeling. Became one with it. Let it continue to pass through her until her mind accepted it and moved on. Zorn was full of amazing tricks for horrible things. Fuck, though. This hurt worse than anything she'd ever even dreamed of.

The last of the briars seemed to wave goodbye... and then the tunnel cleared of them completely. Not just in front of her, but behind as well. It was as if the whole obstacle had been an illusion, and once she was out of it, it vanished completely.

Breathing heavily, her mind fracturing to skirt the throbs of excruciating pain, she turned back to Tarian.

He'd fallen onto a knee, his good hand braced on the ground, his bad arm held in close to his chest. His dark, curled mass of hair fell over his face as he bowed his head. His sides ran freely with blood-tinged liquid, and his ribs expanded and contracted quickly with each labored breath.

Can I come to you? she thought, but the distance was too great. He couldn't hear her thoughts. She repeated herself out loud.

"No," he responded gruffly. "If you cross the threshold you just exited, the obstacle will flare to life again. I'll come to you. I'm just…taking a break."

The break lasted another few minutes, and in that time, she assessed the throbbing pain that registered in her body. Deep in her soul, it felt like. But as time passed, it didn't get worse. It didn't spread or affect anything that might steal her life, like closing her throat. The liquid had pierced her shirt, not her skin, and dripped onto her. That was it, and that wasn't enough to kill her.

That answers that, she thought as he slowly stood, like a man on the brink. Each movement took a lot of effort. Agonizing, she knew. His steps were halting, not at all exhibiting the grace with which he so often moved. His sword was in its sheath and each hand flexed and clenched, over and over, as he handled the pain.

His gaze was downcast until he got close, and then it flicked her way. His eyes were bloodshot and the thin gold line around his pupils had turned red. She furrowed her brow at it, wondering why it had changed color. What that meant for a fae.

"It's so others may assess our state of being in the event we can't respond ourselves," he answered, back in range.

"So red means..."

"Gravely injured. In this case, in extreme pain with the possibility of being poisoned."

"But..." She reached out for him, to give him something to lean on.

"No," he whispered raggedly, pushing her hand away. "I might have some of the poison on my skin. Keep your distance, dove. You are ten times more fragile than I am."

She clenched her teeth stubbornly, having heard that since she was fourteen and hating it just as much now. But as with her early days, he was right. In this, she was vulnerable. Any open cut and that liquid might find its way into her bloodstream. She was lucky the other drop hadn't.

"I thought this plant wasn't poison to you—"

His head snapped up, and his eyes hyper-focused. "What did you say?" He squinted marginally, and then he yanked her around before grabbing her shirt in two fistfuls and ripping down the back, rending it in two except for a small section at the very bottom.

"What—" she started.

His left hand—the undamaged one—clamped

down on her shoulder. The other grabbed her clothed hip. He bent her over. A finger touched down on her skin, and it felt like her knees might buckle from the pain. The finger moved through an area she couldn't really feel, numbed from the poison, before coming away. He was wiping up any lingering liquid.

"Is it having any other effects besides the pain?" he asked, running his finger over her again. He took up her shirt and analyzed it before wiping her off.

"No. I think it's fine." She straightened, needing to slap his hands away to do so. Then she cleared her throat to stave off the shuddering breath at the sight of him. His front was obviously fine, but his arm was swollen and puffy along tracks where the needles had pierced his skin and then dragged along it.

"I thought this plant wasn't poisonous to you," she repeated, swallowing heavily.

"It isn't poisonous in small doses, I think," he replied, walking stiffly toward the end of the tunnel. "This...doesn't feel like a small dose."

As he passed, she got a look at his back. She sucked in that shuddering breath.

The stuff oozing from the wounds was singeing unmarked skin. The plant had released so much poison inside of him that it was now bubbling back out. Given how much it hurt for just a drop to touch her unblemished skin, she couldn't fathom the amount of agony he must be feeling with it inside his body in that magnitude. To still be on his feet...

He'd endured that poison—he'd stood there and let those thorns empty more and more into him—so she could get out. So she would be safe. He could've run and made it. He could've pushed his way out when he'd realized it was more than he could possibly tolerate. He'd saved her life at great peril to his own. That was more than a desire to keep a toy in one piece. That was someone looking after the wellbeing of another. Daisy didn't have the time or energy to dissect what it all meant, or how she felt about it, but she knew his selfless actions deserved her doing everything she could to return the favor. She didn't have much in the way of a moral compass, but this was the decent thing. The right thing. End of story.

"You're on your deathbed, fine," she said crisply, getting to work. "Let's get this sorted out, shall we?"

She could have used her shirt to wipe away the poison oozing down his side. Instead, she put it back on, awkwardly tied the back to keep it put, then ducked under his good arm. If poison started to soak into her shirt, she'd know. Then she'd use the other side of it to wipe him up before tossing the thing away entirely. They needed to hasten him toward water or something that might help clean this gunk off. Speed was life.

"Where are we headed?" she asked. "Closest safe spot will do. Also, I need your weapon. If we run into trouble, you won't be much good to me."

He huffed out a laugh that turned into a series of

coughs. He put his weight on her, and she held on to his arm to keep from reaching around his side and coming into contact with more of the ooze. Her knife was tucked away, and she held his in her free hand. She'd drop him like a sack of garbage if she needed to meet an attack.

A sack of garbage? he thought as they reached the end of the tunnel. *I thought the human saying was sack of potatoes.*

Another saying is—when the shoe fits. Pain still thrummed in her back, somewhat localized but making her vision distort in pulses. That probably wasn't good.

It's happening to me, too, he said as he pointed southeast. *Only, it's darkening my vision, like it's threatening to cut out my ability to see entirely.*

Not good.

Probably not, no.

The night lay still and dark around them. The land curled up into a bank on their right, where strange trees with twisted trunks towered over them. Their branches reached out like skeletal arms, their leaves long, weaving together like an oddly colored quilt. Light fog hazed the uneven path, hiding sharp rocks and loose logs so that travelers might stumble and hopefully fall. Once they were on the ground, they were easier to deal with. Easier to bleed.

Fangs brightened her mind's eye, sharp and dripping with saliva. Red eyes, the pupils circled with yellow. Bristling bodies. Hair tipped with razors, watching them. Waiting for them.

One was sick.

Another was weak.

The eating will be good.

Are you hearing these thoughts? she asked him with a slight quickening of her heart. *Or is this the poison presenting me to myself and I'm just now realizing I should've been going to therapy these last few years?*

It is not the poison. It is not your thoughts, and I am once again surprised and impressed. You have an innate ability to understand the subtle or hidden atmosphere of your surroundings, it seems. Or maybe you are meant to be in Faerie.

I am most definitely not meant to be in Faerie, and I'd greatly love some insight into what's going on.

He coughed again, his body heaving. *There are any number of creatures around us that could be thinking those same thoughts. Your mind is giving the consciousness of the wylds one face, when in reality, it presents as many faces. The trees there drink the blood of the fallen, rejoicing when death soaks into their roots. A great many things in this area kill for sport. Many more feed on only rotting carcasses. Still more will enchant you and lead you away to dance and play until you are dying of starvation and thirst, never having remembered to eat or sleep. Certain parts of the wylds are very treacherous. You must always stay vigilant.*

She sighed and continued on. Same shit, different

realm. She'd have to learn a whole new set of warning signals and danger beacons but...well, what else did she have to do? Might as well start now.

Start fast-thinking about everything you know, she said, stepping over a rock and feeling a sigh of annoyance that she should find it. They seemed fairly simple, these wylds. They must deal with stupid creatures fairly often if her seeing a rock was their big letdown. *You know how you did in the Faegate, when you flicked through images and experiences and—*

The memories came fast, almost faster than she could handle. Once she got into the flow of it, though, she was able to sift through his various experiences, noticing the creatures, their dangers, their tells. As they trudged on, tired, weary, soon-to-be half-naked because she could feel the poison soaking into her shirt and tingling her skin, she did her homework on this new and not-as-terrifying-as-she-had-previously-thought place.

The wylds are not terrifying, no, he said, the tone of his thoughts weakened even more. *They are treacherous, as I've said, but then, so are we. So are you. They are beautiful if you see them the right way. Majestic. Really fucking disturbing, though, most of them.*

So then...like you, she surmised with a grin, pausing to rip off her shirt, wipe him down with it, and toss it aside.

He didn't so much as spare her near-nudity a glance. *Like you.* He paused as they reached a fork. He thought about the direction, leaning against her heavily. He was fading fast.

I'm good, he said, and if he thought his admission was believable, he was sorely mistaken. *I'll make it,* he tried again, and maybe that was truer. *It's not far now. The wylds have rules, and the Celestials mostly do their duty in managing the balance. This part is a bit... deranged, which is why they end up in the catacombs, but that's because it's an extension of the fringe. In other parts of the wyld, there are some truly beautiful places with lovely creatures and kind beings. They're in secretive places that not many of my kind know about.*

Your kind?

The highborn and gentry and above. The nobles, you'd say. The upper class, even. My kind doesn't seek out the mysterious places of this land. They don't communicate with the lesser fae and certainly don't lower themselves to encounter the faeries and wyld things that make this land thrive. And that leads me to the real dangers of this realm. The really scary places that will take more than vigilance to survive. It'll take cunning and planning, backstabbing and betrayals. Alliances, many of whose throats you'd cut if needed.

The courts, she surmised.

Yes. The courts, ruled by the various thrones making up Faerie, and no court is as cunning, as conniving, as that ruled by the Obsidian Throne.

That sounded a lot like the dealings of Demigods

in the human realm. She filed that away for future reflection.

How do you know of these secret wyld places? she asked, her side throbbing. Fuck, that poison was intense.

I have traveled all over this realm seeking the chalices. Before I knew the most powerful of them had been hidden in the human realm, I sought them in my lands.

The most powerful...were hidden? By whom?

He pointed to the right. She barely registered a path leading away. It was only after she had changed their trajectory that he answered.

By past Celestial kings and queens. The legends say that the gods would not destroy their objects of power, and so the Celestial High Sovereign hid them across the Great Barrier—the fringe—never to be found and used against their kind.

Which never works.

In the end, it seems not.

And so all you did was follow the breadcrumbs.

That is an enormous oversimplification, which discounts all the many hours I spent under the guidance of the most boring scribe ever to walk the enchanted lands—which is saying something, because they are all mind-numbing—but sure, I followed breadcrumbs.

She felt a smile bud through the pain, barely able to feel her legs now.

I'm starting to question whether the poison that touched my skin is actually fatal, she reflected.

I can't feel my legs at all. I'm telling them to move, and it seems to be working, but they also seem like a separate part of me.

Oh. Well, I'm not so bad off as that. Good news.

For you, yes. Unless I die. Then you're equally fucked.

Very likely. At least she had the disgruntled wylds to keep her company. They really did hope she tripped on one of the rocks.

The embankment rose on both sides, the trees not having changed but the leaves growing fuller on the branches. Ivy wrapped around the trunks of some, and as she watched, the vines uncurled slowly. They sensed visitors and wanted to check them out, maybe claim a prize for the trees that were so fond of squeezing creatures to death and drinking the spoils.

This place is going to drive me mad, I think, she whispered, realizing belatedly that it was a thought and not actual words. *I wonder if Lewis Caroll took a trip through Faerie before he penned his stories.*

I don't know who that is.

She crinkled her nose as a mysterious echo ghosted by the trees. Not a sound so much as a whisper of a thought. A dark and murderous desire as yet unvoiced.

Don't bother. She was still mentally whispering. *Being used to all this, you'll probably find it boring. I might be changing my mind about how scary this place is.*

He didn't respond, and the images in his mind,

having gone from the wylds to the court they'd be heading toward, had stopped. He staggered, stumbling more frequently, and reached out with his bad hand to brace on things that weren't there.

How much longer? she asked in alarm.

He shook his head, breathing too fast, pushing himself on. She could feel it in his lean forward, his desire to go faster. She complied, taking more of his weight, wilting under the onslaught.

Up ahead, peeking out through dense vegetation and half nestled into a little berm, dull brown wood announced a structure. Tarian reached for the door when they were still a ways off, grabbing for the handle.

Almost there, she said softly, clutching the presence of his mind within hers and trying to keep it with her so he didn't drift away entirely. She didn't know if that was possible or if it was working, but it made her feel like she was doing more than shambling and lurching toward their hopeful safe haven. *Just a little farther.*

He barely nodded, his head drooping. Then his back bowed, still oozing gruesomely. She pushed on, breathing heavily with his weight, refusing to allow her legs to buckle. She could still at least feel them...kinda. She willed herself forward. A little faster.

He mumbled something.

What? she asked.

He mumbled something else, the words not taking shape, barely reaching her ears. His hand came out again, flexing. The presences around them, the voices and feelings, the creepy sensations and negative motives, fell away. Scattered. She barely heard or felt them now. Instead, warmth existed in front of her. That was what it felt like, anyway, as if they were marching through a blizzard and a fire roared just up ahead. The colors softened, or her perception of them did, and the feelings grew welcoming.

Magic, obviously. His magic or his activating some other kind of magic.

Perceptive. His thought felt flimsy, less solid. His amusement was only a passing wisp, lost to the darkness a moment later. He was fading fast.

Here we go. She gripped the feeling of him in her head harder. *Almost there. Rest will help. You just need rest.*

She hoped that was all he needed, because in this realm, she had no idea which plants might act as medicine, and which plants might finish him off.

Chapter Twenty-One

Step by aching step, she wrestled him toward that glowing shack at the end of the tiny path, not much more than a game trail, but for *really* large game. On one of his stumbles, he reached out to grab her. His hand didn't touch down. He quickly pulled it away, probably so his arm wouldn't drag her closer against his side, crushing any lingering poison onto her skin.

I'm sure it's all oozed down your body by now, she said, nearly there, reaching around his big back.

"No." He shoved away from her and fell into the door. "No—"

The door gave way under his weight, and he tumbled into the space. His hand peeled off the ancient-looking knob, bronzed and weather worn. His limbs settled on the ground, and he stayed there, cheek against the dusty wooden floor, chest rising and falling much too quickly.

"Fine." She stepped around him, grabbed his wrists, and heaved. It was like moving a concrete pillar. "C'mon, you bastard," she mumbled, using anger to coax adrenaline into her aching joints and tired limbs. "C'mon, here we go." She dragged him a little bit, then a little bit more. "You could also help me. Just go ahead and inchworm forward. A little bit more and I can close the door."

With a world-weary sigh, he did as she said, not moving much, but enough for her to use his momentum to inch him all the way into the modest space. That done, she stepped around him to close the door, but imagery started tumbling into her mind. She paused, hand on the knob, focusing on the beautiful images filled with light and sunbeams and vibrant hues of color. A path wound through them, following the natural landmarks, turns, and finally ending at a babbling brook.

The imagery changed to the space they occupied. Cupboards and baskets filled with supplies and—

She stepped over him, finding the cupboard in question and pulling out the water skin.

More images—no, the same as before, going over the directions, instructing her to get water.

"Got it," she said, turning.

Still more images came, this time ending in a field near the brook and looking down on a very pretty flower with an explosion of vibrancy. Magenta and amethyst petals framed a core of fiery marigold, emitting beads of light that drifted into the air and hovered all around. Just off the center, the petals looked like leaves, with veins of luminous tangerine, fuchsia, or violet. The leaves seemed ultraviolet, with the blues, purples, pinks, and lime greens.

He went through how to pick it twice, how to tuck it into the pack she needed to grab in a minute, and how to prepare it. So handy, this way of communicating. It made information transfer so much quicker and less tedious.

When he was finished, and before she could leave, images of creatures flashed into her mind. His feelings indicated how she should respond to them, if she should fight, run, hide...

Finally, the images stopped, his feelings subsided, and she lifted her brow to make sure that meant she should go.

The image of the door hitting her in the ass on the way out filtered into her mind.

"Cute," she said dryly, grabbing the pack, strapping it and the water skin to her person, and checking her weapons.

She didn't have a shirt, which would make a quick draw of her knife easier, but it would also expose that she had a knife. Of course, she had yanked Tarian's belt and sheath off him and secured it around her hips, so it wasn't like she would be hiding anything anyway. She was at least thankful she'd been abducted after a job and not after an event. Her nipples showing through a lacy bra was not what she was going for. The sturdy cotton she currently wore checked the right boxes.

"Okay wylds," she murmured, setting off. "Let's see if you can sneak a rock in my way."

It felt like his memories were stamped into hers, which made traveling the path feel like she'd done it before. Done it often, actually, although...looking around, noticing the tree with the hollow at the bottom, or the strange knot in that trunk, or the small outcropping of rocks that had no hope of catching her foot, she had to own that he saw things a lot differently than she did. His imagery was so colorful and pretty, with dancing filaments of plants and the silvery sparkle of moonlight or random glowing orbs. In reality—her reality—the same objects were dark and gloomy, with murky shadows pooling at the bases and the press of eyes from unseen places. She felt like the storm cloud to his blissful, sunny day.

She heard the brook before she saw it, and once she neared, she desperately tried to notice the shimmering light dancing on the slowly flowing water, or the gurgle of rapids across the smooth stones down the way. She wanted to match his poetic observations, if only to prove she wasn't so horribly dour. Instead, she heard a twig snap away right. Something rustled to the left. Ripples of ill intent washed over her, and that was about as poetic as she could get with the whole thing.

They drifted out of the dark grasses, five creatures that looked like a misguided scientist had tried to clone a wolf and ended up with a wolf/jackal hybrid. They snarled, showing too many canines too large for their mouths. Their front legs were longer than their back, with a robust chest leading back into scrawny withers. She took out her knives, one weapon in each hand, and waited for them to elongate into swords. They did so at exactly the same time and pace.

Her legs hurt like hell, her middle throbbed, her vision wobbled, but she had zero fear as she walked into the center of them and let them surround her. She didn't move her swords or choose a stance just yet, watching their movements and the transfer of their weight. Watching how they worked together and which one called the shots. She'd learned to interpret the pack mentality from training with various shifters. That would help her here.

The ground pulsed subsonically. The effect rattled her heart. Magic?

The creatures around her hunched. Their lips lowered, their snarls losing their viciousness. That feeling hadn't come from them. They weren't looking around, though. If it had come from some other creature, they weren't looking for it.

She walked in a small circle, swords lowering, points level with their faces. Three of them snarled. The other two lowered their heads a fraction as another pulse hit, this one crawling up her spine uncomfortably. Fear wavered her resolve. She didn't like that pulse. It felt like a bad omen, like something big and bad was wandering this way.

One of the creatures took a step back, its tail curling between its legs. The others noticed, their ears pricking up. They all suddenly lifted their heads, gazes directed across the brook, as though startled. In a moment, they scattered, having come from positions surrounding her and now all fleeing in a singular direction.

Another pulse. Treetops in the distance moved within the moon's glow. A branch broke, torn from on high and echoing as it plummeted to the ground. Whatever was coming was fucking enormous.

"Fuck that," she said as her heart picked up pace. She didn't care if this clawing fear was magically induced. She didn't want any part of it.

She stowed her weapons away as she ran to the brook. She unslung the water skin, twisted off the cap, and submerged it in the water. Another pulse and her breath came quickly.

"Come on, come on..." Trees groaned, and another branch went down. Something large was definitely moving through the landscape. "Be a brontosaurus. Be a gentle giant that only eats plants."

That pulse worked at her nervous system. Adrenaline dumped into her body, her flight response active. It had to be magic. She wasn't generally afraid in these kinds of situations. Or many situations, really. Training had mostly chased the fear out of her. But fuck if she wasn't shitting herself right now.

A rock wiggled across the brook. As she filled the water skin with a shaking hand, it grew before her eyes. Could the wylds make them fly? Like, throw it at her somehow?

It rolled. All by itself, the rock rolled to the right. Another, first enlarging, did the same, but this one went left. A couple more. They met on the other side of the bank, forming a tiny wall between her and the creature. A message. The feeling in the area changed.

Run.

It was almost like someone whispering it in her ear. Or Tarian in her head. But this wasn't a voice, and it wasn't him, and it wasn't human. It was sentient, though.

The pulse was getting closer. That thing didn't move quickly, but it traveled fast. It definitely had to be enormous.

Run.

She yanked the skin out of the water. Three-quarters would have to be good enough.

She ran away from the massive thing cutting a path through the trees. Memories crowded her, vibrant and bright and pretty, and she'd just missed the turn for the plant.

"F*uh*-ck," she drew out, stopping. She turned back. She needed that plant. *He* needed that plant. He'd endured immense pain to save her, and now she would save him. And while that didn't make all the sense in the world, given he'd gotten her into this mess in the first place, her survival also depended on him. She didn't have any food or fire. She didn't have any way of getting out of here. Also...there was a small niggle in the back of her mind that worried if he died, a part of her would miss him. Miss the feelings she had when she was around him.

Regardless, he needed to live.

She raced down the little path, and all the rocks rolled out of her way. What did it say about her that the most deranged of the wylds were working with her like some sort of teammate or friend? Probably not great things. She needed to look into her mental health when she eventually got back to the human lands.

The field of those faerie plants was like a cactus farm in New Mexico compared to what Tarian had mentally shown her. The shape was the same, though, so she stilled herself for the moment and carefully harvested three, like he'd shown her.

The pulse felt like a hand had physically grabbed hold of her legs and shaken them, trying to knock her to the ground. The subsonic sound materialized into the air, a push of pressure that had her looking over her shoulder, expecting something twice the size of an elephant to be bearing down on her. Nothing was there.

Run!

"Okay," she whispered, her hands shaking so badly

she could hardly stow away the plants. It was important to keep the petals attached.

Never hurry, Zorn always said. *Never rush. That's when you make mistakes. Keep control, and just move faster.*

But the fucking shaking would not go away.

Being afraid is a waste of—

"I fucking know that," she muttered to herself furiously, taking the time needed to stow away those plants. "You try being in the fucking faerie wylds with your body magically on fire from a poison you've never experienced and in debt to your captor with a huge fucking beast bearing down on you and the actual fucking *wilderness* telling you to run. You do that, Zorn, and then we'll fucking talk, huh?"

Plants stowed, she ended her tirade and popped up. She spun and took one step before she saw it. Its massive head was even with the tree line, and the deep brown of its shaggy body nearly blended in with the surrounding fauna. It was still beyond the brook, but the break in the trees gave it a clear view of her, because glowing yellow eyes were focused her way, a pinprick of black in their center, the rest of the face lost to darkness and shadow even though the moon should've been showering it with light. Its huff moved the leaves around it, and a snuffle said it was inhaling, sampling the currents.

It took her a harried heartbeat to realize the direction of the wind. She was upwind and smeared with

Tarian's blood and magic, her own sweat and blood. If it had any sort of olfactory ability, it would know everything about her.

Moving slowly, because predators liked to chase, she took a step toward the path. Another. Those luminous eyes followed her. It didn't move.

Maybe it wasn't interested in her? Maybe—

Its roar froze her solid, locking up the very fibers of her being. Except her heart. That thing had never beaten so fast in her life.

Run! that presence urged.

"But what if it likes to chase—"

RUN!

The creature launched forward a moment before she did.

"Fuck, fuck, fuck, fuck—" she murmured as she swung the pack onto her back and tore out of the clearing. The pulsing quickened, footsteps, each one rattling against her ribcage like a xylophone. Her stomach tightened as she hit the main path.

Left.

"But Tarian—"

LEFT!

She did as the wylds instructed. They'd tried to barricade her behind the brook with stones, after all. They couldn't be all *that* deranged…

Branches slapped her face. Something stung her arm.

Right.

The small game trail was hard to find. The pulsing grew more intense and louder, even though she couldn't actually hear it. Fear consumed her, and she let it. It might make her run faster.

Right.

"Please don't take me in a circle," she said, throwing up her hands to block a wall of bushes. Another game trail. Vines moved quickly, outlining her way.

Another roar made her cry out. Tears streamed down her face. She was so afraid that she was choking. Not even the Celestials had magic like this. It was beyond anything she'd ever experienced, anything she could tolerate.

It would be really great if Tarian suddenly felt better and came to save me, she thought desperately, getting another direction from the wylds but having already figured it out from the vines. Through the foliage, it looked like cliffs rose on each side, like she'd entered a canyon. *I'd be totally fine being the damsel right now.*

Who was she kidding? She *was* the damsel. No way was she fighting something that enormous and terrifying. No way. She knew her limits.

Stop.

"What?" she said, out of breath. Vines reached into the path to block her way. She could've pushed through, but she was getting too far from the general location of the shack.

Trees crashed. Branches tore. A roar blasted across the space, but not like before. It didn't scare her. It made her want to duck. To hide. The creature sounded frustrated.

She looked around, seeing the thick trunks and stringy vines, solid masses of flora and the sheer rock faces to her right and left, going up over her head. She didn't feel closed in—there was plenty of space around her—but she was also a grain of sand compared to that enormous creature. It couldn't get through.

Wait, the voice that was not a voice said.

She stepped toward the nearest bush and hunkered down, catching her breath. Both the pack and water skin were still on her back. The creature out there thrashed and bucked, offering another roar. After a while, though, the noises slowed. The pulses did, too. Then everything quieted. Deadly quiet, as though every living thing had vacated this area.

Go.

She rose slowly. The wylds had saved her life. The nameless, faceless, natural, sentient...thing had helped her escape. She should've been bewildered. Utterly perplexed. Maybe scared. Instead...she smiled. Then chuckled. Then full-out laughed. It seemed...so fucking awesome. Awesome wasn't even the right word. It was—

Go!

"Pushy, that's what it is..." she mock-grumbled, still

smiling to shake loose some of the adrenaline still sizzling her nerves.

A rock moved at the last moment, catching her foot. She tripped over it and fell on her face. She could feel the swell of victory all around her.

When she got back to the shack, Tarian was standing, leaning at an angle, his hand braced on a countertop. His eyes were tight and filled with pain, with worry, as they landed on hers. The circle around his pupils was a deep blood red.

"Hey." She closed the door behind her and noticed a glow from a bronze bowl at the back corner. It provided enough light for her to dimly see the modest and meager surroundings of the one-room space. A bed was pushed into the corner in the back, and a rocking chair sat empty in the other corner, a thick layer of dust over the back and seat. "What's..."

She glanced around. None of the cupboards had been opened since she'd left, and nothing new seemed to be on the countertop.

"What are you up to?" she asked. "Headed out for a jog?"

His torso flexed, and he swayed before catching himself. His hair fell into his eyes as he dropped his head. *I heard the darkrend. I worried you might be in trouble. It took this long to stand. I'm not quite up to my usual standards.*

"I'm going to go ahead and talk out loud, if that's cool." She unslung the pack from her shoulders. "I'm assuming I'll get warned if something else big and mean is coming, and then I'll quiet down."

If you don't mind, I'll still speak like this. She could hear the fatigue and pain emanating through his words. *I set the ward. You are safe within these walls. Nothing can get us in here, not even a group of Celestials.*

"That's good to know. And yes, I was in trouble. That thing saw me across the brook and closed in. I... am going to be really honest here..." She unslung the water skin and placed it on the ground before helping him back down. A rocking chair would not feel nice on his back, and there was nothing else to sit on, save for that bed—and if one of them had to lie in it, she didn't want water or crushed plants making it gross. "It scared the absolute shit out of me. I haven't frozen in fear in...I don't even remember how long. But I did. Froze solid."

He winced as he settled, bowing over his legs. *What did it go after?*

"What do you mean?"

It roared its battle charge. What was it chasing?

"Me. It saw me across the brook. I was getting those plants—which look nothing like your mental images, by the way. Do you habitually take drugs, should I get my eyes checked, or am I just a gloomy person and that's the only filter I have to see the world through?"

His body shook with silent laughter, and then he

started to cough before groaning. *Please don't be funny. It hurts to laugh.*

"I wasn't meaning to be," she muttered softly. She was just in a buoyant mood after the whole wylds situation.

What situation? More importantly, what do you mean it charged you? It couldn't have. You'd be dead.

She told him what happened as she found a bowl and grabbed the plants. She carefully picked off the petals and paused in her story to repeat the instructions the wyld had given her. Then she sat down behind him with the bowl and interior of the flower.

"A chalice," she said, suddenly understanding.

What?

"The cup-shaped interior of a flower. One of our meanings of the word chalice. That's what I'm using to help you heal, right?"

He tried to turn and see but winced and stopped himself. *Yes. That didn't even dawn on me.*

"Oh." She left it in the bowl, unfolded a thick and soft cloth she'd found in a cabinet, and picked up the water skin. "Can I use this water to wash your back, or does it have to be boiled first to get rid of all the bacteria? If the latter, I'm going to need more supplies because I don't know how to make fire with just sticks. Zorn has always been very verbal in his frustration about that fact."

He started to shake silently again before taking a deep breath. *Stop. Please stop. You're killing me. And yes, you can use the water as it is. Water in Faerie is safe for all species to drink, directly from the source.*

Tarian sat on the dusty, dirty floor with Daisy kneeling behind him. She told him the story as she squeezed water over his skin, watching it run in rivulets down his tattoos and tense muscles. Her knuckles occasionally grazed his skin, eliciting goosebumps across his body.

He stayed stoic through the process but didn't speak while it was happening, very likely trying to handle the pain. The good news was that almost all the oozing had stopped. What was persistent was mostly blood, the wounds surely clean of poison at this point.

She took the flower, working in the balm with her fingertips, slow and gentle, careful not to hurt him. She worked the gel-like substance across his back. When she got to his neck, his head lolled forward. His breathing softened, now more controlled. He was clearly enjoying the sensations. Her touch.

"Is it helping?" she asked, her voice not much more than a whisper.

"Very much," he replied in an equally soft tone. "Tell me again what that voice sounded like."

"*Felt* like, actually—"

She cut off as her fingers ran over something hard on the back of his right shoulder, about an inch in diameter. Looking closer, she saw it was an octagonal shape and smooth and shallow, but not skin. Not ink, either, though the color was almost identical. When it caught the light, it glittered.

"What is this?" she asked, seeing four more evenly spaced across the shoulders and upper back. She traced the others, feeling a current within her fingers.

His reply was so low she barely heard. "Obsidian."

His court. Where he was an assassin and an errand boy and apparently a captive, and she would be a plaything. Maybe a dangerous toy.

She pushed the reality of their situation away. She was too exhausted to think about it. To worry about it. She needed rest. Sleep. She needed a fucking break, and she'd only get it if she hurried this along and finished up.

Chapter Twenty-Two

"Okay." She finished his arm and plopped down next to him, holding up her hands to look at the gel-like substance coating her fingers. The bowl still had a bit of the amazingly bountiful flower left. "I guess we have some to reapply should we need it."

She looked up to ask if it would be safe for humans, but the words died on her lips when she met his eyes, so deep, so beautiful. Vibrant, like the memories he shared. Like his humor. The red circling his iris was gone, only burnished gold remaining. The soft glow illuminated his handsome face and lush, full lips.

Thank you. His mental voice was a whisper, but it still relayed his heartfelt sentiment. His gratitude.

"You saved me. It was only right that I help you."

I got you into this in the first place. I put you in danger by forcing you into the catacombs. Into the wylds. You could've let me suffer. You could've held off and only stepped in if I would actually die. You should've, probably. Instead you risked your life to ease my pain. You constantly surprise and amaze me, Daisy. You think of yourself as black-hearted and morally bankrupt, but you're not. You're good at your core. You are the best of your kind. The very best.

She was frozen for the second time that night as he leaned forward slowly, his deep gaze opening her up inside. Her stomach fluttered. His eyes were hooded as he neared. She swayed, pulled toward him like a magnet. Her eyes were trained on his lips. He reached for her with his good hand and gently cupped her face in his large palm.

Their lips met softly at first, tentatively. Exploring. Their mouths moved together, savoring each other's tastes, the electric feel of their touch. Slowly, it deepened, the intensity growing. Passion mounted. His hand slipped down to the side of her neck. She lightly touched his jaw, his stubble scratching her skin.

A spark ignited. The world outside faded away. Her breath quickened, mingling with his. His tongue met hers, dancing at first, then a slow, purposeful thrust.

Her hands fell to his chest, meeting his warm skin. His slipped around to the back of her neck, pulling her in a little harder. Their kiss turned fervent. Her palms dropped farther, as did his hand. Her hunger for his touch grew. She wanted his weight to settle over her body. Wanted—

He stiffened. Then she felt it. A pulse. Subsonic movement, a push from unseen forces.

He pulled back, the gold running around his pupils catching the light and sparkling like a real substance. A small crease formed between his eyebrows.

She started to shake. She couldn't help it. She couldn't stop it. He looked down at her body, seeing it.

"You didn't see that thing charging," she said in explanation, embarrassed.

"Don't—" He placed a hand on hers where it had stopped in the middle of his stomach. He gave a smile, of all things. "The last thing you want to be is embarrassed about this reaction. I've seen battle-hardened warriors piss themselves when that thing comes around. It takes a team of powerful Celestials to bring one down. Few usually escape when it sets its eyes on them. And you had to brave it all alone."

"Ah, but..." She shrugged, grinning, trying to get around the magical fear that had again taken hold of her body. "You were standing by."

He barked out laughter and then groaned, leaning forward into her. "More like *leaning* by. By the time I reached my feet, I didn't know how I'd take a step without passing out. Thankfully, you were able to save yourself."

She threaded her fingers through his hair, tucking a strand behind his pointed ear. Her fingertips softly drifted down his cheek, over the stubble. His forehead rested against her shoulder, his hand still over hers.

"How do you feel now?" she whispered, wanting to tilt his head up and taste him again.

Hearing her thoughts, he straightened, and she could tell the movement took a toll.

"Not great," she surmised as his gaze stamped her lips.

"Better." His deep voice had reduced to a murmur. "It went from drowning me to merely consuming me. The plant helps, though it's not a miracle. It does work on humans, by the way. Let's put some on you."

"Nah." She leaned forward and touched her lips to his. He tilted his head, allowing for more contact. Their lips fit together like puzzle pieces clicking into place. "I've got a handle on the pain."

His tongue swiped through her mouth before circling hers. She fell into it, her control wobbling. Her desire swept away rational thought.

He sucked in her bottom lip before backing off again. "Your turn. With that darkrend roaming around, we can't do much but sleep, so let's make sure we get some genuine rest. Minimizing the pain will help with that."

"What if you need more, though?"

His grin was soft. "I guess I'll have to go out and get some, hmm?"

He moved around her slowly, laboriously. With the bowl in hand, he inspected her back and then her side where she'd been in contact with him. His touch was warm and delicate, giving her goosebumps when he spread the cool gel. Almost immediately, the dull ache minimized if not subsided, working down into her body and quieting the pain.

She closed her eyes with a sigh and, when he'd finished, leaned back against his chest. He set the bowl down, and his arms fell around her, drifting down her stomach and back up, staying in safe areas. She didn't *want* his hands in safe areas, though. She wanted to feel him where it counted, his kisses all over.

"Not tonight, little dove," he whispered, his lips against her cheek. "We need to sleep. Tomorrow we have half a day's walk before we can ride. Besides, we're in a bubble of safety and teamwork after some hard battles. We still currently have a mutual goal: to survive. You're forgetting the reality of your situation. As soon as you come to your senses, you will have regretted my touch."

She could hear the traces of pain in his words. The call back to what had happened with his first—and only—love.

"I don't regret your kiss," she whispered.

He paused, his hands stilling on her stomach. "Because you assume you'll kill me and free yourself from my influence?"

"Obviously. Until then, it feels good."

"And taking my body into yours won't make it harder to kill me?"

She tilted her head to look up at him. "Do you know me, like, even a little bit? If there is a choice between myself and my captor, I'm not going to decide I'm the one that should go. Would you?"

He studied her for a moment as a smile budded. His gaze slipped to her lips. "Obviously not. We seem to be the same sort of creature. Sadly, one of us is still very much in pain and trying not to show just how difficult it is to sit like this. I'm no good to you right now, which is a real pity, because once we get to my kingdom, you'll no longer want me like this."

"You're so sure of that?"

"Yes. Now c'mon. Let's get some sleep while we have the luxury of safety. We won't always."

Somewhere in the distance, another pulse pushed at the air. The darkrend was staying close.

"What are those pulses?" she asked as she stood and helped him up. "I thought they were footsteps, but it can't be moving so infrequently."

"It's sonar, essentially." Tarian grunted as he stood and swayed, better than before but not great. Even if the coast were clear, he wouldn't be going anywhere. "The darkrend uses it to seek out its prey and assess for danger. It's supposed to freeze the prey in fear, I've heard, but I've never seen that happen. Usually, every living thing is running right along with me when its presence draws near."

"The roar freezes you," she said, steadying him. "I don't usually freeze, but...yeah. There wasn't much about my interactions with it that I'd want to share around a campfire, I'll tell you that much. I was freaked out and running like my life depended on it. I didn't even have a thought about fighting."

"Wise. And just so we're clear, if you see one again, don't expect me to save you. In fact, you best be faster than me or I'll trip you and leave you for dead so it doesn't catch me first."

The sparkle in his eyes said he was joking. His smile quickly dulled from the pain, still evident in his hunched lean and stiff movements.

She turned to survey the bed in the corner. "I assume you're going to deny my advances and force me to stay in close proximity?"

"Exactly, yes. Just more torment to keep you on your toes." He ambled, his hands curled into fists.

She wondered how bad it actually hurt. How close he'd come to death. Then, a moment later, her world crashed down in a red haze of mind-splitting agony, cutting out the feeling of her legs, twisting her stomach, and making it seem like her spine and ribs were crumbling under the pressure. He was showing her what he was currently enduring. She staggered and fell to a knee, her head bowed as she tried to compartmentalize what was happening.

The feeling vanished, leaving only its memory behind. Her body twitched in the aftermath.

"So...it hurts," she said lightly, out of breath. Her stomach churned like she might throw up.

"A bit." He popped the button on his trousers.

"Would you have died?"

"No. Not from the poison, in any case. I might not have made it here to safety. Any number of things might've attacked and eaten me out there. You very well might've saved my life."

"Then we're even. In that, at least. There's still the matter of my needing revenge for what you did at the Demigod convention all those years ago, and then taking me captive and using me as a toy…"

"My goodness. You're still mad from all those years ago? You really do hold a grudge."

"Revenge is a hardy pastime."

"Indeed."

They pulled off the dusty top sheet and slept in their underwear, him on his stomach with his arms down at his sides so he wouldn't take up the whole bed. She stayed on her back, hating to sleep on her stomach, the pain nothing but a dull ache. A large space existed between them, and she didn't even have time to think about his touch. As soon as she laid her head on the striped, soft pillow, a heaviness dragged down her lids.

She awoke with a start sometime later. Light filtered in through the shades drawn over the small windows. It was impossible to tell the time. Warmth radiated at her side, and the pain from the poison was all gone, the plant having helped and her body handling the rest. A weight settled across her upper belly, a band of heat right below her breasts.

Tarian still lay on his stomach, but during their slumber, they'd each moved, closing the gap between them until his side was against her arm and his arm was draped across her body, as though holding on to her to ensure she stayed near him.

She let her head drift to the side, catching his handsome face, so serene in sleep. So peaceful. All the fine lines of stress or pain had eased away into sculpted perfection. His back rose and fell rhythmically—he was still deeply under.

Nervousness flitted through her. She wasn't a person who engaged in intimacy like this. She hadn't had partners over or stayed the night at their places. She hadn't woken up next to them, their bodies attached to her like a tether. Confusingly—horribly?—she had to admit...she liked it. She liked the feeling of his touch upon waking. Watching him sleep.

That couldn't be good...right? That couldn't be normal, staring at someone sleeping like a creeper?

It prowls.

She frowned at the voice. Tarian didn't stir. He hadn't said it.

But then, she knew that. The other voice—the presence—didn't sound like him. Didn't even sound like a person, really. It was like...an echo of a thought. An abstract drifting in her mind, somehow making sense, but she couldn't pinpoint why.

It senses you.

She didn't bother asking what it was talking about.

What are you? she asked instead. *Why doesn't Tarian hear you?*

I am everything and nothing. I am the forgotten and the found. The fabric of the world that is no longer needed.

And speaking gibberish. Are you the wylds? A split part of my personality? Some other entity?

I am not you, but you are me.

Time to change topics. She'd never been very good at nonsense or riddles.

How does it sense me? she asked. *Because of earlier?*

It senses danger. It senses its demise. It feasts on carrion and destruction. Its time is nearly at an end, and it knows it.

The pulse was faint. The creature wasn't close and the voice wasn't making any sense.

She realized she'd been staring at Tarian while talking to it, and now he opened his eyes slowly. His pupils shrank into pinpricks as he focused on her.

How do you feel? she asked as her stomach rumbled.

His gaze touched her lips and slid down to where their bodies touched. Where his arm was slung over her. Finally to her stomach. He was either feeling or hearing her hunger.

Decent. Not in tip-top shape, but good enough to be moving.

He didn't move for a moment, and then his elbow bent, as though he were about to pull it away. She thought about putting her hand on it to stop him. Thought about rolling to him to capture his lips again. She didn't need to make either choice.

His hand slid across her stomach, the touch firm, his fingers splayed.

We need to get going, he thought, his gaze tracking his hand's progress. His thumb ran along the skin of her stomach.

Yeah, she thought as goosebumps erupted along her flesh.

We need to get you some food. His hand traveled upward. His fingers grazed the bottom of her breast. He paused, as though uncertain.

She put her hand on his forearm and gently tugged his arm. His hand covered the swell of her breast. His thumb rolled the peak.

She sucked in a breath from the pleasure that coursed through her body. He rose and scooted closer before pushing her bra up and exposing her. He leaned over and fastened his hot mouth over her sensitive nipple, sucking gently and rolling it with his tongue.

She groaned, her eyes fluttering closed. She tried to reach down and grab his length, but his body was pressed too tightly against hers. His hand slid down as he moved to the other breast. His fingers trailed over her panty-covered apex, stopping in the right place and rubbing in a circle.

She spread her legs wider and ran her fingers through his tangled hair. He pushed up and took her lips with his own. His fingers moved a bit and traced the edge of her panty line. They pressed a fraction, dipping under the fabric. He felt along her wetness before dipping in.

Her moan was tortured. The need to feel him deep, all of him, overwhelmed her. She devoured his lips and tried to work him over her body. Tried to wriggle her hand down in between them to touch him. To stroke him.

His digits plunged in and out. His thumb pressed down above, jolting her with pleasure.

"Let me get to you," she said, gyrating against him. She pushed her hand down as far as she could, only managing to get to his stomach.

"Not this time," he murmured against her lips, working her hard and fast. The sensations tightened her body. She was already so close. "I want to feel you come around my fingers." He kept going. The sound of her wetness filled the room.

He pulled his head away to watch her. His eyes sparkled with deep lust. "Come for me, dove," he commanded.

She unraveled, saying his name as she shook against him. Pleasure engulfed her, and she clutched him.

He gave her a few more strokes, another few turns with his thumb, before pulling his hand away. He brought it up, never breaking eye contact with her, and sucked the fingers into his mouth. For some reason, that fired her up all over again.

"Let's go," he said, ready to turn away.

"No, wait." She tried to keep him put. "Let me use my mouth on you."

His smirk held all sorts of secrets. She wasn't sure what he was thinking. He finished pulling away.

"Come on," he said. "You're hungry. We can get water on the way and food at the next station."

After she'd gotten out of bed, she stared down at her pants on the floor. She really didn't want to put those back on. They were filthy and crusty in places. Any more dirt and they might be able to stand on their own.

Still, they were one more defense against whatever plants and creatures existed in the wylds. Dirt and grime were better than brushing up against something toxic with her bare skin.

Tarian waited for her by the open door, looking out. Listening, it seemed like. Two water skins were draped over one large shoulder and an empty pack was slung over the other.

"Ready?" He turned to her but didn't step out of the way. He'd be leading.

She nodded and followed him as he set out.

"Why don't you have supplies and food items in there?" she asked as her stomach rumbled again.

"That station is rarely used. Any food items would go bad. It has a collection of tools, but nothing with which to make a fast meal. It's easier and faster if we move to the more commonly used station."

The sun gradually increased in warmth, morning heading toward afternoon. They'd only gotten a handful of hours of sleep, but as she took in all the green and blossoming flowers and strange, thorny vines crawling up rough brown bark, she didn't feel tired. Or fatigued. Honestly, she felt totally refreshed.

About an hour into their walk, she said, "What color is that flower?"

Tarian glanced back before noticing her pointed finger. *Don't use your voice. It's pink. I can see you know that.*

She narrowed her eyes at the back of his head as they walked. *Show me an image of how that flower looks to you.*

He looked back again, confusion and bewilderment plain. He did as she asked, though, and the beauty and vibrancy of his sight unfurled in her mind.

Is that really how you see everything? In Technicolor? she asked.

I don't know what Tech—what that is, but yes, that is how I see things. Humans can't see the range of light waves we can. Your vision is dulled in many ways.

That was lame. She liked his images so much more.

Wait, but if my eyes can't see those things, she said, *why can I see them in my mind?*

When you use an instrument to help you see things, like the northern lights or ultraviolet light, your brain can process them, correct? My eyes are your instrument. I'm showing you what it looks like through my lens. Your mind can process that.

She supposed that was true. If she'd thought for two seconds, she could've realized that.

One would hope, he thought wryly.

His humor was back. *Goodie.*

No rocks moved into their path as they traveled, and their surroundings remained unnaturally quiet. No critters or creatures scurried within the brush. No birds or anything that might resemble them called out in the sparse canopy. She noted details, the ripe air in some places, smelling of moss and decaying trees, and in others the clean and fresh fragrance of blooming flowers. Strange plants covered the forest floor, some leafy and green, others spindly and browning, still more with an array of colors, like the flower she'd picked the night before. Thick substances, like spider webs, dripped from leaves like cold syrup. Gooey, lace-looking stuff dangled from certain trees.

Her mind drifted as they walked, always listening for that voice-presence but not hearing it. Looking for its influence but not seeing it. Tarian pointed out things that were poisonous, at least to him. Vines to stay away from. Hollows and dark places that might harbor an unwelcome surprise. Nothing bothered them, though, something that made him increasingly agitated as time passed.

At one point he slowed and looked behind them.

What? she asked, stepping out of the way in case he needed to move.

He shook his head, but a crease had formed between his brows. *Nothing. Not long now. Keep your vigilance.*

But there was nothing to trouble them. No noise, aside from the wind moving tree branches or an occasional, unexplained drip. They filled their water skins at a small creek he assured her was safe to drink from.

Never drink what you are offered, Zorn's voice said in her head as they continued on. *Only drink from a friend's cup, meant for their mouth alone.*

Tarian held out his water skin.

That rule doesn't really apply in this setting, she thought dryly.

She held her water skin, the lid off, debating. Humans usually couldn't drink from a water source like a river or creek because of the animal feces and bacteria upriver, but she had an enhancement that other Chesters didn't. She healed quickly. Her body was hardier, which surely included her interior. She'd never really questioned that part of things before, but it stood to reason. She could withstand poisons more easily than normal Chesters because of the upgrade. One would assume bacteria would be nothing.

Still, this wasn't just a bacteria issue. It was water in an entirely different realm, meant for faerie kind, not humans. The very makeup of it could be different.

Though that would be true of all water in Faerie. She'd have to drink something sometime, so she might as well start with the purest sample. Maybe go slow and see if she shat herself in a few minutes…

Your mind is truly a dizzying place, Tarian said when she'd put the container to her lips.

There's always a lot to think about.

It seems so, yes. It hasn't been quiet since we started traveling together.

Maybe just walk farther away, where you can't hear my thoughts. That would be quiet. We'd both be happier then.

He tsked. *I didn't say I was* unhappy *with the proximity. Quite the contrary. Besides, what if something jumped out at us? Who would I throw in the way if you weren't in arm's reach? I quite enjoy your saving yourself while I stand by.*

Lean by, you mean.

He laughed softly, his big back shaking. His inked skin glistened in the sunlight, a light sheen of sweat coating the healing flesh. The obsidian circles glimmered, and it seemed like they were part of him. Not placed there but born there. She was about to ask about it when he stiffened.

What is it? She scanned right and left, then looked behind. Nothing.

It's too quiet, he said, picking up his pace. *It's never been this quiet.*

Are you always attacked when walking this path?

Seldom, but that is because I am usually warding creatures away with magic. I'm not doing that now. I haven't been since we started, actually. Even when I am, I usually hear signs of life. This area is more unbalanced than most, but there are still benign creatures. There are prey animals and insects. It is still an ecosystem. I haven't heard any of them.

The memory of the voice-presence echoed in her mind. *It prowls.*

She pondered that as they walked, remembering the pulse when she'd woken up. Remembering when the creatures had fled by the brook before the darkrend revealed itself. Remembered being charged.

She called up each detail, how they had made her feel, the parts that had to be magic. Her mind churned over the memory as they walked, nothing else to do but analyze, thinking of ways in which she could beat the feeling in the future.

It wasn't until the pale blond sun had reached its zenith, when her stomach felt like it had started sucking in her ribs, she was so hungry, that something niggled her awareness. Souls popped up on her radar, along the sides of the path, two on each side. Humanoid, not animal/creature.

Her knife had been low while her mind was distant, but she brought it back up. The movement in the trees was a whisper, the steps nothing more than a *coosh* of compression. Something was there. Lexi's gift, though Daisy was far from mastering or sometimes even remembering it, gave her a fantastic edge.

She stopped Tarian with a thought. Her knife turned into a dagger. A leaf wiggled on the other side where it shouldn't.

Someone is there, she murmured.

They stepped out as one, four large men—males—equally spaced and surrounding them in a square. She quickly scanned for the information she needed: shoulder size, muscle mass, stance, weapons, height, reach, leg size, footwear. A couple other things also trickled in—long hair, large necklaces and adornments practically begging her to choke the men with them, tattoos in a similar configuration. Their weapons were not the faerie blades she and Tarian held, so she assumed they wouldn't change shape. The men held them comfortably, though, with obvious familiarity. They'd be good with them. All the other information pointed to their being fast, experienced, and good swordsmen. They'd give her some trouble.

Luckily, she had Tarian.

But he put his blade away. "She's all yours," he told the males. Then to her, "Good luck, dove. Sorry for tricking you, but...it was necessary. I told you that you wouldn't want my touch for long. Betrayal tends to do that. It was a treat knowing you. I'm sure they'll be gentle."

Chapter Twenty-Three

Zorn's voice: *If you can save yourself, don't wait. Being on the run gives you better odds than being locked in a box.*

Tarian stepped away. One of the largest males stepped forward to grab her.

She knew a moment of pain and confusion at the deception. A moment of vulnerability as she struggled to process his actions. Tarian had been lying about several things, and she'd stupidly let down her guard. After all they'd been through, after how well they'd worked together, he'd always planned to screw her in the end.

But she only took that one moment, because he'd always said he would do it. She should've been ready for this. She should've known this was coming. She'd been a fool for forgetting the dire situation she was in that *he* had created.

So she bottled up the fleeting hurt and quickly morphed it into rage and action.

She launched at them. They were big and strong, but she was quick and had extensive practice in fighting multiple people at the same time, almost always larger than her. *Thank you, Kieran, for the gift of your guys training me.* She'd only do enough damage to get out from under them, and then she'd run. She needed to get far enough, fast enough, to hide. Or hell, take her chances with the wylds.

She darted at the two bringing up the rear, then ducked and jabbed, stabbing the first in the underside of his thigh. That spot hurt like a fucking bitch. He staggered.

The other got hold of her hair, and she stabbed him in the gut. He yanked hard, but she didn't need hair, so she let him pull out as much as he wanted. It would grow back. She slashed him under the arm, kneed him in the balls, and wished she had another weapon so she could get him in both sides at once. Instead, she had to rip across his stomach, not as deep as she'd have liked, but it would take him out of the fight until he could heal enough to keep his intestines.

Another came from behind her, advancing before she could get away from these two. She grabbed the ornaments encircling the neck of Hair Grabber and yanked him closer. He staggered forward in surprise, holding his stomach. She quickly twisted and head-butted the one coming from behind to grab her. She slipped out from between them, catching the legs of the new guy. He staggered, tripped, and got tangled with Hair Grabber. They were not used to catching hogs, and it showed.

She sliced off the ornament she held and thankfully didn't also have to slice off her hair. Hair Grabber let go to hold his stomach and shove off the newcomer at the same time.

She went for the first guy, his expression dark. He held his sword up this time, his legs set in a fighting stance.

The ornament, a sort of heavy amulet, hit him in the nose. He flinched too late, and the pain in his face registered. Before he got around it, eyes watering and squinting shut with the nature of the wound, she'd sliced his forearm, relieved him of his sword, and stabbed him in the shoulder because she fucking missed his neck. She yanked the light and well-made sword back out and threw it at the fourth one, who was wading into the melee. It would have to do.

She was around them in an instant, a moment away from a burst of speed, when magic froze her body, and she teetered over to land on her side. *Fuck.* In times like this, it would be really nice to have magic of her own. She'd own the world if she could compete in a fair fight.

A slow clap echoed along the path.

Her blade pulsed before curling over the back of her hand and into the spell. It kept growing, freeing her arm. Damn she loved this blade. Tarian was a fool for giving it to her.

Except…

Work for me just this once, she begged it. Couldn't hurt. It wasn't like she had any alternatives. *Just this once.*

She held herself still as the blade returned to normal, hoping Tarian hadn't noticed it elongate with the other males groaning and spitting and talking. She waited for Tarian to walk up close to her, his boots near her face, her anger burning hot.

"My goodness, little dove, you—"

She dug her knife into his calf, higher than she'd wanted. Wasting absolutely zero time, never having moved so fast in her life, she slashed down her body to cut away the magic and ran. Ran so hard and fast she could barely feel her legs. She just needed to get out of his range. Just needed—

Her legs locked up, and she was barely able to twist so that she didn't fall on her face. But her knife still worked. She freed herself and hopped up again, then once more, struggling for distance. Trying to—

Her knife was knocked out of her hand, and her whole body was caught. *Fucking magic!*

She breathed hard, thinking about struggling. About twisting or inchworming or anything to get away.

Worry only about that which you can control, she told herself, needing to hear the words in her head. Not

Zorn's this time, but her own. *Learn how to adapt to everything else.*

She relaxed further. She'd lost this battle, but she had not lost the war. She'd see Tarian again. She'd kiss her way through those big guys, with the long hair and half man-buns. She'd kiss her way through a castle, if they took her to one. Through a dungeon. She didn't give a shit. Until she died, he'd be constantly busy. *Constantly.*

She knew it was him by the shoes. And the limp. Then the lean. He was getting good at the leaning...

Her face was frozen, so she snickered in her mind so he could hear it.

Blood soaked part of his pants and dripped down his shoe to the ground. The knife had gone in deep.

"Ouch," he said as he picked up her weapon. "Your love bites really do sting, dove. That one worst of all, I think. And look, now it's my pants you've ruined! I could've just washed these, but holes? I can't pull off a patch. It's simply not my style."

The magic surrounding her disappeared, and she sat up slowly, tilting her head up to offer him a look of loathing. His eyes were dancing, shining brightly, like Daisy fighting for her life had all been one big joke.

"You really do help me make a statement," he said in a murmur, reaching down.

"I have no interest in helping you make a statement."

Daisy's teeth ground together, her expression

displaying utter disgust at Tarian's obvious amusement. He hadn't been betraying her; he'd been once again playing games. He'd been using her for his entertainment, or maybe just showing his people what she was capable of. Because they *were* his people. That was obvious now. Not buyers or traders, but part of his outfit. He'd never intended to give her up, but to have a little fun as they integrated into this next faction.

And she'd fallen for it, hook, line, and fucking sinker.

"All the same," he said. "Here, take my hand. The station is not far away. There's food there. And rest. And healing ointments that everyone will now be needing. You almost killed one of my *Fallen*." He said the last word in a strange accent, almost as though it were a name and not meant to be translated by her blood gift. "I had to freeze the sword you threw in midair. Good aim. Perfect rotation. It's not a magical sword, but it almost seemed like it was…and on your side. Like this clever little knife here." He studied it for a moment. "It likes you better than me. Imagine that. And all the fun times we've had."

She shook her head, really fucking annoyed, not least because she'd known that moment of hurt when he first began the trick. She was an idiot, and he'd proven it. Zorn would slap her silly, and rightfully so.

Images and words and emotions tumbled through her mind from his point of view, starting from when she'd noticed the strangers' presence until right before

Tarian limped over to collect her. These guys were part of his Starwardens, whatever that meant. Four of ten total, they'd been sent out to look for him. The other six were back at the station, like the one they'd stayed in last night, only much bigger. They were all waiting for him. Worried about him.

"Well, bully for you," she groused. "Someone gives a shit about your wellbeing."

There was no denying it, though. She felt their concern. Their closeness to him. They'd known each other for a long time. Since they were kids, if she had to guess.

She saw what she looked like through their eyes, all four. In summary, not much. Scrawny, one thought. Scared, thought another. Weak, pitiful. They didn't seem to notice her filthy hair or the dirt streaking her face. Her pants caked with filth or her bra kinda loose and ill-fitting, on a little lopsided. They might not have noticed, but she did. She scrubbed at her face immediately.

"You don't care that they think so little of your prowess, but you do care about the dirt you collected while trying to stay alive?" Tarian asked, amused.

"My greatest strength is being underestimated," she replied. "I'd much rather do that while looking good. I look an absolute mess."

"You are very vain."

"Like you can talk."

"I can talk, yes. I, too, am very vain. Takes one to know one, as they say."

She took his hand and let him pull her up as the rest of the memories tumbled through.

Can she actually use the knife, or is it just to communicate? Mr. Pitiful asked.

Do all humans look that frail? Mr. Weak asked. *I could snap her in half. How have you even kept her alive?*

Tarian's plan had been simple: threaten her and watch her dance. He'd been trying to show off her skills, for whatever reason. He'd manipulated her into looking like a fool.

"Not even remotely," he whispered, pulling her in close until their energy buzzed between them. Their chemistry set her to vibrating.

The next point of view was just in his eyes, in those vibrant colors, watching her twirl and spin. Dance like a sprite. Like a wild thing. Beauty in motion. She felt the glow of his pride. His smugness at what she could do. He thought she was magnificent, and he wanted to show her off to his people. His toy was a rare and beautiful sight.

She shoved that sentiment away. Fool her once...

"And I assume this means you aren't selling me." She pushed away from him.

"There is not enough gold in all the kingdoms." He held out her knife. "I want to make a deal with you."

"I don't make deals with fae." She paused. "Except for the kissing thing, but you were cheating."

He shook the knife a little. "You will need this. In the wylds and beyond, you will want a way to protect yourself. I want to allow you that freedom. *But*...I can't have you killing my *Fallen*. I know you will try. There are but ten *unloved*." There it was again, that deep accent. "They are all I have. They are all *you* have. They are my protection, and because of that, they are yours. I will ensure you have plenty of enemies to kill. You'll get as much blood as you desire. Just spare their lives. They are innocent in this, just as you are. I am the villain here. Ultimately, if you should kill me, that will be the end of it. You can try killing me as often as you like. I do so love the game. Aim for me, not for them."

She really wished she could read his mind, to see if he was lying. He'd said he couldn't, but how could she believe that now?

Quite easily, he said. *I didn't lie once a moment ago. Think over it and you'll see. I told you I had a cunning way with words. I was not lying at that, either. All fae do, though some are better than others. I've had to become the best of them all.*

She also didn't know why he would barter on behalf of someone else. Almost offering himself up in their stead. That didn't seem like his style.

Despite his words, she didn't know how to trust

him. The recent situation still burned. She needed more pieces of his story.

"And you shall have them, before the end, though you will likely wish you hadn't," he said. "Regardless..." He held the knife higher. "I will return this to you if you do not try to kill the *Fallen*. Not any of the ten. Not ever."

She made a *face* at him. "Really? Not ever? They come for my throat and I just whistle and look the other way?"

A smile tried to peek through his serious exterior. "I will return your knife—"

"For how long?"

The smile grew a bit wider. "I will return your knife...forever, only borrowing it from you if your life is in danger or should you will it. In return, you will not kill or seriously harm my *Fallen*, unless they are trying to kill you. If I should keep this weapon from you, the deal is off."

"Any time I do not have that weapon in my possession, the deal is off."

The smile was in full bloom now. "You continually surprise and impress me. You are also continuing to help me make a statement. Okay, let's see if I can get this right..."

He couldn't. They went at it for a few more rounds, tweaking and adjusting until each of them had a deal they could live with. When they were done, she wanted to sag in fatigue and hunger.

"Yes, let's get back," he said, handing over the knife and the sheath, which had dropped from her person in the struggle.

The others waited where she'd left them, not as straight and tall as when they first stepped into the path. They had a few more holes in their bodies too. A few more cuts and scrapes.

"Daisy, these are four of my ten *Fallen*," Tarian said as he limped beside her.

"What does that mean, the fallen?" she asked.

"They gave up their place in a proper society, and within a proper court, for me. I take their allegiance very seriously."

She wondered why they'd do that for him but didn't ask. She'd undoubtedly learn more through observation and analysis.

Tarian inclined his head, hearing her thought. "This is Lennox." He indicated a male of about six-two with the muscular build that they all possessed, the mark of a warrior. His wheat-colored hair was half tied on the top of his head and then flowed down around his face and over his back and shoulders in gentle waves. A couple braids tamed a portion, but otherwise, it was loose and wild and more than a little pretty. His reddish beard had a ponytail-holder thing right at his chin with a metallic decal. Leather cords and amulets and leather braids circled his neck and hung down his heavily inked-up chest. Except for the one she'd cut off, which was clutched in his fist. A similar mess of tattoos covered his arms and dotted his legs. It was like he'd been in prison and gotten bored and started marking himself up. His nose was straight and came to a fine point, and his light brows hung slightly low over sky-blue eyes. He was a looker with terrible taste in jewelry, and looked exactly like the Vikings in the Chester history books. She wondered if those hadn't actually been fae raiding and pillaging their way through the lands. It would make a lot of sense.

"Ryoden," Tarian said, indicating a slightly slimmer male. He had black hair, straight, with that same topknot, a couple braids, and strands of his thinner hair flowing down his back. His head was half buzzed, with a wavy line through it as a decal. The other two had the same. She assumed the Viking had a similar style hidden within that mane. Ryoden didn't have any facial hair, showing off his square jaw and cleft chin. Also a looker.

Let me remind you, Tarian said with an edge to his mental voice, *what would happen should your lips land on anyone but me. I do not want to have to kill my own men.*

She grinned at the hint of possessiveness in his voice.

The other two, Niall and Darryn, were similar in appearance, as though they might be brothers. A little shorter than the others, they stood at about six feet and had been the last to engage in their skirmish. Niall's long braid rolled over his shoulder and reached down to his stomach. The rest of his wispy hair half floated around his back because it was so thin and light. He really needed a trim. Darryn had a little dusky-brown braid on each side of his forehead with white string or ribbon or something entwined within it. His topknot was wild, as though someone had yanked on it, and more ribbon-entwined braids streaked the otherwise thin and straight hair. They...hopefully had great personalities.

In addition to no shirts, they all wore a sort of skirt with fur around the waistline and a round metallic emblem where a belt buckle might go. The fur dripped down in places, creating pockets or adorning pockets in the otherwise loose and flowing fabric. If Boman was a kilt guy, he'd be interested in this fashion. She wondered if there was anything under it.

Bandages wrapped their various wounds, and blood stained their fingers and skin.

She nodded in hello. They stared back. Their acquaintance was off to a swimming start.

"Let's get moving." Tarian put his hand on Daisy's shoulder. "It's been unnaturally quiet all the way from the station. It has unsettled the *Fallen*."

She and Tarian walked side by side, and the others created a square around them, half tramping in the grasses and brush to keep the formation. It was a bit stupid, really, at least while there wasn't anything hanging around. They could walk on the path like normal people and stop making so much noise.

"You haven't asked if they have the mindgazer magic," Tarian said quietly.

"With you as my jailer, it doesn't matter if they do or don't. I assume you'll tell them anything of relevance if they can't hear it themselves."

"Well, they do. All of my *Fallen* do." He slipped her a side-eye. "You know, in case you want to rein in some of the very blunt observations."

"If they don't want to hear it, they shouldn't be listening to things not meant for their ears. My head is supposed to be a private place. Don't eavesdrop and we'll get along fantastically."

"You practically shout your thoughts. It's hard not to hear the cursed things," grumbled Darryn, the one with a small braid on either side of his forehead. "I do, you know." He glanced back at her, his face hard. "I have a great personality."

Someone behind barked out a laugh.

"Interesting place to put your knife." The other one at the front, Niall, didn't turn to look at it as he commented. "Was that your idea or Tarian's?"

Tarian didn't respond, but after a moment, a couple of them chuckled. Clearly, he'd answered without words.

"It's easier to relay info via the mind, as you've learned," he told her. "You're new to it, so we don't do it as often, but that's the main way the *Fallen* communicate. You can receive our thoughts, and so, when it is relevant, we will share them with you. You can obviously broadcast your thoughts, and so we'll hear them. When any of us wish to keep our thoughts to ourselves, we shield our minds. We'll teach you how to do that."

"Why?" she asked.

"Because you are incredibly distracting," Lennox muttered. "Also, what is a Viking?"

A mangy, unwashed cretin who raped and pillaged his way through Europe, she thought grumpily.

"Her barbs are worse when she thinks them," Lennox growled. "Much more colorful."

"I'd take mangy and unwashed over just plain ugly," Niall called back. "At least she thinks you're a looker, even if you are those other things."

"Careful, Niall," Ryoden said, his voice pleasantly pitched. "You'll lose personality points if you keep it up. Then what will you have?"

"An ugly brother," Niall replied, and they all started snickering...except Darryl, who was pretending not to hear.

"She's like a running commentary of what we're all thinking but too nice to say," Niall said, laughing. "I can't decide if I like it or not."

"When she's not talking about you, I'd say you like it just fine," Lennox said, his voice a deep drum.

"Yeah. That's what I mean."

They kept up their banter throughout the rest of the journey, which thankfully wasn't long. Hot, though. The sun beat down on them mercilessly without so much as a whisper of a breeze. Sweat poured down her face and collected in areas she'd rather it didn't. She finished the water in her skin and denied Tarian when he offered his, not wanting to appear as frail as they'd made her out. Besides, he was the one bleeding, not her. He'd been worse off than her last night, as well. He needed it more.

Occasionally the guys in front would glance back at her, and she'd avert her eyes to the side to avoid their gazes. Obviously Tarian was detailing their journey through their mind communication. No one reacted to any of it, though—not a huff, a laugh, a scoff, nothing. She was thankful. She'd rather not know their thoughts on her journey and her various hiccups and transgressions.

The only good news was that the mind chatter acted like talking to a degree. Two people talking at once was confusing, so while they communicated, they didn't seem to notice her thoughts. She let her mind wander where it would, thinking about various aspects of their journey and noticing the plants and flora they passed. A tune shouldered its way into her mind at one point, and she thought of her family while she mentally sang it. They were probably pissed that they couldn't find her. Scared shitless that something had happened to her. Hopefully they didn't blame themselves. Hopefully they didn't follow her.

That brought a wave of fear that clenched her heart, and so she switched gears, thinking about the scuffle with these fae and how she could've been better. She'd completely ignored Tarian. That had been a mistake. She should've at least thrown a weapon at him to make him scramble. That might've given her those few more seconds to get out of his reach.

Of course, he would've just tracked her down anyway. It had been stupid to run. A waste of energy. But then, she hadn't had time to think, and as she remembered, it was better to run than tuck yourself into a box for someone to bury at their leisure.

When a small collection of shacks, clustered close together, came into view, she was glad for it. The heat and lack of sustenance were getting to her. An electric zigzag appeared in her vision, blocking some of her view—a coming ocular migraine often set off by exactly these circumstances. Her vision would continue to get blotchy, her mind hazy, and a headache would set in. Maybe she'd feel sick or her fingers would start to tingle or go numb. It wouldn't kill her. The cold shivers racing across her body, however, weren't as great. Heat stroke, most likely. Hopefully a slow onset. She hadn't completely stopped sweating yet. She'd need water and shade, preferably cool. As a captive, she probably wouldn't get to make those demands.

It took her a moment to realize the guys in front had slowed, turning around. Tarian pushed in close, one arm around her shoulders and the other scooping her up under her knees.

"What—" She shoved at him weakly, which was

not her finest moment. "I can walk just fine. How'd you even hear that?"

"Mental communication isn't exactly like talking, no," he said, increasing his pace. The added weight made him limp harder. "The mind can do more than one thing at a time. More than two things at once, even. Especially a mind trained to keep track of multiple situations or conversations at once. Your analytical ability is incredibly interesting and a little humbling. Your rambling is entertaining. Your current state is worrying. How bad are you? Don't lie. You're no good at it."

"I'm"—she shoved at him again—"very good at it, actually. I'm a master at it. You just cheat by listening to the truth in my head."

"Yes. Which makes you no good at it with my kind. How bad?"

"Water, food, and a cool and dark place—that's all I need. The possible heat stroke is the only worrying thing, and it isn't too far along yet, I don't think. I'm assuming we're going to stop soon, at the Shanty Township. I'll make it. Please put me down so I don't look like a frail human who needs to be carried through the fae lands by Lord Dick."

He smirked at her. "Lord Dick. I like that. But don't you like being underestimated?"

"I look plenty pitiful, thanks. Plus, I doubt it'll stick after you replay the scuffle earlier. This is your last warning. Please put me down."

"That was a very polite warning—"

In a swift, fluid motion, she swiped her hand up, grabbed the hilt of her knife, turned it blade side up, and bonked him on the head. He squeezed his eyes shut and staggered, letting go of her legs. She twisted to get out of his grip, but anticipating it, he squeezed her upper half to him and grabbed her wrist with the other hand.

I cheat. Remember that, he thought as he secured her. She wheezed within the hold.

He must've directed that into her mind alone, because then he said, "That wasn't very nice, little dove. Now we have to do things the hard way."

His lids slid open, but she could barely make them out. The fuzzy zigzag had grown within her vision, pulsing in time with the oncoming headache, blotting out a solid chunk just off center. She had to look away and see the situation from her peripheral vision. These things were seldom timed well, but in the human world, she had medicine to stave it off. No such luck now.

"Take her knife," Tarian barked, and someone pried it from her fingers.

"Careful," Lennox said in his drum-deep voice. "She has the ability to kill us now."

Tarian hoisted her up and tossed her over his shoulder. A wave of shivers washed over her body, and her head felt woozy. *Yeah, heat stroke. Super.*

"Go." Tarian directed his team on. "Go!"

"I'll...be..." She grunted as his shoulder repeatedly dug into her middle.

"Curse the wingots, Daisy. Do not say you are fine. What are these human maladies? You can't *see*!"

"You guys don't have migraines? Well, technically, it's an ocular migraine. It's a little different."

"No. I need you alive."

"You *need* me alive?"

"Fine, I *want* you alive. I want to show you off to the court as I play with you. I didn't put all this effort into getting you here just for the sun and situation to kill you off. I have plans for you. You will be a much-needed distraction to give me time to work the chalices."

A distraction. She knew something about how liberal he was with those. How deadly they tended to be. That was where he probably thought she'd break.

Well.

She started singing a song to end the thought. Because there would be a way out. She just had to learn the rules, break the rules, and—

Fuck.

So, so bad at telling lies, my little treasure. So bad. We shall see if you can match my cunning. How's that?

He'd regret that challenge. Somehow.

Chapter Twenty-Four

More souls popped onto her radar, and she could hear gasps and feet crunching and way too much silence for a collection of bodies. He hadn't been lying. Six of them came up to greet him. Adding to the previous four, that made ten in all.

She dangled uselessly off Tarian's back, figuring she might as well take a page from his book and *lean* into it. Her arms dangled and so did her head, letting her hair rain down the back of him. Blobs of color entered her limited field of vision, and she closed her eyes against it. She could feel the souls. She knew they were gathering around to take a gander at what he carried in.

His toy, ladies and gentlemen, that was what. His fun little plaything. What joy. *You're all miserable wretches. I hope every last one of you gets foot fungus and dies from complications.*

Someone spat out laughter and another chuckled. She did not see the humor in this situation.

The material under Tarian's feet changed from dirt to something like sand. Something soft that made him limp more. Then a crunch, like gravel or rock. They'd clearly doctored up this homestead. Next his feet thumped on something like wood, hollow like a porch. Metal hinges creaked and cool air greeted them. She shivered against the change but sighed in relief. Her body didn't realize this was a safe haven, but her mind did.

"Here we go." He lowered, his knee hitting the ground and his hands braced against her back. He pulled her away, and she opened her eyes, but it was awkward looking at someone when you couldn't see details. "Here. Here's a bed. Lie down. I'll get you some water."

The image of the room filled her mind. Wood slats for walls, something like a dresser along the side, and two small windows. The bed right behind her took up almost all of the leftover space, about the size of the one in the shack they'd slept in last night. Apparently, they'd be sharing again.

"We don't have any extra lodgings," he said as he poured water. "You are welcome to sleep on the floor, but without a rug, it won't be very comfortable."

"Quite the gentleman," she said sarcastically, and

sat down on the edge of the bed. Her entire body sagged in fatigue.

"I never claimed to be one. Besides, it wasn't just me scooting closer last night."

"Yes, it was. I was on my side of the bed, where I started," she said in a haughty tone.

"Hmm."

She felt his soul approach and opened her eyes when he neared. Around the throbbing lightning blob taking up most of her vision, she made out the definition of his hand and took the glass of water. Her head throbbed. "Thanks."

"Drink. I'll get more. Niall is readying food, and Kalia is preparing something you can wash with. We'll look for some suitable garments from the females. I'm sure someone has something that will fit you."

She drained the glass and waited patiently for him to keep refilling until she didn't think it was wise to drink any more. He placed a damp cloth against her forehead and lingered for a moment, trailing his fingers down the side of her face to rest on her shoulder. Even though she had a continual desire to punch him in the face after his little stunt, the smooth sensation of his touch was more blissful and soothing than the cloth. She felt her muscles unwind.

"I'll be back shortly with food. Rest. We're safe here. Each of these little dwellings has its own ward. Once it is set, it'll keep anything and everyone out. I'll do it when I return. All you have to do now is rest until dawn."

"And then?"

He paused. "We'll worry about that when we need to."

The door closed softly behind him, and she slipped the damp cloth to her eyes and breathed deeply, letting the headache pound.

Then they would be heading to the Obsidian Kingdom, of course, where the next phase of her journey for survival would begin. Brawn and her sword wouldn't get her through that one. Or not only those things. Cunning and treachery, too. It would be cheating and politics. Demigod Kieran had started training her for that at age fifteen. She'd shown a knack for it at the very first Demigod convention where she initially met Tarian. She'd been studying it ever since, helping where she could, sitting in on meetings whenever they would let her. She found it fascinating. Intriguing. Fun, even.

But these past few years, it had always been Kieran and Lexi who'd been playing for keeps. Now it would be her, and she didn't have a team to advise her. She'd be playing solo and seeing how she stacked up against the fae.

She startled awake. The room lay dark and still around her. A strange feeling skittered across her skin.

A look beside her and Tarian wasn't there. He'd come back with food some time ago, when the sun still illuminated the shades he'd pulled, but left again to give her some privacy to wash up. He said he'd be back after he discussed some business with his *Fallen*. There was no telling how long ago that was.

She felt worlds better. Her headache was only a dull throb. She was still tired, needing more sleep and soon maybe more to eat, but she felt mostly normal.

She sat up, that strange feeling unsettling, like something wasn't quite right. Then again, what *was* right? She was a captive in a strange land with an uncertain future. Still...

She squinted in the low light, the murky darkness hinting at unseen horrors. Magic curled and twisted all around her, *thrushing* in the quiet space. Or was that her imagination?

The floor was cold on her feet as she crossed the room and pulled back the shade. The soft glow of moonlight fell across her skin and the fabric slip Tarian had given her to wear. Darkness shifted around the trees and bushes not far away. It blanketed the grassy plain.

Nothing moved out there in the night. Unlike earlier, when she'd been washing, dressing, and eating, there weren't any strange calls or odd-sounding birdsong. No creatures skittered through the brush. Currently there was nothing. An absence of sound, it felt like. Like everything in the area had taken off.

Like a big predator had moved in.

Shivers washed over her this time. Threads of unease started to tighten her chest. She knew it before the voice sounded in her head.

It's here.

Damn right it was here. The darkrend. She could almost feel its unnaturalness as it moved through the fabric and magical folds of the wylds. As it shed *wrongness* within the lush, strange lands. It was a disease to this place, plucking at the natural order and creasing what should have been smooth.

You can feel the danger now, the voice said. *Heed it.*

She could, it seemed. So she did.

She dashed through the room and yanked open the door. The wood porch led down to small rocks, like gravel. She didn't bother going back for her shoes. There might not be time. She ignored the pain as she ran over the rocks, quickly taking stock of the collection of shacks in a large circle, it looked like, with a central hub. If Tarian didn't sleep in that hub, it was the meeting place.

Her heel came down on the point of a rock. She sucked in a pained breath but wouldn't allow herself to lose speed. She wanted to knock against the side or shout for him, but there was no telling where the creature might be. The wall of the hub-shack ended, leaving room for a wide porch. She rolled under the banister and hopped up.

The roar drove fear directly into her heart. Branches cracked and tore. The compression of huge feet slamming down rattled the rocks. She sprinted across the porch and to the door right as it opened. Soft light spilled across her, and a wide-eyed Lennox stopped short. Terror was etched into every line on his body.

"Get to safety, you idiot!" she yelled at him, shoving him back into the room.

His body was ripped to the side, and Tarian took his place, grabbing her around the shoulders, turning in a hurry, and spinning her into the room. He let go and slammed the door shut as another roar shook the walls. Her body began to shake.

"Get below and set the ward!" Tarian yelled as he darted to the corner to douse the light.

She turned to Lennox, who was frozen solid. He'd never been this close to a darkrend before. The learning curve was rough.

A pretty woman sat in the corner, with the same style of hair as the others, her eyes wide in shock. Niall was next to her, appearing perplexed, and that was a very strange response to the current situation.

"Go, go, go!" she yelled, waving her arm.

Lennox unfroze first as a pulse rocked through the room. The creature was seeking them out. Either it hadn't seen her a moment ago, or once she went out of sight, it had lost her location. She hoped the latter, because that would indicate it wasn't a very smart beast.

Quiet, she thought as loudly as possible. They said she could broadcast, so she assumed it was the strength of the thought. Couldn't hurt. *Set the ward. We gotta set that ward.*

Lennox pulled up a trapdoor at the side of the room and motioned her forward. The two at the table rose and hurried over as Tarian bumped into her back. He grabbed her shoulders and directed her on as the others started to descend.

We need to close all accesses to the building in order to set the ward, Tarian explained. *There's no telling how long that creature will stay. We'll go to our bedchambers and wait it out. It's time for bed anyway.*

Shivers crawled all over her. She turned slowly, the feeling of dread arresting her.

"Get below," she whispered, knowing what would happen. Feeling it. "Hurry, Tarian. Get below." The breath was barely leaving her mouth.

He grabbed her hand as she finished turning. As her gaze ventured out the window. As she met the eyes of an enormous creature made of nightmares.

Its body was only partially obscured by the trees. Huge, yellowed teeth curved down from red-and-black gums. Its head was a flatter version of her idea of a werewolf, its nose pulled up like a canine's but its forehead like a human's. Batlike ears rose from its head, and its body resembled a gorilla drawn by a five-year-old who didn't have a firm grip on proportions. Each hand had claws as big as her whole person, and in about two seconds, it would rip into this hub.

Go! Tarian shouted in her mind, yanking her toward the trapdoor.

The compression of footprints shook the ground. Its roar tried to freeze her, but she fought past it and yanked Tarian with her. Lennox waited at the bottom of a ladder.

Catch me, she hollered, dropping into the hole. He gripped her sides and hurriedly moved them out of the way.

A cacophony of destruction rattled the floorboards above her. It drowned out all sound. Wood splintered and metal whined. The creature had charged into the structure. There'd be no setting the ward here.

Tarian jumped in, holding the edge of the trapdoor. He let go at the last moment. The slap of wood as it hit the frame was lost to the rest of the carnage. All light cut out. She felt his hands on her, holding her to him, then saw images filtering in her mind, a tunnel partially lit in ultraviolet.

She closed her eyes as he directed her. A structural groan filled the tunnel. Dirt and rock shivered away from the walls. The ground shuddered.

Another roar, this one frustrated, like the first time she'd lost it. Then a pulse.

Lennox slowed, ready to pause. Ready to succumb

to that magical freeze button. To the fear. The two in front of him had as well. She pushed them on, Tarian with her.

The tunnel reached a circular area with four paths. Two stopped at the first on the right, looking back at Tarian. His hand tightened on her shoulder. She could see his nod from his point of view, but he didn't share what was said. The female branched off left and paused as well. Another roar and more crashing walls. It sounded like it was stomping through the rubble.

Let's go, dove, Tarian said, stepping in front of her and taking her hand. It was back to the action hero again.

Despite the terror of the situation, she felt his amusement.

The tunnel curved, and he followed it before they hit a fork. He didn't hesitate to go left. Here he slowed, sneaking, being quiet. She followed suit, holding his hand, eyes closed, watching through his vision and trying not to trip on his feet.

The tunnel dead-ended at a ladder, not unlike the one under the ruined shanty-hub. He paused with one hand on a rung and the other holding hers, looking back the way they'd come. The earth trembled.

She saw herself in his gaze and couldn't believe how confident and badass she looked, with her determined expression and set jaw. She looked like she was ready to go out and confront that beast single-handedly. Muscle memory, obviously. Show no fear so the enemy or bully or magical person who hates Chesters doesn't think she's weak and easy pickin's. Internally, however, she was absolutely shitting herself.

Did you leave the door open or closed? Tarian asked her.

She racked her brain, trying to remember.

He touched her face delicately, his thumb tracing her cheek. *It's okay,* he said. *I can look in your memories...*

Open, I think, she admitted.

Here's the situation. I need us both upstairs, with the trapdoor and main door closed, in order to set the ward. Once I do, the ward will render this shanty-hub, as you so lovingly call it, indestructible. It can stomp on it all it likes and only get a sore foot for its trouble, okay? Then we'll rest.

I should be the one to go, she said grudgingly, clutching his soft tunic. He'd freshened up as well. *I know what its version of danger feels like. Let me go—*

His thumb moved over her lips. *You'll be right behind me, little dove—*

But she'd already slithered and pushed her way past him to the ladder, feeling it in her gut that she needed to do this. That she had dialed in on that creature and was the best person to ensure their survival. At least in the first phase of this endeavor.

She felt his head shaking, confused yet intrigued that she should be able to ignore him and get her way so easily. She felt his complete unwillingness to let her take the lead, but they'd made a pact in the caverns to trust each other when their lives depended on it. So he sighed. And shifted his weight. And finally said, *Okay. But Daisy, be careful. If we can't do it, we'll sleep in this tunnel.*

Can't we go ask for admittance into one of the other shanties?

Not after their ward is put in place. They won't be able to hear us knocking and will be beyond the reach of mind touch. But that's okay. That creature won't stay out there forever, and it can't blow fire or fit into these tunnels. If we can't get that door closed, we'll just pass an uncomfortable night together. It'll be fine. We have options.

Assuming she didn't get seen at the wrong time and killed before she could get back to the tunnel.

Assuming that, he said.

She shook her head and saw the flash of uncertainty on her face before it hardened again. How often did she let that expression through, she wondered? That physical glimpse into what was really going on in her mind.

Every time you do something that requires great courage, he whispered in her mind, like a caress. *We are all mortal with the right wound.*

It must've been one of the fae's sayings, immortal until they were killed.

She nodded and felt for the rungs, made it to the top, and shoved him out of her mind. He fled immediately, having felt her desire for space. Or maybe she was getting the hang of things.

Her hand curled around the latch, and she clued in to her surroundings. The wylds were waiting, tricksy and playful and ready for games, violent or fun or both, one never knew. Within that, though, was the darkrend. Twisting and rolling and turning the lush life around it to ash. A scourge. Unbalance. It was plain as day, like being able to tell if someone was magical or not just by watching them move. Watching them interact. At the heart of it, that was nothing more than a feeling, too. Like this.

She had great instincts—Zorn had always said so. She'd lived by them, as he'd always said she should.

The darkrend searched. Looked. Destroyed. Its attention was elsewhere, but the gaping hole that was the doorway to their shanty stood open. The moonlight from the window danced across the dark space.

She edged the trapdoor open slowly. Tarian moved over her feet, his chest touching her bare ankles. He was ready to go up right after her.

If it doesn't see, it doesn't know, she thought to herself.

The trapdoor opened away from the wall, shielding her. She peered around it, only able to see a slice out of the front door. Through it, the moonlight showed the darkrend in all its glory, ripping through the wreckage it had caused, trying to scratch its way to the bottom. It knew she and the others had disappeared within it.

She crawled out to minimize obvious movement, watching where she put her hands and careful not to slide against the floor. She bear-crawled to the side of the room before standing against the wall. The window, the shade pulled up, stood to her right. Tarian waited in the trapdoor opening, watching her. She nodded at him, giving him the all-clear.

Except for stalling to gently close the trapdoor after him, he came faster but just as quietly, flattening against the wall with her. Nothing to it.

A pulse rocked the room, dense and focused, looking for its prey. The sounds of scratching and stomping in the destruction slowed, the creature's focus shifting. Another compression came, then another, beating into them. In a moment it would know where they were, if it didn't already.

Shit, she mentally bit out as her teeth chattered with fear. Tarian's fingers curled around her wrist. *Go,* she mentally barked, and ran.

He was right behind her. The compression of huge feet shook the ground, heading right for them. Tarian and Daisy reached the opened door together. The darkrend lunged, ten feet away, half the length of its body.

"Say the magic," she shouted, her palms hitting the door as his did. They slammed it shut together. The lock latched, the last word leaving his mouth at the same time as the darkrend hit. The wood bowed as though in slow motion, started to split, and then all went still. Silence filled the space.

The small slice of light that the split in the door allowed showed moving shadows. A flurry of activity. In moments, however, the creature slowed. The slit in the door turned pitch black, and then the huge mass was gone. The light bled through.

Tarian released an audible breath. *We made it—*

A concussion of air made Tarian and Daisy jump. She reached out with shaking hands, grabbing his tunic. He took hold of her wrist and reeled her in.

"We shouldn't feel that," he whispered, staring at the door. He stepped away, keeping her close. "The ward stopped it from coming through. It held. We should be good. We shouldn't feel..."

A soft thumping sounded from the roof. Their heads jerked that way, and she could feel him shaking right along with her. He wasn't impervious to its terror, or the terror of the moment.

Another thump, this one louder. A little dust shook loose from the roof.

Tarian's fingers tightened against her.

An eye filled the window. It darted around until it locked on them. Its pupil contracted.

They jumped together. Tarian swore under his breath. The creature leaned back. Teeth flashed in the window, and a roar bled through the ward. The eye appeared once more before it lunged forward, its teeth gnashing at the window. At the walls. Thumps and scratching got through the magic. The structure groaned and bowed.

Tarian dragged Daisy toward the back of the shanty. She clutched at him.

"Leave or go," he said softly. "Leave or—I mean, stay or go. Strengthen the ward or pull it down entirely so we can get through the trapdoor."

"If you pull it down, all of this will come crashing down on our heads in a matter of seconds. One of us would make it down. The other would not. There wouldn't be time, and the space isn't big enough for both of us at once."

They looked at each other, his eyes so open. He wouldn't leave if it meant she'd die. She saw it there, lurking, confusing him but true. She could see he would not leave her to that creature. Not after what they'd been through. Not after what they'd endured and escaped together.

And he could read in her mind that she wouldn't either. He might need to die eventually, but not like this. Not after saving her. She'd made this decision before, and here she was making it again. Maybe it didn't make sense, but she didn't care.

"I can try to strengthen it," he said softly, looking at the bed. "With a chalice. I haven't yet tried to wield the power directly, but I can try."

"Try." She looked at the bed as well. "But...where are they?"

He squeezed her arms and hurried past her. He

ducked beside the bed as the shanty rumbled and her heart hitched. He dragged out first one pack, then the other. He'd magically sent them to this location while in the cavern. She'd been sleeping on top of the crystal chalice and hadn't even known.

"That was removed," he said as he pulled out a flat object speckled in black. It gleamed in the low light. "I didn't want to go traipsing after you when you inevitably grabbed it and ran."

He reached for her hand, and she took it without thinking, allowing him to drag her toward the front door.

"If that thing gets through, we might as well run for it," he murmured in explanation. "No sense delivering ourselves in a box."

His smirk said he was paraphrasing her. It was still true, so she didn't respond.

He paused, looking down on her. He grabbed her around the waist, pulled her against him, and kissed her, hard, branding his kiss on her lips. It didn't take a genius to know he worried it might be their last.

"Stay near me," he said after he'd grudgingly released her, turning toward the door and half looking over his shoulder at her. "Touch me so I know you're there."

He could hear in her thoughts that she was there, since her mind never stopped spinning, but she did as he said, flinching with the next thump. The creature moved away from the window, climbing onto the roof again. The structure groaned under its weight. Tarian's whole body shook against hers—or was that hers shaking against his? She clung to him as he dropped his head, the chalice held in both hands, his eyes closed.

She heard its vibration before she felt the buzz in her body, running from him into her. Sloshing around inside her, churning and fizzing, electrifying her blood before rolling back through to him. Soon all she felt was that buzz, everywhere, inside and out, in her ears and wavering her vision. It felt like it was shaking her teeth loose, it was so powerful. He gasped, feeling the same thing.

She released her hands to push away, to shrug off this horrible feeling, but in a moment, it subsided. The thumping from above dimmed. The silence resumed.

He dropped the chalice and breathed deeply. It landed heavily and bounced away. A droplet of sweat fell from his bow as he sagged.

"Well," he said into the dim interior, glancing at the ceiling. Still no sound. No thumping or dust shivering down. This time his ward would hold. They could be sure of it. The extra boost of power had helped.

And now he knew how to use the chalices.

"At least we didn't piss ourselves when confronted by a darkrend." He reached for her hand. "Take that, Celestials."

Despite her last realization, she heaved out a laugh, her face buried into his back. "I thought you said those wards could handle anything." She still shook, but the tremors were receding. That reaction was magically created. Next time, she'd need to push harder to ignore it, mind over matter.

Next time? He twisted to look at her. *Blight destroy me, there better never be a next time.* He shook his head while pulling her away from the door. "Usually, I would never admit vulnerability but...I need to hear our voices right now. And nothing else. That was... I don't have words for what that was. That creature wasn't balanced. It had magic way beyond its capabilities."

He tugged her toward the window, going at an angle. At the side of it, he glanced through, pulled his head back quickly, then did it again. He breathed a sigh of relief.

"It's somewhere else at present."

"Probably on the roof," she said.

"Yes. Thank you. I was trying not to envision that."

She spat out a laugh as he lowered the shade. Once done, he tugged her to the back of the room toward the bed. He turned to face her, looking down into her eyes. The dim interior made the gorgeous green of his irises impossible to see, but softened his sharp cheekbones and severe jaw, enhancing his handsome face. "I can't imagine enduring one of those alone. Lennox, battle-hardened and afraid of absolutely nothing, froze. I've never seen that in all my days. Look"—he held up his hand—"I'm still shaking."

So was she. She felt the tremors all through her body.

"But from just one meeting," he went on, "you learned enough to keep your cool. You saved lives tonight. Lives of those who would imprison you. Lives of those you had no obligation to save. For that, I thank you."

She hadn't thought about things like that. She hadn't thought about anything at all. She needed to get help, and she knew Tarian would be that help.

"Survival," he whispered.

Survival, she thought, because what else would it be? What else would any of this trip be? Stay alive long enough to get free. To save herself. She had family back home, wondering where she was. Wondering if she was okay. She hated the idea of hurting them with her death. Of leaving them.

On that note, she looked at the ceiling. At the door. Felt a tremor of uncertainty.

He shook his head and pulled off his tunic, exposing his delicious chest with the single tattoo that looked like a metallic necklace. "No thumps," he said softly, kicking off his shoes and pushing down his pants, showing a human pair of boxer briefs.

She quirked an eyebrow.

He looked down at them and shrugged with a lopsided smile. "Fae don't wear a lot of undergarments. I find these more...comfortable when I'm working."

"You're not working."

He glanced at the window. "Like hell I'm not."

Fair.

He stepped closer to her, and his gaze raked up her body, devouring every inch. It burned a trail from her toes, along the slip he'd given her, to the budded peaks of her breasts. He gave her a sensual and provoking smirk at the fervor he saw lurking in her eyes.

Just his look dazzled her. Fluttered her stomach. His appreciation for her body and who she was glowed in his eyes.

The smirk still in place, he bent to pull back the covers on the bed. Then he straightened, watching her, daring her to go next. Daring her to follow his lead and make the next move.

Breath catching, strangely nervous, she silently pulled the slip up and away from her body. She still wore panties, but only that, exposing the rest of her to the air and his eyes.

His gaze dipped, taking her in. He reached forward as though he couldn't help himself and ran his palms along the sides of her belly and up. His thumbs grazed the edges of her breasts, not venturing any farther.

"Daisy," he said, like he was praying to one of his gods. "Such a dainty name that fits this petite, doll-like creature I see before me. And so perfectly hides the monstrous beast that rages within. It is truly a pleasure."

After a glance to the shade, knowing that if the ward failed they'd be dead anyway, she pushed the outside world out of her mind. Like last night, she focused solely on the moment. This moment. There was no better time to do things she might regret. Things that might not be wise.

Things she'd wanted to do since she'd met him on that ledge. Since she'd first set eyes on him on that beach.

She ran her hands up his arms, feeling the muscle, to his shoulders, dipping her fingers into the grooves. Flowing over the bumps. She moved in closer, angling up her face. Closer still, feeling the heat and electric chemistry jumping back and forth between them. His hands stayed where they were, trembling but not because of the threat outside. Not because of a moment ago. But because of *this* moment. Because of her.

She reached for the back of his neck and applied pressure, pulling his lips toward hers. Her other hand ran along his arm to his wrist, applying pressure there, too. She pulled his palm to cover her breast, feeling the fire in her core when he sucked in a breath.

His lips met hers, and they fell toward the mattress, straining to get closer. She hooked her heel around his thigh as his weight covered her. As his lips devoured hers. He pulled her more firmly onto the bed and settled between her thighs, aligning his body exactly as she craved. She hooked her other leg over his hip, her arms around his shoulders, her tongue dancing with his. His hips pushed forward, and she saw stars. It felt better than she could've ever imagined.

She strained against him, feeling her control wobbling. Wanting to free-fall, as he'd said. It would be as safe now as it could be, a ward away from being ripped apart, trusting magic she didn't know anything about or understand. She'd take life as it came. There was no other way. Not right now.

His hips moved against her erotically, and her legs tightened. Her eyes fluttered. She needed to stop and remove the clothes in their way. Wanting to end this craving for him, feel him deeper. To let him consume her. But this felt so damn good. So damn perfect.

The kiss deepened. Her desire flowered until it grew too large to contain. Too much to understand. She clung to him as she writhed, as he thrust, hard, punishing strokes that hit perfectly. She hit a peak and came apart, shuddering against him. He groaned and shuddered with her, tightening his hold on her, burying his face into her neck.

She shivered while he breathed deeply, kissing her skin and lifting up again to softly kiss her lips.

She reached between them, knowing she could get him ready for round two—for the real thing. As her thumbs hooked into his boxer briefs, though, he reached down and stayed her hands.

"No," he murmured against her lips. "I won't take this from you. You'll hate me before the end. You'll regret this."

"I don't regret your kiss." She proved it by pressing her lips to his. "We might as well revel in this feeling while we can. Who knows if we'll ever find it again. We could never be forever, you and I, since one of us is bound to kill the other, but we will make an amazing *right now*."

He sucked in her bottom lip before backing off. "No, Daisy. I have your kiss. That is enough. That is too much, actually. I swore I would never trap another as I did the first. I lost control and took your kiss, but I will not take any more. Please, let me worship your body tonight. Tomorrow, we'll start the next phase of our journey."

His kiss was deep and intense, and she felt herself melting against him. He kissed down her neck and across her chest, taking in a budded peak and rolling his tongue around it. She groaned as his fingertips slid down the inside of her thigh and dipped into her panties. His lips continued down, trailing heat. She pushed her knees wider, and he dipped two of his fingers in and curved, stroking as his thumb touched down.

She jolted with pleasure, her fingers entwined in his hair. His mouth got to her panty line, and he pulled them down her legs.

"You won't need these," he whispered, dropping them to the floor.

"If we have to run for it, I'll be totally nude and you'll still have underwear. How is that fair?"

He paused in coming back to her. She could barely make out the details of his face in the darkness. With a nod, he twisted to his butt and slipped his briefs down his legs. He dropped them on top of hers. Daisy's mouth watered from what she saw, bobbing hard against his flat stomach. His length was thick and long, enticing her to touch. To taste and explore. Her gaze found and stuck to the metal glinting at the end of that hard shaft. She paused, transfixed. Riveted.

"Fae pierce their..." She squeaked, then cleared her throat.

She could just make out his wicked grin. "Is that a blush? What's the matter, Mistress So-Confident-in-All-Things? Have you never seen a piercing before?"

Truthfully...no, she hadn't. Many other places, but not *there*. She knew it happened, but she'd never experienced it. She would've never assumed fae practiced it.

Daisy salivated to taste it. To flick her tongue across it.

He groaned, obviously hearing her thoughts.

"Remember that desire," he said as he lowered between her thighs, his hot breath washing her apex. "You will get your chance when you are kneeling in front of me. In front of my whole court."

The prospect seemed absurd. Ridiculous. Rage inducing. But she couldn't think about any of that right now. He lowered his mouth to her body and all her thoughts fled. The concerns of her reality were a problem for another day. Right now, she was occupied. She'd survived a vicious monster—again—felt vicious magic, and really needed a release and then sleep. Right now, she needed his tongue to do exactly what it was doing.

He licked up her center and sucked, swirling his tongue around her most sensitive area. He threaded his fingers into her and her eyes rolled into the back of her head. She yanked on his hair a little, groaned, and arched enough that it would probably make her sore the next day. Magic washed all down her body in the most complex sensations she'd ever experienced, and it felt like his weight covering her. Him inside of her. Him everywhere. The air danced and sparkled with his power, electric sizzles that ran across her skin and down into her body. His mouth pulsed glorious suction; his fingers and magic worked in dizzying tandem until she lost all semblance of self-control. She turned into the wild thing he'd predicted, moaning and begging and maybe once calling him a god. Near the edge, when she was braced on the cliff and strung out in bliss, control long gone, her dignity a thing of the past, he pulled away to blow softly on her wet and tortured core.

"You fucking—" She writhed like a woman possessed, nearly crying with need. "Please. Please. *Please*."

His magic took hold of her, his mouth touched back down, and she came utterly undone. The gush of pleasure was so extreme that her sensibilities wobbled. His following love bites gave her torturous aftershocks, and then he was beside her, gathering her limp form up into his arms and hugging her close.

"At least let me use my hand," she murmured, turning into his warmth, her eyes drifting closed. "Let me touch you and explore that terrific body."

"No. I worry that if you touch me, I won't be able to keep in control. I won't be able to keep you free of another tether to me. Earlier was enough. You need your sleep. Rest, dove, for tomorrow everything will change. There will be no more obstacles in our way. Tomorrow, we go into the viper's nest."

Chapter Twenty-Five

It was dawn when they awoke again, entwined together, wrapped in each other's arms. Light flared against the drawn shades in pulses of color.

Tarian sat up quickly, startling her. He untwisted his legs from around hers and swung them over the edge of the bed. In a moment he was striding, nude and glorious, to the window. He pulled up the shades and looked out, turning his head to the right and flexing his whole body.

"It looks like the Celestials are taking care of the darkrend problem," he murmured into the din.

She pulled back the sheets and met him there. He turned, leaning his shoulder against the wall at the side of the window. With his other hand, he drew her in so she could see, her back against his front, his palm spread against the bare flesh of her belly.

Just across the clearing, in the sparse trees of the area, the darkrend struck at the sky with its huge claws. Even without sound she could recognize its roar trying to freeze its prey. Or, in this case, his attackers.

Against the lightening and changing colors of the sky, pink tinging the pale blue, beautiful, winged shapes dove and spun around the great beast. Explosions of light hit off its great head or hulking shoulders, knocking it back or forcing it to hunch down. They spiraled toward it in pairs or groups, slicing into it with their weapons and their magic.

She stood there, transfixed. Riveted. The beauty of their movements, of their wings, absolutely entranced her. They were efficient in their viciousness and deadly in their strikes.

The creature raged at them, slashing the air. The Celestials dove to avoid its claws, never ceasing their strikes. Full dawn blazed by the time the beast went down, the twisted tormentor no match for the protectors of the wylds.

The silence felt heavy in the wake. Like the sound had deadened not just outside the room, but within as well.

She turned back to find Tarian staring, his eyes hard but hollow. He looked frustrated but also... forlorn. She studied him harder, wondering about those conflicting emotions.

He glanced down at her, and his expression cleared. "That's the darkrend taken care of. We're free to—" His gaze shot back to the window. His whole body tensed, and he moved quickly, running his hand through the air. The sound from outside rushed back in, wind shaking the leaves, wings beating against the sky. He'd taken down the ward.

Confused, she looked back out and started. Three Celestials were coming their way, their long, straight hair blowing back from their faces, skin so smooth it looked like she was viewing them through a soft focus lens. Their clothes were elegant and refined, declaring sensibility and nobility even though two of the three were heavily splattered in a strange, greenish goo. The creature's blood, maybe, or a defense she'd never seen.

"Get away from the window!" Tarian barked, and magic shoved her back.

She reached out to brace her hand on the wall.

He'd stepped into his pants and now donned the tunic he'd worn last night.

"Come here. Quickly." He beckoned to her, and she complied. "Here." He draped her garment over her head and helped her into it before bending with her and directing her under the bed. "Hide. *Quickly*. Do not show yourself, no matter what. I'll cover you with magic to hide the stamp of the crystal chalice."

"I thought once we were beyond the Faegate, we were safe here."

"*I* am safe here, as a fae. You are a human who doesn't belong and who slashed a few wings and punctured a few Celestial bodies. They won't be as inclined to give you impunity."

She slid under, grabbing her panties as she did so. He moved toward the door, though she was only able to see his boots and then his ankles. No sooner had he reached it, a knock came.

The door swung open, allowing in a blast of chilly morning air fresh with the scent of blooming flowers and crisp green flora.

"What is it?" Tarian asked in a cold voice laced with authority.

"Pardon me, your—" The female voice cut off, the tone going from apologetic to utterly confused. Her voice then hardened to commanding. "What is the nature of this outpost?"

"It is a lawfully established way station belonging to the Obsidian Court, brokered by me, Tarianthiel Drystan Windryker, stationed prince of the Obsidian Throne, bearer of the five seals and carrier of royal, unseelie magic. If you had been doing your duty and scouting the land as you ought, you would've known of this place ages ago. But at least you finally brought down the darkrend, hmm? One only needed patience, it seems. That creature had obviously been twisted for some time. Out of balance. It destroyed one of my buildings. I'll be seeking compensation from your Dusk Sentinel. Now, don't trouble me again. I have important matters to see to."

Daisy's world bled of color as silence met Tarian's response. One of the Celestials offered a crisp retort, but Daisy's ears had started ringing. A prince? She'd been captured by a fucking *prince*? No wonder his power level and magical ability were off the charts. No wonder he had the mindgazer magic. He was at the top of the kingdom's hierarchy.

Her status as a toy, as a pawn in his political games, took on a more dangerous edge. He wasn't just a player. He could rig the game.

"A prince, yes," Tarian said softly, crouched next to the bed. He flattened to the floor so he could look in at her. The door had been shut, the Celestials apparently appeased and on their way. She hadn't noticed. "A lofty title for someone who is little more than a thief for that court."

"So am I, but I don't have a crown to affix when I go to work."

He didn't crack a grin. So serious. So somber. "You should."

She shook her head before resting her forehead against her forearms. Her situation seemed so much bleaker.

"You said the Obsidian Throne was set to be inherited by rotten, strategizing children. The scourge of the realm."

"Yes. And it holds true."

"Yet, to have that title, are you not one of those children?"

"I was not born into this title. I was given it. Trapped with it. Taunted by it. My power granted me admittance, among other things. I am not in line for the crown. They would not suffer my sitting on their throne. I am exactly as you thought, Daisy. A powerful thief with a title to open doors. An errand boy for royalty. A crook. A murderer. A jester who doesn't tell jokes, but who is one. I am their blunt tool, and they titled me for the pleasure of their disdain."

"And the king and queen?"

"They are no parents of mine." The viciousness of his tone washed cold down her spine. "Come on," he said. "It's time we go."

A heavy weight lodged in her stomach as she climbed out and slipped on her panties. His gaze was cold, like ice. Hard. No amusement showed through his steely gaze, no teasing laughter in his flat voice. Right now, he looked the noble royal he claimed to be.

She slipped on her boots and followed him without a word. Without a thought, really, if that were possible. The others joined them next to the ruined hub, debris scattered every which way. She looked where the darkrend had been felled, but no beautiful, winged fae filled the sky. They'd done their job and left.

No one spoke out loud or to her at all. Tarian grabbed her hand, his soft touch the only thing reminiscent of the man she'd gotten to know in the last few days. The one who had never physically hurt her—the one with a tender side and who was prone to tease and quick with a witty reply. The one she'd wanted deep inside her last night, a stark contrast to this prince headed back to his court. Maybe he'd been right to refuse her. He'd shown her an act of mercy. Maybe he'd done her a favor.

It is the last favor I will ever do for you, he said into her mind, that hard tone cracking just around the edges. *The last I can do for you, Daisy. Forget the man you've known these last couple days. That man is about to be put aside. Has to be, if I hope to survive. In his place will be a monster. A master manipulator. Your tormentor. I will do it so it looks like fun. So it looks like I enjoy it. I'll do it for an audience. And I will be convincing.*

Shivers coated her body, but not from the words. He'd said many things since she first reconnected with him on that ledge. Some true, many not. Right now, it was his dull, hard, dead tone. His lack of humor. His hopelessness. He was tucking away his personality so he could fill whatever role was expected of him—a role he loathed, with fae he despised.

They stopped beside one of the shanties, this one the largest of all, almost like a hulking black barn. Lennox and a female she hadn't seen before pulled open the doors. Inside waited great, winged beasts with shaggy hides, wide backs, and four legs. One shook its great head like a horse might shake its mane.

The others filed into the barn and immediately

started to get the animals ready. They'd be flying to the kingdom, it seemed.

"Why me?" Daisy blurted, the question having always been at the fringes of her mind, always nudging her thoughts—but, with everything going on and their struggles to survive, not having room to be fully brought out and analyzed. "Surely you could find another toy. There are a million magical people better suited to royal games and political maneuvering. I actually have a list back home. I'll give you the ones you can be satisfied in killing. There's a bunch of real assholes in the magical world. I'm nothing. I don't even have magic. I won't be much of a contender against fae in a royal court. Anyone would do. Why me, the weakest of the magical world?"

He turned so his back was to the barn and animals. Regret filled his eyes. "You are so much more than anything the human magical world could ever offer."

"Is it because of the crystal chalice?"

"Yes," he whispered. "It was always about the crystal chalice. You are tied into this because of it. There is no escape, not for either of us."

"But..." She shook her head frustratedly. "I still don't understand why it has to be me. Anyone could've found that thing. Someone else did, as a matter of fact. You killed him, but his friend was harboring it. Why not take him? I basically stumbled upon it—because of you, I might add."

His hands closed around her upper arms, calloused

and warm. His deep green gaze delved into hers. "*I found that thing. It is not an object, Daisy. It is a human. It is you.*"

"Wha—" She swallowed. "I don't understand."

"The crystal chalice was always meant to be a person. A thinking, talking prism by which the other chalices react. In every human generation, there are millions of people who might ascend, but only when all the criteria are met does there become a crystal chalice: a non-magical human, enhanced by man, with the blessing of the gods. In your case, a dedicated trainer enhancing your natural abilities, and a godly gift of blood magic, freely given. When that human dies, a great many more possibilities are born, and one of them is eventually realized. On and on, death and rebirth, forever. Only the gods can stop the endless cycle."

"But what if more than one is realized? Can't you use one of the others?"

"By the decree of the gods, only the first can ascend. There is only ever one crystal chalice at a time. One prism."

Her gut twisted. She felt sick. She dared not even think about how she'd gotten here, but it popped into her mind anyway. As before, he spoke the truth that she was unwilling to show to the light.

"Your mother figure tried to save you, but she doomed you instead. It is not her fault. The gods made this so. Most crystal chalices never end up in this position. I toiled to find information about it all."

"So then, I got really unlucky with timing."

"Story of your life, right?" His grin was slight. His eyes lost their twinkle almost immediately. "When I found you first, I was surprised to learn you didn't have the godly magic. I thought maybe the pull of you meant you were what I sought. But then when I saw you next...the prophecies had been fulfilled. The crystal chalice had been formed. You had completed your transformation. I found you before the diamond chalice, though—the object you tried to destroy. The final object I needed. So I kept track of you. Played games to test you. When you set your hand upon the diamond chalice..."

"No, I—" She kept shaking her head. This was not making any sense. It was completely preposterous.

His tone softened. Turned gentle. "The chalices don't light up for me, Daisy, or for anyone else. The objects don't hum. Not unless you are present. I know what they are by sight alone. You ignite their ability. For you, they buzz. They hum and glow. They come alive. The first time I felt the buzz was on that ledge, when it was tucked into your bra."

Her brow lowered. "No, they do that with other people. When other people pick them up, it happens. I've seen and heard it."

"Because you were present. The crystal chalice was present. The other chalices are useless without their prism."

She tried to back away from him, her mind reeling.

"I'm not magical. They tested me to be sure. You're probably thinking of that diamond stone thing with the hole in the middle. That's the chalice."

"That is your amplifier," he said without hesitation. "Each type of magic has a corresponding chalice that works best with it. Water creatures will lean on chalices corresponding to the sapphire gem. Fire creatures veer toward the ruby. Spirit with amethyst, and so on. That's how our kingdoms align. The chalices mirror Faerie. Your amplifier is the diamond."

"But diamond..." Was the throne of the High Sovereign. The Celestials.

"Yes," he whispered. "With your diamond chalice, and the other chalices arranged around you representing Faerie, you can boost a fae's power level—mine, in this case—to impossible heights. You can make me as mighty as a god. You can help me free this whole realm of the High Sovereign's royal influence."

He paused, and her brow lowered. "Free" the realm...and then take over the humans? Like fucking hell she'd help do that. If he was telling the truth, she had the power to destroy the crystal chalice after all. She had the power to destroy herself, and she would if she was the reason her family was in danger.

His nod was slight, and his lips quirked up at the corners. "Yes, I thought as much. I know you better now, and so I know I can not only trust you with this, but that you'll help me." His jaw was set in determination. "I never intended to help the Obsidian Kingdom's king and queen over the fringe. It was an excuse to give me freedom in my search for the chalices. For their prism. Your realm was never in danger from me. But it is still in danger. I mean to strengthen the fringe. To build it back up. To first free myself of the Obsidian Court, then use the heightened magic to restore the balance of Faerie. When the time comes, you will fulfill your destiny and help me. I'll be cleaning out the filth and remaking it anew with my crystal chalice. The diamond is *your* amplifier...and you are mine."

"And your claims of breaking me?"

Regret once again filled his gaze. "Unfortunately, the amount of power that will run through you is that of a god. No mortal can handle it, or so the archives say. If you help me, you will safeguard your family and Faerie...at the cost of your life. There is no other way. I must sacrifice two beings to save many. It is not only my duty. It is my destiny. *Our* destiny. As I said...there is no escape for you *or* me."

Her brow furrowed as she continually shook her head. This seemed too massive for her to grasp. Too foreign. She couldn't comprehend how magic could restore balance in an entire realm. Balance, as if that were a tangible thing. It didn't compare to the human lands. That she'd ever heard, anyway.

Instead she latched on to the one thing she *did* grasp. "Sacrifice *two* beings?"

His eyes hardened. The burnished gold around his

pupils flared gold before dying back down. "Yes. You... and myself."

She put her hand on his chest. Despite the situation and all he'd said, her heart ached. *"You?"*

He was quiet for a long beat. "The history leading to this moment is long and complex. It comes down to this:

"With my birth, I stirred the gods. An experiment gone badly, we'll say. Through no fault of my own—just by being born—I created a fissure within the High Kingdom. *I* created the rift within the royal family. And when there is rift and instability, the gods sense a game. They seek greater entertainment. To that end, they meddle. Oh, how they meddle. They create favorites and pit them against the favorites of other gods. We are pets, really. Pawns. My existence created the desire for treachery within the royal house...and the gods exploited it. That treachery—a betrayal—saw me to my grave. But on my deathbed, as I was watching the beautiful colors of dusk wash me away, Equilas came to me—"

"Equilas?" She remembered him using that name but had never asked more about it.

"Equilas, Goddess of Balance. One of three sisters in the Trinity, the most powerful of the gods in Faerie. She sits on the High Seat in the Divine Collective. She pulled me from the abyss and reset my path. But first, while I was delirious and desperate for one more breath, we made a deal."

Obsidian

Shivers arrested Daisy. It seemed the fae had learned how to make deals with humans from the gods themselves. And by his tone, it sounded like the gods were no less cunning and ruthless, not even with their children.

He nodded. "I am bound to this destiny. I was tasked with finding the crystal chalice and restoring the balance of Faerie, regardless of the obstacles. Regardless of the degradation and horrors I was thrust into. I am a pet of the Obsidian royals...and a pawn of Equilas. A puppet, some think, beholden to the gods while being crushed under the boot of the Obsidian Court. Exiled from my home and lands, and my friends with me, until I can reset what my birth imbalanced. I'm being blamed for the sins of my parents, but still, I must atone. *That* is my life, Daisy. That is my destiny—what I'm up against. Why I need you. For if I can escape my imprisonment in this filthy kingdom and use you to reinstall balance, I will ultimately have to sacrifice myself for the good of the realm. I am entertainment for gods right now, but eventually, I am hope for the realm. We both are. We must be the dawn to end the starless night."

Cold washed through her at the resignation in his eyes. She wished she could read his mind to find out more. His birth had disrupted the royal family? A birth out of wedlock, maybe? That would be a human reason in the olden days, at any rate. But that was hardly an experiment. Maybe something like the son rising up and overthrowing the father, like what used to happen a lot with Demigods...

"That was the fear, yes," he said softly. "It wasn't a desire in my heart, but I had the power to do it, and so it was assumed that I eventually would."

The cold froze her solid, and her whole body stilled. His gaze was deep and imploring.

"But that would mean..." She let the words trail away as she went over everything in her mind again. All he'd said, what it had to mean. "You're not..."

"In the Obsidian Court, I was given this title as a mockery of my rightful station. I was trapped into that court with the five obsidian seals. They tempered my magic so that I couldn't rebel, forced the rules—the curse—onto me, erased my name and existence from the memories of everyone but the Obsidian Kingdom royals, and bled their magic into mine to strip it of its luster."

"Bled their magic into yours?" She remembered the spectral brilliance that was his glamor, with the warm orange, amber, lavender, cerulean, and golden hues. Then his magic as it had danced and played around her, sparkling and gorgeous, like the sky at dawn. It was only when he used larger degrees of his power that she saw the black cut through or take over. Even then, sometimes it still shimmered with gold.

Another memory flashed through her mind, this time of wings. Delicate dragonfly wings big enough to lift a man. A fae, actually. The colors were the same, dawn-like...or dusk-like, one and the same. Like his glamor. Like his playful magic.

No, not a fae. A beautiful Celestial.

"Your mind moves so quickly," he whispered, stepping toward her. His tone was warm, oh so gentle. Grateful. "I am always so impressed."

She couldn't stop blinking rapidly. "No. You can't be. You don't have wings."

"They are banned from me. Wings represent freedom, and I have none."

"But how? How did they do all of that?"

His look was sardonic. "Why, with the help of Equilas, of course. She will use me for the good of the realm, but as she does, she will revel in my struggles. They all will. Some will invent ways to make my suffering greater for their own amusement. They are ever so bored, the gods—they desire entertainment almost as much as they need our worship and devotion. Sometimes...they get greedy for the former. As I said, I am a pawn. Titles mean nothing to me now. They are empty brags of birth."

"So you're...you're a...?"

"My birth name and title is Tarianthiel Drystan Windryker, Prince of the Diamond Throne, High Sovereign and Sworn Protector of Faerie, Guardian of the Fringe, Keeper of Balance, Brought Forth with the Dawn, Commander of Dusk, and Blessed with Ancestral Magic of Sevens. I added more titles as I completed each stage of my training, but you get the gist. I had such pride in them all, and now...they are useless. I am a ghost. My memory was stripped from the minds of the people I love. I did not die...I ceased to ever exist. My king—my father—and my court do not know me. My brother, who nearly succeeded in rooting me out of the royal line of succession, has no idea of his betrayal. My brethren, the Celestials, with whom I trained, drank with—now they try to kill me on each fringe crossing. All but ten of my friends—who allowed their wings and social standing to be stripped by Equilas so they might help me—don't know who I am." He paused for a beat. "Who I was. It was made clear that there would be no help for me. You are my only way out, Daisy. You are my only means of salvation. A human—who must play the games of the court against magical fae—is my only hope. On my end of things, the deal wasn't a great one..."

She was struck mute. She hadn't been able to process the whole chalice thing, and now *this*? This was way beyond her. She'd need a cup of coffee and a quiet room for a few hours to make sense of any of this. It was all too massive in scope to take in. To comprehend. A Celestial? This was only a fraction of his magic?

A *Celestial?!* They were nearly gods themselves, fierce and beautiful and terrifying. Then again...wasn't that always how she'd viewed him?

"Have no fear," he murmured, sliding his thumb along the edge of her jaw. "You'll forget all I've said in a few moments, like everyone else. It will be plucked from your mind by the magic trapping me. Soon I'll go back to being a hollowed-out, princely assassin and thief, the mockery of a filthy, out-of-balance court where evil continues to flower and corrupt and twist the minds and magic of its inhabitants."

She remembered all his memories from Celestial training—how much he knew about their kind. How much he revered the position and the value he placed on their duty to protect the realm. Those were his values. That was *his* way of thinking. It now made so much more sense why he'd make any kind of deal at all. Why he'd fight, and toil, and hold himself above the rest so he could accomplish what he needed to in order to save his beloved Faerie.

He'd be doing this, deal or no deal. She didn't know him well, but she knew that much. She would do anything to save her family, and he was the same, except his family was the whole of the realm.

She let out a slow breath. "This is a lot to take in."

"As I said, you'll forget. I am exiled from my home and trapped, but I have my *Fallen*. I am not alone, or maybe I would've gone mad, as the Obsidian royals desperately try to get me to do. But yes, I have a duty to these lands. I will help these people. It is my birthright."

Some fucking birthright.

She shook her head for the millionth time. A god saved him, only to trap him in horror, expecting him to then save the realm? To sacrifice himself to do it? What kind of fucked-up donkey show were these dipshits running here? If a god had done that to her, she'd desecrate a temple or two. If the court mocked her for it, she'd fuck up the whole place so they'd be trapped just as much as she. Fuck 'em, there were other ways to play the game besides hunting down relics and hoping a magic-less human could get you out of a deal gone wrong...

A smile worked at his lips. *So adorable,* he thought softly.

"But yes, that is the nature of our gods," he added. "They delight in torment. They give you a boon and expect repayment in blood. Faerie is worth it, though. You'll see. Within the brutality exists the truly magical. Even if it were a shithole, though, your family would be worth the sacrifice, would they not?"

Her gut twisted as she remembered what it had felt like to touch that diamond orb. What it had felt like when she'd been next to him at the door of the shanty, feeling the magic run through her. She very much believed him. If she was forced to hold on to that diamond orb, the effects would rip her apart.

But what was the alternative? Regardless of his issues, the Faegate was letting more fae and their magic through. If the Diamond Throne had unrest—and with meddling gods looking for entertainment, that would continue—that would get worse. It would endanger her home. It would put her family at risk, just like she had already.

She let out a slow breath, trying to still the nervous fear running through her body.

"How do I know you aren't lying to me?" she asked.

"I told you, I cannot lie to you now." He opened his mind to her, letting her feel the truth of his claims. His determination and his pain. His mortification at the life he was forced to live in the Obsidian Court and how he hoped to right that wrong. She could also feel the niggling fear deep down, something like what she was feeling right now. He didn't know if he could accomplish his destiny, as he thought of it. He worried his failure would damn them all. *We are all mortal with the right wound.*

To even use Daisy as a chalice, he first had to free himself from the Obsidian Court. He wasn't sure he could. He'd need her help to do it, and she was incredibly unqualified. She wasn't arguing about that assessment, either. The other issue was that any fae could use the crystal chalice. She could help anyone boost their magic. The second they knew what she was, they'd seek to kill him and use her for themselves. Given they wouldn't put the time and effort into learning how, they'd kill her while trying. The death would be grisly, and she wished she hadn't learned that last bit.

"So, fuck, this is just a really shitty situation all

around, then," she surmised flippantly, pushing away from him and turning. Looking out at nothing. Letting her mind wander.

He thought this was a long shot, from start to finish, which was just a little funny in a dark, "I hate my life" sort of way, because she had a lot of experience with long shots—leaving her care home when she was too young to look after herself, helping keep a roof over their heads, keeping Mordie alive, and the big one... helping one Demigod overthrow his crazy dad with half as many forces and a sliver of the experience level. She'd been down this road before. She had faced, and helped beat, insurmountable odds. Every time, she'd done it to help her family. This time would be no different. Hell, maybe this time she'd be their savior.

Suck on that, Mordie. Your no-magic sister is going to save the magical people's fucking day. Go ahead and tell Lexi I swore, too. I'd welcome a punch in the face right about now. It would feel better than the thought of what's in store for me.

She sighed. He'd absolutely *hate* this for her. It would tear him apart. But she also knew he'd step up right beside her if he were here. He'd walk into the twilight with her without looking back. Any of her family would. In the same situation, each and every one of them would step forward.

"If I help you," she said, "I want your guarantee that it will strengthen that Faegate. That it'll keep my family safe. I want to strike a deal."

They didn't leave for another hour, hammering out the particulars. But once they did, she felt the gravity of the situation. She felt the uncertainty of the games yet to come.

Only one thing was left.

"So this feeling between us..." she said. "It is magic. Right? It's because of the chalices and everything?"

His eyes roamed her face before settling on her lips. "I thought so at first, like I said. I thought it was meant to help me find you. And maybe that's true. The gods do love to play their games. They made the fae in their image, cunning and vicious and ruthless, most of us. What better joke than to entice me with something I will eventually have to destroy and watch me struggle to do it? Regardless, this feeling, this *need*, is between you and me. It is ours. Our torment, maybe. The price I will pay for hurting you. The price you will pay for desiring your tormenter. I can envision their giggling about it now." He put a hand on her cheek. "It might be magical, but it is solely ours. No other fae feel it the way we do, even though they have just as much of a connection to the chalice as I do. So, if it *was* the gods, it was meant distinctly for us. Just you and me. It is our gift...until it turns into our pain."

She didn't know if that was better or worse.

His smile was slight. *Neither do I. Maybe we'll be happy in knowing that it is.*

"What is *definitely* magical, however," he said, "is the...link you have with the wylds. I intend to restore balance with you, and the wylds must feel that, in the same way that the darkrend feared it. You'll notice it was only interested in you, the darkrend. The rest of my *Fallen* were at their windows, looking on, and though it noticed them, it didn't seek them out. It only sought you. This realm feels your presence. You are more than a mere Chester now, little dove. More than even a magical human. In this realm, you will hold the power of a god."

Yeah, but...a power she couldn't use herself. What good was that? A power that would destroy her. The old adage "be careful what you wish for" could not be truer. Could she have a do-over and grab the necromancer magic, maybe?

She shivered, but lifted her chin. The chessboard was set. He needed to free himself of the Obsidian Court, and he needed her help to do it. Fine.

She held out her hand. He took it in confusion.

"Teammates again, it seems," she said.

His brow cleared. In his travels, he'd somehow missed the human custom of "shaking on it."

"Yes. We work together. We trust each other. We survive. For a while, anyway."

"I still intend to be the one to kill you in the end, not the other way around. Just so you know. I have vengeance to claim. I hold a grudge."

"I'd expect no less," he murmured, tracing his thumb across her skin. "The fates chose perfectly in you. Life pressed upon you, but could not break you.

Your past would've destroyed most, but in you, from the pressure emerged a glimmering, shining diamond. Who knows, maybe you will best this power after all. If there is anyone who could keep from breaking, it is you, little dove."

"And if there is anyone who can swindle the gods, it's going to have to be you."

Yes. And now...the games must begin. The fate of Faerie is in our hands.

About the Author

K.F. Breene is a *Wall Street Journal, USA Today, Washington Post, Amazon Most Sold,* and #1 Kindle Store bestselling author of paranormal romance, urban fantasy and fantasy novels. With millions of books sold, when she's not penning stories about magic and what goes bump in the night, she's sipping wine and planning shenanigans. She lives in Northern California with her husband, two children, weird dog, and out of work treadmill.

Contact info:
www.kfbreene.com
kfbreene@gmail.com

www.ingramcontent.com/pod-product-compliance
Lightning Source LLC
LaVergne TN
LVHW040130080526
838202LV00042B/2864